White Columns...
Dark Secrets

M. Ellis Edwards

M. Ellis Edwards

American International Publishers
4015 Washington Road
Martinez, Georgia 30907

Originally Published by American International Publishers: April 2003

Prologue

The storm brought the hot fetid breath of Africa to the isolated graveyard. Huge tree trunks groaned as they swayed before the force of humid tropical winds. The sounds that they made mingled with the constant howling of wind, and gave voice to souls ripped from the bodies of dead left in the hurricane's wake. Other restless spirits, some as old as the earth itself, had been born along on the storm tide to this dark and remote place. Here, more than eighty miles inland, the storm would die, but souls and spirits live on. Some wander aimlessly. Others seek to fulfill a definite purpose.

The little white girl huddled closer to the old black woman as the two made their way among the stark white grave markers. An angry bolt of lightening burned a white hot scar across a black sky that suddenly opened, and released a torrent of rain. The flare momentarily made the old tin lantern unnecessary, as it lit the Dunforth cemetery with the clarity of midday.

Perhaps the storm also brought the dark dream that caused Amy Dunforth, Granny Dunforth to her grandsons, to toss and turn restlessly, sweating profusely despite the powerful swirl of air circulating in the bedroom. On the other hand, the terrible events of the past few days could have brought the nightmare. Without a doubt, the grisly murders of Mrs. Dunforth's son and daughter-in-law were enough to bring bad dreams, or worse. They had been butchered in the very house in which the woman now tossed and dreamed.

The old woman resolutely braved the storm. In the dream, she appeared exactly as Granny Dunforth remembered her from childhood. Tea Kettle Hattie. That's what everyone called her. A former slave, now well into her nineties, she was never seen without the mysterious kettle. Superstitious people, black and white, claimed that she was a witch, and avoided her. She lived alone in a run down shanty deep in the Alapaha River swamp. There was no road to Hattie's place, only an overgrown footpath, and it wasn't traveled often. No one knew how she managed to survive, but she clung to life, and her kettle with a tenacity that was frightening.

The little white girl whimpered in fear as another bolt of lightening shattered the night, and reflected off of the granite statues of twin riders on rampant stallions, guarding the entrance to the cemetery. The Spanish moss swirling from the trees as they danced with the sultry wind appeared as hoary ghosts, conjured from rest by the violent storm, and by an unholy presence in their midst. "Hush Honey! Ole Hattie ain't goan let nuthin bother you. You one of my babies. Yo Granddaddy done made me promise to look after you. Come on chile! Step lively now. Ain't much time. Ole Hattie goan have to shake de bones one moah time." The old woman clutched the kettle closer to her body and pulled the child along.

When the pair reached the far side of the cemetery, the old woman took off her apron, spread it over a low hanging tree branch, and propped the other end with her cane. "Get up under dis, out of de rain while ole Hattie does what's got to be done."

The little girl gratefully settled in under the makeshift shelter, marveling that it could stand against the wind and rain. Miraculously it did, and soon Tea Kettle Hattie joined her. She had gathered an armful of honeysuckle vines, and began weaving a basket. In seconds the material, responding to supernatural craftsmanship, began to take on the shape of a cradle.

Hattie talked as she worked. "I always had de gift. De first time it was revealed to me, I shook so hard I like to died. It scairt me to de edge of my life. Yo Grandaddy come to me in a dream. He say. 'Hattie, you go out to de cemetery and dig up my body. You take de bones from my right hand, den you bury de rest. You put dem bones in a big tea kettle, den you go down to de river bout midnight, and you rattle and shake dem bones. Words goan come, and you say dem words over my bones.' The old woman's hands weaved magic as the cradle neared completion.

Hattie cocked her head to the side remembering. *"I was scairt out of my wits. I didn't want to have no truck wid no dead body. I sho didn't want to disturb Colonel Dunforth, but he come back de very next night, and he say, stern like, he say. 'Hattie! You do what I done told you!'* The gnarled old fingers worked faster. *"So I done it. I done what he say do. De words come, and I said dem over de bones. Dat's when de riders come."* The cradle was finished. *"You wait right here honey chile. Ole Hattie goan be right back."*

The child was torn between the fear of being left alone and the fear of what Hattie would do next. Her eyes were drawn to the kettle clutched in the old woman's hand. Now that she knew what it contained, it held a morbid fascination stronger than ever. She could barely see the old woman's outline as she moved away. After a moment's hesitation, the girl followed., being careful not to allow herself to be seen. She watched as the old woman began scrapping dirt away from a tiny grave. The work proceeded with an unnatural swiftness, as had the construction of the cradle. Within minutes, she saw Hattie cupping something carefully in her hands. The child's imagination provided the details. She knew that the grave belonged to a stillborn infant. She imagined that it was the tiny bones that Hattie placed so carefully in the cradle, along with a single rose.

The wailing voice came as a shock to the frightened girl. The words spoken were like none that she had heard before. They weren't English, nor any other European language. They had the guttural earthiness, and the sing song hissing and clicking of an ancient African dialect. Soon however, the words were drowned out by the unearthly rattling of bones emanating from inside the tea kettle. At last the sounds subsided beneath the noise of the storm raging around the child. She was suddenly aware of the old woman groaning as though in agony.

Tentatively the child started forward. She was terrified, yet she desperately wanted to help Tea Kettle Hattie. The old woman's groans were tearing at her heart. And then another sound made its way across the cemetery, as though carried on the wind itself. Clearly, the sound of a baby crying.

****

Granny Dunforth sat bolt upright in bed listening. She was

drenched in sweat, and shaking with fear. Her dream came to her in a rush. She hadn't thought of Tea Kettle Hattie in years. What on earth had made her dream such a bizarre dream. She threw back the cover, and got out of bed. She tipped to Matt and Drew's room. Peering in, she could make out their figures sleeping peacefully, their chests rising and falling with each breath. She breathed easier, having satisfied herself that her two grandson's were safe.

Feeling foolish, yet compelled to reassure herself, she padded quietly downstairs. She paused before the the boy's parents bedroom listening. They were the last of her children. She had to know that they were safe. Quietly she pushed the door open, and tiptoed over to the bed. She watched the handsome couple sleeping in each other's arms. Tears fell as she remembered her other son, and his beautiful wife, gone now, and with them the unborn child that she had already begun to love.

She was retracing her steps when the eerie sound reached her. She paused and listened. It couldn't be. It was impossible. Then she was sure. She knew what she heard. She had heard the sounds of two many Dunforth babies not to know the unmistakable sound of a newborn crying. She rushed headlong to the front door, and jerked it open.

There, beside the door on the wide porch was a cradle made of honeysuckle vines. Inside, clutching a single rose was a tiny man child. She stooped quickly and picked it up, cuddling it to her breast.

She stared out into the night. There! Someone was moving at the edge of the yard, hurrying away toward the river. She cried out. "Who's there?" When there was no response, she hurried down the steps and out into the yard. She ran as best she could carrying the baby. "Wait! Wait up. Please!" She called.

She could barely make out the shapeless figure that paused and looked back at her. It appeared hunched over, like an elderly woman leaning on a cane. When the figure resumed its retreat, she called out again. "Hattie! You wait up, Hattie!" She didn't recognize her own voice, so tense with hysteria that it didn't belong to her any longer.

The figure stopped. Very deliberately it turned to face her. She had an impression that the face was smiling, but there was no way to be sure. It was shrouded in darkness, but she did see the barely perceptible nod of the head, and then the figure was gone, swallowed by the night.

She stood for a long time trembling, afraid to move, unable to believe what she had seen, but acutely aware of the warmth of the bundle in her arms. Her breathing finally slowed, and the hammering in her chest subsided. The thought went through her mind— the last thing I need is a heart attack, especially now with another child depending on me. She looked down into the baby's face, at the solemn eyes that seemed to study her in the faint light. What should she name it? The name of her grandfather rolled off of her tongue. "Gabriel Calvin Dunforth. You ready to go home, Cal?" She turned and started back toward the imposing mansion glowing eerily against the night sky.

CHAPTER 1

The ringing of the telephone jarred Cal Dunforth out of a light sleep. A glance at the clock on the bedside table revealed that it was 11:45. He gently untangled himself from the slender tanned arms of Beth Addison, and swore softly as he lifted the receiver. A phone call at this hour, on a Sunday, probably meant that he'd have to leave the comfort of his bed, and the beautiful woman who shared it. At least the caller had the decency to wait until their lovemaking was finished.

"Yeah," he growled into the phone.

"Cal, it's Heywood. I'm sorry to disturb you so late, but I'm worried. I didn't know who else to call." The voice on the line was anxious.

"What's the problem Heywood?" Cal was wary. Heywood Carlson and Cal's cousin, Marla, were going through a divorce. The last thing he wanted was to become involved in their troubles.

"I was supposed to meet Marla here in Macon at 9:30. I've had Paula for the weekend, and Marla agreed to meet me to save me having to drive all the way down to Emerald, and she hasn't shown up. I can't imagine what could have delayed her for over two hours. I've called her several times, and I get her answering machine. Frankly Cal, I'm worried sick. I'd like for you to help me check on her."

"Sure Heywood. I'll get right on it. You were right to call me. Give me your number there. I'll give you a ring back when I have something." The Alapaha County deputy was out of bed now, the phone squeezed to his ear with his shoulder as he searched for his clothes.

Paula would be three years old next week. He had been trying to decide what to get a three year old for her birthday, and still hadn't bought her present.

"Thanks Cal. I appreciate your help." Heywood still sounded nervous.

"No problem. I've been bailing Marla out of trouble since we were kids. Don't worry, I'll find her," Cal assured him as he hung up.

"Who was that?" Beth asked.

"Your boss, Heywood Carlson," Cal answered, pulling on his trousers.

Beth sat up, "Heywood? What does he want at this time of night?"

"Marla was supposed to meet him in Macon two hours ago. She hasn't shown up, and he wants me to check on her," Cal was tugging on his shoes by now.

"Damn! Marla's a big girl. I'm sure she can take care of herself. Why do you have to get out of bed to chase her down?" Beth pouted.

"I shouldn't be long. I'll put in a call the to State Patrol. The way Marla drives, the chances are good that she got picked up for speeding. If that's not the case, I'll drive out to White Columns and check on her. I shouldn't be more than an hour or two," Cal was buttoning his uniform shirt over a muscular chest.

"Well, as soon as you locate sweet, innocent little Marla, you better get yourself back here. I've never trusted that sultry bitch. I think she's got the hots for you," Beth snapped.

"For God's sake Beth, Marla's my cousin. Give it a rest!" Cal snarled.

"Third cousin, Prom date, first love?" Beth mocked, a trace of bitterness creeping into her voice.

"Beth, be serious. I never dated Marla. She wasn't dating anyone her senior year in high school, so she asked me to escort her. I was home on spring break, so I took her to the Prom. It was no big deal," Cal was getting angry. Beth could pick the most awkward times to fight. She had been harassing him about Marla since his sexy cousin had moved back to White Columns six months earlier, when her marriage to Heywood started breaking up.

"You're awfully defensive about something that wasn't a big deal," Beth retorted.

"Listen Beth, I don't have time to fight about this right now. Marla could be in trouble. She's done some pretty wild things in her time, but with Paula involved, she wouldn't screw around. I've got to find her. We can fight any time," Cal growled.

"She'll turn up. Bad pennies always do," Beth turned away from him; pulled the covers up over her as if to shield herself from the angry look that he shot her way.

As soon as Cal was in his patrol car he put aside his anger and radioed State Patrol headquarters. He requested that Troopers along the stretch of I- 75 that Marla would have traveled to Macon be on the alert for her car. He gave the dispatcher a description of her guards red Porsche, and then turned onto the highway that led from Emerald to the plantation that Marla had inherited.

As he drove along the deserted stretch of highway, his mind drifted back to the night that he and Marla had raced along this same winding road in the Sting Ray convertible that Granny Dunforth had given Marla as a graduation present. He had been home from The Citadel on spring break, and against his better judgment, he had agreed to escort Marla to her Senior Prom. They had arrived at the Prom late, after all of Marla's classmates. She had been determined to make a grand entrance; to display not only the new car that drew envious stares from the boys, but also the tall handsome escort with the face that had hardened into manhood, and who's shoulders and chest rippled with muscles. He had parked the gleaming new car, pocketed the keys, and walked around the vehicle to offer his arm to Marla. She had gripped it possessively as they had pushed through the throng of teenagers gathered around the sleek sports car.

Marla had insisted that rather than renting a tuxedo for the Prom, he wear his Cadet uniform instead. The two of them had made a striking couple. Marla's long, raven tresses cascaded down over her bare, bronzed back in stark contrast to her snow white gown. As he had led her in a graceful fox trot across the gymnasium floor, gawking pimple faced teenagers had stared in awe at the two of them dancing gracefully together.

The seductive way that Marla had molded her body to Cal's, and the smoldering heat in her eyes had made it plain to the whispering knots of her female classmates that the aristocratic beauty, who had everything that life had to offer, was about to add another prize to her collection. At midnight, the band had played "Theme From a Summer Place", and Marla had whispered in Cal's ear that White Columns was their summer place, and that they should be there, under the moon light. Cal still remembered how Marla's slender body had melted against him, and could still hear her low moan of anticipation as she'd felt him stirring against her flat, muscular abdomen.

They had raced the powerful car back to White Columns. As they had wound their way up the gravel driveway toward the imposing mansion, the Alapaha, below and to their left, had appeared as a dark ribbon oozing along at a leisurely pace until it reached the shoals directly in front of the house. There it suddenly shed its lethargy, and roared among the granite boulders in a spectacular display of power before emptying into a deep quiet pool, where slab sided channel catfish, bass, and red breast thrived in the aerated water.

When they'd parked in the yard beneath the mossy oaks that stood like bearded sentinels guarding the big house, Marla had leaped out of the car and dashed across the lawn toward the river. By the time Cal had caught up with her, she had been standing beside a snowy mound of clothing that she had discarded in reckless haste on the granite outcropping that overlooked the pool. Cal had anticipated her next move, and was reaching for her when she had let out a Rebel yell and dived into the river.

He had tried unsuccessfully to coax her out of the water, but had finally stripped off his own clothing and went in after her. She'd tried to escape by swimming away from him, but he'd managed to grasp her ankle. Suddenly she had wrapped her cool, slippery legs around him, and he'd felt her flint hard nipples pressing against his chest. Then, without warning, she had kissed him; her lips and tongue arousing a fire that had burned inside him since that night.

Now, as Cal turned into the gravel driveway, he forced himself to concentrate on the present. He had to put the pleasant memories aside, and focus on finding Marla. He eased the patrol car to a stop in the dark shadow of the towering oaks, and glanced at the old servants quarters that had been converted into a garage. Inside he could make out the outline of the Porsche, crouched in the shadows like a tiger waiting to pounce.

He was relieved that the car was in the garage. It eliminated the nagging worry that Marla was lying in the twisted wreckage of a traffic accident. Cal had investigated enough car crashes to fully appreciate their horror.

As Cal stepped out of the car, he found that he didn't need his flashlight. Overhead, the three quarter moon bathed the house and yard in silvery light. A warm August breeze stirred across his face, and brought the musky smell of the river with it. With the sounds of the night serenading him, he stared for a moment at the imposing structure before him.

The house, with its looming white pillars, seemed to glow with the reflected moonlight. Its many windows stared out at him like glass eyes watching his approach. White Columns was a beautiful relic from a glorious past by day. At night it seemed to Cal to become animated, no longer simply an inert structure of wood and glass, but a living creature with a soul and spirit of its own; a preternatural entity that exuded a malevolence toward strangers that was palpable. An involuntary shiver racked Cal as he approached the porch.

He climbed the marble steps and started across the porch toward the front door. He glanced down at the floor, polished smooth by generations of Dunforth feet. The varnished boards gleamed in the moonlight except for the dark spot on the floor beneath the sturdy beam that supported the second floor balcony. The thin hairs on Cal's neck stood up as he remembered the legend that revolved around the mysterious spot.

He had been eight years old, Marla five, when he'd first heard the legend. Granny Dunforth had read the two children a story, tucked them into bed, and kissed them good night. After making sure that they said their prayers, she went to her own room. Cal had heard a furtive sound outside of his door, and was about to investigate when Marla had whispered from the darkness, "Cal, are you sleepy?" He had replied that he wasn't, and she'd quickly slipped into bed beside him, and asked him to tell her a ghost story.

Cal had made up a rambling tale, and when he'd finished Marla had solemnly announced that she knew a real ghost story. Cal had been skeptical when she had told him about the mysterious spot on the porch, visible only in the moonlight, and reputed to be human blood. Marla had insisted that it was true. He had demanded that she show him.

Later that night, as the moon rose, the two of them had sneaked downstairs, and out onto the porch. They had waited, Marla clutching his arm, as the shimmering light had inched across the porch. Cal's breath had caught in his throat as he'd noticed the dark area that seemed to drink up the moonbeams instead of reflecting them as the rest of the floor did. Without thinking, he'd put out his foot to touch the dark circle. When his bare foot entered the darkened area, he'd felt a sudden powerful force tugging at it, threatening to suck him into a soul devouring black void from which he had been certain there would have been no escape. A frightened shriek had escaped his lips before Marla, with a strength that he hadn't known she possessed, had jerked him away from the danger.

With terror squeezing their young hearts with an icy hand, they had dashed back inside the house, up the stairs and into Marla's room. They had clutched each other beneath the covers while their hearts pounded with fear, and their ears listened for the sound of pursuit. When a board outside in the hall had creaked beneath someone's weight, Marla's teeth had clamped down on his shoulder to prevent a scream from escaping. Only when Granny Dunforth had called out to them from outside the door had they resumed breathing.

With these thoughts racing through his mind, Cal pressed the doorbell. He heard the melodious chime echo through the vast old home as he waited. When several tries elicited no response, Cal fumbled with his key ring until he found the key that Marla had given him. He unlocked the heavy oak door and pushed it open.

"Marla! It's Cal. Are you home?" He called, stepping inside. He walked over to the control panel of the security system that he'd installed when Marla had moved in, and noticed as he keyed in the four digit code that deactivated the system that it had been set to the ARMED: HOME mode.

He flicked on the light, and the overhead chandelier flooded the spacious living room, revealing original Victorian furniture. He moved to the base of the spiral stairs that wound toward the bedrooms on the second floor. As he ascended, he looked down on the gleaming hardwood floor of the room below, polished smooth by the boots of Confederate officers dancing with elegantly gowned ladies.

In its early days the room had been warm and friendly; a gracious hostess, basking contentedly beneath the soft glow from the sixteen oil lamps of the chandelier. Now it seemed to Cal that the room spit the garish, artificial light from the incandescent bulbs fitted in the crystal back at him with spiteful contempt. It was as if the room felt itself to be a whore now, too brightly painted, and adorned with silly draperies that were too frivolous for its taste.

Cal knocked firmly at the door to the master bedroom, and called out to Marla before he pushed the door inward and stepped inside. He found the light switch, and a brass lamp on the night stand beside the queen sized bed flared on. Cal took in the neatly made bed, the antique dresser and chest gleaming with a fresh coat of polish on the cherry wood. A Sony thirty inch television set, and a new Onkyo stereo with huge Cerwin Vega speakers filled the entertainment cabinet along the wall opposite the bed. The modern electronics seemed like a vulgar violation of the room's dignity.

Cal's eyes were drawn to the answer phone on the night stand beside the lamp. It's wary red eye blinked at him, and the digital message display showed six messages on the machine. He walked over, pressed the playback button and listened to the messages. All six were from Heywood. In the first couple, Heywood's voice registered mild annoyance. By the last terse message, a note of desperate anxiety had crept into his tone. At that moment the phone rang, startling Cal. He reached for it with a sense of relief, hoping that it was Heywood calling to tell him that Marla had arrived.

****

The house in Mountain Brook was cool with its thermostat set at 68 degrees. Outside the temperature was still in the high eighties, with humidity shooting the heat index into the stratosphere. It had been another scorching day, unusual even for the city of Mountain Brook, nestled just south of Birmingham. The upscale suburb was no stranger to hot summer days. Its residents coped by staying indoors, enclosed in their plush homes made comfortable by central air. No one in Mountain Brook worried about their utility bills. It wasn't that kind of neighborhood. They worried about their stock portfolios, their law practices, and maybe about their spouses fidelity, but not about how much it cost to keep their homes frigid during the hot days of summer.

In spite of the cool air circulating in the bedroom of the house nestled in the shade of towering oaks, Shanon Lee was drenched with sweat as she tossed restlessly in the queen sized bed. She fought at the powder blue sheet draped over her as if it were a creature from the deep, trying to ensnare her with groping tentacles. She cried out, a frightened, whimpering sound; a testament to the horror of the nightmare that held her in its grip.

In Shanon's dream, Marla Dunforth's lips were turning blue as she struggled to draw air into her lungs. The rasping intake of her sorority sisters breathing was becoming irregular, choked off by the length of hemp rope slowly, relentlessly tightening around her slender throat. The woman's dark beautiful eyes had started to bulge out of their sockets. The ring of white around the brown irises had expanded to startling proportions.

Shanon watched in horror as Marla's once beautiful face slowly turned into a hideous mask. Blood from her mangled tongue, by now protruding grotesquely out of her mouth, streamed down her chin, stained the fabric of her night gown, and dripped audibly onto a stone floor. The macabre sound was punctuated by an occasional agonized groan of the rope against the beam that supported Marla's lifeless weight.

Shanon strained against the invisible barrier that separated her from her friend, unable to penetrate what appeared to be an incredibly strong, clear film. She was able to force her way within inches of her friends face, but then the barrier stopped her, frustratingly close, yet unable to reach through to help Marla. She saw Marla's eyes glaze over as death claimed her. She screamed with pent up rage and unreasoning terror, and woke up trembling, another scream forming in her throat as she sat bolt upright in bed.

Shanon's hand trembled as she sought the light switch. As soon as the lamp was on, she rolled out of bed and walked to the bathroom. She studied her face in the mirror, noted the remnants of terror etched there, and quickly splashed cold water from the faucet on her face. Walking to her study, she shivered from the cold sweat that made her night gown cling to her long tanned legs in a clammy embrace. Ignoring her discomfort, she thumbed through her address book and found Marla's number. She dialed the phone, hoping to hear Marla scold her for calling so late.

The phone rang once, then a male voice, terse with anxiety was on the line.

"Yes, may I speak to Marla?" Shanon asked tensely.

"I'm sorry, Marla doesn't appear to be here right now. I'll be glad to give her a message when I locate her though," Cal spoke into the phone.

"What do you mean, Marla doesn't appear to be there? Who are you, and what are you doing answering her phone?" Shanon tried to control her voice, but couldn't. Her query came out almost hysterically.

"My name is Cal Dunforth. Who's calling please?"

"Cal! Marla's cousin, right?" Shanon felt a wave of relief.

"Right, and you?"

"Shanon Lee. We were roommates at Auburn. Where the hell is Marla?"

"I don't know. That's why I'm here. I got a call from her ex-husband about half hour ago. She was supposed to meet him at 9:30 and she hasn't shown up. Have you heard from her?" Cal asked.

"No. Listen to me Cal. Marla is in trouble, desperate trouble. You've got to find her before it's too late," Shanon urged.

"How do you know that? You said that you haven't heard from her. What do you know about all this?" Cal demanded.

"I can't explain it Cal. Don't ask me to. Just find her. Please!" Shanon begged.

"If you have information that could be helpful, please tell me. I don't know where to start. All I know is that she hasn't met Heywood as planned, and her car's in the garage. I haven't searched the entire house, but my gut feeling is that she's not here. Can you help me Shanon?"

Shanon felt a wave of fear threatening to engulf her, fought it, and said, "She's somewhere in a dark place. She's strangling or smothering, and having terrible difficulty breathing."

Cal felt a stab of fear, followed by suspicion. "How do you know this? I'm warning you! Don't play games with me if her life is in danger."

"Cal, Please! Just listen. I have visions sometimes. It's a gift, or a curse. I don't know which, but whatever it is I sometimes see things in my mind that are actually happening. I just had a hideously vivid dream of Marla being hanged! I don't know where she is, but she's in a close, confined area. It's dark, with stale air, and she's dying! Please! You must believe me!" Shanon fought for control, knowing that what she was telling Cal would be hard for him to accept even if she was calm and rational. She realized that the hint of hysteria in her voice might cause him to dismiss her as deranged, but she couldn't keep all of it out of her voice.

There was a pause at the other end of the line. "Let's say that I believe you. Could she be in the trunk of a car?" Cal asked.

"No, I don't think so. I saw a stone floor of some kind. It was dark, gloomy, and overhead there were beams, and thick timbers of some kind. I don't know any more. All I really saw was Marla's face, twisted and hideous. Please Cal. Help her!" Shanon implored.

Cal forced himself the think. Could this be some kind of cruel hoax? Did the woman on the other end of the phone really have psychic abilities? He thought back to a conversation that he'd had with Marla during her college days. A phrase buried in his memory flashed into his consciousness. He could see Marla clearly, laughing, a wine cooler clutched in her hand, "Cal you've got to meet a friend of mine from school. The two of you would be perfect together. She's beautiful, tall, blonde, with big boobs. She's just your type. There's only one problem," Marla had paused infuriatingly at that point, and Cal had started guessing.

"Don't tell me. I can guess. She's married? A lesbian? Frigid?" When Marla had kept shaking her head, still laughing, he'd made his final guess. "Oh No! No! She's a Damn Yankee!" he had joked.

16

Cal remembered Marla's peal of fresh laughter at his response.. "No silly, she's a witch. You could never cheat on her, because she would know. She would know that you were going to cheat on her, and who you were going to do it with before you even decided to do it. She'd put a spell on you, and that magnificent cock of yours would shrivel up, turn green and fall off."

Cal had reddened with embarrassment at his cousin's shockingly frank and intimate language, and had made a lame reply that he didn't remember now. He did remember the reference to Shanon the witch however, and now the words echoing in his mind instilled an icy fear in him.

"Shanon, when you have these visions, are they about things that have already happened, or are they sometimes about events that are going to happen in the future?" Cal held his breath, awaiting her answer.

"That's what's so frightening about them Cal. I never know. Sometimes they are about things that have happened in the past. Sometimes about the present, and on a few occasions they've been about the future. I can never be sure."

"What's your gut reaction to this one? Has it already happened? Am I too late, or can we still help her?" Cal pressed her desperately.

"Oh God! I don't know Cal. I don't know!" Shanon wailed.

Cal felt frustration mounting. All that Shanon's call had succeeded in doing was to unnerve him, and fill him with a sense of impending doom. There wasn't a shred of information that he could use to help him find Marla. "I'll do everything that I can to find her Shanon. If something else comes to you that could help me find her, call me here, or call me through the Alapaha County Sheriff's department. They can patch you through to me on my car radio. Before you call though, think it through and be sure that what you have to tell me is going to be helpful, otherwise don't call. Let me have your number and I'll call you back as soon as I have some news." Cal said.

"I'm giving you my car phone. As soon as I can dress, I'll be on my way there." Shanon gave him the number, then added, "Thanks Cal, I know you'll do your best."

"Let's hope it'll be good enough." Cal murmured as he hung up.

Cal debated with himself on whether to call the dispatcher at the department. Official policy stated that missing persons reports were not acted upon until the person reported had been missing for at least twenty four hours. In almost all cases, the person would turn up on their own within this time frame. The exception of course, was in those cases involving a child, or where evidence of foul play was present. Cal reflected that the only evidence that he had of foul play was the unfounded fear that had swept over him since he'd talked to Shanon Lee. Still, his instincts told him that something was very wrong, that Shanon Lee was not some crank caller. Setting aside the fact that he personally believed that the woman had indeed had a frightening vision, her call could be construed as evidence of foul play. If she was a fraud, and had not had a paranormal experience, the only way that she could have known about Marla's disappearance was if she was involved in some way. It was thin evidence, but enough. He placed the call.

After he finished explaining the situation to the dispatcher, he called Abe Lucas, the departments dog handler. He was relieved when Lucas agreed to bring a hound right over. While he was waiting for Lucas to arrive, he'd finish searching the house.

Cal went through the remaining rooms on the second floor, then pulled down the attic stairs and climbed up into the musty storage room. He shined his light over the boxes and trunks that he had helped Marla store when she had moved in only a few months ago. He remembered helping her sort through Granny Dunforth's effects, and how the experience had taken them back to memories of their childhood as they'd sorted the family photographs, keepsakes, and other odds and ends.

They had spent hours looking at old photographs that they'd found, some so old that they were printed on metal, and in the case of some of them, on glass. The most interesting picture was a faded one depicting their Great Grandparents. It had been taken with White Columns as a backdrop. The man had an austere expression on his face, and he was dressed in a faded cotton shirt, calvary trousers, and worn calvary boots. On his head, at a jaunty angle, he wore a battered hat with a polished brass emblem in which CSA was barely visible in the picture. A huge revolver was stuffed into his waistband, and Cal had pointed it out to Marla, explaining that it was a LeMat revolver, a weapon that had originated in France. The gun had been a nine shot revolver with a shotgun barrel beneath the rifled barrel. It had been a favorite weapon of Southern calvary officers.

At that point, Marla had opened one of the steel trunks, and withdrew an object wrapped in an oil impregnated rag. With a smile she had handed it to Cal, and watched as he unwrapped the cloth, and found himself staring at an original LeMat revolver, in very good condition. Marla had given him the priceless heirloom as carelessly as she would have shared a piece of candy when they were children.

Cal backed down the stairs, swung them back up out of the way and resumed his search.

After searching the kitchen, dining room, and library on the ground floor, Cal walked down the hall toward the back door. As he walked he was aware of the clear blue eyes of four generations of Dunforths looking down at him from their portraits along the wall. He wondered what their thin, unsmiling lips could tell him if they could suddenly come to life and speak. Collectively, the men and women in the portraits had witnessed almost two centuries of life at White Columns. The only ancestor that he had a clear recollection of was Granny Dunforth, who had passed away only last year. Her portrait smiled down at him from the end of the hall.

Cal walked out onto the back porch, and stared out across the back lawn into the dark gloom where forest surrounded the manicured yard. He remembered the foot bridge spanning the creek that emptied into the river a few hundred yards upstream from the house. The bridge was about forty yards long, and ended at the base of the ridge that ran perpendicular to the river. High on the ridge, across the gurgling stream, was the family cemetery. Cal suddenly remembered the heavy beams that supported the bridge, and the rock strewn floor of the ravine through which the creek flowed, and a horrible picture painted itself in his mind.

He hurried across the lawn, found the stepping stones that led to the footbridge, and with the image of Marla suspended from the bridge in the dark gloom of the ravine torturing him, made his way down to the creek.

Once there, he scrambled into the ravine, and with an act of will forced himself to aim the beam of his flashlight at the underside of the bridge. His breathing froze when he saw the dark shape hanging from the bridge. The image in his mind was so strong that for long seconds the broken tree limb that had lodged beneath the bridge during a period of high water took on human form. Only when he moved closer did he realize that his mind had played a cruel trick on him. His breath exploded in a sigh of relief.

Cal scrambled up the opposite side of the ravine, and walked out onto the foot bridge. He paused and looked over his shoulder to the top of the ridge. There, outlined against the sky by the moon light, two rampant granite stallions whose riders guarded the entrance to the cemetery with drawn sabers, were visible. Cal could clearly visualize the wrought iron fence that encircled the graveyard. Rose bushes used the sturdy fence as a trellis, and veiled the graves with a lush screen of red and white petals. Inside the enclosure, dogwoods gently dusted the earth with snow white flowers, and honeysuckle scented the air with a delicate fragrance.

Cal thought of the generations of Dunforths sleeping peacefully in their garden, and felt a premonition that another would soon join them. He shuddered involuntarily. Marla's parents had been there for over twenty years. They had been murdered in their White Columns bedroom by an intruder when Marla was only three years old. Granny Dunforth had raised their three children in the big house; two older boys and Marla. Marla had been her favorite, and she had spoiled her hopelessly. Granny Dunforth had been the only mother that Marla ever remembered.

Cal stood on the footbridge, and stared down toward the river. All around him the night was alive with sound. Whippoorwills celebrated the evening with their shrill, incessant calls. The mournful, seven noted call of an owl echoed down the river. Behind him, a deer had caught Cal's scent and snorted repeatedly, punctuating the shrill sounds with an impatient stamp of its foot. Fire flies burned hundreds of holes in the darkness as they wandered about, seemingly at random. The creatures of the night were celebrating life, aware that it was a precarious commodity. Unlike man, they harbored no illusions of life after death. To them, death was final, and absolute; their flesh would either be consumed by others to sustain their own life, or decay and enrich the soil that gave life to each of them. Cal wondered fleetingly if it was the same for man. Was the concept of a soul simply a defense mechanism invented by man to help allay his fear of death?

He was jerked out of his macabre reverie by the sound of Abe Lucas's aging Jeep Cherokee laboring up the driveway. He hurried back across the bridge, along the footpath and around the house, arriving in the front yard just as Lucas killed the truck's engine. He stood silently as a grizzled old hound climbed out of the vehicle, urinated noisily on the hubcap of Cal's patrol car, and sat down waiting for Lucas to snap his leash onto him.

"That tells you what old Bugle thinks about police work, " Lucas grinned.

"I guess it does." Cal couldn't help smiling.

"We'll find her Cal. Don't worry. Old Bugle'll find her." Lucas face split into a reassuring grin, white teeth gleaming in his black face.

"Let's take him around the house, see what he can find." Cal said tersely.

"Let's go Bugle, it's time you earned your keep, you lazy old bum," Lucas said fondly.

The dog worked from side to side ahead of the two men as they circled the house, showing no interest in anything until they reached the back steps. There he suddenly stopped, the hair on his back rising, and a low uncertain growl escaped him.

"What the hell's the matter with you Bugle? Let's go." Lucas said.

The hound whined, and cowered against the deputy's legs, refusing to move. He raised his nose and drank in the noxious odor that had stopped him in his tracks— had filled him with terror. Putrefied flesh mingled with the odor of wet decaying wool, and something rank and evil filled the dogs nose. Usually a scent was followed by a visual image in the dog's mind, but now all that he could visualize was a dark swirling mass moving across the lawn, a gray ill defined shape with a darker core that was comprised of congealed evil. The scent brought with it the same unreasoning fear that the hound associated with bad dreams that he sometimes experienced. He pressed closer to his master, whining and shivering violently.

"What's wrong with him Abe? He acts like something's scared the hell out of him," Cal said.

"I don't know Cal. I've never seen him act this way before."

"Could he smell someone under the porch?" Cal asked, his hand hovering over the grip of his service pistol.

"I don't know Cal. I don't think so. Hell, Old Bugle would eat out of Charlie Manson's hand. I don't think it's a person that he smells."

The hound was staring out into the funereal darkness of the forest, following the progress of the frightening specter by the unclean scent that drifted on the breeze. As the odor moved away into the woods, the dog's trembling lessened.

"Whatever he smelled walked across the lawn Abe. You could see him watching whatever it was, but I didn't see a damn thing."

"I didn't see anything either. Could have been some kind of animal, a coyote maybe. Let's give him a few minutes to settle down." Abe reached into his pocket and withdrew a crushed pack of Marlboros, shook one out for Cal, then another for himself.

Cal noticed that Abe's hand was shaking when he lit the cigarette. He had inhaled the harsh smoke before he remembered that he'd quit smoking six months ago. He let the nicotine calm his jittery nerves, despite the mild dizziness that the drug caused in his desensitized system. He prayed silently for the dog to pick up a trail leading into the woods.

Marla hadn't been living on the plantation for very long, and the surrounding acres, five thousand of them to be exact, had changed since she had played there as a child. Open fields that had been in cultivation when the two of them were small were now overgrown with pines. Landmarks that they had used to find their way were no longer visible. Even the swamp along the river had grown more densely tangled with vegetation. If she was lost on the plantation, and kept her wits, no harm would come to her. The dog would lead them to her.

"Let's see if we can get him moving again Abe," Cal said, grinding the cigarette butt beneath the heel of his boot.

"Come on Bugle, ain't nothing out there gonna bother you. Let's go!" Abe urged the dog on.

The hound wagged his tail, and tentatively moved out ahead of them. At the steps leading down into the cellar, he paused. The foul scent trail was unmistakable, leading from the cellar out into the gloom of the woods. The old hound's scrotum tightened, and he felt icy droplets of adrenaline trickling through his viscera. A nervous whine escaped him, and he hesitated.

"Come on Bugle, get with it!" Abe commanded impatiently.

At that moment another scent drifted into the dogs nose. A blend of delicate fragrances emanated from behind the cellar door, and the image of a woman formed in his mind. He wagged his tail expectantly, shoved his nose against the crack of the door and inhaled, waiting for the rush of warm body odor to fill his senses. Instead the odor was cold; a mixture of dried, fear tainted sweat, feces, and blood. A deep melancholy invaded the old hound. He raised his nose skyward, and voiced his sorrow with a mournful howl.

"Christ Abe! Can't you shut him up. He's making my flesh crawl." Cal shuddered.

"Oh shit!" Abe's face blanched ashy grey, and he looked at Cal with a mixture of grief, anxiety, and guilt.

"What is it Abe? What's wrong?" Cal's heart hammered in his chest, and a sense of foreboding swept through him like the cold wet fog that sometimes drifted in off the river.

"It's no good Cal. It's no damn good," Abe was looking down at the tops of his boots.

Cal reached out, grasped the big man by the lapels, and shook him. He felt terror grip him as he noted the flaccid, unresisting response. "What is it Abe?" What's he found?" A profound sense of dread was building within him.

"A body. He smells a body behind that door." Abe choked.

Cal turned, slipped away from Lucas's clutching hands, and bounded down the steps to the cellar door. He jerked at the door knob in exasperation, then gathered himself. He lunged against the door, ignoring Abe Lucas's plea to stop. The door jam splintered, and Cal tumbled into the musty cellar.

He sprawled face down on the cold wet stone floor, in total darkness, disoriented, mad with fear. As he rose to his feet, something filmy descended over his face. Cool, hard limbs surrounded him, smashed into his face with loathsome, meaty impacts. He cried out, and fought at the tentacles that sought to smother him, staggered backwards, and sat down awkwardly on the floor just as the beam from Abe Lucas's flashlight illuminated something suspended from the timbers overhead

Cal stared up at a human form, slowly twisting on a cushion of air above him. He saw the grotesquely bulged eyes, bloody lips, hideously swollen protruding tongue, features that were unrecognizable at first. Then he registered the mane of raven hair cascading down over the translucent night gown, took in the swell of firm, rose tipped breasts straining at the thin fabric, and in an indelible instant was aware of even the dark shadow of pubic hair faintly visible beneath the gown. It was Marla, transformed by death into a ghastly house of horrors mannequin.

CHAPTER 2

Shanon bored through the night, pushing her BMW hard. She had taken highway 280 South out of Birmingham, and the sleepy rural towns blurred by, Sylacauga, Alexander City, Dadeville, Auburn, and then Columbus. She had flashed past the point where 280 veered off to Plains, Jimmy Carter's home town, when it happened. The highway blurred, then evaporated as she started seeing with her mind instead of her eyes. She saw the form of a child, curled peacefully asleep on the back seat of a car, nestled comfortably into tan leather upholstery. The child was covered with a gray sports coat which had a white handkerchief carefully tucked into the breast pocket. The initials J. H. C. were monogrammed in Navy blue on it. Clutched in her arms was a small black and white Teddy Bear.

The image was benign, yet Shanon sensed something sinister. A choking, irritating odor permeated the air in the vehicle. Exhaust fumes! Shanon's eyes roamed the interior of the car, paused at the partly open rear window, observed the length of garden hose pinched against the window and door frame. A barely visible haze of deadly emissions drifted into the automobile.

Shanon felt the wheel of the sports sedan pull against her as it drifted off of the pavement, and onto the shoulder of the two lane highway. The disturbing vision evaporated as she fought to get the car back onto the highway. Her eyes focused on the road again, and a shaft of fear sliced through her as the rear of a tractor trailer rig loomed before her. She wrenched the steering wheel left, felt the big radial tires bite hard into the asphalt, then pressed the accelerator to the floor. The car shot across the center line, drew abreast of the truck, and Shanon found herself staring into oncoming headlights. The white hot orbs rushed at her as if to harvest her soul for a trip to eternity. She twitched the wheel right, and heard the tires yelp in protest. The truck's headlights flooded the car with light, like twin death stars. She sucked in her breath, awaiting the crunch of metal that would start a collision, and wrap her in the steel jaws of death.

The oncoming car flashed past, and for a searing instant stark white faces, caught in the glare of headlights, and frozen into death masks, burned into Shanon's conscience. The blare of the car's horn died as it vanished in the receding shadow of the truck. A glance at the speedometer revealed that the powerful sedan was traveling at over a hundred miles per hour. She let off the gas, and breathed for the first time in what seemed like eternity. She was alive!

A sudden attack of cold shivers surprised her. Death, cheated of its prize, walked up her spine like a spider retreating back to its lair after a failed hunt, each hairy leg tracking ice as it inched along. She felt her stomach turn, threatening to spill its contents onto the upholstery. The lights of the truck closed on her again, and stared threateningly down on her as the driver let out a startling blast on the horn. Shanon turned on her flashers, slowed, and as soon as she could, pulled onto the shoulder. The blast of air when the truck passed shook the car violently before the fiery glow of taillights disappeared over a hill.

Shanon clutched the wheel with white knuckles, fighting the sensation that her viscera was inhabited by living creatures that were clawing desperately for their freedom. She had survived a harrowing experience. But the child? Would she survive? Although Shanon tried to focus on the vision, desperately wanting to know the identity and fate of the child, but it was no use. Her own terror, and physical illness from her brush with fate were too powerful. The vision had faded, and although the scant seconds that had claimed her attention had almost cost Shanon her life, they had not provided enough information for her to act on.

God! I'm a wreck, she thought. She hadn't heard from Cal, although she had constantly signed onto each new cellular carrier as she'd entered the coverage area. Several times she had been tempted to call him, but had refrained, telling herself that no news was good news. Deep down however, she knew that Marla was lost. She'd seen her eyes glaze over in death.

After steeling her nerves, she pulled back onto the highway and continued driving. The memory of the vision of the little girl haunted her. She would probably never know its outcome now. She tried to imagine what kind of person it would take to lovingly cover a little girl with a jacket, then insert a hose connected to the car's exhaust and leave her to die. She remembered that she hadn't been able to look into the front seat. Could she have witnessed a murder suicide? Had someone been in the front seat? A mother, or father, suffering from such deep depression that they had decided to take their own life and that of their child? It happened all too often, and the worst of it was that she was helpless to prevent it. Damn! She smashed her palm down onto the steering wheel in frustrated anguish.

****

Cal sat on the back porch of White Columns stunned. Around him, talking in hushed tones, were his fellow deputies. Occasionally one of them would come over, put an arm around his shoulders and try to comfort him. Cal found himself unable to comprehend the reality of the nightmare scene around him. The activity was familiar enough. He had been the first officer to arrive at several death scenes, traffic accidents, a suicide, and two years earlier a homicide. It was so familiar in fact, that he could not grasp the fact that the body being loaded into the hearse for a trip to the state crime lab was Marla's, and how final the event unfolding around him was.

It had now been over three hours since he'd discovered the body. The coroner and medical examiner had each been summoned, had carefully examined the body, and made the decision that an autopsy would have to be performed.

Cal hadn't understood at first when Coroner Bob Shields had questioned him about whether he had found a note. Then it had struck him with gut wrenching force. Suicide! Shields thought Marla had committed suicide. He had started shaking his head immediately, had in fact went into a rage at the suggestion, and Lucas had restrained him physically. He knew Marla intimately. They had shared enough secrets through the years that he knew that if something had been troubling her, she would have discussed it with him. Furthermore, Marla, whatever her faults, was courageous, and would have faced whatever trouble she was in head on. Marla had been murdered. Cal was certain of that, and as that realization began to take hold, a deadly anger began to build within the young lawman.

Cal got up and wandered aimlessly through the big empty house. He was passing the door to the library when he heard voices, and paused outside. He recognized Heywood Carlson's New England accent, and overheard his words. He was telling Bob Shields that Marla had been traumatized by their separation and pending divorce.

"Yes," he said. "Marla was quite upset the last time we talked, but I didn't realized the depth of her depression at that point. I feel simply terrible."

Cal felt his face flush with anger. He was tempted to push the door open; confront Heywood, and expose the monumental lie that he was telling. Marla had been like a prisoner freed from her cell since she had left the despicable little bastard. Cal controlled himself, and moved on down the hall. He went into the kitchen where someone had brewed a pot of coffee, helped himself to a cup, then started thinking like a cop for the first time since he'd found Marla.

He was appalled at the traffic through the house. The investigation was a farce! The house should have been sealed off. Instead, uniformed officers were roaming through it at will, curious no doubt about the mysterious mansion. Cal fought down rising anger and went in search of Harold Collins, the department's chief investigator.

He found Collins in the library with Shields and Carlson. He noticed little Paula, eyes wide with fright, peering out from behind Heywood as he leaned forward on the sofa talking earnestly to the two officials.

"Collins, I'd like to speak with you please." Cal said evenly.

"Sure Cal, I'll only be a minute more with Mr. Carlson," Collins said, not bothering to look in Cal's direction.

"Now Harold. It can't wait." There was an edge in Cal's voice now.

"What is it?" Collins faced looked pinched, impatient.

"Outside, if you don't mind," Cal jerked his head toward the hall.

"Shit!" Collins muttered under his breath. He followed Cal out into the hall. "What is it Cal. I'm a little busy right now." He spoke shortly. Harold Collins was keenly aware of the fact that most of the deputies in the department thought that Cal Dunforth was better qualified for the job that he had been awarded.

"What the hell are you doing?" Cal asked.

"What do you mean?"

"Why haven't you sealed the house? It's like a three ring circus in here. There's people wandering all over. Someone's been in the kitchen and brewed coffee for God's sake!"

"Settle down Cal. We'll have everything wrapped up soon, and you can go home, get some rest. You've had a rough time tonight. I understand how shocking this must be for you, but you've got to let me do my job here. Okay?" Collins said.

"Let you do your job! I've been in shock, I'll admit that, but even I can see that you're not doing your job! You're treating this like it's cut and dried, letting people walk all over potential evidence! What the hell's the matter with you?"

"Evidence? What evidence? The only evidence is in the cellar. That's been sealed. I'm in the process of taking a statement from her husband, a process that you interrupted, I might point out. As soon as that's complete, we'll be through here. Now my advice to you is to pour yourself a stiff drink, and settle down somewhere out of my way," Collins was becoming angry by now.

"Have you requested a forensics team from the state crime lab?" Cal pursued.

"The body is being sent there for an autopsy as we speak."

"But you haven't asked for a team to sweep the house for prints, fibers, trace evidence?" Cal asked stubbornly.

"Hell no, and I'm not going to. Have you seen the bill they send the department for that?" Collins chin jutted out resentfully.

"Have you seen the property tax bill for White Columns?" Cal regretted his last statement as soon as it was spoken.

"I don't give a damn how rich your family is, Cal. I'm treating this case like any other. If you start throwing your weight around, I'll be all over your ass like ugly on an ape. Now I hate to have to talk to you like this, at a time like this, but that's just the way it is," Collins turned for the door.

Cal reached out and grasped his arm. "Listen Collins. This is murder. I'm sure of it. All you need to start an investigation moving is to find one set of prints that doesn't belong, or trace evidence that indicates that another person was in the house. That's all you need. By allowing all of this traffic, you're making it almost impossible to determine that. Can't you see that?"

"Cal, I'm sorry, but this looks like a suicide. I know that's hard for you to swallow, but that's what it appears to be. The sooner you accept that, the better things will be for you, her husband, her daughter, Matt, Drew, everyone. Don't make this harder on everyone than it already is."

"I'll admit that you could be right. On the other hand, there's a lot of loose ends that don't add up. One, there was no note. Two, there's no evidence to suggest that Marla was depressed about anything. Hell, Marla never had a depressing thought in her life. She sure didn't have to worry about money. She's got a beautiful little girl, who incidentally, shouldn't be in this house now under any circumstances. Three, you can't even be sure of the cause of death yet. Those are enough compelling reasons to treat this as a homicide, or potential homicide. In any event, the scene should be protected as though it were."

"One, not every suicide leaves a note. Two, I just took a statement from her husband that indicates that she was very distraught over the breakup of her marriage. Three, it's pretty obvious that she died of strangulation, the result of hanging. Four, Marla Dunforth has never been the most stable person around." Collins ticked off his points on his fingers, his face flushed with anger.

"Heywood Carlson is lying through his teeth. Marla was relieved that the marriage was over. She couldn't stand the son of a bitch. The only thing that made Marla seem odd was that she enjoyed things in life beyond swilling Budweiser from the bottle, going to hog calling contests, and riding around in a jacked up four wheel drive pickup. In this shitty little town those are the normal entertainments, and anything more exotic is frowned on. Now you get on the horn and get a forensics team on their way, and get these gawking, red neck farmers masquerading as police officers the hell out of here!" Cal roared with fury.

Abe Lucas was suddenly beside Cal.

"Abe, get him out of here." Collins said, turning away.

"I'll take him home, but there's something you should know, Collins."

"Yeah?"

"Cal's right. You're stepping all over your pud here," Abe Lucas said coldly.

"Your opinion is meaningless Lucas. That's why I'm Chief Investigator and you're a road pounder. You're just the department's token nigger. You'd be wise to remember that." Collins spat.

"You're Chief Investigator because in this ass backwards department, rank is inversely proportional to intelligence, and directly proportional to body fat. Let's go Cal, before I punch this racist pig." Lucas eyes had filled with heat, and he bored into Collins with them. He wasn't sure whether the racial slur, or the way that Collins was treating his friend made him angrier. Either way, he decided that Collins was a word away from getting the jaw jacking that he deserved.

"Why leave now, Abe? Collins will probably cook a barbecue, and invite the whole county over before he's through," Cal said, thoroughly angry by now.

Collins gave them a final menacing look, turned and went back into the library. Cal could hear him apologizing to Heywood Carlson for the interruption.

The sound of high heels clicking against the oak floor alerted the two deputies to the woman's approach. They turned and sucked in their breath, watching the most shapely pair of legs that they had ever seen propelling a tall generously proportioned blonde toward them. Cal groaned as he realized that he had forgotten to call Shanon back. He had let her walk in on the scene unprepared.

Shanon walked into Cal's arms, hugged him fiercely, exposing him to her delicate scent. "I'm so sorry Cal. So sorry." She stepped back and brushed tears aside. She sensed the aura of aggression radiating from the two deputies, and wondered about it.

"I'm sorry Shanon. I should have called....I just forgot," Cal felt miserable. He wondered if the faint odor of her perfume would remain on his clothes. He hoped not. It was the same brand that Marla wore. The fragrance brought memories of the times that he had spent with Marla to the surface. He still hadn't reconciled himself to the reality that those times were over, a part of his past.

"It's okay. I knew. I knew when I placed the call. There was nothing we could have done. If only I'd had more warning, or had sensed her danger, I might have been able to help." Shanon soothed.

"We were just about to leave. There's nothing to be done here. We'll go over to my place, and make coffee. I've got phone calls to make, family to notify," Cal said.

"Fine, but you let me know what to do. Anything. I'll help any way that I can." Shanon offered.

"There is something. Paula. If you can help with her, I would appreciate it. Heywood is such a jerk. He's brought her here, of all places. I'll convince him to send her with us," Cal went to fetch the little girl.

For once Heywood displayed good judgment, agreeing to let Cal take Paula without a fuss. As Cal lifted the three year old, a faint unpleasant odor reached him. He dismissed the acrid smell of exhaust fumes clinging to the child's hair without another thought. His mind was reviewing Heywood's response when Cal had called to tell him of Marla's fate. He tried to analyze the degree of sincerity in Heywood's voice as he had stammered in shock and disbelief. He decided that he couldn't access the little man's reaction over the phone. He would have liked to have looked into Heywood's eyes as he told him. That way, he might have been able to fathom Carlson's true feelings.

Outside, Abe inquired whether there was anything else that he could do. He seemed pathetically impotent, a giant of a man reduced to helplessness by circumstances.

"You've been great Abe. I appreciate your help. Now go on home, and try to stay out of Harold Collins sight for a few days. He probably didn't understand when you called him a lard assed fool, but racist pig he understands. Stay clear of him."

"I'm not worried about Collins. He's obnoxious, but so stupid that he's harmless. I just hate to see how he's screwing up the investigation," Abe replied.

"Nothing we can do about that now. Anyway, we've got an ace up our sleeve. We'll find out what really happened. You can bank on it." Cal smiled grimly at his friend.

"An ace? You got to be joking. We didn't even get dealt a hand, as usual," Abe said bitterly.

Cal watched as the deputy got into his Jeep, gave the old dog a pat, and started the engine. He turned to Shanon then. "I really appreciate your help Shanon, and I'm sorry for not calling you. It's inexcusable."

"Lets just get Paula away from here."

"I want Pandy!" Paula suddenly cried.

"Pandy?" Cal looked perplexed.

"Pandy! I got to let him out," Paula repeated.

"Is Pandy in the car?" Shanon asked.

"I've got to get him out or he'll die" Paula looked stricken.

"No problem, we'll get Pandy," Shanon smiled at the little girl.

Cal led the way toward Heywood Carlson's silver Jaguar XJ6. He found the door unlocked, and was reaching inside to get the black and white bear when he heard Shanon's sharp intake of breath, and realized that she had been peering over his shoulder, inspecting the interior of the car. He glanced over his shoulder, and saw her eyes glued to the brown leather upholstery.

"What is it Shanon?" He asked, watching her beautiful frightened eyes darting over the interior of the vehicle, as if searching for something.

"What is Heywood wearing?" She asked, a note of desperation in her voice.

"Navy slacks, pink shirt, burgundy tie, grey blazer. Why? Is it important?" He responded..

"What's in the breast pocket of his blazer?" Shanon asked.

"How should I know? You tell me." Cal answered.

"A white kerchief, with the initials J. H. C. in Navy blue letters," Shanon answered grimly.

"Very good. What does all that mean?" Cal asked.

"It means that Paula's in mortal danger," Shanon shuddered involuntarily.

CHAPTER 3

Bob Shields reviewed his notes for the inquest with a sense of uneasiness. They simply did not add up. The report from the crime lab had confirmed his suspicion that Marla Dunforth died of strangulation as a result of being hanged. Other bruises present on the body, and the raw bloodied hands were consistent with injuries that she could have sustained if, at the last instant, she had changed her mind, and tried to abort the effort. The fact that her neck was not broken also pointed to a last second change of heart.

The physical evidence was solid; it was the motive that left Shields unconvinced. There was no note, and he wasn't convinced that Marla was depressed about her failed marriage. He'd known Marla long enough to believe that she would be happier single. He'd never figured out what she'd seen in Heywood Carlson from the first day that he'd met him. Perhaps that was because he personally detested the man. Another strike against the likelihood of suicide was the nature of the Dunforth family. They were an old proud family, with a rich tradition of leadership dating back to the Civil War. There had never been a suicide in the family, nor any hint of impropriety of any kind. The Dunforth's were far more likely to fight than to run from a problem. He remembered Marla as a happy child, full of life and longing for excitement. He'd talked to her since she'd moved back to Emerald, had actually flirted with her in his good natured innocent way. She seemed glad to be home. He had a big problem ruling her death a suicide.

A knock at his office door stirred him from his thoughts. He hoped Matt Dunforth, Marla's older brother, could shed some light on the situation. When he'd called earlier he had assured Shields that he had information that would be helpful at the inquest.

"Come in Matt. Sit down," Shields said as the middle aged man entered the office.

"Bob, I want you to promise that what I'm about to tell you goes no further than this office. I don't want it discussed at the inquest, or anywhere else for that matter. This is for your own use, to help you make up your own mind about what happened. Understand?" Matt said as he settled into the chair across from Shields desk.

"I understand. It would be more helpful if you testified at the inquest, but I can understand if what you're about to tell me is too sensitive for that." Shields said.

"I feel guilty discussing it with you. I'm only going to do so in order to put this tragedy behind us as quickly as possible."

"I understand Matt. Now, you indicated that Marla may have been under some kind of stress that I'm not aware of. I must confess that I don't feel that her broken marriage was sufficiently stressful to cause her to take her own life. Please be as specific as you can be, with the assurance of course that what you tell me will remain in strict confidence," Shields settled back in his chair.

"Marla talked to me about three weeks ago about her relationship with Cal. Most of what she told me wasn't news to me. I've seen the two of them together since they were kids. They've always been close, too close as it turns out. Anyway, Marla's had a crush on Cal since they were old enough to have thoughts about sweet hearts. As I said, that wasn't news to me. I knew that when she was growing up, and I even used to kid her about it, you know, like an older brother naturally would. I didn't worry about it at the time. I thought it was kind of sweet, innocent enough. After all, kids grow up and laugh about playmates that they had a crush on, and think about how silly they were. Anyway, Marla grew up, and suddenly things weren't innocent. She was in love with Cal. I think Cal tried to do what was right, I really do, but I believe that they were.... intimate, on a number of occasions. I'm convinced that Marla seduced him. She almost admitted as much when we talked. I believe that the only reason that Marla moved back to White Columns was to be close to Cal. She believed that she couldn't be happy with any other man. I believe that she had made up her mind to marry him. Marla always had her way. Always. Whatever Marla wanted, she got. I think Cal finally told Marla that he couldn't marry her, that they were blood relatives, and it just wouldn't be right. I think that when she finally realized that she couldn't change his mind, she went over the edge," Matt Dunforth shifted uncomfortably in the chair.

Shields got up and paced the room. He thought about what he had just heard, and put it together with what he'd suspected about Marla and Cal Dunforth's relationship. He decided that at last he was seeing a glimmer of explanation for why a beautiful young woman, with a comfortable lifestyle, might take her life. "How much of this is speculation on your part Matt, and how much did Marla actually tell you about her relationship with Cal?" He asked.

"She asked me flat out how the family would react if she and Cal got married. I advised against it, as a matter of fact, I was quite adamant that it would be wrong," Matt answered.

"How did she react to your position?"

"She seemed resigned, kind of quiet, as if she already knew what I'd say. Damn! I should have known then something was wrong. It was so out of character for Marla to accept anything that kept her from getting her way without a fight. I should have talked to her again about it. I should have realized that it was driving her crazy." Matt clenched his ham like fist in frustration.

"Matt, there was no way for you to know how unstable Marla was at the time. You can't blame yourself. You just can't," Shields felt the deepest pity for the man.

"Thanks Bob. I appreciate your saying that. I've told myself a hundred times that I'm not responsible for Marla's death, but somehow I still feel guilty."

"I know Matt. Those feelings are normal. Everyone who was close to Marla is feeling the same way. Don't let it get to you Matt. There was nothing that you could have done. A person's decision to destroy their own life is theirs to make. Only the individual who makes that decision is responsible. Those of us left to cope with it can never understand how they arrived at such a tragic conclusion. The only way to deal with it is to accept the fact that it was their decision, made for reasons that none of us will ever fully understand. The pain of her loss is bad enough Matt, don't let guilt enter into your thoughts. You're not responsible. No one is."

"Thanks Bob. Thanks for hearing me out. It's a burden off of my shoulders," Matt stood up, reached for Shields hand, and placed the other hand on his shoulder briefly before turning and walking out.

Shields sat back down. Marla Dunforth wouldn't be the first woman to take her life because she couldn't have the man that she loved. History and case files were full of them. He suddenly felt much more at ease about the inquest that would be held in just two hours. He felt a debt of gratitude to Matt Dunforth. It had taken a lot of courage to come forth with that kind of information.

****

Currents of air swirled across sun baked desert, lifted minute particles of sand from the parched earth, and molded them into an angry cloud that swept toward the coast. Along the way, the cloud grew darker as the soul of Africa flowed into the mass of shifting air. Upon reaching the coast, the sand gradually fell away, leaving only the fiery blast of air, and a host of spirits who joined hands and danced upward as the air mass fed on the steaming hot vapor rising from the dark waters below.

The low pressure cell moved off of the coast, out into the South Atlantic, where it first became an embryo nestled into the womb of mother nature, nurished by the upward spiral of warm moist air. For a time, it wandered aimlessly, suckling at the swollen udders of the restlessly tossing ocean below, but after gaining a measure of strength it started on its journey, the spirits at its core spinning and dancing, howling like a pack of animals on the hunt.

****

When Cal and Shanon had arrived at his house, he had remembered Beth Addison for the first time. He was relieved to find a note on the table explaining that she had gotten up early, showered and started back to Atlanta.

Beth worked for Heywood Carlson's advertising agency. Perhaps that was one of the sources of friction that had always existed between her and Marla. Heywood spent more time with his executive assistant than he did with his wife. Marla, perhaps in a perverse reversal of roles, spent more time with Cal than Beth did. Beth was genuinely jealous of Marla, who only feigned concern about the time her husband spent with his beautiful assistant. Cal didn't think that she cared what Heywood and Beth did when they worked late, or went out of town on business trips together.

Shanon had told Cal about her vision of Paula while they drove. The little girl had went to sleep almost as soon as they had left White Columns, still unaware that she would never see her mother again. Cal had pulled the child closer as Shanon related her vision, and his mouth had set in a grim, determined line.

It was Friday now, and Cal, Shanon, and Paula were finishing lunch. The inquest was scheduled for two o'clock. Shanon was planning to take Paula shopping while Cal attended.

It was hard for Cal to believe that Shanon had been a part of his life for only a few days. Their mutual determination to protect Paula and find the truth about Marla's death made it seem that they had been friends for much longer.

Heywood had seemed relieved that Shanon was willing to keep Paula while he returned to Atlanta to salvage an account that was on the verge of moving their business to a rival agency. Cal had been relieved also. He had already made up his mind that he wasn't going to allow Paula to leave with Heywood, even if it meant taking the child into hiding. He was that convinced of the authenticity of Shanon's vision.

Now Paula was sitting in the middle of the living room floor, coloring in a book that Shanon had bought for her. Cal and Shanon were clearing the dishes, working silently, the prospect of the inquest weighing heavily on their spirits.

Shanon was the first to speak. "What do you think will happen at the inquest?"

"There will be testimony from the medical examiner. The autopsy report will be summarized. Harold Collins will give his report, then the six members will vote. They're going to rule it a suicide," Cal spoke bitterly.

"You don't know that Cal. Keep your chin up. Bob Shields seems like a decent man. I'm sure he'll weigh every shred of evidence, and who knows, maybe keep the case open," Shanon said.

"Shields is a decent man, an honest man. The problem isn't Shields. The problem is Collins. Unless he can bring some evidence to the hearing that indicates that someone else was present in the house the night Marla died, or find a reasonable motive for someone wanting to kill her, the others have little choice in their decision. Collins hasn't done anything. He refused to bring in a forensic team to sweep the house. He hasn't made any attempt to identify a motive on anyone's part. He's just content to let the case solve itself as a suicide. It's less work for him."

"What are you going to do?"

"Today I'm not going to do anything. If they rule suicide, then I'll pretend to accept it. If Collins doesn't think I'm trying to build a case he won't get in my way. If he thinks I'm working on it, he'll do everything he can to screw me up. You can fight City Hall Shanon, but if you do you've got to be cunning about it." Cal said.

"So. What will you look for when you begin your own investigation?"

"Motive. Motive and opportunity, those two ingredients are always the key. First you look for the motive, then you weigh it against the opportunity. If both elements are there, you've got a suspect." Cal explained.

"Elementary my dear Watson" Shanon affected an English accent.

"In concept, but not in reality. It involves a lot of leg work. I'll have to examine all of her financial dealings, her will, any business ventures that she was involved with, investments, then I'll have to examine her personal habits and associations under a microscope. Sooner or later, I'll find someone who benefits by Marla's death."

"Maybe we can take some short cuts. How would you like to have your very own witch working the case with you?"

"I've never thought about having my very own witch before. Since I've met you though, I think I could like it very much," Cal said.

"You had better get moving if you're going to be on time. I'll finish cleaning up and I'll see you after the inquest. Remember, be cool. Don't let Collins get under your skin," Shanon smiled at him.

"Heywood will be at the inquest I suppose. If he expresses an interest in taking Paula back to Atlanta with him I'll agree to it, invite him over here to wait for your return. Don't bring her home until I call and tell you he's on his way back to Atlanta. I don't think he wants to be bothered with her truthfully. We can stall him a little longer, but sooner or later we're going to have to decide how to handle him on a permanent basis." Cal said as he started for the door.

"We'll handle it Cal. I don't know how, but we will, "Shanon placed a hand on Cal's arm.

Cal felt a tingle of electricity where her delicate fingers were touching his bare skin. He looked into her eyes, and saw a spark grow into something more. Impulsively he pulled her to him and kissed her, felt her return the kiss with equal passion, felt the life returning to his spirit for the first time since he'd found Marla's body.

Shanon broke the embrace and stood close, looking into his eyes. "Better hurry Cal. Let them get their official charade over with, and then we'll find the low life that killed Marla. I promise." She pushed him gently away, and turned back into the house.

As she watched Cal leaving, she let the vision of Paula in Heywood's car replay in her mind. Heyward seemed to be taking the death of his estranged wife in stride. Still, one could never tell. She was aware of instances where a surviving spouse had been so distraught about the loss of a life partner that the survivor had killed the remaining family and taken their own life. She knew instinctively that Cal was right to keep Paula away from Carlson. She wondered briefly if the handsome deputy suspected the ex-husband of murdering Marla. He seemed quite cold toward Heywood. He would also be experienced enough to look at those closest to the deceased to find a killer. Remembering the haunted look in Cal's eyes, she realized that when he did find Marla's killer, she would face another daunting challenge. How to convince him to let the criminal justice system mete out the punishment. It was unlikely that a court's idea of justice would coincide with Cal's. She hoped that she was wrong.

****

After Cal left, Shanon finished in the kitchen, checked on Paula to be sure that she was still content, then quickly went through the rest of the house, giving it a quick clean up. She felt a sense of warmth in the old frame house that Cal had carefully restored. Like most of the farm houses built in the late 19th century, it had only two bedrooms, a living room, kitchen and dining room. Each room, however, was spacious, with high ceilings, and large windows that lent an airy, comfortable feeling to them. Cal's bedroom also served as his den, with sofa, chair, entertainment center and bed all sharing the room in perfect harmony. A stone fireplace promised cozy warmth, and atmosphere on dreary winter nights. Above the fireplace the mounted heads of heavy beamed Whitetail deer looked out over the room. On the wall over Cal's bed, a gun rack held a Ruger model 77 rifle, with a Leupold scope, a

Remington Model 700 fitted with a Tasco scope, and a Winchester model 12 shotgun. Over the entrance door on a brass holder, a Thompson Center Hawken muzzle loader glistened black with oil. It was the kind of room that men dream about escaping to for the first week of deer season. A rustic place where the only dreams allowed involve frosty mornings hunkered down beside a white oak tree peering into the swirling mists for a glimpse of the mystical big buck that would be along any minute.

Shanon savored the strength that the room exuded before moving into the guest bedroom that she had occupied for the past several nights. It was furnished to more feminine taste, with earth tone wall paper blending with tasteful drapes, and a comfortable Persian rug covering the floor.

The bed was covered with a beautiful hand made quilt. The room reminded her of a picture from *Country Living Magazine*. The kind of room that suburban housewives longed for.

Shanon found herself wondering what it would be like to be invited into the other bedroom; the lair of the man who had aroused a long dormant desire within her. The place where he dreamed his dreams, and shared them with.... The thought of Beth Addison with Cal suddenly brought a rush of unwelcome emotion. With an angry toss of her blonde hair, she put the thought out of her mind.

She selected a pair of white walking shorts, a matching top, and changed into them. She slipped into a pair of deck shoes and repaired her makeup. She gathered her purse and keys from the marble top dresser, and was ready to leave. She felt compelled to be on the move. She was thinking too much, and the wrong kinds of thoughts as well. Cal Dunforth had enough on his mind without getting involved with her at the moment.

Paula's eyes lit up when Shanon announced that they were going shopping. She scrambled up, grabbed up Pandy, and reached for Shanon's hand.

Paula clutched Pandy as Shanon buckled her into the safety seat on the passenger side. Shanon had started the car and backed out of the drive before she realized that she hadn't decided where to go. The shopping potential in Emerald seemed pretty slim. After consulting her mental map, she decided that Albany was the nearest town of substance, and she aimed the powerful car in that direction.

"Did the Boo Man get Mommie?"

Shanon was surprised at the unexpected question and looked over at the child. Paula's eyes pleaded with her for an answer. "I don't know Paula. Tell me about him."

"He jingles." Paula said.

"How does he jingle. What jingles about him?" Shanon asked.

"His feet jingle. I always know when he's coming because I can hear him jingle."

"Did he come to your house often?"

"Yeah. I think he lives there."

"Tell me what he looks like Paula. Do you remember?"

"He's got hair on his face, and he always looks at me like this." Paula turned her face so that only one side of it was visible, and and she was looking at Shanon out of the corners of her eyes.

"Why do you think he does that?" Shanon asked. Her mind was racing with possibilities. Could the child have seen Marla's killer?

"He's got a big hole in his face, and he's only got one eye. He smells bad."

"What else can you tell me about him Paula?"

"He's got a big long knife. He wears it on his belt." The little girls eyes were wide now.

"Were you afraid of the Boo Man?" Shanon asked.

"Real scared!"

"What did you do when he would come?"

"If I said my prayer he would go away."

"Can you say your prayer for me?"

"Now I lay me down to sleep, I pray the lord me safe to keep. If I die before I wake, I pray the lord my soul to take." Paula intoned.

"That's sweet Paula. Thank you." Shanon's eyes misted over.

"You say it Shana. Say it every night. I don't want the Boo Man to get you."

"Nobody's going to get me Paula, don't worry. Okay?"

"Promise you'll say it Shana. Promise!"

Shanon hesitated, she didn't want to make a promise that she might not keep.

"Promise Shana! Promise!" Paula was near tears.

Shanon decided. "I promise," she smiled at the wide eyed little face staring up at her so earnestly.

Paula smiled. "Can we get some ice cream Shana?"

"We sure can. What's your favorite flavor." Shanon was relieved. She was afraid that she had pushed Paula too far trying to find out if she could tell her something that might help point the way to

Marla's murderer. She didn't know what to make of what the little girl told her, or what it meant, or if it meant anything at all. It sounded so much like a frightened child's nightmare, yet Shanon wasn't ready to dismiss it just yet. With nothing else to go on, it might be a place to start.

Shanon and Paula spent the afternoon in Albany shopping. Shanon picked out several shorts and blouses for herself, realizing that she would need them since she hadn't brought many clothes with her. In fact, she had literally thrown the contents of several dresser drawers into a bag in her haste. She also bought a suitable dress in Navy to wear to Marla's funeral.

Next they found a cute store that specialized in children's clothes, and Shanon helped Paula pick out some outfits for herself. She chose most of the clothing for practicality, but couldn't resist a dainty little dress with lace flowers on it. It was available in several colors and she decided to let Paula pick the color that she preferred.

"Which one do you like best Paula? Shanon held the dresses up for the little girl.

"I want the boo one." Paula said decisively.

"Blue? You like the blue one best?" Shanon asked.

"I want the boo one Shana." Paula answered emphatically.

Shanon realized for the first time that Paula had trouble pronouncing her L's. She had called the man that she said she saw at White Columns the Blue Man. That was more specific than Boo man. A Blue Man could be someone wearing a uniform. A mechanic, mailman, even a police officer. When she got back to Emerald, she would ask Cal what color uniforms the various utility companies wore. It might not pan out, but it was the only thing that they had to go on.

Shanon paid for the purchases with Visa, glanced down at Paula and met the child's eyes. She read the trust there, and reminded herself that she had to work out some way to insure the child's safety. Taking the girl's hand in hers, she was keenly aware of the void that had existed in her own life.

Paula was quickly filling a big part of it. Unexpectedly she thought about Cal, and wondered if he could fill another emptiness in her life? Would he want to?

As they walked across the parking lot, Shanon reflected that Cal's life was probably more complicated than she'd realized. She remembered from her college days that Marla had been deeply in love with Cal Dunforth. She wondered if he'd felt the same about the vivacious Marla. Probably, she decided. Marla had the looks and charm to make any man that she wanted fall in love with her.

Shanon was well aware of her own striking beauty. It was her personality that let her down in relationships with men. They found her too serious, one had even went so far as to describe her as morbid. Some were intimidated by her intelligence, others by the eerie sense that she understood them all too well. In college she had earned the reputation of an ice queen, pleasing to look at, but dangerous to touch, a bruiser of egos, an emasculator of men. She had tried to change, but had never been able to take men as seriously as they did themselves. They all had resented it. Some had rebelled against it, and sought either to dominate her or, failing in that, had simply faded out of her life. Others hadn't been men at all, rather oversized little boys who wanted another mom. It was a pattern that still plagued her relationships, and was the reason that she found herself still single as she approached her late twenties.

The Golden Arches of MacDonalds beckoned from across the strip shopping mall, and she smiled agreement when Paula begged her to go there for a burger and fries. After they finished their meal, Shanon sat quietly, lost in thought as she watched Paula playing excitedly in the little enclosed playground outside the restaurant.

Whatever Cal's involvement with Marla had been, he also had a girl friend. One who spent weekends in his house, even staying over Sunday night, savoring his company enough to arise in the early hours of Monday morning to drive over a hundred miles to work rather than leaving his bed Sunday night. With that thought, another unpleasant reality pushed its way into Shanon's mind. It was Friday, another weekend. The girlfriend would be back, and it would be awkward for Cal to have a stranger, a blonde stranger at that, in his house. She felt deflated, unhappier at the prospect of Cal spending the weekend with another woman than she had any right to be.

She thought about renting a room in Albany for the weekend. She had bought enough clothes for herself and Paula to get by. She could pick up shampoo, toilet articles and other necessities and settle in. Paula could watch television while she read. As soon as the thought developed, she rejected it. Paula deserved better than that. She thought about Panama City, and the fun that she had shared there with Marla. It couldn't be far. She could drive down and spend Saturday at the beach. The more she thought about it, the better the idea sounded. She visualized Paula playing in the sand and made her decision.

Chapter 4

Cal dialed the number of Shanon's car phone and waited. On the second ring she answered, the sound of her voice bringing him a measure of comfort. "Heywood's found pressing business to attend to so it's all clear now," He spoke into the phone.

"You were right about him. He's a busy man. I expected your call much later," Shanon said.

"So, when should I expect you?" Cal asked.

"How about Sunday morning?" Shanon said smoothly.

"Sunday morning? What have you got in mind?"

"I decided to take Paula down to the beach at Panama City. I thought you might have some things that you needed to take care of, and besides, we're having a ball. She's got more shopping stamina than I do," Shanon listened for the sound of relief in his voice.

"Well, I guess that's okay. I'm sure it's okay, but I was kind of looking forward to taking the two of you out to diner," The disappointment was obvious in Cal's voice.

Shanon was surprised, and a little guilty at the satisfaction that she felt when she heard his tone. She realized that she would have been hurt if there had been relief in his voice. "I thought it would be a good idea. Paula will enjoy it, and it will keep her occupied and out of Heywood's grasp in case he shows up unexpectedly. Besides, I suppose you're having company for the weekend."

"Beth's coming in later tonight. That's not why you're going out of town is it?"

"Just one of the reasons," Shanon answered.

"Gee, I'm sorry Shanon. You should have discussed it with me before you took off. Your being here would not pose a problem, really," Cal said earnestly.

"I didn't want to put you in an awkward position. Anyway, we're breezing through Bainbridge so we'll be there soon. Truthfully, I haven't been to the beach this year myself, and I thought that some time spent quietly walking on the beach, listening to the surf might be good for me. Maybe it will clear my head a little," Shanon thought that if she were dating Cal Dunforth, and some strange blonde moved in there would be a big problem. She doubted if Beth Addison would feel any differently.

She changed the subject, approached the one that they had been putting off. "How did it go at the inquest?"

"Just the way I had it figured" Cal said, a trace of bitterness in his voice.

"I'm sorry Cal. At least you were expecting it."

"Yeah."

"I may have something for you to check out. Something that Paula said. She mentioned something about a blue man being at White Columns several times. She was afraid of him, whoever he was. I thought that it might be somebody in a uniform of some kind, a utility worker, maintenance guy, something like that. Paula said that he jingled when he walked. What do you think?"

"You may be on the right track with the maintenance type. Maybe it was tools, or keys that made the sound. I'll check on it." Cal said.

"Cal, your voice is breaking up. I'll ring off now, and I'll call you later to let you know when to expect us."

"Sure. You guys relax, and have a good weekend. I'll see you Sunday."

Cal checked his watch as he hung up the phone. It was 7:30. He'd have just enough time to shower and change before Beth arrived. He thought about Shanon's clothes in the guest room, shrugged and started stripping off his clothes. He wasn't doing anything wrong, had nothing to hide. If Beth noticed the clothes he'd just tell her the truth. She shouldn't be upset about Shanon. Hell, what would he have done with Paula all week without her help.

When he'd phoned Beth Monday to tell her about Marla, she had been surprised and shocked. She had tried to comfort him on the phone, but she had not offered to come back down to help him. She shouldn't be upset because Shanon had stayed. Although his line of reasoning made sense to Cal, he knew Beth would be upset— would probably act like a bitch all weekend. He suddenly wished that she wasn't coming. He didn't need a fight with her now, not with everything else on his mind. He stepped into the shower, and let the hot water massage some of the tension out of his body.

Cal took his time in the shower, enjoying the refreshing spray. He had just stepped out, and was toweling off when he heard Beth walk in. She gave him an appreciative look as he stepped out of the bathroom with a towel wrapped around himself, walked over and brushed his lips with a kiss.

"I picked up some sea food salad, a bottle of wine, and a movie on the way in. Why don't you open the wine, and pour yourself a glass while I shower. I'll only be a minute."

Beth kicked off her shoes, stripped, and leaving clothes in her wake, disappeared into the bathroom.

Cal slipped into an old soft pair of jeans, a t-shirt, and walked barefoot into the kitchen for the corkscrew. He opened the wine, got two glasses from the cabinet, went back into the den, and curled up on the sofa. He could hear the water running in the shower as he poured himself a glass of wine. Usually he started feeling aroused when he thought of Beth's sleek, tanned body soaking under the stream of water. Now, he thought about it only because he realized that he wasn't aroused at all. In fact, he found himself dreading the moment that Beth would emerge from the shower, and if she followed her usual routine, snuggle against him on the couch and begin licking and nibbling his nipples.

He got up from the sofa, walked over and picked up his service pistol, and started stripping it. The weapon was already spotless, but cleaning it again would give himsomething to do, and send Beth a subtle signal that he wasn't ready for sex. He hoped that she would take the hint and get dressed, or at least partially dressed. Maybe after the wine relaxed him he'd feel more like his usual horny self, he thought.

Beth emerged from the bathroom, glanced at him, a slight frown creased her brow, then her face relaxed. She retrieved one of his shirts from the closet and buttoned it around herself. She glided over to the sofa, poured herself a glass of the white wine, tucked her long legs underneath her and gave him a long look. "Cal, I'm really sorry about

Marla. I feel terrible. All week long I've felt guilty about last Sunday night. I kept thinking that the last thing I said to you when you left to look for her was something tacky. I'm sorry. I didn't realize...."

"I know Beth. The worst that I expected was that she had been in a traffic accident, or arrested for speeding. Don't worry about it. I haven't given it a thought. I don't even remember what you said," Cal answered.

"I didn't mean that she was a bad person. It's just that she was always interfering in our lives. I realize now that I only felt that way because I was jealous of the closeness that the two of you shared. I think that's something that we need to talk about. I mean, I always felt that you were withholding a part of you, reserving something that's very special about yourself for her. I really don't know how to say what I'm trying to say. Maybe I just want us to be better friends. Can you understand that?"

Cal stopped what he was doing. Was there a real person hiding behind Beth's frozen beauty contestant smile after all? Had he failed to see it because of his relationship with Marla? Was it possible that he had unconsciously compared her with his cousin, and weighed her against an impossible standard? He conceded that it was possible. "I'd like that too Beth."

"So. How do we to start?"

"Maybe we just did."

Beth smiled. "This is supposed to be a really good movie. I'll fix us some salad, and we'll eat while we watch it," She got up, and in a blur of legs disappeared into the kitchen.

Cal reassembled the Glock 19, operated the slide, and pointed the pistol at the floor. He pulled the trigger, marveling at the rubber band sound as he always did, and then inserted the magazine into the weapon. He returned it to his duty holster, paused and then decided to oil the LeMat. He'd never shown it to Beth. Maybe she would be interested in some of the history behind the old weapon.

Beth returned with the food, and they watched the movie as they ate. It was one of the better ones that Beth had picked. Usually her taste in movies ran to the boring. They munched on the crisp tasty salad as the plot unfolded, each seeming relieved not to have to carry a conversation.

After Cal finished eating, he wiped down the LeMat, then sat with the huge old pistol across his lap as he watched the movie. The wine began to take its toll on him and he relaxed, leaning back against

Beth's firm breasts. The movie ended, and neither of them made a move to change the channel. Beth was stroking the firm muscles of his stomach, her hand beneath his shirt, when the phone rang.

Cal heaved a sigh, and reached behind him for the receiver which Beth offered. "Hello."

"Cal Dunforth." The voice was crisp, business like, unfamiliar.

"Speaking"

"This is Electronic Security Systems central monitoring station. We have an intruder alarm at White Columns. When we call the residence we get an answering machine. We have alerted the Alapaha County Sheriffs department, and they have indicated an E.T.A. of twelve minutes. Please give us a call when you reset the system."

"Thank you for calling. I'll check it out, and get back to you." Cal handed the receiver back to Beth.

"Who was on the phone Cal?" Beth asked.

Cal was up now, striding across the room, reaching for his duty belt. "That was the central station. The alarm just went off at White Columns. I've got to check it out."

"Shit! Can't the department handle it?" Beth pouted.

"I've got to reset the alarm. I shouldn't be gone long." Cal was starting for the door.

"Damn it Cal, there's always something else more important for you to do than spend time with me," Beth showed her frustration.

"It's not that it's more important Beth. It's just that right now this has priority. I won't be gone long, maybe 45 minutes," Cal said evenly.

"It has priority! It's not more important, but it has priority. How the hell do you think Webster's defines priority?" Beth demanded.

"I've got to go Beth. I'm sorry. Priority means that the intruder's not going to hang around all night. With a little patience, you should be able to sit tight for 45 minutes." Cal didn't wait for her answer.

On the drive out, he called the dispatcher, and told her that since he had to reset the alarm anyway, he would respond for the department. If he needed backup, he'd call. The dispatcher was a cute young political science major from Valdosta State. She was working the summer with the department for the experience, and because she needed the money. Cal happened to know that she thought Abe Lucas was the hottest guy around. Usually he teased her about his friend, but tonight he wasn't in the mood. He accepted her condolences regarding Marla, and replaced the handset.

****

Matt Dunforth splashed a generous amount of Jack Daniels into a glass, dropped in a couple of ice cubes, and rummaged through the office refrigerator for a can of soda. He stirred the drink with a thick forefinger, then noisily sucked the liquid off of the finger before sampling his handiwork. With a satisfied nod, he walked into his office, sat down behind his desk, and leaned back in the comfortable leather chair. He didn't spend much time in the office, most of his work was outside, cruising timber, or supervising control burns, or showing a tract of land to a potential buyer. He loved the work. It provided a sense of freedom, and kept him constantly outdoors and on the go. Unlike his younger brother Drew, Matt wasn't the studious type. When he wrote a letter, or a ten page sales proposal, the first draft was the final draft, but remarkably, when his secretary proof read his work she seldom found an error.

He had formed Alapaha Land and Timber in the fall of 1972, within weeks of his return from Vietnam where he had been a platoon leader in the 101st Airborne. From the green second leutenant fresh from ROTC at the University of Georgia, he had quickly developed a reputation as a hardened soldier who got the job done, and kept his men alive. Soldiering had come naturally to Matt Dunforth. He was cool and determined under fire, and had an uncanny feel for the ebb and flow of battle. Other men placed their faith in him, and he always delivered, accomplishing his missions, and taking minimum casualties. He had used the same interpersonal skills and ability to forge a business that dominated the real estate and timber business in a five county area.

Matt wasn't a worrier by nature, but for the past several days his nerves had been on edge. Marla's death, and the investigation had taken its toll, and now, with the day behind him, he needed the drink, and time to think. All of the attention focused on the cellar at White Columns had almost spooked him. Only one other person knew what he had buried there forty years ago. Now as he sat sipping the whiskey, he wondered what was left, wrapped carefully in a newspaper, and tucked inside of an old coal bucket. Enough he decided. A forensics team would have little trouble determining that the gaping hole in the human skull was a forty five caliber bullet hole.

He slid open his right hand desk drawer and removed the Colt Peacemaker from its oiled leather holster. Moving the hammer to its half cocked position, he opened the loading gate and rotated the cyclinder, pushing the fat cartridges out one at a time with the ejector rod. He counted five rounds, then rotated the cyclinder another complete revolution to be sure the weapon was unloaded. The ivory grips filled his big hand as he extended the weapon toward an imaginary assailant standing in the doorway. He thumbcocked the hammer as the weapon came to bear, and was rewarded by a sinister series of clicks as the old gun settled on target. A gentle trigger squeeze dry fired the weapon without moving the front sight from the target.

He reloaded five of the cyclinders, leaving the one under the hammer empty for safety, then returned the weapon to its holster. He closed the drawer and sat thinking. They wouldn't find anything. There was no reason for them to dig. The dirt would have settled in by now, leaving no trace of having been disturbed. No. They wouldn't find anything. There was nothing to worry about. Still, he would feel a lot better when things settled down, and the cops finished poking around.

****

Cal had checked the house thoroughly, reset the alarm, and had walked back to his patrol car. He was about to drive away, but changed his mind. He stared at the ghostly pale mansion, iridescent in the moon light. Why was the alarm system suddenly going crazy? He knew that an alarm system of the quality that Marla had purchased for the old house shouldn't give trouble if properly installed. Occasionally, a window or door contact would give a false alarm in an old house if the woodwork swelled from excess humidity unless it was aligned properly, but he had checked them all when he'd made the installation. He'd found nothing wrong with them.

When he had first arrived, he had quickly circled the house, looking for signs of forced entry, and found none. Upon checking the alarm's control panel, he had found that it had been a motion detector that had sensed an intruder. That hadn't made sense either. How could anyone get through the perimeter system without triggering it? Motion sensor's were a hedge against an intruder with lots of ingenuity, who felt that the loot inside justified going through a wall, the roof, or coming up through the floor. Cal had found no sign of forced entry, yet the panel had indicated an intruder in zone 6. A passive infrared device with a dual detection system consisting of a microwave sensor coupled with the passive infrared, cast its extremely reliable trap pattern along the upstairs hallway, designated in the system control panel as zone 6.

Cal started walking back toward the house as these puzzling thoughts ran through his mind. He'd deliberately chosen the dual detection motion sensor because of the inherent safeguards against false alarms. In order for the device to go into alarm, both the passive infrared sensor, and the microwave sensor had to sense movement simultaneously. Since they functioned off of completely different technologies, the chance of both sensor's being fooled by a false condition was remote in the extreme, yet that had apparently happened. It was beginning to be a frustrating enigma for Cal.

The entire scenario was a little spooky. It was as if someone was hiding inside the house, or had found a secret entrance that wasn't covered by the contacts of the perimeter system. Cal was convinced that the alarm was working properly. Someone had tripped it. The question was, who? And why? He had searched the house with a fine tooth comb, both for a hidden intruder, and for signs of anything missing. He'd found nothing. Some one was playing games. Sick perverted games. Could it be someone obsessed with the grisly murder of Marla Carlson? Did who ever it was have anything to do with her death. Cal still had not accepted the coroners finding of death by suicide. He never would. He was the only one besides Shanon who was convinced that she'd been murdered. The episode with the alarm system reinforced his gut feeling that someone had murdered his cousin. Cal Dunforth intended to find whoever was responsible for Marla's death. Motive, that was the key, and so far he hadn't been able to find one. He was sure though, that if he kept digging one would emerge. Then he'd have something to build a case on.

He'd reached the front porch by now, and he sat down in the cane back rocker that had been Granny Dunforth's favorite. He realized that he had picked up the Lemat revolver, intending to move it across the seat out of his way, but he had instead carried it back in his hand to the house. Now he hefted it's considerable weight. He'd been cleaning it for the hundredth time since Marla had given it to him when the alarm had gone off. He'd left in such a hurry that instead of replacing it in his gun safe, he'd carried it with him to the patrol car. He stared down at it, wondering what stories the big weapon could tell if it could talk. Had it ever killed? Chances were good that it had. Revolvers had been the primary weapons of the Confederate calvary, used extensively in close quarters combat. The gun exuded a faint odor of Rem Oil from his painstaking maintenance that he'd lavished on it. Abruptly Cal wondered what his life would have been like it he'd lived a century earlier. Probably a hell of a lot simpler, he thought.

For one thing, women had been simpler then. They'd known

what they wanted. A good secure home, a man to worship them, children; they had been predictable, comprehensible. Well, that had sure as hell changed. In these times they either didn't know what the hell that they wanted, or they couldn't get enough of it when they found out. He thought about Beth Addison. Sometimes he thought that she loved him, then again, he felt as though he were simply an amusement in her life. He was beginning to believe that the only thing that she was capable of loving was herself, and her career. Fuck her, he thought. No, forget her. Fuck somebody else, that was what he needed to do.

With that thought, an image of Marla, a young Marla, with high proud breasts rubbing against him in the cold water of the river leaped into his mind. Damn! I really am fucked up he thought. When I think about sex, a dead girl is the first image to come to mind. Pretty sick Cal, pretty damn weird. Suddenly his eyes filled with bitter wetness. Relentlessly he shoved his feeling back down into the recesses of his mind. He didn't have time for feeling now. He had a killer to catch. After that, maybe he'd have time for feeling.

He hefted the big pistol, aimed at an imaginary figure stealing across the front lawn in the moon light, and thought about how simple, how pure the revolver was. A product of a better era, he thought, comparing it in his mind with the Glock 19 pistol riding in a ballistic nylon holster on his right hip. Now the revolver is facing obsolescence, overshadowed by wonder nines, and the even newer 40 Smith and Wessons, crammed with magazines holding fifteen rounds of high velocity jacketed hollow points, or perhaps some exotic load like Glaser Safety Slugs. To top it off the damn things were made of plastic, black ugly brutish polymer plastic. Without grace or beauty, modern handguns had become utilitarian tools, like a damn air wrench or something. For all of its modern design and efficiency, the Glock in his holster had never been fired in anger. He knew that the Lemat had. Somehow that made the old Civil War relic seem more potent than the extremely accurate, and very reliable automatic that he wore.

He noticed the moonlight creeping onto the porch, and suddenly remembered the dark mysterious spot, reputed to be human blood. He stared at the place where its outline was supposed to be. He saw nothing, yet he knew that it was there. He shivered remembering the sucking, devouring feeling that it had exerted over him when he'd been a child.

The little involuntary shudder made him angry. Imagination, that's all it had been, yet somehow, he'd allowed the fear that it had inspired in him that night go unchallenged for all of these years. In a sudden move of defiance, he dragged the rocker over to the spot and sat there, daring whatever he'd felt to try and take him now. Almost as soon as the thought entered his mind, he realized how childish it was. Still, he didn't move the rocker.

He sat motionless for a long time, allowing his mind to work on the possible motives that someone may have had to kill his beautiful cousin. Nothing he thought of made sense, and he soon gave up, preferring to sit patiently, his mind in neutral. The only productive thing that he could think of that he might accomplish was to actually be present when the alarm went off. Unlikely, no one would play games with the system with him sitting on the porch, he thought. If it went off now, it would be an indication that it was somehow defective.

Midnight found him still there. He had no intention of going home to fight with Beth. He preferred to sit enjoying the cool night breeze, and the sounds of wild creatures stirring along the river. His head slowly bowed until it was resting on his chest.

Disconnected images raced through his mind for a few seconds, then sleep claimed him— closing on him like a down comforter, and wrapping him in a cloak of darkness as all of the day's tension drained out of him.

While he slept, the moonlight crawled slowly toward him, like a predator stalking unwary prey. Silently it cast it's pale glow across his sleeping form, sifted beneath the chair, and reflected off of something on the smooth floor beneath him.

****

Cal leaned forward in his saddle, allowing his body to synchronize with the powerful motion of the grey stallion beneath him. He could hear the horse's heavy breaths timed with his long powerful stride. Each time the muscular neck stretched forward, a guttural huhungh erupted from the horses dilated nostrils. Cal felt flecks of foamy saliva from the horse's mouth whipped back into his face by the night air rushing past him. On all sides, churning, striving horses propelled grim determined riders dressed in gray uniforms with gold braid toward some vital destination that he couldn't picture. All he knew was that he was part of this headlong charge, and he felt a fierce rush of emotion that brought the sting of tears to his eyes. His heart swelled with excitement until his chest felt as though it might explode.

Ahead, he could make out the dim outline of the river, saw slivers of light explode in the moonlight as the first wave of horses thundered into the water. In seconds, his horse was in the stream. He felt cold water rushing into his calvary boots as the river spilled over them. The powerful horse churned forward, slowed but not discouraged by the resistance of the river. Cal took the opportunity to study the men around him as they spurred their mounts through the stream. Their faces were drawn and haggard, as if they hadn't slept, or eaten in days. The ones without beards sported grime soaked stubbles of whiskers that shaded their faces dark in stark contrast to the brightly shining eyes focused out of dark hollowed sockets. The gleam in their eyes had a maniacal intensity that he had never before witnessed except in combat veterans about to close with their enemies. It was clear that he was riding toward some momentous event that drew the men around him like a magnetic force.

He saw White Columns ahead of him, rising from the bluff like a white beacon overlooking the surrounding cotton fields. It seemed to glow out of the darkness; absorbing the energy of the full moon to light its white towering walls for the approaching horsemen to guide on. Whatever was to happen would take place there. He knew it intuitively, and the house was alive, urging the riders on, a white pure icon, or perhaps a ravished virgin, silently crying out for redemption. Cal felt the house reach out and touch his heart, drawing him inexorably into whatever was about to happen.

The first of the riders were out of the water now. Cal saw the tall golden haired officer leading the charge draw his sabre. His horse reached solid ground, and gained momentum. All around him Cal heard the sinister metallic whisper of sabers leaving their scabbards. When the troop reached the house, their leader rode his horse onto the porch, then through the closed front door of the house, and vanished inside. In minutes he reappeared, dragging a cursing struggling prisoner.

Several of the horsemen dismounted, and surrounded the struggling man. Within seconds they had looped a hangman's noose around his neck. One of them tossed the rope across a heavy beam that supported the balcony overhead. He remounted his horse, and spurred it forward until the prisoner was suspended in the air. While the hanged man kicked and convulsed, he made the end of the rope fast to the porch railing.

Cal sat on his horse in front of White Columns, and watched the carpetbagger slowly twisting at the end of the rope. The bastard's hands clawed desperately at his fleshy neck at first, then his struggles became weaker. Cal watched fascinated as the man's tongue lolled out of his mouth, and seemed to enlarge to grotesque proportions.

The golden haired officer drew a huge revolver from his holster and fired, point blank, into the body strangling at the end of the rope. He fired nine times— the force of the balls causing the body to buck and kick with each shot. The tenth shot was a much louder, more powerful blast, and one side of the man's face disintegrated under the charge of shot.

Cal tore his eyes away from the man swinging slowly at the end of the rope, and stared at the house. There, with his face pressed against the glass of the window, was a youth who appeared to be about sixteen. The look on the boy's face was one of naked hatred. It took Cal several seconds staring into the boys eyes to realize that the youth was looking at the body of the man dangling at the end of the rope. His bile seemed to be aimed at the hanged man.

The Rebel officer holstered the huge pistol, turned his horse, and stared at Cal. He rode down the steps of the house, stopped in front of Cal, and gave him a mournful look. "Why couldn't you stay at home, with Ma and Sis like I begged you? I tried to tell you that the war was over, and as good as lost. I thought you'd listened, then I got Ma's letter. I prayed that you'd get wounded, captured, anything but this. I guess it wasn't God's will. Damn! If you'd stayed home, like I told you, none of this would have happened. Now Ma's dead. Sis! Oh God! Sis! My soul aches when I think about that filthy Yankee pig's hands on her! After he was finished with her, he gave her to his rabble. God damn him to hell!"

The officer stared at Cal through eyes that burned with an unnatural light. Cal felt like he was looking into a mirror that was talking back to him with a stranger's voice. "Well, we've done what had to be done. Let's ride little brother." The officer spurred his horse past Cal, and lifted his fist into the air. The troop of calvary fell into formation behind him, and moved back toward the river.

Cal felt a wave of confusion. Who was the officer leading them? Why had he called Cal little brother? How could the two of them look so much alike? As alike as brothers! He took one final look at the man twisting at the end of the rope. He studied the pool of blood forming on the porch beneath him, then turned and spurred after the receding riders.

As he neared the river, he smelled a smothering sulfurous odor. He noticed a layer of shifting smoke hovering over the water, and realized that the odor was coming from the river. The first of the line of riders disappeared into the haze, and the entire column followed, swallowed up by the smoking cauldron. As Cal neared the stream, he felt a wave of heat rush out to engulf him, and felt an awful force drawing him into the smoke. Then he was inside the smoking layer of heat that covered the river, and discovered to his horror that the river itself had turned to molten lava, with dancing blue tongues of flame along its surface. The smoke surrounding him burst briefly into flames, then went out. He tried to scream, but couldn't. He tried to fight the force that sucked him toward the fiery eternity that was swallowing the troop of calvary, but found it irresistible. He smelled his horse's flesh burning, and felt the frenzied scream of the animal as a physical force as the creature waded into the river of fire. Hot gases rushed into his lungs, took his breath, and stifled the scream that was trying to escape from his throat.

Cal woke up trembling in terror. He looked down, saw the last of the moonlight inch away from beneath his chair, and screamed. His nightmare still held him in its grasp. Off to his left he saw a movement. Swiveling his head to look, he realized that it was only a shadow, and tried to calm his racing pulse. He almost succeeded until he realized that the shadow was that of a man's body dangling by a rope. He looked up, terrified of what he would see, but his eyes were drawn upward despite his fears. His breath escaped his lungs in a rush when he saw that there was nothing there. When he looked back to his left, he saw only his own shadow. Several seconds elapsed before he could move. When he was able to shed his paralysis, he lunged out of the chair, staggered and almost fell. He heard the Lemat revolver clatter to the floor. He stood on wobbly legs for a few seconds with his heart racing wildly. Only when he realized that he'd had an unusually realistic nightmare did he breathe easy and relax.

He reached down, picked up the pistol, and made his way on less than steady legs to his car. He climbed in, sat there for a few minutes, then started the engine and drove home.

He used his flash light to light the way into the house. The flare of the overhead light as he hit the switch had never been so comforting before. He slumped down in a chair at the dining table with the old pistol on the table before him. He was still marveling at the clarity of the nightmare when he became aware of the smell of sulfur. No. It had to be his imagination. The odor persisted, and he glanced down at the black powder revolver. He noticed the residue of burned powder on the nose of the hammer. He picked up the weapon and sniffed its bore. In morbid fascination he inspected each of the nine cylinders. All had the unmistakable residue of black powder in them! My God! It's been fired. All nine cylinders and the shotgun tube underneath! Just like the dream! How! The realization that it had not been a dream after all, that he had been within one step of hell sent cold chills down his spine.

He went to the kitchen, opened the cabinet, and took down a bottle of George Dickel. Not bothering with a mixer or ice, he poured two fingers of the amber liquid into a glass, and swallowed it in quick gulps. Only then did he fill the glass with ice, pour in a shot of whiskey, and fill it with coke from the refrigerator. His hands shook so badly that he spilled the drink on the kitchen floor. For the first time in his life, Cal Dunforth doubted his own sanity.

Chapter 5

Beth Addison awakened to the sound of the television's steady hiss. The channel had signed off the air. She got out of bed and turned it off. She rubbed sleepy eyes, and checked the clock on the bedside table. The numerals blurred without her contacts, but she could see that it was after five. Where the hell was Cal? She had watched television the previous night until sleep had claimed her. She remembered clearly that she had watched the late show, and that he still hadn't arrived home. She felt a knot of worry forming in her stomach as she threw on her robe, and started wondering what he had found at White Columns.

She found Cal leaning head down on the dining room table, an empty bottle of George Dickel beside his elbow. The room had the faint smell of whiskey as Beth walked over to Cal. She put a hand on his shoulder and shook him gently. When he didn't respond she shook him more vigorously.

It was then that she noticed the singed tips of his hair, smelled the acrid, unpleasant odor that clung to him.

"Cal! Cal! Wake up! For God's sake! What the hell happened to you?"

Cal's only response was an irritable groan.

Beth decided that he was stinking drunk, passed out. She tugged on him, half dragged, half lifted his two hundred pound body out of the chair. "Cal! Wake up! Get in bed. Come on now, you've got to help me."

Beth was deceptively strong for a woman, but it was a struggle for her to drag him into the bedroom, and dump him across the bed. She positioned him as best she could, then stood back staring at him. His eyebrows and mustache were singed as well as the tips of his hair. She wondered with rising alarm what had happened. It wasn't like Cal to drink until he passed out. He seldom had more than a couple of drinks. Whatever had happened to him tonight must have been pretty awful. At least he didn't seem to be hurt.

Beth decided to sleep in the guest bedroom. There was no way that she was getting into bed with Cal. He was sprawled all over the bed for one thing. He smelled horrible, and still had his clothes on, including his duty belt.

The aroma of perfume greeted her when she opened the door to the guest bedroom. She felt the hair on the back of her neck tingle as the smell of Marla Carlson floated around her. She felt for the light switch, flipped it on, and her bright blue eyes darted around the room, expecting to see her old nemesis. When she found the room empty, she felt slightly foolish. Her keen nose had not betrayed her though. The scent was definitely Marla's. She wondered how long it would linger, marveled that it could last this long.

Beth slid between the sheets and lay thinking. There was something disquieting about the atmosphere in the house. It was as if a subtle change had taken place— a change that made her somehow less welcome. It had started last evening. Cal had been cool to her, as if he were trying to put a certain distance between them. Then there was the mystery of his disappearance. He had stayed out until Beth had finally drifted into sleep well past midnight. Adding to the enigma was the condition that she had found him in. What had happened to him? How had he been burned. Not so much burned as scorched, as though he had barely escaped an explosion, or fire.

Beth got out of bed. It was useless trying to go back to sleep. She was too uneasy and worried. She decided to brew coffee. Cal would surely need some when he finally awakened.

She smelled Marla again when she stood. There was no question about it. She followed the haunting scent to the closet, and opened the door. She drew a sharp intake of breath when she saw the women's clothing. Confusion was her first reaction, then slowly a chilling thought wormed its way into her mind. She leaned into the closet, inhaled Marla's perfume and shivered.

She walked across to the antique dresser, and opened one of the drawers. She gasped in revulsion at the sight of delicate lace panties and bras. Beth backed away, horrified at what she had found. She felt a mixture of anger, betrayal, and morbid fascination. What, she wondered, had she stumbled upon? Why would Cal bring Marla's clothes to his house? Was it part of some diabolical plan on his part to spook her, to infuse her with guilt so that she would make a mistake and implicate herself?

No. I'm being paranoid, she told herself. Marla's death had been ruled a suicide, just as they'd planned, besides how could she be implicated? She had played only a small role in the overall scheme. She had simply agreed to stay over Sunday night, and to keep Cal occupied and out of the way. Their plan was flawless. It would succeed, and each would get what they wanted. For her, that meant not having to share Cal with a bitch from his past that had hooks in him so deep that there was no shaking them off. She didn't care about anything else.

She didn't care about White Columns. It wasn't important to her. What did matter was that now, with her rival out of the way, she would have Cal Dunforth. She had gone along with the plan for that reason alone. He was worth the risk.

Beth decided that there was another reason, one that frightened her even more than the prospect of being an accessory to murder, that accounted for Cal bringing the clothes here. An image of Cal fondling Marla's silky panties, or sniffing the perfume laden garments in the closet—using them to conjure up memories of the raven haired beauty, tortured her. She clenched her fist in anger so hard that her nails drew blood from her palm. In that instant, she regretted that it hadn't been her own hands that had strangled Marla.

Suddenly Beth felt the need to vent her pent up rage. She had to get it out of her system. She changed into a pair of shorts and a loose fitting shirt, pulled on her Adidas running shoes and left the house. Cal hadn't stirred when she'd rummaged in her bag for the clothes, sat down on the bed beside him to pull on the shoes.

She had to get out of the house before she surrendered to the urge to shred the offending clothes.

Outside, the first faint glow of dawn revealed low dark gray clouds against the eastern horizon. Beth stretched her tight muscular legs carefully before beginning her run. Her lithe body was honed to a razor's edge of fitness, stronger, more durable than most of the soft, and pampered executives that she worked with. She found most men weak and contemptible. Cal was different. Cal had the hard muscular body to match her own, and beneath an easy going exterior, she sensed that his will was also a match for hers.

Her stretching exercises completed, she started running, feeling the blood rushing through her veins, purging her frustration. She thought of Cal as she pounded down the tar and gravel road. She wondered if he had a darker, more perverse sexual nature than she had realized. What kind of fetishes had he indulged himself in with Marla? Was that the secret to his attraction to her? Was he able to perform acts with his cousin, someone that he'd known since childhood, that he was embarrassed to initiate with other lovers? Beth decided that it was possible. She decided to find out.

****

Cal felt molten lava dripping onto his bare skin, pooling in the thick patch of hair that covered his chest before running unchecked down his sides. He opened his eyes, looked down and saw the thick candle burning on the center of his chest. The licking orange flame was the only light in the darkened room. Immediately he was aware of the restraining leather thongs that held him securely to the bed, immobilized. He stared entranced by a flowing rivulet of melting wax that slowly oozed down the candle, and settled with a burning stab on his flesh.

He tried to cry out, but found his mouth full of something that tasted of rubber, and could not force the sound past the gag. With a surge of panic, he struggled against the restraints, succeeded only in writhing enough to spill hot wax onto his quivering abdominal muscles. His eyes roamed the room in desperation, trying to gain a clue about the bizarre and frightening circumstances that he found himself in. The flame danced in front of him, enabling him to see only his own naked, form. Beyond that, only darkness, and a vague shadowy outline.

Suddenly a piercing crack, like a pistol shot rang out.

He flinched involuntarily, but felt nothing. A low agonized moaning somewhere in the shadows reached his ears. Another gunshot report, a little whimpering cry, followed by a moan that could be pain, or perhaps pleasure filled the darkness. The pace quickened, with the cracks coming in quick succession, each followed by a whimpering cry that dissolved into a groan of what was now unmistakable pleasure. As the tempo increased and Cal recovered slightly from the shock of his captivity, the sounds became distinctly erotic— taking on the proportions of the sound track from a pornographic movie.

The noises suddenly ceased, and the silence lengthened until it became ominous. The sound of measured steps approaching sent a shiver of fear mixed with anticipation through Cal. He strained his eyes against the darkness, desperately seeking a vision of what was approaching. A shaft of white hot light reached out, and reflected off of a mirror that had been positioned behind him, and illuminated the figure of a woman. A black leather corset that thrust her pale naked breasts forward, as if aiming them directly at him, gave her a sinister look. Leather straps fastened to black shiny boots that encased long muscular legs to mid thigh, and exposed a generous amount of milky flesh above them stood out in bold relief against deathly pale skin. Thick luxurious hair, as black as the mask that concealed the woman's features, fell past well formed muscular shoulders.

As the apparition moved closer the light died, leaving Cal to measure her approach by the sound of heels on the hardwood floor. Gradually she moved into the light of the candle, and he saw that she held a silver goblet in her left hand. Steam was visible, rising off of the liquid in the vessel. Cal stared in shocked disbelief as she raised the goblet to her lips, and sipped from it. His eyes bulged when he saw rivulets of crimson blood staining the corners of her mouth.

By now the woman was standing over him. She smiled, took a huge mouthful of steaming liquid, and leaned down until her raven hair brushed against Cal's erection. He felt a scalding hot sensation as the contents of her mouth was replaced with his manhood, and the liquid flowed down over him. He screamed, a barely audible sound escaping past the gag.

He writhed on the bed in exquisite agony as voracious lips devoured him. Hot flecks of melted wax splattered across his chest as he moved, but he could not restrain his pumping hips. Cal lost all sense of time, surrendering to the surreal sensations as if his mind refused to accept any other stimuli.

His mysterious partner suddenly straddled him, impaling herself, and established a delicious rhythm of movement. She leaned forward until the candle started painting irregular patterns on her breasts with the soot that it gave off. Cal was mesmerized by the swaying globes circling above the licking tongue of fire. His eyes strayed to the masked face, locked with the eyes behind the leather, but could not discern their color in the uncertain light.

As if sensing his purpose, the woman increased her tempo, riding him faster until he closed his eyes, and shuddered with pleasure.

In the throes of his climax, he didn't feel the needle inserted into his straining arm. All he felt was a wave of intense pleasure, and then he was drifting into a sea of darkness that finally closed around him, and carried him into oblivion.

The exercise hardened muscles of Beth's abdomen stood out in bold relief, jerking spasmodically as a powerful orgasm engulfed her. She blew out the candle and slumped forward, experiencing little aftershocks of pleasure. Her lips moved against Cal's ear. "You like it kinky don't you baby. That's good. Good. You can have it anyway you want as long as it's me. I'll even let you screw Marla sometimes. Dear, departed Marla," Beth Addison's eyes glowed maniacally behind the mask.

She went into the bathroom and removed the leather outfit. With painstaking care she spread cold cream over her body, removing the white body make up that had given her the pallor of the dead. Next she removed the wig, turned on the water, and adjusted it until it was hot enough to redden her skin. She stepped into the steam and allowed the hot water to rinse away the residue of cold cream and paint. In minutes her bronze vitality returned and her eyes cleared. When she stepped from the shower and wiped the steam off of the mirror above the lavatory, Beth Addison, successful career woman looked back at her.

****

The telephone beside the bed finally jarred Cal out of a catatonic sleep. He fumbled for it, dropped the receiver, finally got it oriented and mumbled, "Hello."

"Hi Cal, it's Shanon. I'm just calling to let you know that Paula and I are driving through Albany. We'll be in Emerald in about an hour."

Cal was silent, still unable to untangle the cobwebs from his mind. He could hear someone moving around in the kitchen.

"Cal?"

"Yeah, I just woke up. I'm not quite with it yet."

"I understand. Do you still have company?" Shanon asked.

"Yeah, at least I think so. Damn, my head feels like someone's been pounding on it with a hammer."

"Too much to drink last night?"

"I guess. I'm still in a fog, but I can't remember."

"Cal, are you all right?"

"Yeah, I'm fine, just a little groggy. I thought you guys were going to spend the day at the beach. Did you decide to come back early?"

"Well, we won't really be early by the time I get Paula and myself dressed for the funeral and get lunch. I was wondering if it was okay for us to stop by and rest up a little and change at your house."

"Sure it's fine for you to come by, but the funeral's tomorrow." Cal sounded puzzled.

"Cal, do you know what day it is?" Shanon sounded worried.

"Saturday."

"It's Sunday Cal. Are you sure you're all right?"

Cal looked down at his watch. Sunday! He'd lost a day. The disturbing dream like memories began to surface in his sleep fogged mind. What the hell had happened to him? "Listen Shanon, can you give me about ten minutes to get showered, and a cup of coffee down? I'm sorry. I'm really screwed up. I don't know what's wrong with me, still asleep I guess."

"Sure Cal. I'll call back." Shanon said, concern in her voice.

As Cal was hanging up the phone, Beth walked in with a tray filled with scrambled eggs, sausage, and toast. The aroma of coffee curling up from the steaming cup was tantalizing. Cal gave her a worried look. "Damn Beth, I'm sorry. I feel like Rip Van Winkle. What the hell happened to me anyway? I've never slept 24 hours before."

"You've never downed a liter of sour mash whiskey before either. You really put away the booze. I was worried about you. Something happened Friday night. I don't know what time you got in, but I woke up at five in the morning, and found you passed out at the dining table. Your hair was scorched, and your clothes were filthy. I put you to bed, and you've been out of it since. Don't you remember what happened?"

"I don't know. There's a lot of stuff bouncing around in my head that I can't get a handle on." Cal replied.

"Who was on the phone?" Beth decided not to press Cal about Friday night just yet.

"That was Shanon. She was Marla's roommate at college. She's been keeping Paula for the past few days. She's on her way here. She's had a long drive, and they're going to rest up and change for the funeral." Cal eyed Beth warily.

"Well, in that case you'd better eat your breakfast and get dressed. Personally, I prefer your present attire, but it's not suitable for welcoming guests." Beth smiled and playfully groped him.

After finishing breakfast, Cal showered; adjusting the water so that it was cold enough to bring goose bumps to his flesh. The nightmare that he'd experienced at White Columns gradually took shape in his mind as the water revived him. Mingled with the terror of the memory, was some kind of erotic dream that he'd had later, during the following night. In it Marla had appeared, masked, dressed in black leather, and with scalding blood dripping from the corners of her mouth. She had made love to Cal while he was bound and helpless. In many ways the erotic dream seemed more real than the experience at White Columns. He wondered if he would ever be able to separate reality from the nightmares that he'd experienced. He'd never felt such a cauldron of emotions before. He decided that he would have to put it out of his mind for now, until after the funeral. Then when he was alone again, he'd sort it all out.

He hadn't heard the phone ring with the water running, but when he stepped from the bathroom, Beth was talking to someone. He overheard Beth telling the person on the line that he was a mess. She was right about that.

"It's Shanon. I told her that you might be back among the living after you emerged from the shower. Here she is," Beth handed him the phone.

"Hello."

"Feeling better?"

"I'm starting to function again. By the time you guys get here I'll be back up to speed," Cal spoke with more confidence than he felt.

"You're sure its okay for us to barge in?" Shanon asked.

"Sure, No problem. We'll be looking for you."

"Fine. We'll see you in about half an hour. Beth seems like a real nice person."

"Sometimes."

"Have you thought about what we can do with Paula to keep her safe?" Shanon changed the subject.

"No I haven't. I'll come up with something though," Cal promised.

Cal hung up and started for the closet.

"Shanon seems nice. I'm sure Heywood appreciates her helping out with Paula. What does she do anyway?" Beth asked.

"She said the same about you. Shanon's doing research at the University of Alabama, Birmingham. She's got some kind of grant for a study that she's doing. She's interesting. You'll like her." Cal said as he started getting dressed.

"I'm looking forward to meeting her. It was thoughtful of you to remember to call her."

"I didn't call her. She tried to call Marla while I was at White

Columns looking for her. She sensed that Marla was in danger. As a matter of fact, she told me when she called that Marla was strangling. It's the spookiest thing that's ever happened to me," Cal explained.

"My God! How terrible. How did she know?"

"Her field is ESP, Paranormal Studies formally, but it's ESP. She's convinced me that she has special abilities," Cal was trying to decide whether to go ahead and put on a suit for the funeral, or to slip into something casual until later.

"I'm intrigued." There was a current of uneasiness in Beth's voice that Cal recognized now.

The phone rang as Cal was about to reply. He answered the phone instead. It was Marla's brother, Drew. He invited Cal and Beth to come over to his house for lunch. There was tons of food he insisted, and relatives that Cal hadn't seen since Granny Dunforth's funeral. Everyone was asking about him.

Cal explained that he was expecting someone any minute, but that didn't deter Drew. He insisted that Cal bring everybody over. They would leave from his home for the funeral home. Cal agreed. Drew was a decent guy. He was six years older than Cal, and had just made partner in a prestigious law firm in Macon.

When Shanon and Paula arrived, Cal made introductions. He noticed that Beth's demeanor turned frosty when she saw how beautiful Shanon was. He couldn't help but think that if men were as jealous and spiteful as women, they would kill each other off in a matter of a few years and the species would vanish.

After Shanon and Paula changed, they rode over to Drew's farm in Beth's Mercedes. The ten mile trip was uncomfortable despite Shanon's obvious efforts to be friendly. Cal despised Beth's bitchy moods, and lapsed into silence. He spent the time trying to decide what to do about Paula. He wasn't going to let her go with Heywood after the funeral, but could not come up with a way to avoid it without an ugly confrontation. He worried about the problem in silence.

Drew's farm consisted of two thousand acres of mixed farmland and pine forests. Soybean fields fanned away from the gravel road on either side until they abruptly gave way to towering pine covered ridges that surrounded the fertile valley that had, in years past, produced vast harvests of snow white cotton. The house was a ranch style home that Drew had built on the site of an old share croppers shack. The only reminders of the old home was the grove of Pecan trees that shaded the new house and manicured lawn.

Drew, his wife Carolyn and their daughter Angie, spent weekends on the farm. They owned another home in Macon, close to Drew's office. Drew hired seasonal labor as needed to run the farm, and had been modestly successful with it.

Cal was grateful when Carolyn took Shanon and Beth under her wing when they arrived. She was a gracious hostess because of her breeding, and a naturally outgoing personality. Cal had always thought that she and the good natured Drew were as close to the perfect couple that he had ever known.

After greetings and introductions, Drew ushered Cal into his study. He closed the door behind them and poured each of them a brandy.

"I haven't had a chance to discuss this with you Cal, but Marla left you a life trust in White Columns, with the provision that any income produced by the standing timber go into a trust account for Paula. Any income that the plantation produces as a result of your own efforts are yours to keep. Had she discussed this with you?"

"No. I'm surprised that she would do that." Cal said.

"I'm not. She always felt closer to you than she did to Matt and myself. Frankly, the life trust was my idea. She would have left it to you outright if I hadn't talked her out of it. I wouldn't have been concerned about her willing it to you either, understand, except that marriage, or divorce rather, the unfortunate outcome of so many marriages, complicates the picture when it comes to the division of property." Drew explained.

"I understand. You were acting in her best interest to protect Paula." Cal sipped the brandy.

"Absolutely. I've seen too many marriages fall apart and each spouse wind up with half ownership in a home or property, and neither of them be able to afford to keep it. As a consequence it gets sold off, and lawyers wind up with the lion's share of the proceeds."

"Sometimes I envy you Drew. You sit back and analyze things dispassionately, and plan your whole life. Hell, sometimes you plan other peoples lives. It must reduce stress to a minimum, knowing exactly what's going to happen in your life twenty years from now." Cal said with a trace of bitterness in his voice.

"That was a cheap shot Cal. I didn't deserve that one."

"Sorry Drew. You're right, you didn't. I've just been under a lot of stress lately. I apologize." Cal said sincerely. He hadn't meant it as a cheap shot. With the turmoil in his own life, he honestly did envy the calm sedate pace of Drew's structured lifestyle.

"No offense taken. Anyway, we're going to have trouble with Marla's insurance. She had a two hundred fifty thousand dollar term policy, but it's not going to pay under the circumstances. We're going to have to find a way to reopen the case, and get Marla's death ruled accidental. I've talked with a colleague who thinks that we've got a shot at pulling that off." Drew said.

"Drew.... Maybe this isn't the time to discuss all this." Cal was beginning to resent the calculating dollars and cents approach to Marla's death that Drew was taking.

Drew suddenly looked vulnerable. A helpless, crestfallen look fixed itself on his face. "I'm sorry Cal. You're right. I guess it's my way of coping with what's happened. I'm no good at anything else." His eyes suddenly brimmed with tears and his voice shook. "I'm going to miss her so much. I still can't believe she's gone. Why Cal? Why would she do such a thing? If I had known how troubled she was, I would have tried to help her. Why didn't she let me help her? Why didn't she let you help her? She trusted you above all people Cal. I can't understand it. It's so horrible."

"Drew. Listen to me. You've got to keep what I'm about to tell you in confidence, understand? Drew nodded.

"Marla's death was no suicide, and it was no accident. She was murdered. I intend to prove it." Cal's voice was hard, forceful.

"My God! Are you sure?"

"As sure as I'm alive and breathing."

"Who?"

"I don't know that yet. I've got to find out why first. You can help me with that Drew."

"What can I do?"

"You were her attorney. You handled all of her financial dealings. I'll have to go over them with a fine tooth comb. You can provide me with the documents that I need. You can also help me to understand who might benefit from Marla's death. If we find that, we'll be only a few steps behind her killer."

"I'll get to work on it as soon as I can. Tomorrow morning as a matter of fact." Drew said.

"We can use the insurance case as a cover. Believe me, we'll need cover. Officially Marla's death has been ruled a suicide. Cops, prosecutors, judges, and the entire power structure will work ten times harder to cover their ass than they will to solve a case. They have rendered their professional opinion on this case. If they think we're trying to prove them wrong, they'll fuck us over every way that they can. I've seen the wheels of justice turn for too many years. They have no reverse, only forward, very slowly forward."

"We'll pull out all the stops, approach it from every angle. If there's a motive for someone to have killed Marla, we'll find it. My firm has the best investigators in the business. They know all the tricks. Damn it Cal! I should have known! Marla was too damn tough to let life get her down. We'll find the bastard who murdered her. We'll find him, won't we Cal?" Drew's blue eyes had hardened, and a determined glint reflected from them, reminding Cal of the severe uncompromising expressions of their ancestors staring down from the walls of White Columns. Drew Dunforth was ready for battle.

Cal reassured Drew that they would indeed find Marla's killer, then went looking for Shanon and Beth. He hoped that the shaky truce between the two women was holding.

****

Drew leaned forward and buried his face in his hands. What a mess, he thought. Just when he had almost resigned himself to Marla's death, he learned that she had been murdered, and that Cal was going to continue the investigation. The local cops, lead by that incompetent Collins, wouldn't find anything, but Cal would They should just go ahead and tell him. He would talk to Matt about it first, but that was the best thing.

Why hadn't they left the damn thing where they had found it? He remembered the event as though it had been yesterday.

The big storm had roared through during the night, dumping six inches of rain on the plantation. After breakfast Drew and Matt had hurried with their chores, anxious to try to catch some of the fat channel catfish that would still be feeding in the rising waters of the Alapaha. As they had raced for the river, the sun had burned through the clouds and glistened off of raindrops clinging to leaves like tiny diamonds. Drew could feel the squish of black river bottom mud between his toes as he ran barefoot along the trail leading to their favorite fishing spot. He was struggling to keep up with Matt, who was twelve that summer, and beginning to shoot upward like a bamboo sprout. At ten, Drew hadn't started to stretch out, and his short legs were churning as fast as they could, trying to match the faster pace set by his older brother.

As they moved deeper into the river bottom, Matt began to stretch his lead. Gradually Drew slowed to a walk. It was hopeless trying to keep up. He was trudging along, wondering if he would ever grow as big as Matt, when he heard a yelp of pain from ahead. He felt a stab of dread when he thought about the big water moccasin that they had seen in the trail a few weeks earlier. He started running again, hoping that Matt hadn't stepped on it.

He found Matt sitting beside the trail examining a bleeding cut in his foot. With a sigh of relief, Drew plopped down beside his brother to catch his breath. Looking down, he saw a rusted piece of flat tin protruding from the ground where rainwater rushing down the slope had uncovered it. He knelt and pried the piece of metal from the wet earth, and felt a sharp edge. "Look Matt. This is what cut you. What do you think it is?" He asked.

"Who cares!" Matt snatched the tin away and hurled it into the woods.

"Why did you do that? I want to see what it is!" Drew cried angrily. He went to fetch the piece of tin while Matt wrapped his handkerchief around the cut on his foot.

Drew found the piece of metal, about six inches high and approximately a foot in length. Its surface beneath the coating of mud was irregular, as though letters had been stamped into the metal. He used his pocket knife to scrape away the mud, while dipping the tin into a puddle to clean it as the clinging dirt came free. In minutes he realized that he was holding an automobile licences plate. Working diligently he was able to distinguish a T, but the following four letters had rusted over. He carried it back to where Matt was sitting.

"Well, what is it?" Matt asked.

"A car tag. Texas," he proudly announced.

"You can't read it."

"I can see the T, and then there's four letters after that. That has to be Texas," he declared stubbornly.

"Lemme see." Matt reached out for the plate. "Wow! Texas, how do you suppose it got here?"

"I don't know. You think there may be more?" Drew asked excitedly.

"I don't know. We could dig around and find out. See, the water pouring down off the ridge washed away a lot of dirt. We got to have a shovel," Matt said.

"I'll go get one. But don't start digging until I get back!" Drew warned.

"What am I gonna dig with, my fingernails? Get moving, before I bleed to death," Matt grinned.

When Drew returned, the two boys took turns digging in the muck, rooting around like a couple of hogs. Instead of more metal, they found a long slender bone. "What do you reckon this was?" Drew asked, studying the bone carefully.

"Probably a cow or something. Keep digging," Matt grunted.

"It don't look like a cow bone to me," Drew said.

"Maybe it's pirate bones."

"Don't be stupid. Pirates wouldn't bury nobody this far inland," Drew scolded.

"I know butthead. It's a cow bone."

"Bet it ain't." Drew carefully placed the bone along his lower leg. It was about six inches longer than the space between his foot and knee. "Hold still," he demanded, and placed the bone along Matt's lower leg. There was only a couple of inches difference.

Their eyes met, and each saw a measure of fear in the others. They continued to dig, but more carefully now, and when they spoke it was in hushed whispers. Soon they were standing beside a growing pile of bones, and Drew's eyes had widened with fright. "What are we gonna do Matt?"

"I don't know. First let's be sure we've got all of it. Keep digging," Matt ordered.

"Maybe we should go get Granny."

"No! She won't let us keep it if she finds out."

"What are we gonna do with it?" Drew whispered.

"We'll put it in the tree house, to keep everybody out."

"Bullshit!"

Matt turned hard eyes on his little brother. "Boy, you better not let Granny hear you say something like that. She'll blister your butt good."

"That's nothing compared to what'll happen to us if she finds us with a skeleton in the tree house. She'll kill us, then we'll go to jail," Drew said.

"We ain't going to jail. Nothing's going to happen to us if you keep your mouth shut about this." At that moment the shovel hit a larger, more solid object. Carefully, Matt scraped the muck away to reveal the unmistakable shape of a human skull. With trembling fingers he worked it out of the clinging mud, and lifted it free. "Oh shit," he breathed.

Drew started backing away, his eyes glued to the grinning skull as though drawn by a magnet. He stumbled, then sat down hard in the mud. He started scooting backward, away from the horror that Matt held in muddy hands. The empty sockets seemed to glare at him menacingly. He felt tears begin to stream down his face. He would have turned and raced for the house, except that his legs wouldn't work.

Matt carefully set the skull down on a stump, then sat down and stared at it. While the bones had been spooky, he hadn't really believed that they were human. The skull left no doubt. He was looking at the remains of a human, and the hair at the back of his neck stood on end. Even more ominous than the skull, was the neat round hole the size of his finger centered just above the vacant eye sockets. Whoever the skull had belonged to had been murdered, shot in the head in a cold blooded execution. He became aware of Drew crying. "Shut up crying, Drew. Act like a man. We've got to figure out what to do now," he said softly.

Drew's memory was so clear that he could feel the same cold worm of fear squeezing his gut that he had felt when he had first felt the skull's empty eye sockets glaring at him. He had the same trapped feeling. He had been unable to convince Matt that they should leave the skull where they found it. Matt had insisted that they keep it, and it had hung inside the tree house above the entrance for over a year.

Now Drew remembered the day that Granny Dunforth had discovered the macabre trophy. He shivered involuntarily at the scene. He had expected some terrible punishment—an outpouring of wrath such as the two boys had never witnessed before. Nothing that he had imagined could have been more chilling than what had actually happened. He had watched Granny Dunforth's normally kindly face turn to stone, and her ordinarily warm eyes turn to glittering orbs of ice. She had impaled the two petrified boys with a cold glare, and hissed, "get rid of it."

Matt had buried the skull in the cellar, and the incident was never mentioned again, but Drew knew from that day that a Dunforth had fired a bullet through the victim's head. He had felt his world shift beneath him, and when he looked into a mirror, he imagined that anyone who looked closely could see that his haunted eyes were guarding a terrible secret. For most young men, the loss of innocence comes with a sexual encounter. That fateful summer the shadow of death stole Drew's.

He worried at the idea of telling Cal for a few more minutes, then decided that it wouldn't be a good idea. Cal was in law enforcement, and his instincts would be to search for the identity of the skull, and how the victim had died. Drew decided to keep quiet, the secrets of White Columns were best left buried. He heaved a resigned sigh, and went to join the family.

Chapter 6

The family had agreed upon a grave side service for Marla. The hearse skirted the house and stopped on the back lawn of White Columns. The pall bearers, Cal, Matt, Drew, and three of Marla's uncles, carried the coffin down the trail, across the foot bridge, and up the ridge to the family cemetery. It settled over the freshly dug grave, and the six sturdy men stepped back, sweat pouring down their faces, and soaking their shirts. The Pastor of Emerald Baptist Church waited until those in attendance settled around the grave before beginning his sermon.

Cal couldn't focus on the preachers words. His mind replayed images of Marla, alive and happy. He saw her as a child, swinging out over the river on the rope that they had attached high up in the big water oak that stood on the river bank. He watched as she drove away from White Columns in the Sting Ray convertible, eager to experience her freshman year at Auburn. He could see her sitting cross legged on the attic floor, poring over old pictures, keepsakes, and the numerous sentimental treasures that Granny Dunforth had left behind.

Only when the service ended, and the rich black soil of White Columns had swallowed her body, did the memories fade, and only then because of the procession of people who made their way to him, trying to console him with words that he wasn't listening to. He smiled, returned handshakes, hugs, and mumbled barely coherent responses. He was vaguely aware of Beth Addison at his side, her arm encircling his waist as he made his way down the foot path, back toward the imposing mansion standing forlorn and empty among the bearded oaks that had shaded it for over a century.

When he and Beth reached her car, he saw Shanon's BMW pulling out onto the highway. Inside, her face pressed against the back window, staring back toward White Columns, he could see Paula. The realization that he hadn't thought of a plan to keep her away from Heywood flashed into his mind, and brought him back to reality.

He thought about the two women who were still a part of his life. Beth Addison, his girl friend of the past two years—a sensuous intelligent woman who could be charming when she tried. Shanon Lee, beautiful, exciting, and slightly mysterious. Which of them should he trust to help him protect Paula?

He knew that Beth Addison was probably in love with him. He also knew that she was a self centered callous bitch most of the time. Besides, she was too close to Heywood. Her loyalty might lie with her employer, rather than with her lover. Her career meant everything to her. Cal knew that he couldn't trust her to go against Heywood.

Shanon on the other hand, seemed trustworthy, but he realized that he knew very little about her, and had learned nothing more since he had been with her for the past few days. Still, she was the one who had convinced him that Paula was in danger. She would keep Paula with her, depending upon him to talk Heywood into allowing the child to stay in Emerald for another week, rather than accompanying him back to Atlanta. It might work for another week, then again it might not. He racked his brain for a solution.

His thoughts were interrupted by Beth's voice. "Cal I'm worried about you. Are you going to be all right?"

"Sure. I'll be fine. Don't worry," He reassured her.

"I know that you can't forget about Marla, and that's not what I'm suggesting, but you've got to let go of her, and get on with your life. I know it's going to be hard for you. Do you want me to take a few days off, and stay with you?"

"That would be nice Beth, but I know how busy you are with your job. I think what I really need right now is to have some time alone, and take a canoe trip down the river or something. I've got to let nature heal this wound, and nature's medicine is usually time. Sometimes I can get a better perspective on things when I spend time alone in the woods. I think I'll give it a try. Everyone has been so understanding, so kind, but what can anyone do? This is something that I've got to learn to live with in my own way. I appreciate the offer though."

"I don't know Cal. You still haven't told me what happened to you Friday night, why you started drinking, and just kept on until you passed out. That really worries me."

Cal had prepared a story to explain the scorched hair. "I did something really stupid. I loaded and fired that old revolver without covering the cylinders with grease. I had a flashover. One of the cylinder detonated and blew hot gas back in my face. Luckily, I was wearing my shooting glasses, otherwise I could have been blinded. I guess that it shook me up worse than I thought. Anyway, when I got home you were asleep, and I decided to have a couple of drinks to calm down so I could sleep. I guess I got carried away."

"You've got to promise to be more careful. I'll worry all week about you alone on the river. Are you sure that you want to go?" Beth asked.

"Yeah, I think I will. I need the quiet time." The rest of the ride passed in silence.

Beth dropped Cal at his house, packed her over night bag, and after having him reassure her that he would be careful, drove away.

After watching Beth's car disappear down the highway, Cal went inside, picked up the LeMat revolver, and with a slight trembling in his hands, started cleaning it with hot soapy water. The smell of black powder haunted him, and brought back the horrible odor that had surrounded the river. He shuddered when he remembered the molten river swallowing the troop of Confederate calvary.

As he scrubbed each of the massive handgun's cylinders and its bore, troubling thoughts plagued him. Why had the soldiers rode into the fires of hell so willingly? It was as though their destiny was preordained. Had the lynching of the Union General caused their damnation? He wondered if he had been a part of some dark pact between the souls of the dead soldiers and Satan. Had the Devil freed their spirits from the confines of their tombs so that they could take their vengeance on the man who had defiled their home and family in exchange for possession of their eternal souls?

He swabbed the pistol with a generous amount of black powder solvent as his thoughts raced. Perhaps the spirits of the soldiers had violated the law of the realm of the dead by laying their hands on a living soul. Maybe their consignment to hell was inevitable once they had taken a life. Maybe there was a set of prescribed laws that governed the spirit world that was unknown among the living. Cal shuddered as a vivid picture of Marla, ghostly pale, frightened, and alone, standing before a dark shrouded tribunal of judges entered his mind. "Thou shalt not touch the flesh of a living soul." The words echoed in his mind like the roll of thunder. Fear closed its icy hand around his heart, and squeezed until beads of cold sweat formed under his arms and rolled down over his ribs.

"Marla Dunforth Carlson, you have violated the law of the dead. Your spirit returned to the realm of the living, and in flagrant disregard for the law, did engage in unlawful intercourse with the body of Gabrial Calvin Dunforth. For this crime against the law, I hereby sentence you to burn in the fires of hell!" The words roared through his mind with the force of a hurricane, sweeping his sanity before them.

"No!" Cal roared, slamming his fist down on the table with such force that the skin covering his knuckles split open, showering the oak table top with his blood. He lunged up, staggered to the kitchen cabinet, and reached inside for the bottle of Meyers rum. He unscrewed the cap with trembling fingers, and poured the contents down his throat.

He made his way into the bedroom, slumped down on the sofa, and waited for the warm glow in his belly to chase away the fear that held him in a paralyzing grip. The alcohol worked swiftly, mercifully. In a few minutes he was able to think rationally again.

Paula. The smiling innocent child catapulted into his mind. What to do about her?

The solution came in a burst of auburn hair, a spray of freckles, and bright green eyes. He searched in his wallet until he found the card. Executive Protection Services, the first letters of each word enlarged, with the rest of the words spelled out beneath them in a flowing script. He looked at the name that went with the face smiling at him from his memory. Hannah Groone. He dialed the phone number on the card and listened to ring back tone. On the fifth ring Hannah's recorded voice thanked him for calling EPS, and invited him to leave a message.

"Hannah, this is Cal Dunforth. Give me a call as soon..."

"Cal! I haven't heard from you in ages. How have you been?" Hannah asked.

"Hey girl, what are you doing working on Sunday?" Cal asked playfully.

"I was just in the office trying to get organized. I have to get out tomorrow and try to rustle up some business. You know me, always hustling. It's good to hear your voice Cal. It's been a long time." Hannah said. There was a hint of breathless excitement in her voice.

Cal and Hannah had dated for over three years. They had been good years until she had started pressing him about marriage. Finally she had issued an ultimatum, marry her or get the hell out of her life. Cal could still see the flashing anger in her green eyes when he'd told her that he wasn't ready for that kind of commitment. She'd walked out of his house, and his life that day, had trying to get away before he saw the tears, but hadn't quite managed it. A week later she'd called and said that she wanted to talk.

They had met for coffee at the truck stop outside Emerald. As they had sipped the bitter brew, she had told him that she was moving to Atlanta, accepting a job with the Decalb County Sheriff's office. She'd explained that she understood how he felt, and had accepted it. She'd told him that at first she had been furious with him, but had finally realized that she shouldn't blame him for being honest about the relationship. Far better she'd said, to find out that a relationship couldn't work from the start than to awaken rudely to that fact three years, and two kids into a marriage.

They had parted friends, each with a deeper appreciation of the other than they had ever had before. That was five years ago. Since then, Hannah had started EPS, a security service that specialized in protecting high profile witnesses in criminal trials, executives and their families who felt the need for security measures, but who wanted to keep the watch dogs low profile. Her specialty was becoming part of their families— being a friend to their kids as well as a bodyguard. She was very good at what she did.

She also performed routine investigative work, divorce cases mostly. She had quickly earned a reputation as the person to hire if you needed to check on an errant spouse.

"You know me Hannah. I only call when I need a favor." Cal said, only half joking.

"What's wrong, your wife fooling around?" Hannah laughed.

"Still single Hannah, you ought to know that." Cal said.

"Same old Cal, breaking hearts and notching your pistol. There ought to be a law against men like you," Hannah laughed with only a trace of bitterness.

"Seriously, I'd like to hire you to protect someone. It's kind of a strange situation. Can you spare some time?"

"Sure Cal. Right now all I've got is time, past due bills, and a lot of overhead. What have you got in mind?"

"You remember my cousin Marla?" Cal asked.

"Sure I remember. I heard she got married a few years ago." Hannah's tone was guarded now.

"She died a week ago. I've just got back from her funeral."

"Oh No. I'm sorry. What happened?" Hannah was shocked.

"Officially her death's been ruled a suicide, but I'm convinced that she was murdered."

"I'm sorry Cal. I know how close the two of you were. Are you okay?"

"I'm a little screwed up right now, but I'll be fine with some time."

"How can I help?"

"She has a three year old daughter that I have reason to believe is in danger. I want to hire you to protect her." Cal said.

"You don't have to hire me Cal. You know I'll do it as a favor. Where's the child now?"

"A friend of Marla's has her. We've been keeping her away from her father, Marla's ex- husband, however we can. We have reason to believe that he might harm her." Cal said.

"My God Cal! Do you think he'd hurt his own child? What kind of a monster is he?"

"I'm not sure. I intend to find out though. In the meantime, I need you to help me Hannah."

"You can count of me to do my very best Cal. What's the set up?"

"I've got to think of a way to get you involved without Heywood suspecting what's going on. Any ideas?"

"Marla had custody before her death?"

"Right."

"What kind of work does the guy do?"

"He owns an advertising agency in Atlanta. I don't know that much about it."

"I bet his schedule is pretty hectic. He won't have much time to take care of a little girl. He'd probably jump on the chance to hire someone to give him a hand."

"He's a cheap bastard, and I don't think things are going all that great for him. Truthfully, I think Marla's money was keeping him afloat. I'll be looking into that more in the next few days. Anyway, I don't think he would spend any real money to see that she's taken care of. He will probably want to put her into a day care center, then hire part time baby sitters to take care of her when he's out of town." Cal explained.

"She needs someone that she can feel close to. Poor baby. I'll take good care of her if we can find a way to get him to agree to it."

"We'll have to trick the bastard into it. We can't let him know what you do for a living. He'll be going nuts for the next few weeks, worrying that I may find a way to prove that he killed Marla. We can't let him know that there is any connection between the two of us."

"That does present a problem. I'll think of something though, don't worry." Hannah said.

"Thanks Hannah. I don't know who else to turn to right now." Cal said.

"Hey, what are friends for?"

"You're more than a friend Hannah. I think you know that."

"Yeah," More than a friend, but less than a wife, she thought.

"I'll be in touch when I think of a way to get Heywood to agree to your staying with Paula." Cal said.

"Good." Hannah paused, then said, "It's good to hear from you Cal. Take care of yourself."

"I'll be fine, really. Knowing that you're going to keep an eye on Paula will take a big weight off my shoulders."

****

Hannah replaced the receiver gently, and sat quietly for a few minutes thinking about Cal Dunforth. She tried to analyze the pressure building in her chest, the tightening knot that was growing around her heart. Fear. She was afraid that her carefully rebuilt life would crumble if she became involved with him again. She tried to tell herself that it wouldn't happen, but the flashing images of his tanned, muscular body forming in her mind, and the tension building in her abdomen, rebutted her rational arguments.

What the hell, she thought. She'd never let fear and common sense hold her back before. Why not follow her instincts? Maybe Cal was ready for a lasting relationship now. His voice on the phone had sounded vulnerable. Perhaps the invincible Cal Dunforth was crumbling. Maybe that was why she had allowed herself to let her guard down, and allowed the old memories to run unchecked through her mind.

Marla. A picture of Cal's cousin, laughter bubbling out of her sensuous mouth, entered her mind. Dead. It didn't seem possible. Not Marla. She was one of those charmed people that nothing bad ever happened to. Even though Hannah had known that Marla was her rival for Cal's love, she hadn't been able to dislike her. Marla attracted people because she was so full of energy, so confident that life was one long exciting adventure. Now she was dead. It was depressing. If something tragic had happened to Marla, what could one expect life to hold for ordinary mortals?

Hannah forced her thoughts to focus on the problem of how to get Heywood Carlson to accept her into his home. Nothing short of her living in the same household with Paula as she did with the clients that she protected would be acceptable. Especially since the threat to the child was from her own father.

She picked up the phone, dialed information and jotted down Drew Dunforth's number in Emerald. As she dialed, she wondered if Cal had discussed his concerns for Paula's safety with Marla's brother. She listened to the odd sounding ring back tone of the antiquated telephone system that served the rural community.

"Hello." The voice on the line sounded strained.

"Hi Drew. It's Hannah Greene. I just got off the phone with Cal. I'm very sorry about Marla."

"Hannah! How nice of you to call. I really appreciate it. I'm glad Cal talked to you. He's a wreck right now. I'm sure it helped him to talk with you." Drew said.

"I could tell he was upset. I can understand why. Marla was a wonderful person. I was shocked to hear about her death. Is there anything that I can do?"

"Just hearing your voice is enough. Thanks." Drew said earnestly.

"Cal was concerned about Paula. He seems to think that she might be in some danger. Has he discussed that with you?" Hannah plunged ahead.

"No. No he hasn't. We're all in shock down here I guess. I did talk to him before the funeral and he expressed deep reservations about the way the investigation into Marla's death is being conducted, but he didn't say anything about Paula." Drew's voice sharpened.

"He asked me about providing security for her. I'm in that business now. He seems to think that there might be a problem with Marla's ex-husband." Hannah waited.

"Heywood. What kind of problem does he anticipate?" Drew asked.

"He doesn't think that Heywood will agree to having me involved. At least, not if he knows the real reason that I'm hanging around."

"He suspects Heywood."

"I got that impression."

"The bastard!"

"You're the attorney Drew. Put your fertile mind to work, and

81

come up with a way to get me in," Hannah said bluntly.

"Leverage. We need some leverage. Let's see. Marla had legal custody of Paula. Since her death, custody would ultimately be awarded to Heywood. In fact, until you called, I would have simply allowed him to take the child without making an issue of it. Now, I need some evidence to prove that his having custody is not in the child's best interest. If I had that, I could petition the court for a hearing." Drew thought aloud.

"Maybe that won't be necessary. Maybe you could question him about his plans for caring for her, and let him know that you expect him to make acceptable arrangements. The implied threat of legal action might make him receptive to your suggestion of a nanny for Paula. I could pose as a college student, willing to trade room and board in exchange for caring for her while he's at work." Hannah said.

"Perfect. The cheap bastard will jump at such an arrangement." Drew answered.

"Yeah. From what Cal told me I think he would. It would give me a chance to check him out on the Q. T. as well."

"Damn right. It'll fly Hannah. You know, I never could figure out why Cal let you slip through his fingers. You're smart as a whip, just the kind of woman he needs."

"Hey, let's not go into that." Hannah answered.

"Sorry Hannah, I was out of line with that comment.
 Still......"

"You're a sweetheart Drew. Give me a ring when you get
 things worked out. I'll be ready."

"Thanks Hannah. You send your bill to me and I'll handle it on a weekly basis. Heywood won't suspect a thing."

"Fine. I'll be waiting for your call." Hannah said.

Drew hung up the phone and sat back. He pictured Hannah in his mind. She wasn't a big girl, but she was a tough nut. Her green eyes, and the splash of freckles across a face framed in shoulder length auburn hair made her look like a cute college coed, but when she was angry, those same eyes darkened, and seemed to smolder with heat. Full warm lips that could pout seductively, could as easily twist into a thin cruel line, and the merry tinkle of laughter turn to a harsh rasp as she barked commands during an arrest, and the muscle tone that gave her figure such attractive curves enabled her to weild an impact weapon with deadly efficiency.

Paula was in good hands, he decided. Cal would have been

better off settling down with Hannah than dating that Addison bitch, he thought. Mentally he compared Hannah and Beth. Hannah had a lot of class. Why couldn't Cal see that, he wondered? What was he doing with something like Beth Addison? He had to know that she was trash. He heaved a sigh, what the hell, if Cal wanted to go slumming for a while, who was he to judge.

CHAPTER 7

Cal had mixed himself a rum and Coke after he got of the phone with Hannah, and relaxed on the sofa for half an hour, allowing the drink to calm his jangled nerves, while letting memories of Hannah run through his mind. It hadn't taken long for his thoughts to return to Marla however, and he had gotten up, and started packing his camping gear, preparing for his trip down river. He applied a fresh coating of camp dry to the seams of his North Face tent, rubbed mink oil into his well worn boots, sharpened the hunting knife that he would carry, all in a vain attempt to keep his aching feelings at bay.

Drew had phoned to tell him that he had talked to Hannah, and the two of them had devised a plan that would make it possible for her to provide security for Paula. When he had hung up the phone, he had mixed another drink, and then started checking his archery tackle. Bowhunting season would open in a few weeks, and he planned to do some preseason scouting during his trip down the river. He had missed a shot at a nice buck the previous season, and momentarily the memory of the majestic animal claimed his attention. His vision of the ghostly buck oozing silently beneath his treestand was interrupted by the phone.

It was Shanon. He told her about the plan that Drew and Hannah had worked out, and she agreed to drop Paula off at Drew's house before stopping by to pick up her clothes. Cal found himself listening for the sound of her car in the driveway, anticipating seeing her again.

When she arrived, he already had a drink mixed for her, and met her in the driveway. She followed him inside, and sank down on his sofa with a sigh of gratitude.

"How are you doing?" She asked.

"I'm okay."

"You didn't sound okay this morning. Want to tell me what happened?" Shanon fixed him with her clear blue eyes.

"I'm not sure that I know." He shrugged.

"I'm not trying to pry into your personal life Cal, believe me, but if you want to talk about it, maybe I can help."

"You won't believe me if I tell you. I'm not sure that I believe it myself now." Cal said.

"Try me."

Cal sat down on the couch, drained his glass, and told about the frightening experience that he'd had at White Columns. When he finished, he searched her face for a reaction.

Shanon didn't speak, instead she reached out and gently touched his singed eyebrows.

"Do you think I'm crazy?" Cal asked.

"Do you think I am?"

"Of course not.

"When you think about it, your experience isn't that much harder to accept than the visions that I have. I've spent hours trying to develop a theory to explain how I'm able to see something happening in my mind as clearly as though I were actually there, on the scene, watching with my own eyes. I haven't refined my thoughts enough to call my conclusions a theory yet, but the basic concept is that time and distance are not the absolute realities that we think that they are. I believe that as physical beings we are trapped within a single dimension of reality that precludes us from participating in the full spectrum of what actually constitutes reality. I believe that our spiritual beings, if allowed to escape the physical confines of our bodies, can sometimes catch a glimpse of other dimensions. In your case, I'd say your spirit left your body for an extended period of time, actually participated in an event that took place over a century ago. I find that fascinating." Shanon was staring at him.

"How do you explain the physical phenomena? The scorched hair, the powder residue on the gun?" Cal asked.

"I can't. It's the first evidence that I have heard about that supports my theory that the spirit world is as real as the one in which we live. I'd like to do research at White Columns. Do you think I could get permission?"

"I'm not sure White Columns should be disturbed."

"Why not?"

"I don't know. Just a feeling. There's something incredibly evil there. I suppose I've always known that. I always thought that it was the house itself. Now I'm not so sure." Cal shuddered.

"There may never be another opportunity to observe the phenomenon that you experienced. Please. I can't tell you how much it would mean to me."

"What do you want to do?"

"First I'd just like to walk through the house, and get the feel of it. Later, I'd like to set up some equipment, an infrared camera, a mass spectrometer, a passive infrared motion detector. I've set up in so called haunted houses before with very little results. Here, I think the aura of White Columns is strong enough that I can register activity. If I can, it would be a break through." Shanon was breathless with excitement.

"What about the danger?"

"There's no danger. There's not a single authenticated case of anyone being harmed by a ghost. It's as if they are as incapable of entering our world as we are of entering theirs."

"I'm not sure that is true at White Columns. I can tell you without reservations that I was within one step of Hell."

"Cal, please. It's important." Shanon begged.

"Okay. Set up whatever you want there. All I ask is that you promise to be careful. There is danger there. I can feel it. You will too."

"Thanks Cal. This means more to me than I can tell you."

"You'll be pretty much on your own. I've got to get started with my investigation into Marla's murder. I'm going to take a canoe trip down river tomorrow, camp out on an island about ten miles downstream tomorrow night. I need the time to try and get my head screwed on straight. After that, I'm going to be tied up until I get to the bottom of this."

"That will work out. I'll have my equipment shipped tomorrow. It won't arrive until the following day. After that I'll be pretty busy myself. I hate to be pushy, but do you think we could do the walk through tonight? I'd like for you to guide me through the house the first time, after that I can handle things on my own— prefer it that way actually."

Cal heaved a sigh. He dreaded the thought of returning to White Columns. He knew that he had to do it sometime anyway, and he might as well get it over with he reasoned. "Sure, let's go."

****

In the South Atlantic, tropical storm Cindy celebrated her birth with howling winds, and driving rain. Like a voracious predator, she searched the barren expanse of water below for a victim to devour. At her core, gray shapes danced and cavorted, exulting in power that transcended the force of the storms winds. They held life and death in feathery hands as they rode the surging storm westward.

****

Dusk was gathering like a charcoal gray shroud when they arrived at White Columns. The house loomed up from the emerald lawn, its white walls assuming the pallor of death, and its shadow a menacing ghost in the failing light. It seemed to be holding its breath, waiting in the absolute silence that afflicts the world in the brief time between daylight and darkness.

As Cal climbed out of the passenger door of Shanon's BMW, he was instantly aware of the total stillness that surrounded him. The air was oppressively heavy, like a physical weight bearing down on him. He felt the hair on his neck rising, and sensed a sudden current of hot air brush his face. The evening grew perceptibly darker, as if a shade had been lowered across the dying sun. He glanced at Shanon, saw her eyes glowing with excitement, and realized that she was processing the aura of their surroundings through senses more acute than his own.

Neither spoke as they made their way across the lawn, climbed the steps onto the porch, and hesitated at the heavy front door. Cal inserted his key into the lock, and had difficulty turning it, as if the lock hadn't been opened for some time. As the door swung inward, it suddenly groaned on its hinges. The warm air that flowed out to meet them was stale, and old, flavored like moldy bread. The interior of the house was in total darkness, and Cal had to use his flashlight to find the alarm control panel. He keyed in the code to disarm the system, and flicked on the light switch. He almost expected to find the furniture covered with dust, and cobwebs clinging to the walls. Instead, the room appeared neat and spotless, just as he had found it two nights earlier when he had checked the alarm.

"It's a lovely home Cal. Marla's taste in decor was very good." Shanon said. She was standing very close to him.

The sound of her voice, and her presence in his personal space dispelled some of the coldness that had settled over Cal. "It's very nice. Marla didn't change it much from the way it was when we were kids. New drapes, refurbished the original chandelier, added a few pieces of furniture." Cal explained.

"Your ancestors would feel right at home if they walked in, I bet. Except for the electric lights, and modern appliances, everything else appears to be original furnishings."

"They are, handed down from generation to generation. Speaking of generations, you may find the portraits in the hallway interesting. A portrait of each of the generations of Dunforths who have lived in this house are hanging there. Come on. I'll show you why I'm so handsome." He smiled.

"I see that your male ego is reasserting itself. That's a good sign, I suppose. I can stop worrying about you now." Shanon laughed.

They walked into the hall together, and Shanon studied each of the portraits carefully. "Who's this handsome devil? You look almost exactly like him, except that the expression on his face is much sterner, cruel almost." Shanon said, referring to the portrait of a Confederate Officer.

"That is my great, great, grandfather. He was killed at Gettysburg. The portrait was done sometime during the second year of the war. That probably accounts for the expression."

"Yes, I suppose it would." Shanon drifted down the hall, and stopped in front of Granny Dunforth's portrait.

Cal lingered in front of the soldier, something stirred in his memory, and then in a flash he replayed the vision of the man in the portrait aiming the huge LeMat revolver— remembered the sunken hollow eyes, burning with hatred as he had fired shot after shot into the body of the man struggling at the end of the rope. He shuddered.

"This must be Granny Dunforth." Shanon didn't turn to look at him as she spoke, but getting no response, she turned to find him staring at the portrait. She noticed that the color had drained from his face, as if he were ill. "Cal, are you all right?"

He took a step backward, still staring. When he found his voice it was a mere croak. "It's him, the leader of the soldiers that I rode with in my dream." He said.

Instantly Shanon was beside him, arm encircling his waist. "Are you sure Cal?"

"Positive. It's him."

"That can't be. You said he was killed at Gettysburg. The event that you were part of happened after the war. You have to be mistaken." Shanon said gently.

"No. It was him." Cal thought about the words that the officer had spoken to him, and understood their implication for the first time. He felt a wave of fear rising within him. "My God. It makes sense now. He thought I was his brother, his younger brother. He thought I was dead too."

"What are you talking about Cal? What did he say?"

"He said he'd tried to tell me to stay home, with our family, that he had tried to tell me that the war was over, then he'd gotten a letter. He said 'I prayed that you'd be wounded, or captured, anything but this.' It didn't make sense at the time, but it does now. He was a spirit, and he thought that I was too. That was what he meant when he said anything but this. He thought I was his youngest brother, and that I had been killed! All of them were ghosts Shanon. The entire troop. Do you know what that means?"

"Tell me."

"It means that your theory that ghosts can't harm the living is bullshit! They dragged a man out of this house, and hanged him right out there on the porch! I watched him die Shanon! I was there. I was a part of it!"

"Calm down Cal, you're shouting."

"Calm down Hell! You don't know what you're saying. You don't know how dangerous the game that you're playing can be! I'm not letting you go through with it. That's final."

"You promised Cal." Shanon's eyes were hard, accusing. She wasn't going to let him back out.

"I can't let you risk it. If something happened....."

"Yes?"

"If something happened to you. I'd never forgive myself."

She moved close to him, shared her warmth, invited him into her space. "Why would it matter?"

"That's a stupid question."

"No that was a stupid answer. Why would it matter?" she repeated.

"I..... Cal struggled for an explanation, found none, and the truth trickled out of his mouth. "I don't think I could go on without you," He finally said.

Shanon reached up, filled her slender fingers with his hair, and pulled his mouth down to her own. Her kiss was fierce, and relentless, releasing pent up passions that had been too long without an outlet.

****

They had made love on the couch, quickly, desperately, as if each were afraid that the spark of passion they felt would evaporate, and never return if they waited. Afterward, they had remained on the couch, Shanon's body stretched out on top of Cal, her head snuggled against his chest. When his rhythmic breathing told her that he was sleeping, Shanon had gotten up, dressed, and started quietly exploring the house.

By now, darkness had descended with its full weight, and outside the night had come alive with sounds. Along the river a chorus of owls called to each other, their eerie hooting and screeching reverberating across the dark water of the Alapaha, and sending chills up Shanon's spine. Impulsively she walked out onto the front porch. Here, the voices of the feathered sentinels of death were clearer.

Shanon walked to the edge of the porch, and stared out across the river. She watched mesmerized as the moon crept stealthily from behind the dark outline of hardwoods along the river bottom, and spread a few silvery spears of light across the lawn. Her eyes searched for movement among the trees in the yard, half expecting to see wraith like figures returning from a day working in the fields, or perhaps a ghostly column of riders slipping silently out of the mist that hung over the river.

She felt a subtle force drawing her eyes downward and to her left, to a spot on the floor directly beneath the main support beam that ran across the porch ceiling. She saw nothing different about the floor there at first, but then a shaft of moonlight struck the edge of the porch and she could make out the outline of what appeared to be a trickle of dark fluid overflowing the edge of the porch. She watched with morbid fascination as the moonlight illuminated more of the floor, and the spot spread toward the center of the porch.

Shanon felt a tremor of excitement ripple through her. She took a tentative step toward the spot, and felt it tugging at her; surrendered to the powerful force, and stepped into the pool of glowing light.

Abruptly she felt a violent force vacuuming her consciousness from her body with a wrenching accelerating motion that blurred her vision. She heard a dull thud, and realized dreamily that it was her own body collapsing onto the hardwood floor, and caught a fleeting grotesquely distorted view of it lying there, an empty shell, while her spirit disintegrated into minute particles that gained speed at an alarming pace.

Moonlight flowed over the particles that made up her spirit until they glowed, white-hot. Then darkness descended over her, sending her into total black oblivion, devoid of any sensation except of incredible forward momentum. The sense of incredible speed grew in intensity until a final barrier suddenly shattered as her spirit accelerated through the speed of light.

****

The first thing that Shanon became aware of was the sound of voices. The sounds were below her, and she focused downward and the scene came into focus. A family, a man, a woman, and a teen age boy materialized.

The woman was clearing dishes from the table, diner obviously just finished. She moved with a furtive grace, like a deer aware of constant danger. Her hair was pulled up in a severe bun on top of her head. The dress that she wore was plain, although much of it was obscured by the apron tied at her waist. Her eyes darted toward her husband occasionally, but refused to sustain eye contact.

The man wore a crisply pressed blue uniform, resplendent with gold braid. A silver star was pinned to each of the epaulets of the tunic. A braided riding whip hung from his wrist and dangled down to his glistening calvary boots. Beside him, an almost empty bottle of whiskey, and a glass sat undisturbed by the woman. He poured himself a glass of the amber bourbon, and sat back in his chair.

When he spoke his words were slurred with the liquor. "To a conquered land." He tossed down the whiskey and poured another. "Next year the fields around White Columns will be white with cotton, a fortune waiting to be plucked. I'll be the richest man in Georgia by the close of the decade."

The woman stopped, a flash of desperation revealed itself in her eyes. "But you promised that by next spring, we'd be home in Boston. Now it sounds as if you intend for us to live here." She whined.

"Boston! To hell with Boston! There's nothing there for me. My future is here. Right here! White Columns is the first gem in a fortune that will soon be mine. The South is stretched out, flat on her back, legs spread, waiting, for someone to come along and rape her. I intend to be that man."

"But Johathan, we're strangers here, outsiders and hated. All of our friends are in Boston. We can never be happy here." The woman said.

"In Boston, I'm at the bottom of the pecking order, just another General, soon forgotten now that the war's over. Here, I'm on top. I'm in control. Don't you see? These people lived like Royalty here before the war. This place is like a kingdom! Five thousand acres of the richest farm land in the country. And it's mine! In a few years, I'll own all the land around here. Hell! I'll have my own bank, stores, factories, I'll be rich and powerful beyond imagination. It's all within my grasp. I intend to wring every drop of blood out of the South before I'm finished."

"Jonathan, please... I'm begging you. You have to forget these grandiose dreams. Soon civilian rule will be restored, then we'll have to leave, we'll want to get back home, to our house, our friends."

"Grandiose dreams! Dreams can be reality if you've got the courage to seize the moment!" The General slammed a meaty fist down on the table to reinforce his statement.

"Like you seized White Columns? You stole it from its rightful owners for the price of one years taxes. Is that what you fought for? The right to steal and plunder, like a barbarian? Was all the talk of freeing the slaves just that, only talk?" The woman's eyes flashed with disgust, and met his for the first time.

"You stupid bitch! You don't understand a damn thing! You don't know what it was like! Smoke, confusion, screams, and bullets whining around me. Nasty stinking Rebels screaming like banshees, pouring up the ridge with mindless determination to kill me! Some highborn Southerner riding alongside them, exhorting the filthy trash on, using their blood to fuel his career. The nights before a battle were the worst— the night sweats laying awake in my tent, wondering if a Rebel bullet would find me, or worse yet, a charge of grape shot ripping through my legs, leaving me a cripple for the rest of my life. The stench of my own fear would drive me out into the night, but out there, I'd see visions of armless men, their eyes glazed with shock wandering around, aimlessly. I would close my eyes, try to make them go away, then I'd see myself among them, cupping my bloody shredded genitals in my hands,

screaming, but there was never an answer to my cries for help, only the pitying look of men who were still whole, quickly looking away as they passed me by." The words tore from his lips with a sob.

The woman stared at him, as if seeing him for the first time. She stalked over to him, put her arm around him, and pulled his face against her breasts. "I'm so sorry Jonathan. I never knew how afraid you were. I'm so sorry". She crooned.

He shoved her away violently. "Damn you! You never cared! No one cared! They still don't! Well I can tell you I didn't do it so a bunch of darkies can run around free! It won't be long before they find out that free and hungry are two words for the same thing. Then they'll have to go back to work. White Columns will be just like in the old days before the war. The blacks will work the fields, clean the house, and work in my factories. Oh, I'll pay them, pay them with one hand, and take it back with the other. They'll live in the same quarters as before, paying me rent, buying their own food and clothes, all at my store. The only difference between the future and the past is that I won't have to buy the black bastards! If one of them gets sick, or injured, or can't work for any reason, I'll just fire him, run him off. I won't have a dime invested in him. Come election time, I'll control all their votes. Have you any concept of how powerful that will make me? No candidate can win without my support. Sure there will be a civilian government, but I'll manipulate it just like I manipulated to get this assignment."

The woman recoiled from him in horror. "My God! How wicked. How revoltingly wicked. I can't believe you could become such a monster!"

He shoved her violently, sent her down onto the floor. Her hands went instinctively to her abdomen in a protective reflex.

The whistle of the whip cut the air, and the explosive crack it made against her face tore a scream of agony from the prostrate woman. One hand went up to shield against the blows, but the other stayed, protecting her belly.

Pregnant! The word jumped into Shanon's mind. She wanted desperately to go to the woman's aid, but couldn't. She was a mere spectator as the whipping continued, unabated and merciless, driven by the soldier's drunken fury. She looked at the youth, and tried to will him to intervene, but he only watched, a cruel pitiless smile creasing his lips.

Another sound, a vague rumbling at first, grew until the sound of galloping horses became clearly audible outside. The beating stopped as the man went to the window, pulled the curtain aside and peered outside. He recoiled backward, stumbling over his moaning wife, A look of stark terror was etched on his face.

Suddenly a horseman appeared in the room, his eyes glowing with hatred from dark sunken sockets. He reached down, grasped the General's collar, and dragged him outside. There a noose was snugged around his neck, and in seconds he was kicking and struggling at the end of a rope as he was jerked unceremoniously off his feet to dangle from a sturdy beam.

The roar of shots ripped apart the stillness. Shanon found herself floating beside the hideously twisted face of the hanged man. Looking down, she saw an older, crueler version of Cal Dunforth aiming a huge revolver up at the body twisting beside her. More gunshots slammed into the body, which jerked and danced with their impact. A final louder shot rang out, and the face beside her disintegrated in a pink spray of blood and vaporized flesh.

As the riders rode away, Shanon drifted back inside, saw the woman struggling on the floor. She was appalled at the flow of blood where the cruel whip had flayed her flesh to the bone.

"Help me". The woman reached a bloody hand out to her son. "Help me," She pleaded.

The youth turned and walked into the library. He returned with a Navy Colt in his hand, and stood for a moment staring down at the struggling woman. He pointed the pistol at the woman's head and murmured, "This is all the help I can give you. It's more than you ever did for me when he used to beat me."

The roar of the revolver filled the room, smoke billowed up, and swallowed the scene. Before the smoke cleared enough for Shanon to see, she felt the sudden onslaught of violent acceleration.

CHAPTER 8

Cal awakened naked and alone on the sofa. He listened for sounds of Shanon moving around in the house, and heard nothing. He dressed, called out to her, and started a cautious exploration of each room. He felt tension building inside him as each room proved empty. He glanced at his watch, and was surprised to find that it was 9:45. He realized that the moon would be shining brightly outside. With a sense of dread he opened the front door and looked out onto the porch. A sharp cry of dismay escaped him when he saw Shanon's prostrate form. He rushed to her, lifted her limp form into his arms, turned her face toward him, and shuddered. Her eyes had the glaze of death in them.

He found a steady, but subdued pulse beneath his probing fingers, and breathed a sigh of relief. He explored her body with gentle fingers, probing for any sign of a wound. Finding none, he shook her gently and called out to her. Her body was seemed lifeless, despite the pulse. He shook her more firmly, frightened now by the sensation that he was holding on to a corpse. He felt again for her pulse, reassured himself that her heart was still beating, then started to lift her off of the floor. An uneasy sensation warned him against moving her however, and he remained where he was, cradling her limp body in his arms.

Cal wasn't sure how much time elapsed before her body suddenly went rigid. He held her and watched as the light of consciousness returned to her eyes. He waited patiently as her eyes darted about for a few seconds, as if she were trying to comprehend where she was. He spoke quietly to her. "Shanon. It's Cal, what's wrong?"

She suddenly clutched him with uncanny strength. Her voice bordered on hysteria. "Cal! Thank God! I just had the most terrible..... the most terrible...." She seemed to be searching for the right word to describe what had happened.

"Let's get away from here." Cal turned and locked the door, and then guided Shanon across the lawn to her car. After she was seated, shivering in the passenger seat, Cal got in and started the engine. Loose gravel spun beneath the tires as he sped down the driveway, anxious to put some distance between them and the sinister old house.

When they had driven in silence for a few miles, Shanon started relating what had happened to Cal. He nodded silently, the events in her experience similar to his own, except viewed from another perspective.

"Now you see why I'm reluctant to allow you to delve into whatever it is that is happening at White Columns. I hope that you've learned that it's best to leave some things undisturbed." Cal said.

"On the contrary. I'm more determined than ever to study the phenomenon." Shanon's voice had regained its strength now.

"Shit!" Cal exclaimed.

"I'm fine Cal. Really. I'm not injured, a little shaken, I'll admit, but I wasn't hurt." Shanon said.

"What about next time? You don't know what is going on at White Columns. What if I'd moved you? Would your spirit have been able to reenter your body, or might it have somehow gotten lost? The risks are just too great. Suppose I had taken you to a hospital? You may have spent the rest of your life in a coma! We don't understand the rules to this game. When you don't know the rules, it's just too dangerous to play," Cal insisted.

"Don't you see Cal? That's what this is all about, to learn the rules, to expand our knowledge of the spirit world. I've dedicated my career to studying phenomena that science can't explain. In many circles, my work is ridiculed. This is my one chance to gather hard evidence that some of my theories are correct," Shanon pleaded earnestly.

"Just what theories are you trying to prove? Earlier you said that your thoughts weren't organized enough to call them a theory," Cal challenged.

"I have my theories. I'm just not prepared for you to laugh, and make fun of them." Shanon replied.

"There will never be a better time to share them with me. I'm ready to accept anything right now that will help explain what's happening to me... to us, lately," Cal said grimly.

"Fine. Deja vu is a well known, much studied subject. No one has come up with a plausible explanation for it yet. I think that I might have an explanation, and what happened to me tonight goes a long way toward proving that I'm on the right track. We think of history as being carved in stone, finite, unchanging. That may be wrong. History may be constantly evolving, events being replayed with slightly different scenarios. If that were the case, the sense of deja vu would be explained by a person having lived the same event that they are experiencing before, within the frame work of another history scenario." Shanon waited for Cal to comment.

"That's an interesting concept, but I don't see any way to prove it," He answered.

"Maybe not. You should at least admit that it's possible though."

"I'll concede that point. In fact, it seems as reasonable as any explanation that I've heard offered."

Encouraged, Shanon continued. "The belief that many people have in reincarnation is another example. Many people who believe in reincarnation sense that they have already lived another life, in another time. What if instead, they have lived some of the same events in their lives within the framework of different history scenarios?" Shanon posed the question, and waited for his response.

"It seems that everything that you've said depends on the ability of history to recreate itself. How does your theory explain that happening?" Cal frowned.

"I can't explain that, but I'm convinced that by studying White Columns, I might find some answers."

"I'm not sure that I can accept history as a fluid concept. Even in my present state of mind, that seems to be stretching a little far."

"Consider this question then. What if you had taken a more active role in the experience that you had Friday night? For example, how would history differ if you had somehow stopped those soldiers from hanging the Union General?"

"I couldn't have stopped them. It was preordained. Somehow I didn't want to stop it. I was part of it, one of them. I felt the same satisfaction watching him hang that they did. I can't explain that, but that's how I felt." Cal said.

"That may be true. The fact remains that you were there, physically. The scorched hair proves it. It is possible then that your participation could have somehow changed the outcome of that event, thus altering the course of history in some way." Shanon insisted stubbornly.

"I can't argue with that," Cal answered. By now they had arrived at his house.

As they walked inside, a tacit understanding was reached. They went to Cal's bedroom, undressed and without further discussion, slid beneath the sheets together. They lay quietly, each savoring the warmth of the other's body. Within minutes Shanon was sleeping. Cal found a phrase that she had spoken replaying itself in his mind over and over.

"You were there, physically. You could have altered the course of history in some way." He lay awake wondering why he attached such importance to those particular words.

****

Beth Addison was surprised to see Heywood's car in her driveway. The light shining out of the living room window revealed that he had let himself in, and made himself comfortable. She felt the slight stir of resentment. She stepped into the foyer, stretched her aching muscles and sighed. She wondered what he wanted this time.

"Heywood, what are you doing here? I'm exhausted. I was looking forward to a quiet evening, and getting to bed early." She snapped as she walked into the room.

"I'm here to explain phase two of my plan to you." He got up and met her, encircled her with his flabby arms.

She shrugged him off, strode past him and kicked off her shoes. She sat down on the sofa, and stared up at him. "What are you talking about?"

"My plan to gain control of White Columns. I don't suppose that you thought that it would be as simple as getting rid of Marla." He shoved his hands into his pockets and rocked up onto his toes.

"Listen, I kept Cal occupied like I agreed to. As far as I'm concerned that's the end of it."

"That's where you're wrong. That was only the beginning. Now the complicated, interesting part begins."

"I'm not going to get involved in anything else." Beth glared at him.

"But of course you are. I'm aware of your reason for helping me this far. You wanted Marla out of your way so that you could have Cal all to yourself. That's fine. In fact it dovetails nicely with phase two of the plan." He paced back and forth in front of her.

"Cut the bullshit Heywood. Get to the point." Beth snarled. She was anxious to get rid of him.

"Now you have to marry Cal Dunforth." He smiled.

"There's one little problem. Cal's not interested in marriage, and neither am I at this point. Besides who the hell do you think you are, planning my life for me?" She asked angrily.

"I am your master. You my dear, are my slave." He grimaced wickedly.

"Bullshit. This isn't one of your sordid little S&M games we're playing. This is my life. I call the shots. Now get the hell out of here, and let me get some rest."

"Maybe you've forgotten one of the little games we played not so very long ago. A game that got a little too rough for your taste, if I recall. Maybe you need a refresher." He pulled the remote control out of his pocket and turned on the T.V. and VCR.

"What is this shit, Heywood? I'm tired, and I'm getting pissed off." She said.

"Just watch."

On the screen a slender young man with dirty blonde hair was tied up naked. A thin nylon cord was knotted around his throat. The sound of Beth's spike heels were audible as she slowly circled the man. His frightened eyes tried to follow her, but lost her as she stopped behind him.

She was dressed in skin tight black leather, her face concealed behind a mask. She raised the leather wrapped cane in her hand, and delivered a stinging blow across the helpless man's buttocks, eliciting a shriek of pain and fear.

"That's enough Heywood. You sick bastard, turn it off." Beth demanded.

"No. No. No. We haven't gotten to the best part yet," he smiled evilly at her.

"You son of a bitch, you never told me that you were taping." She shrieked. Fear had started gnawing a ragged hole in her gut by now. She remembered all too well how the tape ended.

"Sometimes it's best not to tell all that we know."

Beth watched with a sense of dread as the tape played. She saw the red whelps that the whip raised on the man's buttocks swell, turn puffy, then split open and begin to bleed. She listened to the man's pleas for mercy become strangled incoherent shrieks as the cord tightened around his throat. She saw herself hesitate, look with concern at the cord, then respond to someone off camera, and resume her sadistic task.

The camera zoomed in on the victim's face, and revealed bulged panicked eyes, lips that were turning blue. Suddenly Beth's leather clad body loomed on the screen, the camera panned away, showed her ripping off the mask, struggling with the cord buried in the victims neck. The lens zoomed in on her face, and recorded the wild eyed look of fear etched on her features, then settled on the lifeless face of the man.

"You bastard! You set me up. It wasn't an accident. You planned to kill him all along." Beth ejected the tape and smashed it against the floor, breaking the plastic. She tore the magnetic tape from the spool and stood panting with rage, surrounded by the damning tape.

"Temper, temper, temper. You've destroyed your copy. A pity. You could have had that copy for your very own. Of course I've got others." Heywood's voice held a sinister under current.

"What do you want?" Beth was angry and a little afraid, but curious as well.

"Cooperation of course. You'll marry Cal Dunforth, like a good little girl."

"Just how am I supposed to orchestrate that?" She asked.

"You'll tell him that you're pregnant." Heywood made it sound simple.

"Tell him I'm pregnant! Welcome to the real world Heywood. Women don't marry because they're pregnant anymore. They have abortions! You fool!"

"Just tell him, very casually of course. You'll find that he will insist on marriage. If you mention an abortion, he'll come unglued."

Beth thought about what Heywood was saying. It had the ring of truth to it. Cal was old fashioned, with a highly developed sense of honor. He would insist on marrying her if he believed that she was pregnant. The prospect of being married to Cal was pleasant, but overshadowed by the ominous motive that Heywood had for achieving that goal. "How would my marrying Cal help you gain control of White Columns?"

"That part of the plan will be revealed later. For now make sure that you carry out phase two. The Police would have a field day with this tape. To say nothing of the news media. Now that we have defined our relationship, I'll be on my way. You have thirty days to complete your assignment."

He was out the door before Beth could reply. She gathered up the tape, placed it in the fireplace and burned it. She watched the incriminating tape curl and disappear in the flames, knowing that her efforts were futile. Heywood would have another copy. Dread descended over her as she thought about the insecure little man exercising control over her life. Heywood Carlson was a manipulator. It was an obsession with him. She realized that she would never be free of his influence as long as he had the tape in his possession.

A sliver of neurotic fear grew into a knot of anxiety that threatened to choke her. She had thought that she had been in control, using him to achieve her goals, both professional and personal. Now, she was terrified by the prospect of having him dominate her life. She felt a cold chill creep over her. She knew that she would not submit to life under his rules. There had to be a way out.

She walked into her bedroom, stripped off her clothes and started exercising on the Soloflex machine that was responsible for the rigidly toned muscles rippling throughout her body. As the surge of nutrient rich blood gorged her muscles, she started to regain her confidence. Heywood Carlson was no match for her. No one was. That lesson had been indelibly imprinted in her mind the night that she had smothered her drunken, and abusive father with his own vomit encrusted pillow.

CHAPTER 9

The night spent under the stars, listening to the soothing ripple of the river flowing past the island had restored Cal's perspective. He still realized that something eerie was happening at White Columns, but his experience was beginning to fade, and to lose the intimate reality that it had held for him. He had started searching for rational explanations for what had happened.

Now, as he installed the infrared motion detector and aimed it at the doorway to Marla's bedroom, he felt slightly foolish. He had spent the entire day, working under Shanon's expert supervision, mounting cameras, stringing wire, turning White Columns into a maze of electronic sensors. He felt a little like a magician's assistant, preparing the stage for the slight of hand that would deceive the audience. This time the sensors were the audience, the house itself the stage, and he couldn't help but wonder if all of the high tech hardware was simply a sophisticated medicine show.

He could hear Shanon loading the infrared film in the cameras that he had installed in the hallway. He attached the wires to the motion detector, reeled enough off of the spool to reach the camera mounted in the opposite corner, and completed the last installation.

He climbed down the ladder to allow Shanon to load the camera, caught a faint odor of her, and felt her warmth as they traded places. The serious look on her face reminded him that to her, at least, their elaborate preparations were part of a scientific study, the cornerstone of what she had trained years for. He wondered how someone could spend their life chasing shadows, and asked himself if he were prepared to spend his own life in a similar fashion.

"Well, it's all in place. Everything is ready. Whatever activity that goes on at White Columns will soon be recorded for posterity," Shanon said, climbing down.

"If this stuff works," Cal answered.

"Oh, it works. I'm sure of that." She gave him a reproachful look.

"So. What now boss?"

"I'm all finished with you. You've done a great job. It usually takes at least two days to make an installation such as this. I'm impressed."

"Impressed enough to have diner with me?"

"Better than that. I'll cook for you. I seldom have the opportunity to show off my home making skills. I'll write out a grocery list and while you run into Emerald and pick up a few things, I'll be showering and getting into fresh clothes."

"Sounds good to me." Cal replied. He was looking forward to the evening with her.

When he returned with the groceries, he found her in the kitchen. "That was quick. I should get you to do all my shopping," She smiled. She was wearing an oversized T-shirt with a set of tiger paws positioned as if they were fondling her breasts, a pair of cut off jeans, and sneakers. She wore no trace of makeup. Her finely chiseled features, bright blue eyes with long delicate lashes, and full sensuous lips, were so perfect that instead of the washed out look that most women exhibit when caught without makeup, her face only seemed to soften.

Cal caught himself staring. "I like your shirt." He said lamely.

"It was Marla's. I found it in a dresser drawer. We each had one when we were in school together. I can't remember what happened to mine. Marla always held onto memories. She used to say that life was a blend of memories and dreams, without either a person couldn't live." Tears formed in Shanon's eyes as she thought about her friend.

Cal saw the moisture shimmering against the blue eyes, and moved to put his arms around her. "Please... Marla wouldn't want you to be sad. She would want you to hold onto the memories of the times you spent together. She'd want you to be happy." Cal whispered the words against soft blonde hair that caressed his cheek.

"I'm sorry Cal. I can't help it. I still can't bring myself to confront the reality of her death. I keep expecting to look up and see her smiling at me from the doorway. It's hard Cal." Shanon brushed at her eyes, turned and began rummaging in the bags of groceries.

"Maybe we should get away from here. We could go back to my place for diner." Cal offered.

"No. I'll be all right. I have to confront my feelings and deal with them. Marla's gone, and all I can do for her now is to help you find out who killed her. I think the key to that is here, in this house, locked away with the spirits that are trapped here." Shanon had regained her composure. Her face had hardened into a determined mask.

Cal watched her as she began preparing the food. He realized for the first time that she had another reason for staying at White Columns besides her research. She suspected that somehow the supernatural power that resided in White Columns had caused Marla's death. If she believed that, her assurances to him that she was in no danger here was false—a smoke screen to get him to agree to allow her to stay. Cal marveled at her courage. He felt uneasy in the house, even though logic told him that there was nothing to fear from the house. Shanon was convinced of the existence of a world of spirits. To her, the ghosts who had flitted through his imagination when he had been a child were real. Cal realized that her decision to meet them on their own terms reflected a toughness that he hadn't expected from her.

Feeling helpless, not knowing what to say, he wandered out of the kitchen and found himself moving toward the rear of the house. A part of him revolted at the knowledge of where his footsteps were taking him, yet another part was drawn inexorably toward the back porch. Once there, he stood staring at the stone steps that led down into the cellar.

A broad yellow ribbon of plastic with the words Police Line Do Not Cross, stretched across the entrance to White Columns womb. Staring into the darkness, Cal sensed that the mystery of the old house originated within the dark confines of the damp, musty cellar. His legs moved of their own volition, carrying him down the steps to confront the terror that suddenly woke from a light slumber within him.

As he stooped down and groped his way beneath the tape strung across the splintered doorway, his breath whistled through his teeth. His chest expanded with emotion and left scant room for air. He stood in the darkness, listening to his own breathing. After several minutes he regained control of himself, and reached for the tiny one cell streamlight flashlight attached to his key ring. He steeled himself and twisted the light on.

The flashlight's beam explored the empty vault, stabbing the darkness with feeble shafts of light that trembled only slightly. The cellar was almost empty. A single discarded board, lying on the floor, a few quart jars against the back wall. Clearly, the space hadn't been used in years. There was no need. White Columns was a huge home. There were more empty rooms, and space than in most homes. So, why would Marla choose such a dreary place to die? And while it was possible to stand on the entrance, and step into space with a rope around your neck, it would have been far easier to have stood on a chair. The more Cal examined the scene, the less sense that the scenario that Collins had presented made.

Cal knew for a fact that at one time Marla had tried recreational drugs. Some of the circle of friends that she moved in still used them. If she had been contemplating suicide, she would have had access to enough downers to put an elephant under. So why hanging? It wasn't a method that people who had other choices used. It was a gruesome way to go—both for the victim, as well as those who recovered the body. Marla would have known that Cal would have been involved in a search for her, and would have been the most likely person to find her. She wouldn't have allowed him to find her in the manner that he had. She wouldn't have hurt him that way. It was pure bullshit, that's what it was. Marla wouldn't have left without having said goodbye to him. She might have done it subtly, but she would have made sure that they had a last time together. Marla hadn't killed herself. All of his instincts had told him that. Now, hard evidence was backing that feeling up.

The light traveled across the floor and reflected off of a spot that was brighter than the rest of the cobblestone floor. Cal played the light upward and realized that the spot was directly beneath the beam that had supported Marla's body. He moved the light downward and felt something bitter rise up in his throat. He moved forward on legs that barely obeyed the nerve impulses fed them. Only when he was standing directly over the spot, did Cal allow his mind to absorb the meaning of the brightness coating the cobblestones. Marla's blood. A memory of her raw torn lips, the swollen bloody tongue, gripped him and he reached out for support as his legs grew weaker. The full impact of her hideous death mask flashed into his mind, and his own startled cry echoed back at him from the walls of the enclosure. His hand groped empty air, found no support and he slumped to his knees, barely aware of the pain as the stone floor tore skin off of his kneecaps.

He allowed his body to crumble until he settled onto the cold floor. A tortured moan that he hardly recognized as his own escaped him. The light was smothered beneath him, and as he lay in total darkness he heard someone calling for Marla. The voice was filled with anguish and longing. He pressed his face into the cold smooth stones, tasted the musty unpleasant flavor of the cellar floor, and choked off his cries against the unrelenting coldness.

As he lay there in the darkness, the image of Marla's bloodstains formed in his mind. Now White Columns had another indelible stain to its credit. Would it remain visible into the next century? Would future generations of children whisper the legend behind the mysterious spot in the cellar? Would this spot have the mysterious power to transport someone back into time, and allow them to witness the horror of Marla's death as he had witnessed the lynching?

No. The stain on the porch was visible only under the direct glare of moonlight. Here, in the dark bowels of White Columns, the moonlight would never touch it.

The thoughts raced through his mind in a millisecond-second, and he cursed the irony of the situation. He would give anything to be able to return to the night of Marla's death, instead he had been swept across the span of more than a century to witness the murder of a stranger from another era. He reflected that his life had become a living nightmare in which he was unable to separate reality from fantasy.

The clarity that had been restored to his mind by his brief sojourn down the river had shattered within hours of his return to White Columns. Emotions that he had thought in check, were running rampant again. A sadness so deep that if felt like an open wound in his soul pervaded him. He realized that he had to get away from the house to shake off its morbid influence so he could get hold of the reins of his sanity again.

With an effort he struggled to his feet, found the streamlight, and followed its fierce gleam out of the cellar. He paused for a last look back inside the gloom, shuddered, and quickly walked back inside the house.

The odor of food emanating from the kitchen greeted him as he made his way down the hall. He thought of Shanon, and wondered if the atmosphere of the house affected her in the same way that it did him. He paused at the kitchen door, and watched her for several seconds. He decided that the house probably had a more pronounced effect on her because of her acute sensitivity. He realized that she could feel the pulse of White Columns, and sense subtle nuances of spirits moving through the house that he could only imagine.

She turned and noticed him watching her. "Why don't you freshen up Cal. You look worn out. I'll have diner by the time you're finished." She didn't remark about the pallor, and thin sheen of perspiration that clung to him like the cold embrace of a corpse. "Out. I can't cook with you standing over me."

Cal allowed the hot steamy water to cascade over his body, and felt a measure of relief as the clammy grime of the cellar, and his own terror was washed away. Even the sting of it in the fresh scrapes on his knees felt good. By the time he was finished, he had recovered his composure. Still, the oppressive atmosphere in the house chilled him. He hurriedly slipped his clothes on and went downstairs where he found Shanon placing a steaming bowl of stir fried vegetables on the table.

The meal passed in silence. Each of them caught up in their own thoughts. Cal was anxious to be away from White Columns, while Shanon was almost visibly trembling with anticipation of the coming night in the house.

As Cal drove away from the plantation, he couldn't dispel his feelings of cowardice for leaving Shanon alone. Even though she had insisted that he leave, he still felt a trace of shame.

On the horizon, lightning lit up the base of dark ominous clouds momentarily. By the time Cal drove home and made his way inside, the intermittent flashes were beginning to illuminate the familiar and welcome outline of his house, and the rumble of thunder threatened in the distance.

Safely inside, he turned on the television and sat staring at the actors in the sit com. The canned laughter seemed absurd in his present mood. Again he cursed the irony of his being able to hurtle across a century of time to see an event that had little meaning for him, yet he was unable to fathom what had happened in the cellar of White Columns only days ago. With that thought, the germ of a plan began forming in his mind.

****

Shanon curled up on Marla's bed, and picked up the novel that she had brought to read herself to sleep by. After a few pages she set it aside, turned out the lamp, and lay in the darkness listening to the approach of the thunderstorm. Through the bedroom window she could see the old oak trees standing stark and lonely in the flare of lightning.

107

They seemed to be stoically bracing themselves for another of the thousands of thunderstorms that they had endured.

Without warning, a strong gust of wind whistled through the open window, snapped the curtains noisily, then swept across the room, bringing with it the first fine mist of rain. Shanon hurried to the window on bare feet, and pulled it down. She stood in the darkness watching the trees bending before the storms onslaught. They bowed before the first sheet of wind driven rain like bearded old men, sentinels too proud to leave their post. Downstairs a shutter slammed against the side of the house in loud protest against the elements.

Throughout the house an undercurrent of anticipation grew. A low moaning that could have been wind, or the old house itself, was barely audible.

Shanon crossed the room, using the flare of lightning to light her way, slid beneath the covers, and listened to the steady patter of rain on the roof overhead. She closed her eyes, and an image formed immediately. She was staring out of a narrow slit at the rain, swirling in grey sheets against the black sky. She could see trees swaying in a ritual dance whenever the lightning flashed. She had no idea where the scene before her was taking place until a brilliant lightning bolt illuminated the entire sky. She saw them then, unmistakable, swords raised in defiance against the raging torrent, astride rampant stallions whose lips were curled back, teeth bared in a silent scream. The stone soldiers guarding the cemetery rose up out of the darkness.

She felt the hairs at the base of her neck bristle, and a chill course the length of her spine when she realized that she was staring out over the Dunforth graveyard through someone else's eyes. But who's? Who would be lurking in a cemetery at this time of night, in a driving thunderstorm? Instantly she wished that she' hadn't sent Cal away. Fear tightened a hard fist around her heart.

Suddenly the view started moving, threading its way among the headstones. Shanon could see the cemetery clearly— could even read the names on the markers! Whoever it was had a light. She got up and silently groped her way out of the bedroom, down the hall, and into the back bedroom where the window looked out toward the ridge. As she moved her vision blurred, the image in her mind super imposed over her own eyesight.

She stared out of the window, looking for the spot of light that she knew must be moving through the cemetery. Only blackness greeted her eager searching, yet the image seen through a strangers eyes continued, piercing the darkness. Shanon tensed as the image stopped before a fresh grave. The flowers draped over the mound of earth glowed with surreal intensity beneath whatever kind of light source that the stalker was using.

Shanon knew that someone was standing over Marla's grave, perhaps taking shelter beneath the funeral tent that still protected the grave site. Again she wished that Cal was with her, and thought about calling him, then decided that whoever was trespassing in the cemetery would see Cal's approaching headlights, and be gone before he could make his way across the ravine, and up the ridge to the grave.

Without hesitation, Shanon returned to her bedroom, pulled a pair of jeans on, slipped into her sneakers, and made her way down stairs. She had fought back the intruding image now, and concentrated on finding her way through the darkened house by the almost constant flare of lightning. If she could approach quietly, she might be able to get a look at the intruder, and perhaps see him clearly in the flare of lightning.

She slipped silently out of the back door, stood for a moment scanning the ridge beyond the screen of trees in the back yard. She was puzzled by the fact that she still saw no light in the cemetery. She slipped down the porch steps, out into the torrential rain, and picked her way across the yard to the trail of foot stones that led across the ravine, and up to the the gates of the cemetery. She made her way quickly to the footbridge, crossed it during a bright flash, and started up the trail toward the gate.

By now she could make out the outline of the statues on either side of the gate. Still she could not see whatever light source that the intruder was using. She wondered if he had slipped away while she was crossing the distance that separated the house from the cemetery. To reassure herself, she paused, huddled beneath the belly of the stone horse, and clenched her eyes tight waiting for the strangers view to appear. In seconds it was there. With a lurch of fear she noted that he was staring at the gate. Had he seen her? Please God, don't let him!

The strangers gaze remained locked on the gate for agonizing seconds before turning to look back at the fresh grave. It was then that the true horror of what she was witnessing registered in Shanon's mind. There, bathed in some kind of ethereal light lay the body of Marla. Her carefully arranged hair cascaded around a face tranquil in sleeping repose. The satin lining of her coffin encompassed her body safely, the air and water tight seal of the vault keeping her safe from the flood of clay reddened water pouring over it.

The import of what she was seeing through the watcher's eyes took Shanon's breath in one long gasp. Terror closed icy fingers around her stomach, and she began to shake uncontrollably. Without warning, the unholy gaze shifted back to the gate, and Shanon saw herself, dripping water, lips blue with cold and fear, huddled helplessly beneath the statue. A shriek of fear that she barely recognized as her own started her legs in motion. She ran headlong down the trail back toward White Columns. Her feet skidded from beneath her on the rain slickened boards of the footbridge, and she fell heavily on her back with such force that the breath rushed out of her lungs. With agonizing slowness she rose, stumbled along the foot stones, unable to suck enough air into her lungs to keep her oxygen starved muscles working. She sagged to the wet earth, gasping for what seemed an eternity before she was able to continue.

Inside, she flew up the stairs two at a time and slammed the door to the bedroom. She stood for long minutes, listening, ears straining for the sound of pursuit. A wet puddle formed around her as she trembled with cold fear. When her mind started working again she retreated to the bed, slipped off her shoes and burrowed beneath the covers. Her shaking hand reached out for the control panel that activated the motion sensors that would trigger the cameras located throughout the old house.

Minutes dragged by, and the only sound that she heard was the low moan of wind, and rain lashing at the house. Her fear was beginning to recede into something manageable when she heard it— the faint whirring of the automatic shutter of one of the camera's downstairs. Instinctively she reached for the phone at her bedside, punched in Cal's number, and clutched the receiver to her ear. Nothing, no ring back tone.

She depressed the hook switch and listened for dial tone. Instead she heard the faint crackle of static. Her hand tightened around the phone, and she desperately worked the switch. The crackle of static was her only reward. Now she heard with startling clarity the shutter of the camera outside in the hallway. Terror swept through her like the storm's cold wind as she listened to the insidious whirring that told her that whatever was outside was moving down the hall toward her.

The sudden repetitive clicking and winding noise of the camera positioned in the corner of the bedroom paralyzed her. Whatever evil that stalked the corridors of White Columns was in the room with her!

The camera stopped as the intruder stood poised at the foot of her bed. Shanon heard a faint metallic jingle just before the camera resumed its eerie task. Boo Man! The words of Paula crashed into her mind. The innocent sounding question reverberated in her mind. "Did the Boo Man get Mommy?" Paula had asked.

In a flash like a stark x-ray film, she suddenly saw herself huddled beneath the covers, filthy, shivering, hair matted around her face, she lay helpless, viewed through the eyes of her killer. Unconsciously the words leaped into her mind, her lips muttered them into her pillow. "Now I lay me down to sleep. I pray the Lord me safe to keep. If I die before I wake, I pray dear God my soul to take."

A strangled snarl erupted above her, followed by hurried footsteps that were clearly audible, punctuated by a metallic jingle each time a heavy boot struck the floor. The camera mounted in the corner fell silent. The one outside in the hallway whirred furiously for a few seconds, then it too ceased. The footsteps receded down the stairs, greeted by the faintly audible whirring of the downstairs camera.

Shanon snatched her keys from the bedside table, and without pausing to gather up her shoes, fled down the stairs, out the front door, and started across the front lawn toward her car. As she streaked across the wet expanse of grass, and dodged among the swaying oaks, the simple choppy sentences of the prayer played through her mind. Only when she was inside her car with the doors locked, and the engine roaring, did she stop repeating the phrase.

She slipped the car into reverse, backed it out of the garage in a cloud of foul smelling rubber generated by the madly clawing tires, and with reckless disregard for the BMW's gearbox, slammed it into drive. Her foot pressed the accelerator to the floor, and the powerful sedan obeyed with a throaty roar of torque that sent wet sod flying behind it as it shot out onto the gravel driveway, and careened down the winding trail toward the highway. Once there, the car's tires clawed aggressively at the wet asphalt, and shrieked in protest as the relentlessly powerful engine raised its howling voice above the sound of the storm, and propelled its terrified driver toward the safety of Emerald.

CHAPTER 10

Hannah Greene lay awake, listening to the rhythmic breathing of the precious bundle of warmth curled up against her. Paula had fallen asleep almost as soon as they had pulled the sheet around them. The last words that the child had murmured before sleep had claimed her had been a simple bedtime prayer. Her "G'night Nanah," had been slurred as she gave in to exhaustion.

Hannah found sleep difficult. She kept reviewing her security precautions in her alert mind, weighing them against all eventualities. She had established the bedroom that the two of them would use as their safe room. The bed had been moved across the room so that it would take only seconds for her to sweep the child off of it, carry her into the closet and place her on the pallet that she had prepared on the carpeted floor. A flak jacket was ready on a hook to drape over the child, and Hannah's own second chance vest hung beside it.

They had made a game of their practice runs, but Hannah felt sure that Paula recognized the urgency of the preparations, and would obey her instinctively in an emergency.

A sound from downstairs brought Hannah to full alertness. It had sounded like someone bumping into a piece of furniture, furniture that she had purposely rearranged. The sound was followed by what could have been a muffled curse.

In an instant, Hannah was out of bed, gliding across the floor to stand listening at the bedroom door. She knew that there was no possibility of anyone sneaking up the stairs to their room unnoticed. She had made sure of that by placing a layer of bubble wrap packing material beneath the carpet runner that lined the upstairs hall. The weight of the stealthiest footstep would pop the bubbles and awaken her. Because of this, she felt secure enough to open the door a crack, and look out over the den below.

She heard the unmistakable murmur of voices, saw a tiny shaft of light, as if from a penlight. Swiftly, and silently she closed the bedroom door, activated the deadbolt lock, and quietly slipped back to the bed. Waking Paula and cautioning her for silence, she led the child to the closet, had her lie down on the pallet, draped the flak jacket around her, and turned on the nightlight that she had installed inside the closet. She knew that the soft glow of light would keep the child from panicking in the darkness.

Slipping into her Second Chance vest, she moved to the foot of the bed, reached between the mattress and box springs, and withdrew a Remington 11-87 semiautomatic shotgun. The weapon had been fitted with a twenty one inch Rem-Choke slug barrel and a Hastings extra full choke tube screwed in place.

It was equipped with an eight shot magazine extension, oversized safety, shell loading guide, and oversize bolt handle. Nestled in its mount beneath the magazine extension was an Emerging Technologies Laser aiming device. Hannah silently closed the bolt on a Federal Premium copper coated turkey load. The Magnum shot shell would decapitate a man from where she crouched to the bedroom door, yet its two ounce charge of number six shot would not penetrate interior walls, and endanger occupants of other rooms in the house.

Next Hannah drew her Glock 17 nine millimeter from the drawer of the nightstand, and placed it beside her on the floor. She then accessed her situation. Her principal was safely ensconced in the closet to her left, close enough so that she could whisper reassurance if needed, yet far enough away to be out of the line of fire of an intruder who returned her own fire. The mattress would provide her with cover and concealment, and along with the protective properties of her vest give her a high probability of surviving a shootout. She had the shotgun trained on the bedroom door across from her, and when she depressed the actuator switch, the red glow of the Laser's aiming dot was rock steady, centered on the doorway, chest high. She was ready.

Next she reached for the phone, listened for dial tone, and hearing none muttered, "These assholes are serious." Undaunted, she pulled a cellular bag phone from beneath the bed and dialed 911.

"Emergency 911, please state the nature of your emergency." The voice was crisp, professional.

"My name is Hannah Greene, I'm calling from 415 Sycamore Lane in Norcross. I have multiple intruders in my house."

"Remain calm Ms. Greene. I have no trace on your call at that address. Are you calling from a car phone?"

"I'm on a cellular phone. The house phone line is dead."

"Remain calm Ms. Greene. Stay in your car, lock your doors...."

"Shut up and listen. I don't know how much longer I can talk. I'm in an upstairs bedroom, armed and barricaded. The Perps are downstairs. I will stay on line and assist responding officers if possible. Get a unit dispatched."

"Stand by Ms. Greene." Hannah heard the call go out. "Ms. Greene, are you an off duty officer?"

"Ex- Officer with Decalb County. I'm in security now. I have my client secured and will remain in a defensive posture until your unit has cleared the house."

"Very good. Standby while I get an ETA." There was a pause and then the operator was back to tell Hannah that a unit would be there in 7 minutes.

The time dragged by, the silence broken only by an occasional faint sound from downstairs. Hannah wondered what the assassins were waiting for. Whoever had broken in obviously expected someone to be home. Why else would they have disabled the phone line? They were probably being cautious, confident that they had plenty of time as a result of the cut phone line. Did their cautious approach indicate that someone, probably Heywood had tipped them off to the the fact that she was a trained security specialist? She decided that it was likely, and wondered how Heywood had learned her occupation so quickly. He had probably done some checking before he hired the hit men, just as a precaution and had hit the jackpot. While her company wasn't exactly high profile, there wasn't anything clandestine about it either. A few phone calls would have told Heywood all that he wanted to know.

She was thankful for the backup phone. At least now she would have uniformed officers for support in a few minutes. Maybe before the intruders made their move, if she were lucky. If not, she felt secure in her own abilities. No one would get through the bedroom door alive. She gripped the Remington securely and waited. She saw the blue strobe of the approaching police cruiser as a faint reflection off the window behind her.

She picked up the phone again and spoke into it in a low voice. "The intruders are still on the first floor. I don't think they're aware of the unit's arrival. Wait! They're moving... They're headed out the back!"

"I'll relay that information Ms. Greene. Standby."

Hannah heard the back door crash open, fought an instinct to move from her position and pursue, but knew that her one and only job was to protect her client. Apprehension of the intruders was a police matter now.

Several minutes elapsed. She could hear the police pounding on the front door, then she was startled by the sound of a gunshot. It had come from the rear of the house, about where the six foot privacy fence enclosed the backyard. Hannah prayed that the officers were safe. The sound of the single shot wasn't reassuring however. If the intruders had fired on police officers and missed, she knew that they would return fire. It was unlikely that an officer would fire his weapon first. She shivered with worry and waited.

After what seemed an eternity, she heard a voice calling to her from downstairs. She stalked to the door, opened it a crack, and felt a flood of relief when she saw uniformed officers standing in the living room. She crossed to the closet, tossed on a robe and picked up Paula. In seconds she was downstairs.

"Ms Greene?" The cop was a heavy black man with a thick mustache. He was bulging over his uniform belt a little, but his thick chest and arms left little doubt that he was in pretty good shape. "I'm Sergeant Paterson. This is officer Butts." He indicated a lean crew cut man in his mid thirties. "We've run into a strange situation here," he paused and measured her with a cool eye.

"I heard a shot. Is everyone safe?" Hannah asked anxiously.

"We've got a guy stretched out in back, grave yard dead." Paterson said, studying her face.

"Damn. Was it a justifiable shooting?"

"I don't know about that Ms. Greene. You'd have to ask his partner about that." Paterson said flatly.

"You're telling me that his partner shot him?"

"You got it."

"Why in hell would he do that?"

"I don't know. I was hoping you might have some ideas."

Hannah sat down on the sofa and placed Paula beside her. "I can't imagine."

Butts spoke for the first time. "I was going to cover the back but before I got in position, the creeps were already outside. I chased them across the lawn, got a hand on one of the guy's ankle as he tried to go over the fence. The guy yelled for his partner, and the next thing I knew, I heard a shot and the guy I was scuffling with fell on top of me. The slug caught him in the throat. He died in minutes. There was nothing I could do for him."

"You don't think that the other one fired at you, hit his buddy by mistake?" Hannah asked.

"Not likely. I was on the inside of the fence. The guy who got shot was halfway over, straddling it. The shot would have been five feet over my head, besides, I was concealed by the fence. I got the feeling that it was an execution."

"I don't know what to make of it." Hannah puzzled.

"Well, neither do I. Anyway, a homicide detective is on the way. I'm sure he'll have plenty of questions for you when he arrives," Paterson said.

At that moment, a man in a cheap, ill fitting sport coat walked in. He had a lean cadaverous face whose every feature seemed too large. His hair was so light that Hannah at first thought that he was prematurely grey. He wasn't. His hair was so light colored and fine that it appeared almost colorless. He conferred with Paterson, issued terse orders, and then turned to Hannah. "Carl Striker, Homicide." His voice was as colorless as his appearance.

"Hannah Greene. This is Paula Carlson, my client." She pulled the child reassuringly closer.

Striker attempted to smile at Paula, managed what looked like a distasteful grimace. "Tell me what's going on here Ms. Greene."

"We had intruders, apparently one of them shot the other," Hannah replied.

"That simple." Striker eyed her as if she were slightly repugnant to him. "I need to know what you were doing here. I understand you're some kind of bodyguard for the kid. Why does she need one?"

Hannah's reply was cut off by Butts. "The stiff dropped this." He held out a paper bag, hovered nearby while Striker took an inventory.

Hannah felt his eyes on her and gave him a smile. Butts returned it and rolled his eyes behind Striker's back as if to say, "What an asshole."

The bag contained a thin stack of cash held with a silver money clip, a wallet, a stack of envelopes, a passport, and burglary tools. Striker opened the wallet, and studied the drivers licences. "Gordon Chase. Is he the guy who hired you, the one who lives here?"

"Never heard of him." Hannah replied.

Striker stared at her for a few seconds then continued flipping through the wallet, inspecting the numerous credit cards ranging from VISA, American Express, to various oil company cards. He then flipped open the passport, glared at it, and held it for Hannah to see. "You're telling me you don't know this guy?"

"Sure, I know the guy in the picture. His name is Heywood Carlson. He lives here."

"Says here his name is Gordon Chase." Striker's face showed a spark of interest now.

"I don't know a Gordon Chase. I know the man in the photo as Heywood Carlson."

"Maybe he hired you under an assumed name?" Striker raised his eyebrows questioningly.

"He didn't hire me. His ex-brother in law hired me. Carlson thinks that I'm a student, willing to trade room and board in exchange for keeping an eye on his daughter." Hannah explained

"I see. Your employer, his ex-wife's brother, thinks that Mr. Chase poses a threat to his own daughter?"

"Yes, except the name is Carlson. That's the name that he is known to his brother in law by. He runs an advertising agency under the name. That name is in the phone directory, listed at this address. The Gordon Chase identity is news to me."

Striker was becoming more animated now, his nostrils flared as the case started to take on more complexity. He sensed that he had stumbled into something that could make headlines, one that he could ride to a promotion if he played his cards right. "If what you're telling me is true, this bird was getting ready to fly. There's at least five grand in cash here, and probably double that amount in credit under the Chase alias. Why do you think Mr. Carlson, or Chase, whoever, was getting ready to run?"

"I don't know. I think that you're probably going to find out why someone broke into his house, into a hidden safe, if my guess is right, before you get your answer to that."

"Maybe it won't be that difficult. Maybe I can just ask him. You do know where he is?"

"Not really. He told me he had to go out of town on business. He didn't say where. I'm sure that you won't have a problem locating him though. I expect that he made his arrangements under his own name. He shouldn't be hard to nail down."

"This case has a funny smell to me already, and I haven't really started digging yet. Why don't you fill me in on what you know about Mr. Carlson, about this whole affair."

Striker lit a Marlboro, coughed and leaned back in his chair.

Hannah quickly filled in the details of her employment, noted that Striker leaned forward in his chair when she mentioned Marla's recent death, and Cal Dunforth's suspicion that it had been murder rather than suicide. By the time she finished, Striker's cigarette had burned down almost to the filter, leaving behind a column of ashes that clung together tenuously.

"Well, that is an interesting story Ms Greene. Perhaps your friend Dunforth is right about Carlson. Maybe the alias was prepared in case he botched his wife's murder. Now I need to figure out who the stiff is, who hired him and his companion, and what the purpose of the break in was. I think that we know now that it wasn't an attempt on the child's life."

"Why would the dead guy's buddy wax him? I think that is a question that you need to be asking yourself." Hannah offered.

"What do you make of it?"

Hannah was surprised that Striker wanted her opinion.

"I don't know. I haven't given it much thought. The first thing that comes to mind is that the other intruder was the one who hired the dead man. He must have needed the guy's skills. I'll be willing to bet that when you get an I.D. on the stiff he'll have a rap sheet. Burglary, safe expert if my guess is right. The other guy took him out to protect his identity. That means that he took something out of that safe that's more important than what you recovered here."

"How do you figure that?"

"Just think about it. If a third party hires two goons to toss a guys house, crack his safe, why would one of the two risk a murder rap by shooting his partner when it becomes apparent that he's gonna get caught? Suppose the uniforms had grabbed this stiff alive and took him in, sweated him a little, and come up with the other guy's name. How much heat is gonna come down on the guy for a burglary? Not much. Burglary is penny ante shit when you've got the crime that this town has. But now the other perp is hot, a murder rap hanging over him. Now he's got to worry about homicide detectives on his ass. It doesn't add up."

"Unless there's more to this picture than we're seeing now, I agree. You're a sharp lady Ms. Greene. I understand you used to be a cop. When you're tired of this security business, you should get back into the real action." Striker gave her what he must have thought of as a gracious smile. On his face it seemed that he was just giving the slack muscles badly needed exercise.

After the police had left, Hannah carried a sleeping Paula back upstairs, shrugged out of her robe and bullet proof vest, and lay beside the sleeping child. Her thoughts raced through the maze of facts that she knew, jumped across huge gaps that she couldn't fill in, and tried to see some vague outline of the picture that would lead her to the truth. She dozed off with the knowledge that she would soon know every detail of Heywood Carlson's background. She wouldn't rest until she had a complete picture of the man.

With that as a blue print she would start piecing together what was going on now. She wanted to do it to help Cal, but more importantly it had become a challenge to her.

CHAPTER 11

Shanon had arrived at Cal's house, soaked to the bone, with a layer of mud caked on her clothes, and with the remnants of terror etched on her face. He had led her inside, stripped off her wet clothing, and led her into the shower. He waited until she had washed away the grime, and the hot water had warmed her before he had asked her what had happened.

Warm, dry, and with a scalding cup of coffee before her, the story that she told him sounded wild and impossible, even to her own ears as she related it to him. She had been relieved when he had simply nodded, gathered her in his arms, and rocked her against him as though she were a child.

Cal awakened as the first light of dawn began to cast its dim light into the bedroom. He gently unwrapped Shanon's arm from his body, and without waking her went into the kitchen and started brewing coffee. When he walked past the bedroom on the way to the bathroom, he glanced inside, paused and watched her sleeping peacefully for a few seconds.

After showering shaving and brushing his teeth, he slipped into a pair of faded jeans, pulled on a shirt, and went back to the kitchen. He poured himself a cup of coffee, and sat sipping it, replaying the story that Shanon had told the previous evening.

White Columns...Dark Secrets

Thinking about the eerie, invisible light that Shanon had described, he suddenly remembered the SWAT class that he had attended two summers ago. One of the exercises that had stuck in his mind had involved the search of a warehouse for terrorist, and hostages that they were holding. The exercise had been incredibly realistic, with SWAT trained officers playing the role of terrorist, and a group of admin people serving as make believe hostages. Both terrorist and the swat team that was tasked to carry out a rescue had been armed with paint ball guns. Cal's team leader had waited for full darkness, then issued his team night vision goggles, and led them in a daring night time rescue. Cal and his teammates had shot the bad guys with gelatin capsules filled with red paint, carefully avoiding the hostages. The mission had been a complete success, all of the terrorist neutralized without a hostage being hit. Cal had been very impressed.

Now the eerie greenish appearance of the images as seen through the goggles played through his mind. He wondered if Shanon had seen White Columns cemetery through the eyes of some sinister intruder who had equipped himself with night vision equipment. He decided that it was a strong possibility, then racked his brain for a plausible explanation for why anyone would go to such lengths to frighten Shanon. Was it someone's sick idea of a prank? Was the same person responsible for the alarm going off at White Columns? If so, what did the person hope to achieve? He couldn't answer that question, but he reminded himself that twisted personalities were capable of acts that a rational mind couldn't understand. Someone was staking out White Columns, roaming the house at will, but for what purpose Cal didn't know. It was connected in some way to Marla's murder. Of that much he was certain.

It was at this point that Cal suddenly remembered the infrared cameras that were poised ready to capture on film any movement inside White Columns. They would provide a clue, maybe even an identity of the intruder. As soon as the thought flashed through his mind he was up, striding toward the bedroom to awaken Shanon. They had to get the film before the intruder returned and destroyed it. Damn! The film could already be removed. He cursed himself for not returning the previous night. If his hesitation had cost him a look at the mysterious intruder, he would never forgive himself.

Shanon was as intrigued by the possibilities of the film as he was. As they drove toward White Columns, they sat in silence, each preoccupied with thoughts of what the film would reveal.

Shanon glanced at Cal. She hadn't told him about being able to see Marla's body, encased within its coffin. She had spared that detail knowing how it would affect him. Now as she watched the gloom of dawn turn into the soft glow of early morning, she wondered what he hoped to find recorded on her film. She knew that he didn't doubt that someone had been inside the house, but she wondered if he accepted the fact that it had been a spirit. Nagging doubts entered her mind. The presence of the spirit had definitely triggered the motion detectors, but would the film be able to capture a visual image of it?

She noted the grim, determined set to Cal' jaw, the jut of his prominent chin, and reflected that he was as determined to get to the bottom of White Columns mystery as she was. She only hoped that his pride and the physical courage that his face reflected didn't lead him into a reckless course of action that he wasn't prepared to handle. A stab of anxiety pierced her as she realized that Cal's face was almost a replica of his Civil War ancestor. Lack of sleep, and an almost desperate yearning to find Marla's killer was turning him into a ruthless vigilante that she barely recognized. Now he seemed more like a soldier ravaged by the hardships and tragedy of war than the kindly, troubled man that she had met only a few days ago. She tried desperately to think of something to say to break the electric tension that rode with them but couldn't.

When they parked in front of White Columns and she got out of the car, she was startled by a sinister metallic sound. She whirled toward Cal and realized that the noise was the result of his having violently chambered a shell in the Remington 870 pump shotgun that he cradled in his arms as he strode toward the house. Staring at his broad shoulders, she knew that Cal Dunforth was a match for any mortal that might be lurking inside. What filled her with a sense of dread however, was the knowledge that whatever evil White Columns harbored wasn't mortal. She shuddered suddenly, and followed Cal into the house.

With the morning sun streaming in through its expansive windows, the house seemed benign, almost friendly. Only the memory of the previous nights terror kept Shanon from relaxing. She followed Cal through the house as he searched each room with methodical, relentless purpose. Not even when they entered the dark musty confines of the cellar that held such horrible memories for him did she notice any hesitation on his part.

"There's no one here. Get the film while I have a look around outside." Cal said tersely.

He moved across the yard with slow measured steps. First he studied the woods before him, then with a hunter's eye he searched the ground for footprints. He found none.

Although he had noticed Shanon's muddy footprints throughout the house, he had not seen evidence of another set of footprints, footprints that should have been there if an intruder had followed Shanon from the cemetery as she had claimed.

Outside, the heavy downpour of the previous night had washed away any trace of prints. He moved forward more quickly now, eyes searching the woods on either side of the footpath. Arriving at the gate, he bent down and placed a hand in the slight depression where Shanon had huddled beneath the stone horse. Everything about her story checked out except that there was no sign of another muddy set of prints inside the house.

Cal moved into the cemetery, found himself drawn to the raw mound of earth exposed by winds that had swept the flowers that had been lovingly placed over Marla's grave away. The carefully crafted flower arrangements were scattered spitefully across the cemetery, forlorn looking patches of brightness dotting the green lawn.

A heavy burden of sorrow settled over Cal. He found the wreath of roses that he had ordered for the funeral and laid it back across the ugly slash of clay that marked the grave site. Then with an act of will, he tore himself away from Marla's final resting place and moved deeper into the cemetery, seeking any possible hiding place that a man could have used the previous night.

At the rear of the plot, near the back fence, he noticed an unmarked grave, evidenced only by a cement slab that had been placed over it. Closer inspection revealed that years of water flowing beneath the slab had eroded a cavernous vault underneath. With a morbid sense of foreboding, he wriggled beneath the slab and peered out. The tree line along the edge of the cemetery was visible. In an instant he visualized the old hardwoods swaying against the fury of last night's thunderstorm. He felt a coldness invade him as he understood that he was now experiencing the viewpoint that Shanon had described.

Cal forced himself to remain inside the wet mucky enclosure long enough to carefully inspect the ooze that covered his sneakers. He saw no trace that anyone had stoodwhere he was now standing. Water rushing into the gaping wound in the earth had eradicated all signs of someone's presence.

Having made his examination, he pulled himself back up through the opening and inhaled deeply. The fresh sweetness of the morning air purged his lungs of the dank, foul air that he had found inside the grave. He turned and looked back at the open sore that seemed out of place in the well kept cemetery. He thought that whoever had been buried there must have been placed there in a crude wooden coffin that had gradually disintegrated over the years. He refused to think about the dark pasty muck that still clung to his shoes, except to remind himself that anyone who had stood in it last night would certainly have tracked some of it into White Columns.

He had satisfied himself that no intruder was lurking near White Columns when he felt a disturbing sense that someone was watching him. He felt malevolent eyes boring into his back. Instinctively he lunged behind a marble headstone, and trained the shotgun's gaping maw into the woods beyond the fence. His eyes searched in vain for a glimpse of the watcher. He waited for long minutes in motionless silence, until he saw two grey squirrels scurrying about, searching unconcernedly through the leaves for hickory nuts. He followed their progress through the sparse hardwoods, checking for any sign of alarm in the animals.

When they continued to feed without concern. He got up, brushed the mud from his clothes as best he could, and feeling slightly foolish, made his way back toward the house.

He found Shanon kneeling at the foot of the stairs, diligently trying to scrub away the mud that she had tracked inside the previous night. He became aware of his own muddy prints on the gleaming hardwood floor then and frowned. If someone had followed Shanon inside, why would they pause in the midst of a downpour to carefully remove mud from their own shoes? To add to the macabre effect of their presence? He had to admit to the possibility.

"Don't worry about the mud stains for now. Did you get the film?" He asked, not bothering to hide the trace of impatience in his voice.

"There." Shanon pointed to the canisters carefully arranged on a table in the hall.

"How soon can you get them developed?"

"I'll have to use the lab at the University.... If I leave with it right away I may have something for us to look at by Friday." She noticed the look of disappointment on his face. "Thursday night at the earliest." She added.

"Couldn't you fly them over, airfreight?" He asked.

"Maybe, but I still have to drive over and develop the film. There's no way I'm trusting anyone else to do that." She said, showing her stubborn streak.

"Well, let's get going. That will work out anyway. I need to get back with Drew and see if he's been able to dig up anything that will provide a clue as to the motive for Marla's murder." Cal said as he turned and started for the front door.

Shanon followed him to his car, climbed in and felt herself pushed back into the seat as the cruiser accelerated down White Columns driveway. "Did you find anything at the cemetery?"

"I think I found where the intruder was skulking when your vision started," He went on to explain about the washed out grave.

Shanon felt a chill of apprehension. "You will promise to be careful while I'm away, won't you? I think it would be best if you stayed away from White Columns until I get the film developed. Maybe then we'll have some answers as to exactly what we're up against."

"What do you think we're up against?" Cal avoided answering her directly.

"I believe that the intruder is a spirit." Shanon answered and studied his face for his reaction. When he didn't reply she pressed. "Well, tell me your reaction to that theory."

"I'm not ready to subscribe to it completely, although I'm willing to reserve judgment about it. What puzzles me is why I couldn't find a shred of physical evidence of another person being inside the house last night. I mean, your muddy footprints were plainly visible, yet whoever chased, or followed you inside left no trace of his presence." Cal glanced at her.

"You do believe that someone was there?" Shanon sought his reassurance.

"Absolutely. I only wish I knew who and why." Cal answered.

"Maybe the film will provide an answer. Right now it's all we've got."

"You're right. I'll focus my attention on Drew's investigation until you get back. Call me the minute you have the film."

"Only if you promise to stay away from White Columns in the meantime." Shanon said firmly.

"What the hell kind of deal is this?"

"Promise Cal."

"No promises. I'll do whatever it takes to find Marla's killer."

"Regardless of the danger, right?"

"Look, you were the one who said White Columns was safe. Why the sudden change of heart?"

"What happened last night..... It was nightmarish, yet real. The danger was real, and it was more than just physical danger Cal. Whatever is haunting White Columns is angry. I could feel it in the way it looked at me. It hated me, as if it sensed that somehow I'm a threat to it." Shanon answered.

Cal remembered the eerie feeling that had come over him in the graveyard. The feeling of being watched. It had felt like the hate filled stare of a mortal enemy. "Maybe you are. Maybe the evidence already recorded on film is a danger to it. If that's true.... You be careful too, Shanon. Remember what you told me about the limitations of time and distance in the spirit world as you believe it exists."

Shanon felt reassured. She would prefer any danger to having Cal refuse to believe her. "Only if you will." She retorted.

"Okay, Okay" He smiled at her for the first time that morning, and some of the tension drained out of both of them.

The ride back to Cal's house passed quickly. Shanon soon found herself standing beside her car, ready to leave for Birmingham. Part of her was anxious to get started, but another rebelled at leaving Cal. She clung to him for an embarrassingly long time, kissed him fiercely, and then slid behind the wheel of her car. Already she was looking forward to returning, and spending an uninterrupted night wrapped in his powerful arms.

CHAPTER 12

Beth Addison shoved the video tape into her player, and her trembling fingers pressed the play button. For agonizing seconds nothing appeared on the screen, then abruptly the scene that she desperately hoped for began playing. She held the fast forward scan down on the players remote, and watched a ludicrous jerky version of herself, whipping the ill fated young man.

She watched the entire sordid tape up to the part where she had gotten concerned about the well being of her prisoner. At that point, she allowed the tape to play at regular speed. Satisfied that it was a copy of the one that Heywood had threatened her with, she smiled, congratulated herself and then destroyed the tape.

She then undressed, stretched out luxuriously beneath her sheets, and allowed the queen size bed to carry her into peaceful oblivion. She awakened sometime during the night dreaming of her wedding to Cal Dunforth. For a long time thereafter, she lay awake in the darkness, savoring the dream, decided just before drifting off to sleep again that she would follow Heywood's plan that far at least. Knowing that she was free of him was almost as satisfying as the image of herself married to Cal. Only she realized that she wasn't really free of him. Not yet.

Heywood would know immediately who had broken into his house, and what had been taken from his safe. He would threaten to report his knowledge to the police unless she continued to cooperate. Beth smiled dreamily. Very well, she would cooperate, to a point. Then after she had what she wanted, she would deal with Heywood Carlson, rid herself of him forever. With that thought she drifted off to sleep again.

****

Beth opened the office at nine the following morning.

Within minutes, Sarah Haroldson, Heywood's secretary arrived, and the day started with the usual flurry of phone calls. Most were for Beth. She felt a sudden deep satisfaction knowing that Heywood needed her. Without her considerable sales and creative skills, the agency would go under quickly.

This knowledge added to the security that she was already beginning to bask in. In the bustle of early morning business, she had almost put thoughts of the police that she was certain would arrive soon out of her mind. By the time Sarah informed her that Detective Striker was outside, asking for Heywood first, then requesting to speak with her, she had relaxed completely. She smiled grimly, and told Sarah to send him in.

Beth was appalled at Striker's appearance. A skilled mortician could not have made him resemble a corpse more.

"Have a seat Mr. Striker. How can I help you?" She disguised her revulsion behind her most professional voice.

"I need to locate Mr. Carlson as quickly as possible. I was hoping that you would be familiar with his itinerary and tell me how I could reach him." Striker said.

Beth weighed the question in her mind. Sarah was familiar with Heywood's schedule. She could have told Striker how to contact him. Striker was feeling his way around, fishing. "I'll ask Sarah to help you with that Mr. Striker. She keeps a tighter leash on him than I do. The two of us kind of work independently, each handling different accounts." Beth answered. "Is there some kind of emergency? I hope nothing has happened to his family." Beth asked, probing to find out how much information Striker was prepared to share.

"Oh no. Nothing like that. Just a burglary at his residence. I'm sure he would want to know about it as soon as possible." Striker's face twitched.

"Well. I'm relieved." She paused for a few seconds and then added. "I guess that is an indication of how bad crime has become. Heywood's house has been burglarized and I'm relieved that it's nothing serious." She laughed.

128

"How long have you worked for Mr. Carlson?" Striker asked.

"A little over two years now." Beth wondered why he'd asked. She also felt a slight sense of apprehension that he hadn't mentioned the body in Heywood's back yard..

"Tell me about Mr. Carlson's relationship with his late wife."

A stab of fear probed for Beth's heart. "I don't know much about that. Mr. Carlson and I have a professional relationship. I've never discussed his personal life with him."

"In over two years, he never mentioned his wife to you?"

"Well, of course he mentioned her. I knew her as a matter of fact. I'm not sure what you're asking me." Beth said.

"I simply want you to tell me what you know about their relationship." Striker repeated himself rather mechanically.

"Why is that important? I'm not sure that it would be appropriate for me to discuss Mr. Carlson's personal life with the police." Beth said shortly.

"I see. Then you are somewhat familiar with his personal life. Your reluctance is a result of moral qualms." Striker pounced.

Beth looked at Striker with wary respect. Behind the corpse mask lurked a keen and resourceful mind. She would have to be careful. "Yes, that's an accurate statement."

"Let me put your mind at ease on that score Ms.Addison. I'm conducting a murder investigation. As you must know, moral qualms have to be set aside, only the truth is important in such matters." Striker said in a sepulchral voice.

The mention of murder caused her to start, even though she had been expecting it. "I see. Surely you don't suspect him of murdering his wife. I understand that her death was ruled a suicide." Beth parried.

"Do you suspect him, Ms. Addison?"

"Of course not!" Her reply was sharper than she intended.

"Why don't you answer my original question." Striker said.

"Well, in my opinion they were simply too different to make a relationship work. She was a product of the Old South. He was from Boston. He is a very serious, hardworking type of guy. She was a spoiled, rich, over protected child. She always got whatever she wanted. Everything in her life was a toy to her, including her husband. When she grew tired of him, she disposed of him as she would any other plaything that she had no further use for."

"You didn't like her very much, did you Ms. Addison?"

The question surprised her, and caught her off guard. She

answered it honestly. "I don't suppose I did. We had nothing in common."

"I see." Striker's colorless eyes bored into her. "Does the name Chase Gordon mean anything to you?" He asked.

"No."

"Nothing at all?"

"I've never known of anyone by that name." Beth wondered where this line of questioning was leading, and who Chase Gordon was.

"Were you aware that Mr. Carlson sometimes used an alias?" Striker asked.

"An alias?"

"I know that Mr. Carlson sometimes traveled under the name Chase Gordon. Why would he do that Ms. Addison?"

"You'll have to ask him."

"Does that mean that you know, but prefer that I ask him?"

"I've already told you that I've never heard the name before." Beth answered with irritation. She was growing weary of Striker. She had no idea where he had come up with the name Chase Gordon. The knowledge that Heywood used it without her knowledge was a disturbing development. She wondered if it was a part of the elaborate blackmail scheme that he had trapped her in.

"Are you aware of any other business interests that Mr.Carlson has?"

"No."

"Was his relationship with his wife acrimonious enough that he might have tried to hide some of his assets from her by using a second identity?"

"It's possible, but I have no knowledge of that." Beth answered, wondering now herself. After all, how much did she really know about Heywood Carlson.

"I appreciate your help, Ms. Addison. One last question. Do you know if Mr. Carlson had dealings with a man named Claude Raynes?"

"No. Is Claude Raynes another of Mr. Carlson's alias?" Beth asked the question with slight sarcasm, to cover her sudden need to know more about Heywood and his associates.

"No. Claude Raynes is the lowest filth in this city. He deals in pornography, the kind that you can't buy downtown, and I hate to admit it, but you can buy some pretty raunchy filth right over the counter." Striker volunteered information for the first time.

"I'm aware of that Mr. Striker. It appalls me that anyone could deal with material more disgusting than some of the movies playing downtown," Beth answered, sensing that she was on the verge of learning something vital to her safety.

"He deals in S&M stuff, the real deal, The blood's real, the pain's real, and it's rumored that for the right price, he'll sell you a snuff film."

The blood left Beth's face with that revelation. She was ill, struggling to hide the raw fear that she suddenly felt. Fortunately Striker was ready to terminate the interview, and seemed not to notice her sudden discomfort.

When he left, she buzzed Sarah, told her to hold all of her calls and sat behind her desk in shock. She cursed herself for allowing Warren to keep everything that they recovered from Heywood's safe except the tape. The wad of papers that he had stuffed into the bag, and that had tumbled into the yard on top of him when she had shot him, must be the source of Striker's information. Anxiety started building inside her as she wondered what other revelations Heywood's private papers might reveal. The knowledge that Heywood had used her in the making of a snuff film filled her with cold terror. She wondered how many copies of the tape that she had just destroyed were floating around the city, She buried her face in her hands, and cried for the first time in a long time.

****

The pounding beat of heavy metal assailed Striker's ears as he opened the heavy wooden door to Cheeks, the sleazy club that Claude Raynes operated from. He stood just inside the doorway, peering through a swirling haze of cigarette smoke, and artificial smoke emanating from somewhere beneath the dance floor, where a naked blonde with impossibly large breasts undulated to the ear splitting music.

It was only a few minutes past noon, on a Tuesday, but true to the sign hanging outside in the alley, Cheeks rocked twenty four hours a day. The dive was a favorite hang out of guys who worked second shift. Here they could satisfy their lust for topless, bottomless entertainment any time of the day.

Striker paused at the bar long enough to order a Crown Royal and water. While waiting for the bartender to splash the drink into a glass, he looked around. He noticed a couple of under cover vice and narcotics officers, as filthy and degenerate looking as any of the other customers, seated at the end of the bar. They lived a hell of a life, he thought, hanging out in dives like this. He thought that the only socially redeeming value that places like Cheeks had was the fact that they served as perfect sanctuaries for the informants that vice and narcotics depended on so heavily.

He studied the girl performing on stage, was mildly surprised that she was so attractive. He wondered how Raynes got girls as pretty as she was to degrade themselves so thoroughly for the tips that they earned. A look at the budging wad of bills in her garter provided the answer. Some people would do anything for the dollar green, he thought.

When the bartender set his drink down in front of him, Striker downed it quickly, tossed a few bills on the bar, and walked to the rear of the club, through a door that led to a narrow passage that ended in a flight of stairs. At the top of the stairs he pounded on the door to Raynes' office.

"Who is it?" The voice was terse, impatient.

"Striker. Open up Raynes. I want to talk to you."

"Get the fuck away from my door, and out of my club. I got nothing to say to you."

"I can come back with a warrant Raynes, or send in a couple of guys from vice and narcotics. No telling what kind of shit they might find. Open up. I just want to talk. If you piss me off, I'll shit all over your little parade."

Striker heard a chair scrape against the floor, and in a few seconds the door opened a crack. He shoved it inward violently, and stepped into the office.

"What the fuck is this Striker? You can't come in here shoving me around. My lawyer'll have your ass up on charges." Raynes wheezed.

"Shut up and sit down." Striker responded.

"What do you want?" Raynes rested a heavy hip on the corner of his desk.

Striker pulled up an uncomfortable looking straight chair, turned it around backwards and leaned over the back of it. He fixed his cold eyes on Raynes and said, "Tell me everything you know about a guy named Heywood Carlson."

"Never heard of him."

"Then tell me about Chase Gordon."

"What is this, twenty questions? You want something specific, ask. I don't tell you everything I know about nobody, understand?"

"You ever buy films from him?"

"Maybe."

"Rough stuff?"

"Could be."

"Snuff films?"

"Don't start that shit again, Striker. I'll have my lawyer in here so quick that your head will spin. I know my rights. I ain't some two bit street punk that you can bully around, understand. I already told you I don't deal in no snuff. If that's what you come to talk about, you can drag your dead ass back to whatever morgue you escaped from. I got no time for your shit. This snuff film business has gone to your brain. That shit don't go on in Atlanta. Forget it."

Striker withdrew a pair of latex surgeons gloves from the inside pocket of his blazer, and very deliberately pulled them on. Next he reached inside his jacket pocket, and held up a Smith and Wesson model 36 snub nose. He leaned down, and skidded the ugly little weapon across the floor until it came to rest against Raynes shoe. He removed the gloves, and drew his Colt auto from its shoulder rig.

"What the fuck.... are you trying to pull Striker?" Raynes licked his lips nervously.

"We need to reach an understanding Raynes. I know you're no street punk. You're the lowest form of shit that this city has to offer, but you're dangerous, everyone knows that you're dangerous. Now, I'm not one of the candy ass narcs that you're used to dealing with either. My job is homicide. A dirty job, but somebody's got to do it. Right now, I've got a case that stinks like hell, and your name is right in the middle of it. You're either going to tell me what I want to know, or your fat hairy ass is gonna leave here in a body bag."

"You're bluffing Striker. I ain't telling you shit."

The roar of the 45 auto was deafening inside the office, but Striker knew that it wouldn't be heard above the pounding music in the club below. The fat 230 grain slug ripped Raynes earlobe off.

"Aargg! Raynes cry of pain and fear had an animal quality about it. The stench of urine filled the office. "You're crazy Striker! God damn! You're crazy as hell!"

"That's what the department shrink has been trying to tell my boss for years Raynes. Now, you want to talk, or die?"

"I'll talk" Raynes was clutching his bloody ear, still unaware that he had pissed his pants. "What do you want to know?"

"Did you buy a film from a guy named Heywood Carlson, or Gordon Chase?"

"Chase."

"How long ago?"

"Couple a months."

"I want a copy."

Raynes started to shake his head, saw Striker raising the pistol again, and held up his hands. He limped over to the safe, nervous, taking three attempts to get the combination right. He withdrew a video tape and handed it to Striker.

"Thanks Claude. I hope that things can be more cordial next time we need to talk." Striker said, his face twitching. He holstered his automatic, shoved the tape into the rear of his waistband beneath his jacket, and leaving the revolver where it lay, stalked out of the office.

On his way out, Striker had another Crown and water. He sipped it slowly, waiting to see if Raynes would come downstairs. When the smut king didn't appear, he unwound his lean frame from the bar stool and walked outside. His ears were still ringing when he reached his car. He wished that he'd tapped Raynes phone before he'd paid him a visit.

He drove aggressively across town, parked in his garage, and went inside the split level home that he had all to himself. He paused in the kitchen long enough to pour himself another drink, then went into the living room and started the tape. He settled in on his sofa, and watched a lithe, muscular woman clad in black leather beat the living shit out of a guy with dishwater blonde hair. The closing minutes of the tape showed a thin nylon cord slowly tightening around the guy's neck. The final sequence alternated between close ups of a twisted, bloated face, and the mans throbbing erection. It was the sickest sight that he had ever watched. In a blatant attempt at black humor, the tape ended with The End superimposed over a close ups of the guy's glazing eyes.

Striker replayed the tape, focusing on the woman, looking for any identifying mark on her body that might hold a clue to her identity. He found none, and the mask that she wore, in addition to making her appear convincingly menacing, completely obscured her features. All he could tell about her was that she was a well proportioned blonde who obviously enjoyed her work.

He rewound the tape, snapped off the television, and sat thinking about what he had seen. He memorized the face of the murdered man, then went back to his car and climbed in. He would spend the rest of the day searching the missing persons file for the man in the tape. He would not try to contact Heywood Carlson. He'd let him return as scheduled the following evening, and meet him at the airport. He wasn't sure that Carlson would return if he was aware that someone had cracked his safe, and exposed the nasty little porno business that he was involved with.

At least he now had a clue as to the real reason that the house had been burglarized. In addition to being into smut, Striker was willing to bet that Carlson was also involved with some kind of blackmail scheme. He decided that it wouldn't hurt to check into the circumstances of Carlson's wife's death. Suicide, that's what the Addison bitch had said. Lot's of suicides hanged themselves. Carlson was into strangling. If he found that the wife had hanged herself, he would know that it was murder. He would know it, but would he be able to prove it? So far, none of the evidence that indicated that Carlson was into televised murder was admissible in court. Striker had secured it illegally. That thought didn't bother him. First he had to understand what was going on, get a feel for the case, then he would know enough to find the evidence that he needed for a prosecution.

Striker was unique in that he worked on two levels. First he proved a suspect's guilt or innocence to his own satisfaction, by whatever means necessarily. Then he gathered evidence legally, or planted it if he had to. He had solved cases in a few days that other detectives had worked for months, because he had no scruples. Striker was a firm believer in the law of competitive behavior. When faced with adversaries who lied, cheated, stole and murdered to achieve their goals, the only way to have success against them was to engage in the same patterns of behavior. Any other approach would lead to failure. Failure was unacceptable to Striker. His father had been a failure— in business, and to his family. Striker had seen first hand how failures ended up, sucking on the barrel of a revolver. The day that he had found his father lying in a pool of blood and brains on the kitchen floor, he had sworn that he would never wind up a failure, no matter what he had to do to succeed. That childhood oath made Striker a formidable adversary.

CHAPTER 13

Cal called Drew Wednesday morning. He was disappointed, but not too surprised when Drew confided that so far he had not found anything irregular in any of Marla's financial matters. They talked for several minutes, mostly about Paula, and the security precautions that Hannah Greene was taking with her. Cal assured Drew that Paula would be safe under Hannah's care, and promised to call again on Friday.

After he got off the phone, Cal felt an irresistible restlessness. Shanon wouldn't have the pictures developed until Friday. That gave him two days to come up with another angle from which to pursue Marla's killer. He wasn't pinning his hopes entirely on the pictures. He couldn't afford to. They might not reveal anything at all, or they could reveal some crank lurking around White Columns who wasn't connected with Marla's death in any way. The intruder could be a cruel hoax, someone enjoying their role of perpetuating the mystic aura of the old house.

Since learning that Drew was drawing a blank, the only place that Cal had to start from was back at White Columns. As much as he dreaded it, he knew that he had no choice— he would have to start from the scene of the murder, examine every detail again, sift through every grain of sand on the floor of White Columns cellar until he found some clue.

Within minutes Cal had loaded the items that he would need in the back seat of his patrol car, and started toward White Columns. He had been granted a weeks leave from work, and he resolved to make the most of it. He wasn't sure that he would ever be able to put his mind back on his regularly assigned duties until he had found Marla's killer, although he knew that he would be expected to. To hell with it all, he thought. He'd worry about that next week. For now, he would work as if he had been assigned this case, as if Harold Collins didn't exist, and the investigation that had determined that Marla had killed herself had never happened.

By the time he had arrived at White Columns, he had forced his mind to form the barrier of professional detachment necessary to function as an investigator. He didn't bother to enter the house, instead he walked around back, entered the cellar, and strung the lights that he had rigged across the ceiling of the gloomy enclosure. He plugged the drop cord into an outlet on the back porch and entered the cellar.

The array of bulbs bathed the area with harsh light, and chased away the gloom that usually permeated the interior. Cal stood inside the doorway, taking a mental inventory of the cellar's contents. It was depressingly bare, empty except for a single two by six board, approximately five feet in length, that was leaning against the wall opposite the entrance. Two very large nails protruded from each end of it. What was it doing there? Cal would ask himself that question about every object that he noticed until he found something that didn't add up.

His eyes scanned the cellar carefully. He realized that this was the first time that he had seen it in full light. At first he felt a sense of disappointment that the place was so empty. It seemed hopeless. Then he reminded himself that the lack of clutter was good. It meant that the slightest trace of evidence left by the killer would be that much more obvious.

He noticed two stains where water had puddled on the cobblestone floor. He remembered falling down on a slippery wet floor when he had first encountered Marla's body. He noticed how dry and dusty the air smelled, and with his mind now attuned to the slightest variation from the normal, the water stains stood out conspicuously. How did water accumulate in those two spots when the rest of the floor appeared dry?

He remembered something else. He hadn't given it a thought at the time, but there had been something on the cellar floor beneath Marla's body. Something that had torn his uniform pants, and left an ugly gash in his thigh that had gone untended.

He took a small notebook from his pocket and started jotting down his thoughts. He looked back at the board, leaning carelessly against the wall and wrote down: Cellar as neat as a pin, except for board with nails. He thought about Marla. Why would she clean out the cellar and leave a board with nails behind?

He walked over and examined the piece of lumber, smelled the familiar odor of new, freshly sawed pine. He turned it and examined the bright, shiny heads of the nails, compared them with the rusted shafts, rubbed his fingers across the rust and noted that it came off easily, proving that it had just formed. His eyes scanned every inch of the board and stopped at the brown stains splattered across the center of it. He almost lost his cool, methodical detachment when he stared at the blood, but quickly recovered. The blood on the board could easily be his own. He now felt certain that it was what he had fallen on, and one of the nails had been what had gashed his thigh.

With a wry smile, he thought that if Collins found his blood in the cellar, the chief investigator would really go ape shit.

The presence of blood on the board meant that it had been lying carelessly discarded on the floor beneath the beam from which Marla's body had been suspended. It didn't matter if it was Marla's blood, or his own, either way, the board had to have been beneath Marla's body. Cal found that more suspicious than having it leaning against the wall. The memory of Granny Dunforth's voice, warning the two children to be careful of stepping on a nail, when he and Marla had used an old barn as their playhouse came to mind. The barn had long since fallen in and its debris carted off, but her often repeated caution still echoed in his mind. Marla would have remembered it too. She wouldn't have left a board with nails lying in the middle of the floor where someone would step on it in the dark of the cellar.

His spirits lifted. Already he had found two items that didn't belong in the cellar. But how did they fit into Marla's death? How would a murderer use a board and two buckets of water to kill their victim? Kicked the bucket. The slang phrase that had been a euphemism for death played through his mind. In his childhood Granny Dunforth had once told him that an old dog that she had owned had kicked the bucket, meaning that it had died. The term had derived from the practice of those attempting suicide, standing on a water pail with the noose around their neck, and then kicking the pail, or bucket, out from beneath themselves.

Collins report had stated that Marla had stood on the cellar steps and adjusted the noose, then simply stepped off and hung herself. The presence of the board with traces of blood on it should have indicated that she had stood on the board, not the steps.—unless there was nothing found in the cellar to support the board, a pair of cinder blocks, a couple of chairs, for example.

Cal tried to think about a pair of objects that could have supported the board, then vanished mysteriously from the scene. A disturbing picture came to mind. He picked up the board and carried it over to where the water stains were. He laid it down and observed that the ends of the boards extended almost exactly to the ends of the water stains.He looked up and found that the board was directly beneath the beam from which Marla had been hanging. Ice! Two blocks of solid ice would support a board.

Such an arrangement would have allowed a murderer to delay his victims death until he could drive miles away, and establish an alibi for the time of death. The only unanswered question was how the murderer would convince his victim into being docile enough to step up onto the board, and stand there quietly with a noose around their neck.

Shanon's vision of Paula in the back seat of Heywood's car flashed into Cal's mind. Marla would have done exactly what Heywood demanded if he had held her at gun point, and explained that Paula was at that moment breathing exhaust fumes. He would have pointed out that the sooner Marla obeyed his commands, the sooner he would remove the child from the death trap. Cal could see the evil little bastard goading Marla by telling her that if she hurried, Paula just might still be alive.

Suddenly he remembered how Paula's hair had smelled the night of Marla' death. He hadn't given it any thought at the time, but now it suddenly fit. Her hair had smelled of engine exhaust! In a split second the entire picture formed in his mind. Heywood had left Marla in the cellar, pulled the hose out of the exhaust and simply drove away, leaving Marla to a slow and agonizing death. By the time the ice melted and Marla strangled, the bastard had been in Macon, establishing an alibi!

Rage swept through Cal like heat from a furnace. It escaped in a long wail that tore at his vocal cords. His hands clenched into fists, and he could feel an ache inside that he knew wouldn't go away until Heywood Carlson was dead.

He walked out of the cellar into the light of day like a sleep walker. In his mind Heywood's face disintegrated beneath the fury of his flailing fists. Images of the murderer's swollen face, devoid of color, deprived of life giving oxygen by his own powerful fingers clasped around the fleshy neck implanted themselves deep within his mind.

Without bothering to unplug the lights, he walked to his car and slumped down in the seat. Depression stalked him like a dark cloud. As satisfying as the thoughts of what he would do to Heywood Carlson was, he realized that nothing would bring Marla back. The knowledge that she had died alone in the dark, without even the comfort of knowing for certain that Paula was safe haunted him.

All of his professional objectivity was gone, vanquished by the black worm of emotional disturbance known as clinical depression. A disorder that robs its victims of self worth, confidence, even of the will to live, began spinning its insidious web inside his mind. He no longer cared about his future. Only Heywood Carlson's death mattered to him. After that...... He was unable to construct a vision of his future beyond that. Only darkness.

****

Beth Addison's nerves were frayed to the breaking point. She knew that somehow she must maintain a semblance of normalcy in her daily routine, yet she was so keyed up that she made a mess of all of her sales presentations that morning, and had finally returned to the office and taken refuge behind her closed office door. She wasn't taking messages, so she was surprised when the intercom sounded.

"Sarah, I thought you understood that I'm not taking calls." She snapped into the phone.

"I know Beth, but Cal's on the line. I thought you would want to speak with him." Sarah said defensively.

Cal! Beth realized that she really did want to talk to him. Why hadn't she called him? Maybe a few days off, quiet days, with him would soothe her nerves. "Thanks Sarah, you're wonderful. Of course I want to talk to him."

She punched the flashing line and said, "Cal, I'm glad you called. I've been worried about you. How are you doing?"

"Better. Listen, I just called to tell you that I'm going to be out of town for the weekend. I wanted to let you know soon enough that you could make other plans, in case you were driving down."

"Out of town?" Beth couldn't hide the disappointment that she felt. "Is it somewhere that we can go together? I'm having kind of a rough week with Heywood out of the office, and I could use a break myself." She added hopefully.

"Where's Heywood off too this time?" Cal asked.

"Denver. He's working an account out there, some kind of sporting goods manufacturer. If he lands the account, it could mean a big jump in business." Beth paused. "You didn't answer my question Cal. Would you like some company?"

"Sure. Why don't you call and make our airline reservations?"

"Because I don't know where we're going, silly." Beth laughed, beginning to relax.

"How does Wyoming sound?"

"Wyoming? Why would you want to go there?" Beth asked.

"I was thinking about flying into Jackson Hole, renting a four wheel drive, and maybe driving up to Yellowstone. From there I might rent a couple of saddle horses, and scout the National Forest land adjacent to the park. I've always wanted to hunt mule deer. I think that a trip like that is just what I need before I have to start back to work next week."

"Don't you have to have a licences, and all that stuff to hunt?" Beth asked. She had just noticed how flat, and unemotional Cal's voice was. Before, whenever he discussed a western hunt, he almost bubbled with enthusiasm.

"This won't be a hunt. I'll just be looking for sign, trying to find a good area. I won't be able to hunt until next fall. You have to plan this kind of thing almost a year ahead. It's just a whim. I want to go, so I'm going. Are you game?"

"Sure, why not. I'll make the arrangements and call you back."

"I don't want to hang around the phone, why don't I call you Friday morning, and we'll take it from there?"

"Sure Cal. I'll get right on it."

"Good. No reason to let Heywood have all the fun while we sit home. I'll bet he's booked in the plushiest Hotel in Denver, or has he had to curb his taste now that he's spending his own money."

Beth wondered at the bitterness in Cal's voice. If he had ever resented Heywood's lifestyle before he had never let it show. "He's getting a little more down to earth. He's booked at the Sheraton, no palace, but nice. Do you think that we could spend one night in a hotel? I mean, I'd rather be roughing it with you than surrounded by luxury, still..."

"Sure. Make reservations for Friday night in Denver. The Sheraton sounds good. We can catch a commuter out to Jackson Hole first thing Saturday. Maybe we can surprise Heywood."

"Great Cal. You're a darling. The best part though, is that Heywood will already be gone. If I saw him now, I'd probably punch him out for leaving me in such a mess. I've spent more time this week handling his screwups than I have on my own accounts. He's such an asshole."

"Is he really that bad?"

"Absolutely. He's a turd." Beth allowed her newly acquired hatred to filter into her voice.

"Yeah. Got to let you get back to work. I'll call you Friday," Cal said, and the line went dead.

Beth sat for a minute, reviewing the call. It was strange. Cal had never been interested in Heywood's where abouts before. He usually ignored him, as if he preferred that he didn't exist. Beth gradually became aware that she had just given Cal all the information that he would need if he wanted to find Heywood.

There was only one reason that Cal might want to find Heywood, now that she thought about it. If he had uncovered some flaw in Heywoods plan to murder Marla, and had discovered that Heywood had killed her, then he might do anything. There was no question in Beth's mind that Cal was capable of executing Marla's killer. The thought would have been pleasant to contemplate except for two concerns. The first was that Cal might not try to avoid implicating himself. The other was that he might let Heywood live long enough to reveal her own involvement. She knew that a vindictive bastard like Heywood would certainly taunt Cal with that bit of information—he might even try to trade it for his own life. She couldn't afford to allow Cal to find Heywood. It was too risky.

Beth's anxiety rose another notch as she thought about her plight. She had thought that with the incriminating tape destroyed, she would be safe, at least for long enough to carefully plan a way to get rid of Heywood. She had not even been very worried about killing Warren. There was no way for the police to connect her to his death, and the burglary of Heywood's house, except through Heywood. She had known that Heywood would not have gone to the police. He would not have been able to resist holding his knowledge over her head as a threat.

Those damn papers that Striker had gotten his hands on! If she had only destroyed them, or better still, hid them as a hedge against Heywood. She had been careless, and it had cost her. Now she realized that there were dozens, maybe even hundreds of copies of the damning tape. She could only hope that Heywood had edited them so that her face was not visible. She comforted herself with the thought that he must have. If her identity became known, it could lead the authorities to Heywood. He wouldn't risk that. No. She didn't have to worry about the tapes floating around. Striker and his investigation was what she had to be wary of. That, and whatever Cal was up to.

She thought about Cal. Would he simply fly to Denver, wait for Heywood in his hotel room and kill him there? She couldn't be sure. In fact, she realized, she couldn't even be sure that she wasn't allowing her imagination to run wild. She couldn't be sure of what Cal was planning, or even if he knew that Heywood had murdered Marla. She had to find out.

She picked up the phone, and dialed the Alapaha County Sheriffs department. When the dispatcher answered she asked for deputy Abe Lucas. When pressed about the urgency of her call, she insisted on being patched through on his radio.

She waited for the call to go through, and then heard Abe's friendly voice. "Hi Abe. Listen, I'm worried about Cal. Have you talked to him lately?"

"No I haven't. I guess I should have called him, but I don't know. I guess I just didn't know what to say to him." Abe said.

"Why don't you drop by and chat with him a few minutes, you know, see what you think, then call me right back. Don't let him know that I put you up to it. You know Cal, he wouldn't want me mothering him." Beth said.

"Sure Beth. I'm only a couple of miles from his house. I'll swing by and say hello. I'll be back to you in a few minutes. I appreciate your calling. I should have been out to see him already."

Beth hung up and waited nervously, unable to concentrate on the vague outline of a plan that was forming in her mind. She watched the clock as she waited. She didn't know what she expected to hear from Lucas, but any information that she could glean would be helpful.

She saw the intercom light up and pounced on it, barely acknowledged Sarah, then got on the line with the deputy. "Thanks for calling, Abe. How does he look?"

"I guess he's fine. He seemed a little preoccupied. I don't know, probably normal." Abe said.

"So what was he up to?"

"I just managed to catch him. He was packing his Jeep, said he wanted to get away for a few days."

"Leaving right away?" Beth felt her stomach tighten.

"Yeah, he was in a hurry. We didn't talk long. I think he's fine though. He may have the right idea. Me? I know I would get out of town if I had a few days off." Abe said.

"Did he say how long he was planning to be away?"

"No. He just said he'd see me Monday at the office."

"Thanks Abe. You're a sweetheart. I feel much better."

Beth hung up and buzzed Sarah. "Sarah, get Heywood on line for me, will you. I just run across something that I've got to talk to him about. It's important. Don't let anyone give you the run around. Get him on the line, pronto." She glanced at the clock. Four thirty. Heywood would most likely be in the hotel bar by now. Beth knew his work habits only too well.

Ten minutes later Sarah had reached him. Beth clutched the phone to her ear and spoke urgently. "Heywood, something's come up. Cancel whatever you've got on tap for tomorrow and get your ass on a plane, the sooner the better."

"Damn it Beth! Can't you handle things for a few days. You know how important this client is. I don't even want to know what its about, just handle it. You're as familiar with the accounts as I am."

Heywood had already been drinking. It showed in his voice. "It's not about the office Heywood. It's your extracurricular activity that has raised serious questions." Beth said ominously.

There was a long silence. "What's happened?"

"You don't want to discuss it on the phone. Get back here as soon as possible. Don't book the flight under your name, and not under Gordon Chase name either. When you know your flight number, give me a call at home. I'll meet you." Beth felt sadistic glee, knowing the effect that the Chase identity would have on him.

"Shit!" The exclamation was brief, yet the fear in his voice was audible.

"Don't fuck around Heywood. We have to talk, somewhere private. You can't go home either. I'm your only hope."

"Damn. What kind of shit is this? How did you know about Chase?"

"Shut up Heywood. Do as I say or we're both going to be in deep shit." Beth hung up, gathered her brief case and purse, and walked out of her office.

"Sarah, I'll see you in the morning. Have a nice evening." Beth flung over her shoulder as she headed for the elevator.

As an after thought she turned and asked, "Do you know anything about a guy named Gordon Chase?"

Sarah looked surprised. "Of course. He's damn good." She replied.

"What do you mean, damn good?" Beth snapped.

"At sales. His commissions are huge." Sarah replied. She still had a puzzled look on her face.

"How do you know about that?" Beth queried.

"Come on Beth. You know that I work up commission statements, write the checks. Of course I would know."

"You write commission checks to a guy named Gordon Chase?" Beth took a step back into the office.

"Maybe you should take up whatever problem that you have with Heywood." Sarah now had a worried look on her face.

"I'm asking you. Now if you know what's good for you, you'll tell me everything that you know about this Chase." Beth's manner was menacing as she approached Sara's desk.

"Look Beth, I don't want trouble with you. Gordon Chase is our other sales rep. I think that he covers the West. I really don't know. All I know is that he earns top commissions. I thought that you knew about him."

Beth thought quickly. So that's why the Agency was so close to broke. Heywood was siphoning off income. She was furious. "Where do you mail the checks?" She demanded.

"Beth, please...." Sarah's face was white with fear.

"You listen to me, you mindless bitch. There is no Gordon Chase. It's a scam. Now where do you mail the fucking checks!" By now she was towering over Sarah threateningly.

"It's a direct deposit."

"What bank? I want the bank and the account number." Beth snarled.

"Please Beth. I can't go into this with you without Heywood's approval. I could get fired if he finds out." Sarah whined.

"Tell me what you know. I just spent the morning being grilled by that detective creep. If you hold out on me, so help me, I'll see that your ass goes to jail!"

"Oh God. Are we in some kind of trouble?" Sarah was close to tears.

"Hell yes, we're in trouble. I'm trying to find out just how bad it is. Now if you help me, I'll see that you are protected from prosecution. If not..." Beth trailed off ominously.

Sarah typed furiously at her keyboard. She printed out the pay record for Gordon Chase and handed it over to Beth.

"Thank you Sarah. I know I can count on you to do the right

thing. Now, I want you to help me back up all of our financial records onto a zip drive." She said softly.

"Heywood already has a backup." Sarah replied.

"Well that one's not going to do you and I any good is it. There's no telling what information that has been tampered with, is there? Be a good girl and make another backup, right now." Beth demanded.

While Sarah backed up the records, Beth searched for tools. When Sarah handed over the backup, she went to the server and shut the system down. She then began removing the hard drive from it. Once finished, she methodically removed the hard drives from each of the office's work stations. Finished, she walked back to Sarah's desk. "We just had a major disc drive crash. Call a computer repair service, not the one that we've been using, and get them over here to replace these drives. If they ask where the original drives are, tell them another repair service is trying to recover data from them, and that we can't wait until they're finished to get our system back up and running."

Sarah looked apprehensive, but she picked up the Yellow Pages and began looking for a service center. "I hope that you know what you're doing Beth." She said.

"Trust me Sarah. You know that I'm the one that has made this agency successful. It appears that I've done so in spite of Heywood's double dipping. Don't worry. We'll be okay." She soothed. She had to move fast now. It was her only chance.

She tucked the ZIP drive into her brief case, and left the office. She knew that she didn't have to worry about Sarah. The stupid cow had placed her trust in Beth, and having made that decision, there was no turning back. She would do whatever Beth told her until this thing was over. That wasn't a bad trait in an employee Beth decided. Maybe she would keep her on after she dealt with Heywood.

On the way to the parking deck, she contemplated briefly trying to recover the money that Heywood had already siphoned off. She immediately realized that there was no way to get her hands on that money. Heywood would close the account at the first sign of trouble. After further thought, she realized that the account was an intermediate one anyway. Heywood would never leave substantial sums in an account that could be traced. With this realization another thought crossed her mind. She took comfort in the knowledge that the Chase identity was only a vehicle to move money from the agency into Heywood's hands. If that was the case, as she felt certain that it was, then Heywood would have another layer of protection between himself and the long arm of the law. That meant that Striker's knowledge of Gordon Chase would lead him exactly nowhere. Gordon Chase would simply disappear into another identity that Striker would never unravel. She was beginning to see a dimension of Heywood Carlson that she had never suspected. He was a hell of a lot smarter than she'd given him credit for.

This knowledge spurred her on. She couldn't allow him time to determine what kind of problem that he faced. She had to act immediately, while he was off balance. He wouldn't suspect that his real danger was from her, not the law. It was a window of opportunity that she wouldn't let close. Heywood Carlson was as good as dead.

CHAPTER 14

Striker studied the file in front of him. On top was the rap sheet of Paul "Bebo" Warren. It listed five arrests for burglary, one conviction. He was pretty good at his trade. While Bebo wasn't quite in the big time, with enough skills to crack sophisticated vaults that would be used to safeguard really big hauls, he was good enough to open the safes used by small time jewelers to store their clients valuables while they were in the shop for repairs.

The wall safe at Carlson's residence would have been a cracker box for Bebo Warren.

Bebo had just made parole last month. He would have been flat, looking to score. Whoever had hired him wouldn't have had to look too hard to find him. Bebo had probably made his contacts already, and put the word out that he was available. He must have been desperate to have hired out without checking up on his employer. Too bad, Striker thought. Bebo's carelessness had cost him dearly. He had gotten into something that was bigger than he imagined going in.

Striker usually solved murders involving known felons with ease. Almost invariably they got iced by their business associates. A little digging would turn up a motive, and by squeezing his extensive stable of street level informers, Striker would come up with a suspect. He knew that this case was going to be different. He would have to find out about Heywood Carlson before he would get to Bebo's murderer.

Instinctively he knew that Carlson's illicit pornography business was the key to solving Bebo's murder. As far as he was concerned, Bebo's killer would be served up as part of something much bigger. The newsies didn't care about the offing of a small time burglar. The mastermind of a smut ring that dealt in snuff films on the other hand, would be something that he could ride to the top. If he cracked this case, he would be in line for the top job in his department, maybe even Chief later in his career. He wondered if he should leak a hint that he was working something that might turn into a sensational case.

He decided that it was too soon to start any rumors. He wanted to be more certain of nailing his mark before he got the brass stirred up. He would have to hint to Tom Bugosi that he might be onto a major crime ring in order to get the manpower for the legwork that he would need, yet he wanted to leave himself an out in case he drew a blank.

He studied his watch. Five minutes before his meeting with Atlanta's Chief of Homicide. He got up and wandered down the hall, and waited outside Bugosi's door. When it opened and disgorged Al Stewart, he saw a barometer of Bugosi's mood this morning reflected in the angry slash of Stewart's mouth.

"Hope you're wearing your brass underwear Striker," Stewart muttered as they passed. Striker walked into the office exuding confidence. He read the expression on Bugosi's face, and determined how to handle him. "Morning Tom. I can see that you're up to your ass in alligators, so I'll be brief. I need to throw a team together to run down some leads in the Warren case. I've run across some solid information that leads me to believe that there's more to this case than meets the eye," Striker paused, knowing that Bugosi couldn't resist the bait.

"Sit down Striker. What have you got?" Bugosi was in his mid fifties, short, stocky, and his bug eyes and fleshy face reminded Striker of a Teddy Bear. He wore thick black framed glasses that were heavy, and constantly slipped down over his nose. He had worked his way up from the bottom to his current position, and although he basked in the prestige of his office, he missed the action of the streets. Striker correctly guessed that his frequent fits of temper were the result of the frustration of having to rely on his subordinates for results. Bugosi had lived his life in the middle of the action. Now he chafed at being on the sidelines.

"The interesting part of this case turns out to be the guy whose house Warren burglarized. I asked myself why Warren was killed when it was apparent that he was going to be collared. Some documents that Bebo had in his possession when he was nailed provided a clue. The guy who owns the house turns out to have a complete set of false identity papers, including drivers licence, social security card, and passport. I need some people to dig into the guy's business associations under the assumed name." Striker said.

"Shit. Everybody needs more manpower. I remember when I was on the street, we did whatever we had to do. Now, all I hear is, I need more manpower, or computer time, or some such shit!" Bugosi exclaimed.

Striker wasn't concerned. He knew that Bugosi was blowing off steam. He also knew that Bugosi felt comfortable enough in his presence to let his hair down a little. He would get what he needed. "I know boss. I don't see how you handle it as well as you do. I understand what you're up against. That's why I don't ask for anything unless I really need it. You know me. I've got the highest clearance rate of anyone in the department. I stay out of your hair, and do my job as long as I can. When I need something I come to you, because I know that you'll back me, because I back you by getting results."

"Yeah. Thank God somebody around her does. How many guys do you need, and for how long?" Bugosi growled.

"I need a couple of guys for routine surveillance, and a clerk who knows how to find out who owns commercial property, and who they lease it to. I may need more later, or I might be able to cut these people loose in a couple of days. It depends on what I turn up. If nothing shakes out in the next few days, it probably means I'm working the wrong angle, but if I'm right, this thing could get bigger." Striker said.

"I'll get the people assigned. While I'm doing that, I want a complete report of the incident, including a summary of your action plan. Have the report ready by lunch time. We'll grab a bite together, and go over it. Your people will be ready to report to you this afternoon."

"Yes sir." Striker walked out of the office, and reflected that it must be lonely at the top. Bugosi had agreed to provide the manpower because he trusted Striker's judgment, and because he wanted to be cut in on the action.

****

Cindy's winds surpassed 74 miles per hour one hundred thirty miles Southeast of Barbados. The ominous gray mass of destruction bore down on the tiny island nation with shrieks of fury. It had spent the past few days stoking its anger, and now it increased its forward speed like a hungry predator that smelled fresh blood, and was closing in for the kill.

Buried in the layers of billowing clouds, a sinister force awaited a summons from its master. Ever ready to empower a soul that refused the peace of death, it searched for a restless one driven by hate, and thirsting for revenge. The bargain that it offered was renewed life in exchange for eternal damnation. Only those souls tortured by a black and bottomless hatred could be tempted, but occasionally the offer was accepted, and the blood of an enemy savored without regard for the debt of eternal service to the master of fire and destruction.

****

Beth Addison had called Delta and checked on flights departing for Denver. A late flight was scheduled at 10;15 that evening. She estimated Cal's drive time and decided that it was the one that he would book, if her suspicions were right. She was grateful for the fact that it was tough for a traveler to leave Georgia without first going through Atlanta. Equally comforting was the knowledge that Heywood would be on a flight that left Denver at 9:45. The man that she loved and the one that she hated would probably pass each other somewhere in the friendly sky.

She watched the powder that she had emptied from the black capsules dissolve in the glass of water on her sink, then carefully poured the water into the waiting ice tray. She carefully placed the tray in the freezer, and hurried to her bathroom. She showered quickly, slipped into underwear, and sat down at her makeup table. She used bright red lipstick to make her lips appear wider, fuller, darkened her eyebrows, and gave them more of an arch. Next she donned a black shoulder length wig, and a pair of large tinted eyeglasses. She smiled. No one would recognize her in a crowded airport where they weren't expecting to see a familiar face.

****

Hannah Greene had not been idle in the hours since Heywood's safe had been broken into. Using her extensive contacts in law enforcement, she had checked Carlson's background for any criminal activity, had confirmed her suspicions that he was clean, at least officially. She had also run the Chase identity through the computer and found nothing on it either.

She had obtained a copy of Heywood's birth certificate, and on a hunch had plugged his father's name into her computer for a criminal background check. Within seconds the powerful mainframe that she subscribed to searched its exhaustive files, and displayed a screen full of information on her terminal.

Jason Carlson was serving a life sentence in Ohio for the 1972 murder of his estranged wife. Parole had been denied on three occasions. His next parole opportunity would be in 2004. Hannah absorbed the information thoughtfully. Heywood would have been twelve years old when the murder took place. She wondered who had assumed custody at his mother's death. Probably the maternal grandparents. The file revealed that Jason Carlson had changed his name at the age of 11. Prior to that he had been Jason Heywood. So that was where Heywood had gotten his given name.

Hannah frowned. Why would the child's name be changed? Something must have happened to his parents, his father anyway. It so, it must have been something with an ugly stigma associated with it to prompt his new guardians to change the name. Perhaps Jason Carlson's choice of his own son's name had been a sign that he was uncomfortable with his new identity, and resented the loss of his heritage.

Hannah jotted down Jason Heywood's place of birth., Oddesa Texas, 1932. Her computer would not have any additional information. From now on, the genealogy of Heywood Carlson would become more difficult to trace. What she had learned so far was interesting, but didn't seem relevant to Heywood Carlson's current activities. Except for the fact that he had been exposed to the trauma of domestic violence in its ugliest form as a child, his background seemed unremarkable.

Hannah watched Paula exploring the small office that served as the base of operations for Executive Security Services. She had found the child easy to supervise. She seemed to understand that something was changing in her young life, and was trying to adapt to it in her own way. Hannah's heart ached for her little charge. It was bad enough losing her mother, but unlike other children, Paula didn't have the comfort of a surviving parent that could help to ease her pain. She felt more like a foster mother to the child than a bodyguard.

Hannah was about to sign off the terminal, and take Paula for a burger when the phone rang. "ESS, Greene speaking. How may I help you?" She said crisply.

"It's Striker. Listen Ms. Greene, I know I don't have to tell a smart lady like you that this case I'm working is turning into a can of worms. I'm just calling to let you know that I'm having a surveillance team put on Carlson. They'll be watching his house in case I miss him at the airport. If he contacts you, do me a favor and don't mention the break in and shooting. I don't want him spooked. I got a feeling that if he finds out the police want to question him, he'll disappear, or take action to cover some dirty laundry that I've found on him. Can I count on you?"

"Sure Striker. So he looks dirty?" Hannah probed cautiously.

"Yeah."

"I've got a friend who suspects that Carlson may have murdered his wife. Maybe the two of you should talk." Hannah said.

"Could be helpful. How do I find him?"

Hannah gave Striker Cal's phone number. "I also turned up something interesting in his background. Carlson's father is serving life for murdering his wife." She waited for Striker's response.

"Violence begets violence. At least that's what more and more criminologist are saying. I'll give Dunforth a call as soon as I get a chance. How did Carlson's wife die?" Striker asked.

"An inquest decided that she hanged herself. Cal thinks it was murder."

"He's right. Bank on it." Striker hung up before Hannah could say anything else.

She sat wondering if it had been a good idea to get Cal involved with Striker. She thought about Cal's determination to prove that Heywood had murdered his cousin. In Emerald, with limited resources, the odds were stacked against him. If Striker got into the act with the clout of a major department behind him, it could make a big difference. She hoped that she had done the right thing.

****

Beth Addison mingled with the crowd at Hartsfield as she walked briskly toward the departure gate. Upon arriving, she picked a seat in the passenger lounge from which she could watch each passenger as they approached the smiling Delta attendant for a boarding pass. She settled in with her lap top computer, alternately typing, and then staring into space as if lost in though about the sales proposal that she was ostensibly working on. Her real purpose was to look for Cal.

Soon the lounge filled with travelers, each passing the wait in their own way. She noted businessmen studying presentations, making last minute notes, workaholics who squeezed every minute for productivity. Families with young children, an elderly couple, two jocks who eyed her with obvious appreciation. She frowned. She didn't want to attract attention. She should have worn slacks instead of the skirt and blouse that accentuated her figure. She gave the two young men a glance calculated to impress them with her disdain for their youthful good looks, and impart her lack of interest.

After what seemed like an eternity to Beth, the plane finally was ready for boarding. Cal still hadn't shown up, and she was beginning to think that her imagination had triggered the sense of paranoia that she had been experiencing since she had been interviewed by Detective Striker, when he materialized.

He had changed his hair, dyed it dark chestnut, or more likely, the locks protruding from beneath the slouch hat belonged to a wig. It was his ramrod erect posture, broad powerful shoulders, and something about the way that he moved, graceful and athletic in an understated way, that drew her attention to him. She studied the chiseled features, hoping that she was mistaken, and then he turned his head toward her and she was staring into his ice blue eyes. Something lurking within their frigid depths frightened her badly. They were the eyes of the dead, lifeless, uncaring, and predatory. She shuddered, and averted her face, praying that her disguise had been effective for the brief instant that their eyes had met.

When she looked tentatively back, he had secured his boarding pass, and she saw his broad shoulders disappearing from view. She breathed a sigh of relief, but still felt an odd prickling sensation that she knew was fear in her stomach. He knew that Heywood had murdered Marla. It was etched in the cold determined set of his jaw.

As she closed her briefcase and retreated, she wondered how much he knew. Whether he was aware that she had been involved. She remembered the flat, inflectionless voice on the phone, thought about the spur of the moment trip to a remote wilderness area, and felt her knees weaken. The trackless wilderness of Wyoming would be the perfect place to dispose of a body, or to stage an accident, a horse plunging down a ravine, a body swept away by the roaring water of a mountain river. There would be a dozen ways for him to kill her, and make it look like an accident. He knew! She was suddenly sure of it.

She couldn't think clearly as she settled in on a bar stool, and ordered a drink at the bar that she wandered into on numb legs. If she lost Cal, nothing else mattered. She wondered how he could have found out. Heywood had left some trace of evidence behind that Cal had unraveled, she realized that. But how had he found out that she was involved in killing Marla? He couldn't know that, not for certain. Only Heywood knew about her role of keeping him occupied. At worst, he could only suspect. She started to feel better, recovered her composure, aided by the warm touch of Scotch. By the time she had finished her drink, she had regained hope. Heywood was the only link between her and Marla's death, just as he was the only link in the death of Bebo Warren.

The ice cubes waiting in a compact cooler in the back seat of her car would put Heywood within her power. By the time he recovered from a drug induced sleep, he would be thrust up like a pig ready for slaughter. She would learn what she needed to know from him, and then she would kill him. It was as simple as that. She even knew the perfect place to take him for the interrogation. It would take the police weeks to find the dungeon that he used to make his films. Even then, his death could be made to look like a S&M game that had gone wrong. It would work, and with luck she would never be suspected. Except for those damned tapes...

Beth found that she was restless, and debated whether to return later to pick up Heywood, or to wait for his flight. She consulted her watch, and decided to wait. She ordered another drink, sipped on it slowly until their was nothing left but ice. She watched the gleaming cubes with fascination, and congratulated herself on devising the perfect scheme to trap Heywood.

She ordered a light snack, picked at the sandwich and chips absently, then paid her tab and then went to a news stand. She bought a novel and settled in, prepared now to wait patiently for Heywood's flight to arrive.

She met him at the gate, and felt elated when he didn't recognize her until she slipped her arm into his, and hissed into his ear, "let's go."

She took sadistic pleasure in the frightened look on his face as they made their way to baggage claim. She refused to talk about the reason for her call, allowing the suspense and fear to eat away at him. She knew that the first thing that he would want would be a drink. Already, she could smell the cocktails that he had on the plane on his breath. Inwardly, she smiled. It was going to be so easy.

Outside, they loaded his suitcases, and got into the car. Beth twisted into the back seat, and amid the faint tinkle of glasses, mixed each of them a Scotch. She handed Heywood his drink and pulled out of the parking space. She had her eyes on him, gloating as he lifted the glass. He would drain it in a gulp, and be ready for another before they reached the perimeter highway. The mixture of alcohol and barbituates would work rapidly.

Perhaps her preoccupation with her scheme distracted her, but for whatever reason she didn't see the station wagon turning into the lane ahead of her until it loomed broadside ahead of her. She instinctively applied the brakes, but it was too late. The cars collided with a metallic shriek of protest, punctuated by the crash of broken glass.

Beth recovered from the impact, smashed her palm against the steering wheel, and then threw the car into reverse. She backed up, slammed the transmission back into drive, and accelerated past the disabled station wagon. She glanced into her rear view mirror, and saw the driver emerging dazed, to stand beside the wagon. The family wagon reminded Beth of a beached whale, sprawled there in the middle of the parking lot. For the first time, she glanced at Heywood, and saw the trickle of blood on his lip, noticed the broken glass gleaming up at her as tiny shards of glass and ice reflected the street lights that lined the lot.

"What if he got your tag number?" Heywood's voice was shaky.

"He wasn't out of the car until we were past. He didn't get the licence. Besides, a traffic ticket, even a hit and run, are the least of our worries now." Beth said tersely. She wasn't worried about the damage to her car, but the knowledge that she would have to take out a fully alert Heywood troubled her. She glanced down at the spilled drink, and cursed under her breath.

"All right. What is this all about. How do you know about Chase? What the hell is going on?" Heywood demanded, dabbing at the trickle of blood.

"A Detective Striker was by the office, asking about you, when you'd be back, what your connection to Gordon Chase was. I got a bad feeling that he's onto something that can blow you out of the water."

"I'm touched. I didn't know that you cared." Heywood's voice was heavy with sarcasm.

"I don't. Not about you anyway. But this is about your films, and I'm featured in one of them, remember?" Beth turned scathing eyes on him.

"He can't know about them. He may suspect. He can't know. He was fishing and you probably panicked and tipped him. My walking out of those negotiations are going to look incriminating. You dumb bitch!" Heywood returned her stare.

"He knows you're Gordon Chase. He knows Gordon Chase deals in snuff films. Somebody that you're dealing with has turned. You better find out who, and deal with them before its too late." Beth saw the flicker of fear in his eyes, and knew that he was still under her control. She knew that she had told him everything that she could afford to until she found out who he had sold the tape to.

"So what else did he have to say?"

"Enough for me to know that he's ready to come after you. More than I'm telling you until you tell me who else has a copy of that tape, and until I get my hands on your copy. I want out clean. You get off my back and out of my life, and I'll help you,. Otherwise....."

"Don't threaten me, you little cunt!" Heywood's voice was dangerous, and carried a menacing undercurrent.

Beth stared back at him, measuring him. She had caught him at the perfect moment. She knew that he was unarmed, having just passed through airport security. It would be an even fight, and she would win. Her body responded to the adrenalin flowing into her bloodstream and she gripped the steering wheel fiercely. She could hardly wait to sink her foot into his groin, to deliver a knife hand strike to his throat, to jab her rigid fingers into his pig like eyes. Then her trained feet would work him over at will. Side thrusts, snap kicks, roundhouse, spinning reverse side thrusts, a flowing ballet that would destroy his will to resist. The vision of what she would do to him next relaxed her enough to answer. "Shut up Heywood. We have to get somewhere safe, and work our way out of this mess. We don't have the luxury of fighting each other."

"I've got to get to the house. Drop me there, and I'll meet you at the studio about an hour later." He said.

"No. You're house is under surveillance. We'll go straight to the studio. You're going to have to trust me Heywood. I'll get whatever you need from the house after we've decided what to do." She replied.

"Bullshit!"

"You can't be seen, don't you understand? Striker has enough for a warrant. We have to find out how he got his information, and cut it off. We're going straight to the studio."

"Fine. But when we get there, you're telling me everything that you know about this shit. If you're pulling my chain, or if you've fucked up....." He didn't finish the threat.

They drove toward their destination, each seething with hatred, a spider and a scorpion measuring each other.

CHAPTER 15

Shanon's hands trembled as she studied the gradually forming image. She watched it take shape before her eyes, and felt a pang of disappointment as she recognized her own form. She had forgotten that she had tested her setup by walking in front of the motion detectors. She laid the picture aside, and started developing the next one.

This time she gasped at the clarity, and at the subject. The figure of a man, indistinct in a knee length top coat, his face concealed by the dark shadow of a wide brimmed hat, floated in the solution. She dried the picture carefully, shaking with a mixture of emotions, and started developing the next one. At least she knew that her film had captured the nocturnal visitor.

One by one she developed the prints, studying each carefully. By the time that she had the last one developed, an uneasy sense of familiarity with the subject had surfaced. None of the photos had captured a close up of the intruder's face, yet there was something frighteningly familiar about the shadowy figure. A heavy growth of dark beard covered the intruder's face, and the hat disguised the eyes with dark shadows, but their was something about the profile.

Most unnerving of all was the final pictures on the roll from the camera mounted in the bedroom. The intruder showed up as a dark silhouette in the center of the print, with the bed and a huddled lump that Shanon knew had been her, in the background. The stalker stood poised, looking down on the helpless figure shivering beneath the damp covers.

The image was unmistakably menacing. Shanon remembered the numbing fear that she had felt, lying helpless beneath the malevolent stare, and shivered with dread.

With the pictures spread out drying, Shanon washed her hands, and then hurried to her desk. She dialed Cal's number, and listened to ring back tone. "Come on Cal, pick up." She pleaded. She needed desperately to share her discovery with someone. There was no answer, and she slammed the phone down with disappointment.

She stood, indecisive for a moment, and then made up her mind. She went back into the dark room, carefully sealed the prints in an envelope, and gathered up her keys and purse. She locked the lab and strode down the empty corridor that led to the parking lot. She would stop by her house for a few clean clothes, and then start back to Emerald. She knew that Cal would want to see the pictures as soon as possible.

Outside, darkness surrounded her. The metallic clang of the exterior door locking behind her suddenly had an ominous overtone. She remembered Cal's warning, and searched the deserted parking lot with nervous eyes. The blaze of lights mounted high on steel poles provided adequate illumination, yet shadows of the buildings that she had never noticed before cast dark sinister shapes around her. She started toward her car at a brisk walk, heels echoing off of the asphalt.

Halfway across the empty lot, she felt unseen eyes following her progress. A knot of fear hardened, and grew into a suffocating pressure within her chest. Her steps faltered, then stopped. She turned to look over her shoulder, almost expecting to see a lurking figure in a shapeless topcoat watching from the shadow of the building.

She edged toward her car crablike, still searching the shadows for whatever was watching her. She bumped into the side of the vehicle, felt her way to the drivers door, fumbled with the lock in her nervous haste, and then was inside with the comforting curtain of steel wrapped around her. She held her breath as she turned the key, exhaled with relief when the engine started immediately. A brief glance at the gauge confirmed that she had almost a full tank of fuel. The dash mounted clock revealed that it was 12:15 Central time. It would be an hour later in Georgia. Where the hell was Cal, she wondered as she drove out of the parking lot.

She suddenly hoped that he had kept his promise and stayed away from White Columns. In her heart she knew that he hadn't however, and the knowledge spurred her on. Instead of taking the route to her house, she headed strait for highway 280. It would be dawn when she arrived in Emerald, even if she drove straight through the night. She stopped at a

Dixie Quick Stop for coffee just before reaching the highway.

The steaming brew would keep her alert for a couple of hours at least. When it wore off she would stop again. The nagging worry that was starting to grow into genuine fear for Cal's safety would also keep an edge on her reflexes.

Once on the highway she set her cruise control on eighty five, turned on her radar detector, and breathed a silent prayer that all of the Alabama State Troopers were patrolling the interstate instead of the two lane highway that snaked its way toward the Georgia border.

****

Cal studied the ads in the Denver Shopper. He found what he was looking for under the sporting goods heading, a Taurus Model 85 for sale, one hundred seventy five dollars. He dropped a quarter in the pay phone and dialed the number.

"Yeah." The voice was deep, masculine.

"Bill?"

"Yeah."

"You still got that handgun for sale? I saw the ad in the shopper. I hope I'm not calling too early. I work nights and I'm just getting off." Cal said.

"Yeah man. I still got it. It's a niece piece, bought it for the old lady a few months ago. We split up and she left it behind, so I thought I might as well get a few bucks out of it. I'm sure I'll be needing the money when the divorce settlement comes down."

"Sorry man. I was wondering how I could get a look at it. I need something to keep in my car, and I saw the ad. I work nights and getting together might be a problem. I was hoping that maybe you could meet me on your way to work, show it to me, and if it's what I need I'll lay the green on you."

"Yeah, that works for me. There's a little coffee shop just off the interstate, exit 36, Granny's Place. Know where I'm talking about?"

"I'll find it. What time?"

"Better make it around quarter of eight. I got to be at work by eight thirty. How will I know who to look for?"

"My name's Carl, about six two, two hundred, I'm wearing gray slacks and a Navy jacket, red striped tie. Tell me what you're driving, and I'll come over to your car." Cal said.

"I'm in a blue Toyota four by four, big tires, with a lift kit. I won't be hard to spot. I'll see you then. Uh..., I'll need cash, no checks,

160

that a problem?"

"Got you covered. I'll be waiting."

Cal hung up and called a cab. He probably wouldn't need a gun, but it was best to be prepared. He studied the skyline as he waited. Denver was nice he decided. Clean and cool. At another time, under different circumstances, he would have enjoyed seeing its sights. Now he simply had a job to do. He focused his concentration on getting it accomplished as quickly and easily as possible. He had realized on the plane that there would be no chance to indulge in his fantasy of beating Carlson to death. He would have to kill him quietly. Perhaps he would leave him hanging from a light fixture, one of his brightly colored ties wrapped around his neck. Yeah, that would be appropriate.

Granny's turned out to be only a short drive. Cal paid the driver, checked his watch and decided he had enough time for a quick cup of coffee. He selected a table that would afford him a view of the parking lot, and ordered. The smell of bacon frying was tantalizing. He felt hunger for the first time since he had discovered how Marla had died. Until now his stomach had been knotted with tension. As he closed in on his quarry, he felt himself relaxing. It would be over soon.

He was up, heading for the door before the Toyota had stopped. He left money on the table for the coffee and tip, and made his way unobtrusively outside. The gun was in excellent condition, although it wouldn't have mattered as long as it had been functional. Cal counted the money into Bill's outstretched palm, pocketed the pistol and went back inside the restaurant. He walked straight back to the restroom, made his way into a stall, closed the door and loaded the five shot cylinder with Glaser Safety Slugs. He slipped the little snub nose revolver into his waist band at the rear, where it nestled into the small of his back without any sign of its presence. As long as he wore the sport coat, it would take a pat down search to find it. He flushed the toilet, and went back to the table at which he had been seated. The purchase, loading and hiding of the little gun away had taken less than five minutes. When the waitress freshened his coffee, he ordered breakfast.

Cal reflected that he had little time to waste. It was Thursday morning and Heywood would check out today, and leave for the airport from his last meeting. While he waited for the plump young girl who had smiled charmingly at him when she took his order to return, he walked over to the pay phone by the restrooms. He dialed the hotel. A friendly female voice answered.

161

"Morning. I've got a problem." He greeted the desk clerk.

"So early? Maybe I can help." The voice was warm, trusting.

"I am expected to drop a copy of a report by for one of your guests, and I just realized that I don't have his room number. His name is Heywood Carlson, kind of small guy, snappy dresser, a lady's man. I bet you remember him?"

"Oh yes. I remember him. I don't think I would characterize him as a ladies man." She emphasized ladies.

"I know what you mean. He can be a bit of hand full if he's had a few drinks."

"He's in room 215. Do you want me to ring him for you?"

"Sure, I'm running a bit late, guess I better face the music." Cal laughed. He waited tensely for the call to go through. If Heywood answered he would let him think that he was calling from Emerald. He would tell him that he had run across some pictures of Heywood and Marla while at White Columns, and offer to ship them to him if he wanted them. He didn't need the cover story, there was no answer.

He decided that Heywood was probably having breakfast. He went back to his seat just as his food arrived. He wolfed the eggs and bacon, washed it down with orange juice, took a final sip of strong coffee, and paid his ticket.

He walked out of the coffee shop, casually strolled through the parking lot and out to the busy street. He stopped at the traffic light and waited. Timing it so that it would only be a few seconds until the light turned green at the intersection, he walked across in front of the lane of cars waiting for the signal to change. He started across, but when he passed in front of the late model dark blue Thunderbird he suddenly turned, walked up to the drivers door, and jerked it open. Reaching inside, he grasped the slender young executive behind the wheel by the lapels of his suit, and jerked him out of the vehicle. A violent shove sent him sprawling to the asphalt. He leaped into the car, locked the door, restarted the engine that had stalled when the surprised driver had released the clutch, and drove away.

He could see the driver of his confiscated vehicle standing in the street, arms outspread in shock and disbelief. He accelerated rapidly, slowed, and when he saw a break in the traffic shot through the red light and left the cars that had been close enough to see what happened behind. Now he was just another innocent traveler, and he blended into the traffic.

It took him fifteen minutes to make his way to the downtown Sheraton. He parked the stolen T-Bird in a parking garage, and walked the two blocks to the hotel. He bought a morning paper, went into the restaurant and ordered coffee. He scanned the dining area for Heywood, checked his watch and waited for his coffee.

A cold calmness enveloped him as he waited for his quarry. It was only 8:30, too early for Heywood to have already left for an appointment. He decided that the man that he was going to kill was probably back in his room. He paid his tab, walked over to the bank of pay phones in the lobby and dialed the hotel.

He was in luck, the voice on the other end of the line was different from the one that he had spoken to earlier. He hung up, walked to the front desk, and stood waiting with a sheepish look on his face.

"Help you sir?" The young woman was pleasant, not very pretty, but with a friendly smile, and the eyes reflected the smile.

"I hate to be so much trouble, but I locked myself out of my room. I can't believe I walked out without my key."

"Your name Sir."

"Heywood Carlson. Room 215." He waited, holding his breath while the girl's fingers flew over her keyboard.

She smiled. "Here you go sir." She handed over the key.

Cal thanked her and pocketed the key. He took the elevator to the second floor, stepped out, and without hesitation walked down the corridor to the room. On his way he passed a couple of executive types who nodded pleasantly, but paid him almost no attention. He unlocked the door and stepped quickly into the room. His eyes darted over the carefully made bed, swept toward the bathroom as a sense of disappointment grew inside of him. Heywood was already gone. The knowledge caused a sinking feeling in Cal's stomach. The unslept in bed told him that Heywood had left last night, without even bothering to check out. He pushed the bathroom door open, studied the untidy array of toothpaste, shaving cream and aftershave on the lavatory. Maybe Heywood had gotten lucky in the bar, and spent the evening with a lady friend he thought.

He walked over to the closet and pulled the door open. Empty. Heywood wouldn't have moved in with the woman. He had left. No question about it now. Cal sat down on the bed and let his mind work the problem over. Who could have warned Heywood? He had been careful to cover his tracks, yet somehow his quarry had known that he was coming for him.

He thought about Beth. Had she seen through his efforts to find out where Heywood was and warned him? His inquires had been very casual. There was no reason to suspect that he was more than idly curious about Heywood's whereabouts, yet she must have called Heywood. There was no other possibility. The conclusion that he reached caused Cal to contemplate a more sinister posibility. If Beth had been alarmed by his discreet questioning about Heywood, it could only be a result of her being on edge about something. He reflected on her hatred of Marla, her insistence that she stay over Sunday night, the night that Marla was killed. Had her role been to keep him occupied, out of Heywood's way so that he could orchestrate his elaborate plan?

The idea, as repulsive and inconceivable as it was, had merit. Heywood would not have risked the possibility of Cal showing up at White Columns prematurely. The image of Marla, teetering on the board as the blocks of ice slowly melted flashed painfully into his mind. He heard her calling for help in his mind. Her desperate cries would have been muted within the thick walls of the cellar, yet he would have heard if he had dropped by.

Another problem that Heywood would have had to solve was a method to prevent Marla from simply loosening the noose, and squeezing it over her head. A knot tied behind the noose would have made that impossible. Simple, efficient, deadly. He would have to find out if there had been one in the rope that Marla was suspended from.

He put the death scene out of his mind. He had been tortured by it since finding Marla's body. The method that Heywood had used to delay her death had only added to the horror. He had to put all of that out of his mind. He must focus instead on finding the murderer, and making him pay. He would also deal with Beth Addison. He had always sensed that she was a bitch, but he had never considered that she was capable of murder. Obviously he'd been wrong. He asked himself why he had dated her for over two years. He didn't like the answer that wormed its way into his mind. He realized that it had been for the very reason that he didn't like her very much as a person. She had been nothing more than a warm graceful body to have sex with. He was able to maintain an emotional detachment that freed him from any bonds of love that might have developed with another woman. Perhaps he had sensed that Beth was the type of person who deserved no better. His affair with Hannah had been painful, full of guilt. She had deserved someone who could love her faithfully, without reservations. He had known all along that he wasn't capable of providing that love. His heart had always belonged to Marla. Now he supposed that his soul belonged to her too. He had let her down. Failed to protect her, had in fact been lying with the woman who had helped plot her death at the very moment that she was dying.

He had to stop thinking. He couldn't live with the guilt and remorse that threatened to overwhelm him. He picked up the phone and dialed Hannah's office. Maybe she could provide a clue to Heywood's whereabouts, he thought as he listened to ring back tone.

"EPS, Hannah Greene. How may I help you?"

"Hello Hannah. I just wanted to check in with you to see how you and Paula are getting along." He said.

"Cal! Where the hell are you? Shanon's been calling all morning. She's really upset. She drove to your place last night, arrived this morning actually, and when she couldn't find you, she almost panicked. You better give her a call at your house."

"Sure. I'll do that. So, have you been seeing much of Heywood?" Cal tried to sound casual.

"No. He's in Denver, on some kind of business. Listen Cal, Heywood's in deep shit. The police are looking for him. Two guys broke into the house a couple of nights ago and went through his safe. I called 911 and the police almost caught them in the act. One of the intruders shot the other one dead, then escaped. The dead guy was carrying a bag filled with Heywood's personal papers, and get this, Heywood had a complete set of false identity papers, including drivers licences and passport under the name of Gordon Chase. What do you make of that?"

"It sounds like a contingency plan in case Marla's murder didn't wash the way he'd planned it." Cal growled.

"That's what I thought at first, but it seems that Heywood's tied into some kind of pornography business. Sordid stuff. He was using the Chase identity to operate that business. That's why the APD want to question him. Striker, the detective who is handling the break in, thinks that Heywood was selling snuff films."

"Damn!"

"He thinks that Heywood killed Marla, Cal. I don't know what kind of evidence that he has, or if he even has any, but he asked how Marla died, and when I told him, he said that he was sure that your suspicions were well founded."

"I know exactly how he killed her Hannah." Cal said.

"Can you prove it?"

"I doubt it."

"Shit! What are you going to do?"

The hesitation before Cal replied answered Hannah's question. "Cal! Don't do it! He's not worth it. Where are you? You never answered me."

"I'm in Denver. Heywood's gone. He left in a hurry. My guess is that Beth Addison tipped him off. At first I thought she had tipped him that I was coming for him. Now it seems more likely that she called to let him know that the police are looking for him."

"Cal, you listen to me. You get home and let the law handle Heywood. We'll nail his ass. I promise you. I'll work on the case with you. I've already put Striker on it. He won't get away with it, do you understand?"

"I don't know....."

"You're screwed up right now Cal. Promise me that you won't do anything stupid. Promise. You've got your whole life ahead of you. We could...." Hannah stopped herself.

"No promises Hannah, about anything right now. I'll fly back though. Obviously Heywood's not here. He may have dropped out of sight permanently. My biggest problem is going to be the same one that this guy Striker is going to have. Finding the little bastard. If he could come up with one false identity, he can do it again. Call Striker and get him working on any forgers that he may know about. Unless I miss my guess, Heywood has somebody working on new identity papers right now."

"You take it easy Cal, and don't forget to call Shanon. She seemed on the verge of hysteria, worried sick about you. She said she had pictures that you had to see. What's she up to, Cal? Is it something to do with Marla's murder?"

"I'll call her. I don't know what she's come up with. There's something really strange going on at White Columns. I don't know if it's tied in to Marla's death or not."

"Call me when you book a flight back. I'll pick you up at the airport. We need to talk Cal. If I'm going to help you, I need to know what's going on." Hannah said.

"I'll be on the next flight out." Cal hung up. He realized that he shouldn't have used the phone in Heywood's room. If Heywood had disappeared, investigators would examine the phone calls made from his room. It would lead them to Hannah, and pose uncomfortable questions for her. That couldn't be helped now. He'd just have to be more careful from now on.

He wiped down everything in the room that he had touched, locked the door, and walked down to the hotel lobby. He used a pay phone to call Shanon.

The phone was answered on the first ring. He could sense the anxiety in Shanon's voice. "Thank God Cal! I've been worried sick. Where are you?" She asked.

"I'm out of town."

"Where? I'll meet you." Shanon said.

"You don't want to know. It will be a few hours before I can get there."

"I've got the prints. You've got to see them Cal. They confirm what I told you. At least they confirm that someone was inside White Columns. Please hurry."

"Call Hannah back and arrange to meet her in Atlanta. She's going to meet me at the airport. I think the three of us had better put our heads together."

"What's going on Cal? Why did you leave? You knew that I would be in touch with you as soon as the prints were developed?" There was a trace of accusation in the voice.

"I know exactly how Marla died. I was trying to catch up with her killer, but I screwed up. He's disappeared."

"Heywood?"

"Yeah."

"But the pictures. I have pictures of the person who is lurking around White Columns." Shanon said.

"Do you recognize him?"

"No. I didn't get a clear shot of his face."

"Could it be Heywood?"

Shanon thought for a few seconds, tried to word her answer carefully. "No. It's not Heywood." Whatever her film had captured was not a mortal, of that she was certain.

"I got to get moving Shanon. Bring the prints and we'll have a look at them. I don't know how they fit in, but we're sure as hell going to find out." Cal hung up, started to dial the airlines, then changed his mind. He could catch the courtesy shuttle to the airport if he hurried. He'd catch the next available flight.

CHAPTER 16

Striker watched the passengers as they emerged from the Delta flight. The features of Heywood Carlson had long since burned themselves into his mind. He had a knack for faces, not only remembering them as he had seen them, but also a flair for picking up basic features that even the most clever disguise couldn't hide. He had checked with the airline and learned how many passengers was on the flight, and he mentally counted them off as they passed by. He accounted for all 87 passengers, but Heywood Carlson wasn't among them.

He was aware that he wasn't the only one interested in the incoming flight. He recognized Hannah Greene among the crowd of faces waiting for the arrivals. He wondered who the fashion model type accompanying her was, and why the two of them were so anxious. At first he had thought that Greene was here to meet Carlson, and that had puzzled him. Then when she and the Miss America type had rushed forward to greet a tall well proportioned man, he had started wondering who the new arrival was.

There was something about the way that the man moved that spelled cop. He had a hard intense expression on his face that barely relaxed when the two women approached him. His blue eyes had swept the terminal quickly, the unconscious search of his surroundings so common to men accustomed to wearing a gun and badge. He had made eye contact with Striker, held it long enough to issue a challenge, then focused his attention on the two women.

Striker watched the trio walking away, decided that the man was one of Greene's colleagues, and dismissed his arrival as coincidence. He felt a slight sense of uneasiness when he reached the conclusion that Carlson wasn't on the flight. He wondered if he had somehow learned that he was the subject of an investigation, and turned rabbit. He lit a cigarette, and inhaled deeply as he pondered the problem. Only one person could have tipped Carlson off, Beth Addison.

He found a phone and called Heywood's office. When the voice on the phone informed him that neither Carlson nor Addison were in, the alarm bells started ringing. He slammed the phone down, and fought his way through the crowds toward the short term parking lot, and his car. He wanted to alert the surveillance team covering Carlson's house to be especially vigilant.

****

Cal followed Hannah and Shanon through the airport. He felt no particular sense of curiosity about the prints that at one time had seemed all important. He was now certain that Heywood Carlson had murdered his cousin, and the only thing that stirred any emotion inside him was the thoughts of what he would do to him when he caught up with the murderer.

Outside the blazing sun did little to lift the gray depression that hung like a blanket over his mood. He coiled his long legs into the back of Shanon's BMW, and settled in for the ride. He didn't care about their destination, nor did he respond to the presence of the two women. His mind was in a wasteland where no stimulation was sufficient to activate its normal functioning.

"The prints are in the envelope Cal. Take a look at them and see what you think." Shanon said with obvious excitement.

Cal undid the clasp of the manila envelope, and absently thumbed through the eight by ten photos. The sinister, faceless figure was an abstraction. A cruel prankster preying on the imaginations of a frightened, superstitious woman. Ordinarily the thought of someone violating the family home would have sent him into a rage. Now, it was only a minor irritation, something that he would have to deal with at some later date, after he finished with Heywood Carlson.

"Well? What do you think?" Shanon pressed.

"I don't know. It's hard to tell very much from the pictures. Someone's idea of a sick joke, I suppose." He forced himself to answer.

"I don't think so Cal. I showed them to Paula." This statement was made with a trace of defiance.

"Why would you do that. She's been through enough. I can't imagine why you'd want to frighten her." Cal answered, feeling a trace of anger.

"She recognized the person in the pictures." Shanon announced.

For the first time Cal stirred from his mental lethargy. "Who?"

"Boo Man."

"What are you talking about?" Cal shot back, feeling a trace of irritation.

"Don't you remember me telling you that Paula asked if the Boo Man got Mommy? She went on to describe the man in those pictures. She said that he jingled when he walked. Whatever was in White Columns Monday night made some kind of metallic sound when it walked." Shanon said.

"It sounds like Shanon's come up with a clue. If this person was inside White Columns before Marla's murder. He could be our man." Hannah cut in.

"Heywood Carlson is our man." Cal said with finality.

"Could the man in the pictures be Heywood?" Hannah asked.

"The man in these pictures could be anyone. The face is completely obscured by shadows." Cal said.

"The height is right. It's hard to tell about his build from the pictures, because of the coat. He shows up kind of shapeless. One thing's for certain, whoever it is knows his way around White Columns. That would fit Heywood." Hannah argued.

"So if it is Heywood, what's he up to now? Why is he hanging around the scene of the murder. He has nothing to gain by it, and everything to lose. It makes no sense. I'm not sure that this guy's connected with Marla's death. Heywood Carlson is." Cal answered, punctuating his words with a wave of one of the pictures.

"Maybe we should back up a little. Tell us why you're now so sure that Heywood's the killer. You said that you knew how Marla died." Hannah said, noticing that Shanon was very quiet, her face drawn with an expression that she couldn't read.

"I found two water stains on the cellar floor, and a two by six board with two spikes in each end of it. The length of the board matches the spacing of the stains exactly. Heywood supported the board with two blocks of ice, put a noose around Marla's neck, and stood her up on the board. By the time the ice melted hanging Marla, he was in Macon, establishing an alibi. I have no doubt that he can prove that he was a hundred miles away at the time of her death."

A heavy silence descended over the occupants of the car. The only sound was the slight whine of tires on asphalt. Finally Hannah spoke, "There are some major flaws in that theory Cal."

"For instance?"

"She wouldn't have meekly allowed herself to be put in such a position, for one thing. What would have prevented her from loosening the noose and freeing herself for another?" Hannah answered.

"Marla would have done exactly what Heywood demanded if Paula was at risk. A knot behind the noose would have made it impossible for her to loosen it enough to slip it over her head." Cal said quietly. He found it painful discussing the details of Marla's grisly death.

"What kind of threat do you think he used?" Hannah asked.

"He had Paula in the back seat of his car, with a length of garden hose attached to the exhaust pipe, and inserted in the window. The car was running. He held Marla at gunpoint, marched her to the window at the end of the upstairs hall where she could see Paula in the car, then told her that unless she did exactly what he wanted, the child would die. He probably told her that the longer that she delayed, the more likely Paula was to die from exposure to carbon monoxide poisoning. Marla stepped into his trap willingly, anxiously, so that he would spare Paula."

"Damn. It's possible. How in the world did you come up with such an idea? It's diabolical. A defense attorney would tear it to pieces in court though." Hannah said.

"I don't have to convict the bastard in a court of law. Knowing what he did is enough." Cal said bitterly.

"That's where you're wrong. You do have to convict him. For the very reason that you don't think you have to. How could you even contemplate what you were trying to do in Denver without absolute proof?"

"You want proof? Ask Shanon about the vision that she had while driving to Emerald the night of the murder."

Hannah looked from one of her companions to the other in confusion. "Vision?"

"Tell her." Cal demanded.

171

"Well, I saw a child sleeping on the rear seat of a car. It was a luxury model with brown leather upholstery. The child had a black and white Teddy bear clutched in her arms, and she was covered with a grey blazer. I could see a monogrammed handkerchief in the pocket of the blazer. The initials were J. H. C.. It looked innocent enough at first, but I sensed that something was wrong. I saw the hose running into the car window, but before I saw anything more, I ran off the edge of the road and almost wrecked. The vision faded and I couldn't get it back." Shanon said in a level voice.

"You told Cal about your vision?" Hannah said skeptically.

"Yes. That's why we felt that Paula was in danger in the first place."

"I don't know. It doesn't add up. It smacks of...."

"Witchcraft? Voodoo?" Shanon shot Hannah an angry look.

"It sure as hell isn't sound investigating." Hannah said defensively. "You've decided that Heywood is guilty based upon some vision that may or may not have any validity. What you have done is fabricate a theory that dovetails with an unsubstantiated, less than credible piece of evidence. It's unsound. A prosecutor would be laughed out of court if he tried to present a case based on evidence like that."

"We're not in court." Cal reiterated.

"Well you better start getting used to the idea that you will be if you want to nail Heywood, or anyone else for that matter. Vigilantes are never justified, even with certain proof. What you have strung together doesn't constitute any proof at all. I'm appalled."

"You sound like an ACLU lawyer." Cal said cuttingly.

"You're sounding, and acting like an ignorant redneck."

"What the world needs is a few more rednecks, at least that's what the song says." Cal shot back.

"What you need is a psychiatrist."

"What I don't need is a redheaded bitch trying to tell me that I'm wrong about something as certain as death." Cal said cruelly.

"Bastard! How could I have ever loved you? You're a selfish, uncaring bastard, obsessed with your own cousin! She owned you all of her life. You were just another of her toys. You were the prettiest doll in her collection, that's all. You could never see that, but I could. You were nothing more than Marla's anatomically correct doll, waiting with a big hard on whenever she wanted it!"

Cal's right hand shot toward Hannah's face in a reflex that he was unable to check. At the last instant, he was able to open his tightly knotted fist, and strike with his open hand instead. The crack of his heavy palm against her face split the air inside the car like a sizzling lightning bolt. Her slender neck snapped back under the impact, muscles momentarily flaccid. Red hair cascaded over her face like liquid spilled from its container—blue eyes blurred as the shock rendered her senseless for a brief moment.

Shanon heard the explosive slap, turned in time to see Hannah recoiling into the dash. Instead of her usual revulsion when in the presence of violence, she felt a hot stab of satisfaction flow through her. The bitch got what she deserved. The thought shot into her mind. She waited for the remorseful apology, silently praying that it wouldn't be forthcoming. It wasn't.

An uncomfortable silence settled over the car. Hannah wiped her nose with the back of her hand, staring in fascination at the smear of crimson against her milky white skin. She rummaged in her purse for a Kleenex, wiped at the trickle, and stoically turned her smoldering eyes to face the oncoming traffic.

After a mile of silence Shanon said, "Can we find a place to talk like civilized people, or are the two of you going to punch each other out?"

"We can talk now. Find a bar. I need a drink." Hannah said stiffly. Her top lip was starting to swell.

"Appleby's sound good?" Shanon asked.

"Yeah." Cal said.

The hostess looked accusingly at Cal when she showed the trio to a table. Hannah caught the look, hooked an arm through Cal's and said. "Oh God! What will we do if my husband finds me? He's crazy. He might shoot everybody in the room. Do you think I'm doing the right thing, running away from him?"

Cal was caught off guard but Shanon responded. "Don't you worry about a thing Honey. We'll protect you. If he thinks he's going to breakup our threesome, he's wrong. I mean what business of his is it who you're fucking?"

The shocked hostess made a hasty retreat. As soon as she was out of sight Shanon and Hannah burst into nervous laughter. The tension was broken.

"There goes our chance to get any service." Shanon grinned.

"They'll probably ask us to leave." Hannah giggled.

Cal smiled for the first time.

"I'm sorry Cal. I know that you were not sleeping with Marla. I always let my mouth run away with me when I get pissed off." Hannah extended her hand.

"I'm sorry too. I guess you were too close to the truth for comfort," Cal said, and pulled Hannah into an embrace.

Shanon wondered what Cal meant by his admission. Had Marla meant more to him than he did to her, as Hannah had suggested, or did Cal mean that the two of them had slept together? It was a question that she would leave unasked. "Hey, you two. I could use a little of the TLC myself." She said as she joined the embrace.

"People will think that we're already drunk if we keep this up." Hannah said. "But what the hell? I'll share." She didn't say it, but she couldn't help thinking that it would be more pleasant to share Cal with Shanon than with Marla. Shanon was beautiful, intelligent, and obviously in love with Cal Dunforth, but she was mortal. Hannah could compete with that. She wasn't sure if she could handle a woman who still held her lover in her grip from beyond the grave.

"Fun's over guys. Time to get down to business" Hannah announced as she settled into the booth. "What we have is a very thin, unsubstantiated theory that won't even get us a search warrant, much less an arrest warrant for Heywood Carlson." She held up her hands to cut of the protest that she saw coming. "Let me finish. Now, I'm not saying that I don't believe you. What I'm saying is that now we've come down to the hard part, gathering evidence that will prove to a jury that the theory is correct. Can we all agree on that?"

"Let's say that we do. What do you suggest?" Cal asked.

"First, we have to have a sample of the water stain, a tiny amount will do it, even a minute amount squeezed from the dust on the floor, and from the grain of the wood. If we can come up with hard evidence that the water didn't originate at White Columns, we're on first base. That is step one. Step two is to confirm that the rope was knotted behind the noose. If we find out that your theory is correct in those two particulars, I'm prepared to buy it without reservations. I think we can convince the investigator who handled the case to reopen it if we can get that far."

"We've got a real problem there Hannah. You remember Harold Collins?"

Hannah stared at Cal in astonishment. "I'd like to forget him, but I haven't. You're not going to tell me that incompetent asshole is an investigator now?"

"You guessed it."

"Shit. No help there."

"You're right. Now you see what I'm up against. Or maybe you don't. I'll spell it out. No matter what kind of evidence that the three of us come up with, it'll be thrown out of court. You know how strict the chain of evidence rules are being interpreted now. Let's say that we build a case, lay all of the evidence, lab reports, the whole nine yards on Harold Collins desk— the first thing a defense attorney is going to want to know is, how did he acquire a particular piece of evidence. Collins says, my good friend and fellow deputy, Cal Dunforth brought it to my attention. Attorney stares at Collins. Then there's no way that you can attest to the fact that this particular water sample labeled exhibit A, actually was collected at the scene. Am I right?" Collins squirms down in the witness chair and whines, no, I can't establish the origin of this particular water sample. That piece of evidence is in the shit can."

"Then we're going to have to point him in the right direction, hold his hand, and let him discover all of this for himself." Hannah said. She saw the contemptuous look on Cal's face. "Who am I kidding? Harold Collins couldn't find his way to the John." Hannah sighed.

"Even if he could, he'd wait until he almost pissed his pants before he got up to go. That's how lazy the bastard is. But it gets worse. Collins, and the local yokels have already reported that it was a suicide. Not only will they not help us prove otherwise, they'll do everything possible to prevent us from doing that." Cal said.

"There's got to be a way. What about the G.B.I.?" Hannah asked hopefully.

"They're not going to get involved, unless they're invited." Cal said bitterly. "After all, who would work with Harold Collins if they didn't have to?"

"Striker!" Hannah hissed.

"Why would he butt in?" Cal asked.

"You've got to meet Striker. I get the feeling that he doesn't work like most investigators. He does whatever he has to do to get a conviction. If we can convince him that he has a chance to tie Heywood to Marla's murder, he'll jump in with all four feet. He can request everything that Collins has on the investigation. That means that he'll check out the rope. If he finds the knot. He'll buy in. He already thinks Heywood is dirty. He can get technicians down there to get the samples that we need, run the tests, and most important, maintain the integrity of the chain of evidence. He'll find a way to tie it to something that he's working so that it will seem kosher." Hannah said.

"Maybe." Cal said.

"I must be missing something here. What will a lab test reveal about the water stain that will prove that it didn't come from White Columns? Shanon spoke for the first time.

"One simple little detail. If the water is from a block of ice, Heywood either froze it himself, or bought if from a commercial ice distributor. Chances are that he rolled his own. If he did, it's a safe bet that it'll be tap water. City water. Fluoride. White Columns has its own well. A trace of floruide, or any trace of chemical treatment, will prove that the water originated outside of White Columns, from a city water supply." Hannah lectured.

"I see." Shanon frowned.

"Look, I know it's not much. But all we need here is enough to get the ball rolling. Striker already suspects that Heywood killed Marla. I'm not sure why. But he'll sink his teeth in and won't let go if he has the slightest hope of success."

"How do we tie in the vision that I had with Cal's theory of how Heywood got Marla to submit?" Shanon asked just as a waiter arrived to take their order.

After ordering, Hannah continued. "The blazer. If Heywood hasn't sent it to the cleaners, it will have exhaust residue trapped within the fibers. What else? Oh! Paula's clothes that she was wearing that night! Please tell me that they haven't been laundered."

"No. They haven't. I was planning to put them in with some of my clothes, but I've been so busy that I haven't done my laundry. Something else comes to mind also. Pandy. Paula's bear. Wouldn't the exhaust residue cling to the fuzzy little bear?" Shanon was getting caught up in the excitement of the forensics of the case in spite of the fact that she believed that a spirit rather than Heywood Carlson had murdered Marla.

"Absolutely! Along with your testimony, that would be very convincing." Hannah enthused.

"I thought you said that testimony about a psychic vision wouldn't be believable in court." Shanon said.

"Standing on its own, it probably wouldn't. On the other hand, if you have a track record to back up your credentials, and physical evidence backs it up, it would be powerful testimony."

"I can establish my credentials. I've worked with the authorities in Birmingham, Montgomery, and Mobile. I've led them to three bodies, and several murder weapons." A trace of pride showed in Shanon's voice.

"Good. We're on a roll guys. I think we just might put Mr. Carlson away for a very long time." Hannah said.

"We've got to find the prick first." Cal growled.

"Wrong. We've got to get Striker on the scent, come up with the evidence. Then we find him." Hannah said emphatically.

"That may be the hardest part. If he could come up with one false identity, he can do it again. He's probably hard at work on that right now." Cal said.

"Striker was at the airport. I noticed him but he didn't seem to want to acknowledge my presence. He was waiting for Heywood. By now he knows that Heywood has been alerted. He's probably asking himself who could have tipped him. He'll be tied up for the next few days, trying to uncover a trail. He'll be on top of everybody that he knows who's into making paper. He may get lucky. It's going to take a lot of manpower, and interagency cooperation to find Heywood. Striker knows he can't call in a lot of firepower without a means of justifying the effort. So far, he has nothing on Heywood except the fact that his house was burglarized, and that he had false identity documents. The brass won't get too revved up about that. If he could tie him into a murder case, then he could get the size task force that it's going to take to track him down. That's why he's going to help us." Hannah said.

"Eventually he may decide to follow up on the information that we feed him. First, he's going to make every effort to find Heywood on his own. We'll have to wait until he runs into a wall before we approach him." Cal said.

"Right, but that will only be a few days unless I'm over estimating Heywood." Hannah answered.

"What do we do in the meantime?" Cal asked.

"The only thing that we can, get on with our normal lives as much as possible. You've got to accept the fact that this is going to be a long haul, Cal. Promise me that you'll settle down. Let me help you do this the right way."

"I don't suppose there's another choice." Cal said.

"No. I want you to understand that I'm not going to help you find Heywood so that you can execute him. If you want help, and you know that you're going to need it, you'll have to give me your word."

"I'll think about it."

"Not good enough Cal. Your word."

"No." Cal's face hardened. His eyes regarded Hannah with defiance.

"Okay, you're on your own. I guess I'll just have to wait for you to run into a dead end too." She drained her glass, turned to look at Shanon. "If you love this stubborn bastard as much as I do, and I think that you do, you better try to talk some sense into him. He won't do either of us any good in prison. I've got to get back to the office and pick up Paula. My secretary is a great pal, but I can't afford the overtime. She should have been out of the office an hour ago. You guys have a few more drinks. I think you need them. I'll get a cab." She turned abruptly and walked toward the pay phone near the bar.

Shanon rose halfway out of her seat, offered to drive her back to the office but was rebuffed.

"Let her go. She'll be all right. She always did get huffy whenever I refused to see things her way." Cal said, putting his hand on Shanon's arm.

"She has every right to be upset Cal. You have no right to take the law into your own hands. How could you even think about it? All that I could think about when I arrived in Emerald, and couldn't find you was that something terrible had happened to you. I was so excited about the pictures. Now I find that you're not even interested in them anymore. What's happening to you? You're not the same man that I thought that I knew." Shanon said.

"You're right. The Cal Dunforth that you knew is dead. I'm not sure who I am right now, but one thing that I am sure of is that Heywood Carlson's going to pay for what he did. If it takes the rest of my life, I'll find him, and kill him."

"Then what? It won't bring Marla back. You'll still have to face that." Shanon said.

"Maybe then I can join her." Cal muttered into his glass. "Listen, I need some time alone. My Jeep's at Hartsfield. How about driving me over to pick it up. We'll drive down to Emerald in separate cars and maybe by then I'll be more pleasant company."

"Cal, I'm not looking for entertainment. I'm here to help you. Don't shut me out of your life. Let me help you through this." Shanon pleaded.

"I will. The drive will be good for me. Hannah was right about this being a long haul. I've got to try and harness my emotions, and get my life back under control. I'm glad that you're here." Cal left money for their tab and a tip, and walked Shanon toward the door.

From where she stood at the bar, sipping another drink, Hannah watched them go. Already her anger was turning to jealousy. First Marla. Now a damned witch. A real one. She reflected on her lack of success with the men that she found attractive as she waited for her cab. Life's a bitch, and then you die, she thought.

CHAPTER 17

The stiff mask that served as Striker's face was impassive as ever, yet he seethed with anger. He had gotten careless, and Carlson had eluded him. Beth Addison had also vanished without a trace. He had staked out her house until past midnight the previous night, staying in touch with the team watching Carlson's residence by radio. When it became apparent that neither was going to show, Striker had furtively entered Beth's house and conducted a careful search. There was no sign that she planned to be away permanently. Too many personal items were lying around in plain view.

He had decided that she was involved in helping Carlson disappear, and would resurface in a few days. The thought hadn't been comforting. By then Carlson could be anywhere, living under an assumed name. It might take years to discover where he had moved, unless he could get Addison to cooperate. In order to convince her to turn on Carlson, he knew that he would have to have some leverage, something to threaten her with. He had returned to his own home, watched the sordid video that he had confiscated from Raynes, and decided to play a long shot. He would tell Addison that he had proof that the woman on the tape was her. If he was right, she would be frightened enough to cooperate. If not, he hadn't lost anything. Before he could do anything he had to find her.

As he stalked through the busy squad room on the way to his desk, he worried about what he would report to Bugosi. So far, he'd come up empty. Bugosi would hit the ceiling when he learned that Carlson had disappeared. He had taken a personal interest in the case, and would ride Striker hard for results.

At his desk, Striker picked up his phone and punched in the intercom number for Sandra Hart, the clerical type who was working on finding the building that Carlson, posing as Gordon Chase had used as a studio. He listened to her tell him how confusing it was, sorting through the ownership, management companies, and real estate brokers involved. He didn't have to wait for her to tell him that she hadn't come up with anything. The whine in her voice confirmed her lack of progress. He gruffly ordered her to stay on it, and slammed his phone down.

He didn't want Bugosi to corner him, so he made one more quick phone call to Hannah Greene. She agreed to meet with him, and he told her that he was on his way to her office. He didn't give her a chance to set a later time. Instead, he hung up and hurried outside to his car.

As he rode up in the elevator, he wondered what it would be like to have your own office, to be free of the political bullshit of a major police department. Nice. He had been impressed by the distinctive way that Hannah's company had been listed on the building's directory. Maybe he should go into private security, he thought as the elevator ground to a halt.

He stepped out into the clean quiet carpeted hallway, and started walking toward Hannah's suite. It was a hell of a lot different from the prescinct, with its noisy quota of drunks, hookers, and the smells that they brought with them off of the streets. Hannah Greene had been smart to get out of that filth he thought.

When he stepped into the reception room, he was greeted by a pleasant, attractive middle aged woman. She had an air of quiet competence about her that Striker liked. She showed him courteously to Hannah's office door, and discretely retreated.

"Good morning Mr. Striker. What brings you to see me so early?" Hannah smiled at him.

Striker noticed the child playing quietly with a pile of building blocks on the floor behind Hannah's desk, and frowned at the first sign of disorganization that he had seen since leaving the precinct. "I wanted to talk with you again to find out if there's anything else that you can tell me about Carlson that could help me locate him."

"Have a seat." Hannah gestured toward one of the comfortable chairs in front of her desk. "I'm afraid I can't help you with that problem. I might be able to give you some information that you will find useful however."

"You have a captive audience." Striker grimaced at her.

Hannah quickly told him about Cal's theory, explained the problem that Cal was having with local authorities, and waited for his reaction.

"That's a very interesting story. The fascinating thing about it is that it could very well be exactly what happened." Striker said.

"Can you find a way to work it into your investigation?"

"Sure. It'll only take a few days for the lab work. I'll have to drive down there, and convince someone with the local department to go out to the house with me to collect the evidence, and show me the crime scene. Do you think they'll cooperate?"

"Unless I've misjudged you Striker, you'll find a way to make them cooperate." Hannah flashed him her best smile.

"I'm sure I will. One more question. Is it possible that Beth Addison was involved in the death of Carlson's ex-wife?"

"I suppose it's possible. I have no reason to suspect that she was however. Why do you ask?"

"She's going to be the key to finding Carlson. She's dropped out of sight. I have reason to believe that her disappearance is temporary. When she surfaces, I need something to use as leverage to get her to turn on Carlson."

"I see. Let me see what I can dig up. I'll call you if I come up with anything."

"I appreciate it. I best be on my way. I've got a long drive ahead of me."

"You're driving to Emerald today?"

"Might as well. I've got some people working on a few leads here, but it involves a lot of digging. While they're on that, I can nose around down in the swamps." Striker twisted his face into what passed for a smile.

"Good luck," Hannah said as Striker started for the door. A sudden nagging worry started twisting inside her, and she added, "go easy on Cal. He's taking this pretty hard."

"Sure. I'll keep that in mind." Striker flung over his shoulder.

Hannah sat watching Paula playing quietly. She couldn't get over how easy the child was to supervise. She had almost forgotten that she was in the office. She thought briefly about how nice it would be to have a daughter of her own. She thought about Cal. Wondered what to do about him. The only course of action that she could think of was to help Striker find Heywood Carlson before Cal did. She knew Cal well enough to know that once he committed himself to something, he wouldn't stop until he'd seen it through. She knew that he was committed to killing Heywood, no matter what the cost to himself. Somehow she would have to make him see that his own life was too important to throw away. She hoped that Shanon Lee was trying to do that as well.

The thought of Cal and Shanon together was painful, but the thought of Cal alone, plagued by his dark thoughts was worse. She used her standard defense mechanism against pain. Work. She would find Heywood Carlson. She knew where to start looking, or at least she had a hunch. She picked up the phone and called the Probate Judge's office in Odessa, Texas.

****

The knock on Drew Dunforth's office door was firm, insistent. He was reviewing for the tenth time all of the documents that he had prepared that dealt with Marla and Heywood's divorce settlement, trying to find any possible way for Heywood to benefit from her death. He had left word that he wasn't taking calls. He frowned. "Come in."

The door swung open and Matt walked in. "We've got to talk Drew."

"Sure Matt. Good to see you. What's on your mind?"

"I've been hearing some ugly rumors, and I wanted to talk to you about them," Matt said as he eased himself into a chair.

"What kind of rumors?" Drew asked his brother.

"I understand that you've hired a bodyguard to protect Paula. Is that true?"

"Yes."

"I also hear that you're conducting your own probe into Marla's death."

"I am."

"What's going on Drew. Why haven't you talked to me about any of this?"

"I should have. I apologize. Things just kind of moved very fast. I've been busy, and I neglected to give you a call. I'm sorry."

"Why does Paula need a bodyguard? Who would want to harm her?"

"Cal thinks she may be in some kind of danger. I' wouldn't take a chance that something might happen to her, so I hired someone to protect her."

"You still haven't told me why, or who would want to harm her."

Drew pulled his glasses off, polished the lenses before answering. "Cal is convinced that Marla was murdered Matt. He suspects Heywood. He has reason to believe that Heywood might harm Paula."

"Oh shit. I can't believe this."

"Why not? Can anything be harder to accept than the idea that she would kill herself?"

"I don't know. It's hard for me to accept that she's gone. But murder, that makes it even more awful. Has Cal got any hard evidence?"

"He has something. I don't know what, but I trust Cal's instincts. If he says it was murder, then I accept that at face value. What's more, I've been working all week, trying to find a motive."

"What have you come up with?"

"Nothing so far."

"Why does Cal think Heywood would harm Paula?"

"I don't know. Maybe he thinks she knows something about Marla's death, something that she's too young to tell anyone, but it may be enough to make Heywood panic, and do something terrible."

"Can't you get her out of his custody?"

"Maybe, but it'll take time, and a good reason. Right now, we don't have either. That's why I've hired Hannah Greene."

"I know a way." Matt said with a sigh.

"You do?"

Matt nodded. "I wasn't going to tell anyone this, ever. I feel like I'm betraying Marla by doing it now, but if Paula's safety is at stake, I have no choice." Matt squirmed in his chair. "Paula isn't Heywood's child."

"You know that for a fact?" Drew asked sharply.

"Marla told me a few weeks ago. She told me that she had something that she wanted to discuss with me. It turns out that what she wanted to talk about was her marrying Cal. I told her that it was out of the question. We argued about it for almost an hour. Finally I told her to think about any children that they might have. I told her that the chances of cousins having children that weren't normal was greater than for a couple that wasn't related. She said that was an old wives tale. When I insisted that I was right, she blurted out that Paula was as normal as a child could be. It floored me. I asked her what that had to do with anything, and she said that Paula was Cal's daughter."

"I'll be damned! Does Cal know?"

"I don't think so. In face, I'm sure that he doesn't."

"Well, if we could prove that, it would solve the custody problem, but we have to consider how traumatic such a revelation might be for Paula, coming right on the heels of her mother's death."

"I don't think it would upset her very much. She loves Cal. She's spent more time with him that with Heywood. Besides, we could break it to her later, after she's recovered from the shock of Marla's passing. The important thing now is to get her away from Heywood."

"You could be right. I'll have to think about it." Drew said thoughtfully.

"We have to consider Cal as well. How will he take it?"

"I don't know. He's been through hell lately."

At that moment the intercom sounded. Drew picked up the phone, listened for a few seconds and said, "Yes, I'll take it." He covered the receiver with his hand and spoke to Matt. "It's Hannah Greene."

"Drew I want you to talk to Cal. He's in a mess. He's made up his mind that he has to kill Heywood personally. He's already made a trip to Denver to try and find Heywood. Luckily he didn't, but I'm worried. He doesn't seem to care what happens to him. He just wants Heywood dead. Can you talk to him?" Hannah said. She had decided that calling Drew was a good idea.

"My God! Of course I'll talk to him. We can't have him thinking like that, especially now."

"What do you mean, now? Has something else happened?" Hannah asked.

"I've just had a bombshell dropped in my lap. I'd prefer not to tell you about it just yet." Drew said into the phone. He glanced at Matt, saw him nodding agreement.

"Damn it Drew! I'm worried sick. Tell me!" Hannah demanded.

"I can't. I just found out something about Cal that he isn't aware of. It doesn't pose a threat to him or anything. As a matter of fact, it will solve some of his problems, but I feel that it is only fair to tell him before I disclose it to anyone else."

"Will you call me back as soon as you've told him, or have him call me?" Hannah asked.

"I'll have him call you. Thanks for your call Hannah. How's Paula?"

"She's the sweetest thing that I've ever been entrusted with. She's happy and safe. Heywood has vanished. He has some serious problems with the Atlanta Police. I think he may have skipped out."

"Then Cal's right about the son of a bitch!"

"I think so."

"I'm going to drive down to see Cal as soon as I get off of the phone. I'll ask him to call you."

"I'll be waiting."

Drew put the phone back in its cradle. "Heywood's disappeared. It's looking more like Cal's right about Marla's death."

"What else did she say?" Matt asked.

"She said that Cal's trying to find Heywood, and kill him. She wants me to talk him out of it."

"If he's sure Heywoods guilty, there's no way that you can talk him out of killing him. You know Cal. He's always been obsessed with Marla. The best that you can hope to do is to talk him into doing it in such a way that he won't be caught." Matt said.

"I can't believe you said that."

"Drew, we're not talking about some faceless stranger here. We're talking about the man who tortured and killed our sister. If I become convinced that he did that to Marla, Cal will have to beat me to him." Matt's eyes flashed with anger.

Drew leaned back in his chair. He saw Marla, laughing as she talked on the porch at White Columns the last time he had seen her. "You're right of course. If we're absolutely sure, we'll kill that son of a bitch."

Matt stood and reached across Drew's desk. The two clasped hands and uttered words from their past. Words that they had spoken about secrets that they had shared as boys growing up at White Columns. "Swear to God, solemn oath." They intoned. The last time that they had spoken those words was the night that Matt had buried the mysterious skull in the cellar at White Columns. They hadn't discussed it then, but they had known that the grinning bones and ivory had belonged to an enemy. They had known that Granny Dunforth was aware of the identity of the dead, and that she was willing to keep the secret that the black earth had almost given up. Whoever's bones that they had discovered had deserved to die, and a Dunforth had killed him. Now they faced another mortal enemy who deserved death, and as surely as the dark soil of White

Columns had swallowed the victim that they had discovered so long ago, it would easily accomodate Heywood Carlson's useless carcass.

"Let's go see Cal." Matt said.

"Fine," Drew responded. "Say Matt, I've been thinking, we always thought of Cal as our cousin, because Granny Dunforth told us that, but I don't really remember ever knowing who his parents were, do you?"

"No, come to think of it, I don't. I've always thought that they were dead, maybe since he was just a baby. It's odd, now that you mention it."

The two brothers walked out of the prestigious law firm stripped of the civilized facade that they wore every day of their lives. Their eyes burned with rage, and their jaws jutted out with characteristic Dunforth stubbornness.

****

Hannah was about to take Paula for lunch when her phone rang. She grabbed it, hoping to hear Cal's voice. Instead she recognized the lazy Texas drawl of the woman that she had talked to earlier. She felt a rush of adrenaline when the caller confirmed that she did have a birth certificate on record for Gordon Chase. As Hannah had suspected, a death certificate was also recorded.

Gordon Chase had died three days after his premature birth, and was buried in in Odessa Texas. Heywood Carlson had resurrected him to form the basis for his second identity.

As she hung up, Hannah congratulated herself on her insight. Heywood did have some kind of family ties in the town where his father had been born. She hoped that her second hunch would pay off as well. She suspected that Heywood would return to the same source to find another identity now that he was on the run.

She gathered up her purse and keys, took Paula's hand and guided the child out of the office and onto the elevator. Now she had something to sink her teeth into. She would book a flight to Texas after lunch. It wouldn't hurt to learn more about Heywood's background. She would also show his picture to the lady at the records office. She might recognize him as someone who had been in the office recently. When the elevator stopped, she picked Paula up and stepped into the main lobby. She had wanted to take the little girl to McDonalds, but she now felt a sudden sense of urgency, and wanted to get back to work as quickly as possible. She turned down the hall toward the sandwich shop. She'd pick up a quick lunch for herself and Paula, and be back in her office in ten minutes. She found it hard to curb her restlessness now. A sense of excitement was growing inside her. For the first time since learning of Heywood's disappearance, she felt confident of finding him quickly.

CHAPTER 18

Striker's stomach tightened as he examined the rope that had choked the life out of Marla Carlson. He observed the knot in it close behind the noose without comment. The first part of Cal Dunforth's theory was born out. He turned to the oaf beside him. "I want a close up photograph of the rope, and be sure that the noose, and this knot show up clearly."

"No problem. I'll take it myself." Harold Collins said. He had learned that it was pointless to ask Striker what he wanted it for.

"Fine. I want to go out to the house where Marla Carlson died. Can one of your deputies give me a ride?" Striker asked.

"Sure. I'll get Abe Lucas to drive you over." Collins was relieved to be free of Striker. The experienced cop made him feel the way he had as a child when a teacher had graded his homework.

Striker was equally happy to be getting away from Collins. He reflected that Collins fulfilled the movie stereotype of the dumb country lawman perfectly. They were a vanishing breed with even the rural departments, yet their kind was seen just often enough to perpetuate the myth that Southern cops were inept bumpkins. Striker knew that Collins was an aberration, a lazy bastard who took the path of least resistance. He decided that if things turned out the way he hoped, and he found that

189

Marla Carlson had been murdered, he would make Harold Collins look bad.

On the drive out to White Columns, Striker measured Abe Lucas. He knew that he had to work through the local department. He hoped that Lucas would be sharp and ambitious enough to take up the investigation on his own and run with it. He doubted it. Collins would have sent the least likely man in the department to challenge his authority.

As they turned into the driveway, Striker heaved a sigh and initiated the inevitable. "Lucas, you could be stepping into a confrontation with your investigator, Collins. If we find evidence that he missed, he's not going to like it, but it's your duty to collect it, evaluate it, and if it warrants it, reopen the investigation. Do you understand that?"

"I understand perfectly. Cal Dunforth has found a way to get some help from the outside, to get a real investigation started. I don't know how he pulled it off, but I'm glad he did. If we find so much as a fleck of dust that looks suspicious, we're going to jump all over it."

Lucas' answer surprised Collins. "You think Dunforth had something to do with me being here?"

"Are you trying to say that he didn't?" Lucas countered.

"Greene, the security specialist, tipped me on this one." Striker said. He noticed the grin forming on Lucas' face. "What am I missing here?"

"Cal and Hannah go back a long way. They almost got married a few years ago. If she tipped you, you can bet Cal's behind it." Lucas confided.

"Well I'll be damned. What kind of guy is Dunforth?"

"The best in our department. He should be our investigator, would be if the Sheriff wasn't afraid to assign him to something with a visible profile. Cal Dunforth's going to be the next Sheriff of Alapaha County. If Sheriff Garrison had treated him right, Cal wouldn't have run against him as long as Garrison wanted the job. He's put the screws to Cal every way he can though, and Cal doesn't feel that he owes him anything except an honest days work until the next election. When that day comes, Garrison's gone."

"You sure don't mince your words." Striker grimaced.

"No. I get the feeling that you don't either."

"You're right. What we're about to do is going to piss off some pretty important people in this little town, including your Sheriff. Nobody appreciates being second guessed, made a fool of. They're going to make your life miserable as hell if you help me."

"They'll try."

"Pretty cocky aren't you?"

"Some people call it that."

"Collins is even dumber than I realized. I figured that he would send me out with someone who couldn't ties his own shoe laces. Why the hell did he pick you?"

"Simple. In Collins mind, this is a shit detail. You're an obnoxious asshole, so he stuck me with the chore of nursemaiding you around."

"You're right. I am an obnoxious asshole, but I'm also one of the best homicide detectives in the state. Stick with me kid, and I guarantee you're going to learn more today than you have since you joined the department." Striker said.

When they parked in the yard, Striker noticed the silver BMW. "Who belongs to the beamer?"

"Lady named Shanon Lee. She was a friend of Marla's, from what I understand." Lucas answered.

"What's she doing here?"

"She's helping Cal somehow. I'm not real sure what she does for a living."

"Dunforth gets around, I'll say that for him," Striker grunted.

Striker got out of the car, strode toward the front door of the house with Lucas following closely behind. Before he could knock, Cal Dunforth stepped out onto the porch to meet him.

"Hello Abe. What brings you out to White Columns?" Cal asked.

"This is Detective Striker, from Atlanta. We're going to have a look around, see what we can find." Lucas said casually.

"Glad to meet you Striker. Can I help you?" Cal asked as he measured the man that he had noticed at the airport.

"Maybe. First I want to check the scene alone, get a feel for it without any input. After that, we'll talk. Have we met somewhere Dunforth?" Striker asked, trying to place the familiar features.

"No. I don't think so." Cal turned as Shanon emerged from the doorway. "This is a friend, Shanon Lee. You may want to talk to her later also." Cal said.

Striker immediately recognized the woman who had been at Hartsfield with Hannah Greene. In the same instant, he remembered Cal as the man that the two women had greeted. What was going on? Dunforth's hair had been different, his features partly obscured by a hat.

The son of a bitch had been in disguise. He had arrived on the flight from Denver. The one that Heywood Carlson was supposed to be on. Unhuh. What have we got going here?

Striker decided to pretend ignorance of the connection for the moment. "Nice to meet you Ms. Lee. I guess I'll get right to it. Lucas will show me around. You two mind waiting around for a few minutes?"

"No problem. We'll be inside when you need us." Cal answered.

Cal and Shanon watched Striker and Lucas disappear around the side of the house, then turned and went inside. Cal led Shanon to the library. "I see Hannah didn't waste any time contacting Striker." Cal said as he sat down at the reading table and sipped his coffee.

"No. She didn't. What do we tell him about the equipment?"

"The truth if he asks."

"What about the pictures? Do we show them to him?"

"No."

"What if he asks about them?"

"We'll worry about that when it happens. Meanwhile, I think that you and I have to clear the air. You've been withdrawn, maybe a little upset that I haven't shown as much interest in the pictures as you expected. That tells me that you don't believe the theory that I've pieced together about the way Heywood killed Marla." Cal eyed her closely.

"I don't know what to believe. I admit that I'm surprised at your lack of interest in the intruder. He could be important in solving Marla's murder." Shanon replied.

"The way I see it. There's no way that the person in those pictures is Heywood. There's strong evidence that he was in Denver when they were taken. I don't know who's lurking around White Columns, or why. My guess is some prankster with a sick sense of humor. I'll deal with him, but first I intend to find Heywood."

Shanon debated with herself for a moment, then decided to reveal the full extent of what she had seen that terrible night that she had spent at White Columns. She knew that it was cruel, yet Cal's refusal to acknowledge that her cameras had captured the image of a spirit drove her on. "I haven't told you everything about the other night." She saw him swivel toward her, attentive now. "I'm positive that the intruder was a ghost, not a living person." She paused.

"What makes you so sure?" He asked quietly.

"When I was seeing through his eyes, I could look through

objects, as if the vision was an x-ray. He stood over Marla's grave, and I could see her clearly. She was just the way her body was positioned before the coffin was closed. Then when he looked toward the gate of the cemetery, he could see me huddled beneath the stone horse. It was terrifying."

"Why didn't you tell me this before?" Cal asked.

"Would it have made any difference? Would you have believed me?"

"Of course I would have believed you." Cal insisted.

"Then you believe me now?" Shanon asked.

Cal hesitated before he spoke, lifted the coffee cup to his lips, as if to prove that his hand was steady, sipped the hot liquid, then pushed the cup aside. "I believe what you're saying, yes. But if you're trying to tell me that a ghost is responsible for Marla's death instead of Heywood, then I don't believe that." He met her eyes with an even stare.

The phone interrupted at that point. Cal went into the kitchen to answer.

Shanon used the break to gather her thoughts. She wondered how far she dared pursue her own theory with Cal. It was farfetched, and poorly defined, even in her own mind, yet she was more convinced than ever that a connection of some kind existed between the ghost that Paula referred to as Doo Man, and Heywood Carlson. Still, she wondered if Cal would accept the idea that Heywood was the reincarnation of the ghost who haunted the old house. She wondered if she really believed that herself.

Cal stuck his head in the doorway and informed her that the call was for Striker. While he went to give the detective the message to call his office, Shanon continued to mull her implausible explanation for the events that were taking place at White Columns.

She didn't have the opportunity to pursue her idea with Cal however. When he returned, Striker was with him. She remained silent while Striker used the phone in the kitchen.

When Striker got off of the phone, he appeared in the library doorway, his pale face drawn with tension. "I need to get back to Atlanta as quickly as possible. Any suggestions?" He stared at Cal.

"What's up?" Cal asked.

"Something urgent. How do I get back in a hurry?"

"That depends. Tell me what you found out, and I might be able to help." Cal answered.

Striker stared at Cal menacingly, then decided that Dunforth wasn't going to be intimidated, and decided to tell him enough to get him to cooperate. "I got a lead on Carlson. I've got to get back and follow up on it."

"I'll have you on a plane in thirty minutes, guaranteed, with one condition." Cal said.

"No conditions. I need that plane." Striker growled.

"Sorry. In that case the best you can hope for is to catch a charter out of Albany. If you're lucky, you'll be airborne in three hours." Cal informed him.

"But you said you could have me out of here in thirty minutes." Striker said. He stared at Cal, then asked. "What's your condition?"

"I'm going with you." Cal said.

"I can't do that." Striker answered.

"In that case, we'll drive you to Albany. You better call from here, and see what's available."

"Shit! You can go. But I'm warning you, don't get in the way." Striker relented.

While Cal made a call, Striker fixed Shanon with his cold eyes. "How do you fit into this circus, Honey?" He demanded.

"Along for the ride I guess." Shanon smiled at him.

Cal had called Robert Cason, a friend who owned a small Cessna. Cason had responded with characteristic enthusiasm. He seldom missed an opportunity to fly, and when Cal told him that he had someone who would pay for the ride, he'd agreed to close the one man real estate office that he operated in Emerald, cancel his appointments for the day, and set the plane down on the highway that ran past White Columns.

Cal informed Striker that the plane would be arriving in a few minutes, took Shanon aside and looked into her stormy eyes. "I want you to go back to my house. Stay near the phone. I'll call as soon as I know what's going on." He said softly.

"What are you going to do Cal?" Her lip trembled as she waited for his reply.

"I don't know." His answer was honest. He had chosen to answer as though her query referred to the immediate future. In his heart he knew that he would kill Heywood as soon as he got the chance. He hoped his evasion would satisfy her.

"What if Striker finds Heywood?"

"I doubt that it will be that easy. He has a lead, but that's all. Heywood's no fool. He could be miles away by now."

"Cal, please...."

"I have to go. I promise that I'll call though. Don't worry."

Shanon felt helpless as she watched him join Abe and Striker in the patrol car. She caught a glimpse of his face looking back at her from the back seat. His features were drawn into a tight mask of determination.

She started for her car with a heavy heart. She had spent so much of the last few days alone with her fears that she didn't think that she could stand more hours of agonizing waiting. She decided that she would have to find some way of spending the hours waiting for Cal's call productively.

Perhaps some research into the history of White Columns would serve to keep her occupied, and also shed some light on the identity of the ghost. If she knew the origin of the spirit, she could begin to unravel the meaning of its preoccupation with White Columns, and those who lived there. Whoever the spirit belonged to, the living person had hated the Dunforth's for some specific reason. The hatred was so intense that it allowed the spirit to remain within the realm of the living, or at least to revisit it at will.

As these thoughts formed in her mind, she realized that they had no basis in science, no connection to her previous research. Her speculation was based on nothing more than a gut reaction, yet she was sure that she was right.

She got into her car, and sat without starting the engine. She thought about Cal's bizarre account of the event that he had taken part in, her own dreamlike journey into the past. She was sure that the key to the identity of the ghost was buried within that episode. In all likelihood, it belonged to the man who had been hanged. But who exactly was he? Did he have any connection to Heywood Carlson, and if so, what was it?

She was still puzzling over those questions when she heard the drone of an airplane. The pitch of the engine changed as the plane started an abrupt decent toward the highway. As she watched it dip below the trees and out of sight, she thought that its pilot was either very skillful, foolhardy, or both.

In less than half a minute, she heard the engine straining as the plane gathered speed for takeoff. She watched it reappear above the tree line, bank north toward Atlanta, and gradually fade to a silvery glint against the hard blue sky. Only then did she start the car and proceed down the driveway. When she arrived in Emerald, she turned into the parking lot of the library. It was an imposing brick structure. Over the heavy wooden double doors a sign proclaimed that it had been dedicated in 1878. Walking inside, she hoped that it would contain volumes on the history of the town.

She saw a thin faced hunched backed lady with gray hair pulled up on top of her head in a severe looking bun behind the circulation desk. She walked over, aware of alert blue gray eyes watching her progress.

"Good morning. I'm interested in a book about Emerald, specifically one that deals with the history of the town. Can you give me a suggestion?" She asked politely.

The lady's eyes brightened. Shanon realized that she had touched on the woman's favorite subject. "I sure can, young lady. Emerald has a proud heritage, I'm happy to say. We have one book that covers its history from it's founding up to the early fifties. I bet that's just what you're wanting. I'm always happy when someone takes the time to learn about the towns heritage. You must be a newcomer. I haven't seen you around before. I wouldn't forget such a pretty face." The woman shuffled toward a stack of books along the back wall.

Shanon followed a short distance behind. "I'm visiting a friend."

"And who might that friend be? I know everyone in town, at least the older families."

"Cal Dunforth."

"Cal? Well, that's a fine boy. He sure is." The woman stopped and gave Shanon an appraising look. "He always did keep good company, an eye for beautiful women, that boy. Just like his Granddaddy. Why Honey, when that man walked by, I used to get weak in the knees. I swear. We went to school together. He was a fine man. Handsome. But he was kind and gentle. Just as polite as you could ask for. You would have never known he had a dime from the way he acted. He was gentleman from the tip of his toes to the top of his head. It didn't pay to get him riled though! Don't pay to get none of the Dunforth's riled. They got a temper like a wildcat. Underneath those velvet smooth manners, and that soft spoken drawl, there's a backbone of solid steel."

"I'm beginning to realize that." Shanon smiled.

The librarian pulled a worn book off the shelf. "Here it is. *Emerald, The Gem of The Alapaha.* I've read it half a dozen times. I never tire of it. You'll enjoy it too, I bet. Especially if you're planning on mar..., settling down here."

Shanon smiled at the older woman. The idea of marrying Cal Dunforth sent a warm glow through her. "I'm not sure about my future plans. I'm sure I'll find this interesting reading though."

"Modern women don't like advice from my generation, especially the kind I'm about to give you, but I'm going to give it to you anyway. Women now days try to push their men around, try to insist that they can do anything a man can do. Maybe they can do what most men do, but if they can, it's a sign that men are getting weaker, not that women are getting stronger. Don't you try it with Cal Dunforth. He's got too much pride. Of course a man without pride ain't worth having. A man that lets a woman dominate him ain't worth much in my book either. A real man is going to treat a woman with respect and kindness. He'll do anything possible to see that she's happy. He'll do it because he loves her. If a man has to be bullied into treating you right, then he ain't worth your time. The Dunforth men have always treated their women with respect and dignity, and insisted that everyone else respected them too. You'll read about what happens when Dunforth women get mistreated." The lady paused for breath.

"The Dunforth's are mentioned in the book?"

"More than that, you'll find entire chapters about them. They were one of the first families to settle here."

Shanon's heart beat faster. She felt certain that she had found what she was looking for. Suddenly she was anxious to get to Cal's house and start reading. "Thank you so much for your help." She thought for a moment about the glowing words that the lady had used to describe the Dunforth men. "I think your advice is sound also I'll certainly keep it in mind."

"Good. I think Cal's lucky to find a girl like you. I'm happy for him too. He deserves some happiness. He's had enough tragedy in his life. I hope the two of you get along just fine."

As Shanon signed out the book, she wondered what kind of tragedy that the old lady was referring to. She hadn't mentioned Marla's death, and somehow that didn't strike Shanon as what she had been referring to. She started to ask questions, thought better of it, and hurried out of the building clutching the book under her arm. She wondered suddenly about Cal's parents. He had never mentioned them. Had something happened to them? If so, did White Columns fit into the picture? She decided that she would make a few discreet inquiries. Drew would know. She'd ask him.

CHAPTER 19

Cal felt Striker's cold eyes appraising him. He turned in his seat beside the pilot, and returned the stare without blinking. "What's on your mind Striker?"

"I was just wondering if you were smart enough not to cause me any trouble." Striker growled.

"I don't think you have to worry about that. If you corner Heywood Carlson, he's going to be all the trouble that you can handle. He's desperate. Desperate men are dangerous. Heywood's more dangerous than most because he's also a near genius, and he's got a lot to lose. From what I hear about your investigation of him, he's looking at a murder rap regardless of what he did to Marla."

"You're right about that. He produces snuff films, cinematic murder. There's enough aggravating circumstances surrounding the charges that he'll be facing that he'll get the chair if he's convicted." Striker said.

"I know why you're trying to reopen the investigation into Marla's death, Striker." Cal bored into Striker with relentless eyes.

"Yeah?"

"If you had enough evidence to charge him with murder for what you suspect him to be involved with here, in your jurisdiction, you wouldn't concern yourself with a murder that took place two hundred miles out of your jurisdiction." Cal said.

Striker's face tightened. "I'm going to nail Carlson for murder.

I don't care if it's for the ones he committed in my jurisdiction, or the ones outside. I'm going to nail his ass," he said.

"There's only one sure way to insure that Heywood pays for his crimes. I know it, and you know it. The leads you're working at your end have got to be pretty slim. As for what I've turned up, I may not even be able to get an arrest warrant, much less a conviction. The incompetents in my own department have rendered judgment. According to them, Marla committed suicide. They will resist any other conclusion bitterly. I'm not optimistic that anything will come of your investigation, regardless of evidence that you find, short of a confession."

"So what are you suggesting?"

"If we find Heywood, the two of us together, he'll let us take him in. By now, he has to know that we don't have enough to convict him of anything." Cal offered.

"He doesn't know how much we know. He's running scared right now. It's a good time to take him. That's if he can be found." Striker rasped.

"By now he's found out from Beth exactly what we know. You can bet your ass on that. I don't know what kind of hold he has over her, but she'll go along with whatever he wants. She hates his guts, but for some reason, she can't refuse to do anything that he asks her to." Cal thought out loud.

"You think the two of them are on the run together?"

"No. I'm afraid that Beth may be in over her head. Heywood's a hell of a lot smarter than she gives him credit for. Frankly, the more that I think about it, the more concerned for her safety I become." Cal frowned.

"So what have you got in mind?" Striker asked.

"Heywood knows that I'm going to kill him if I find him. If I go in alone, he'll either run or fight. If he feels trapped, I'm sure that he will turn on me with a weapon. If he does, then we don't really have to worry about a conviction, do we?"

"You're pretty damn sure of yourself. What if Carlson ambushes you. What then?" Striker asked the question dispassionately, showing no real concern for Cal's safety.

"In that case, you've got your murder conviction, provided that you're up to taking him." Cal challenged.

"Sounds like a winner to me. When we get to the warehouse, he's all yours. We'll take a rental car from the airport, no backup. If you take him out, our problem's solved. If he takes you down, you can rest assured that I'll kill him, even if I have to burn the damn place down on top of him." Striker promised.

Cal stretched across the seat and offered Striker his hand. The two renegade cops sealed the deal. Both had gotten what they wanted. Striker was accustomed to operating outside the law. He didn't give a damn how he closed a case, as long as it got closed. Cal only wanted an opportunity to kill Heywood Carlson. If it meant striking a deal with the dirtiest cop that he had ever known, so be it.

The pilot was looking at Cal with a mixture of fear and awe. "I can't believe that I heard what I just think I heard." He finally said.

"You didn't hear shit. Just fly this bird and forget this conversation. It never happened, understand?"

"Sure Cal. I didn't hear nothing."

"Just keep in mind that if you ever remember this conversation, and should be stupid enough to repeat it, your ass will be in a sling right along with us. After all, you're part of it now. You know what we're going to do, and you are helping by flying us right to our pigeon. That's called an accessory."

"Shit Cal. I can't believe that you've got me mixed up in this. I always thought that you were a straight arrow.", the pilot grumbled anxiously.

"I always was, up to now. Maybe I will be again after this thing is over."

"There's still time to reconsider. I mean, its one thing to talk about killing some guy..."

"Don't worry about it. It'll go down without a hitch. Carlson's going to try to kill me as soon as he sees me. I'm just going to kill him first, that's all. It's not like I'm going to murder the little bastard like he murdered Marla." Cal tried to reassure his friend.

"Are you absolutely certain that he murdered her Cal? I mean, if you are, I'll go in with you."

"I'm sure, and I know that you would cover me if I asked you to, but that would ruin the plan. Heywood won't fight two of us. In fact, my greatest concern is that he'll cower down in a corner like a rat, and I'll have to shoot him in cold blood."

"You better be careful Cal. He's got the advantage of you. He's on his own turf. There's no telling what you're walking into."

"If he gets lucky, you can go in with Striker."

"If he gets lucky, I'm calling in a SWAT team. With an officer down, they'll squash him like a bug." Striker smiled evilly.

The rest of the plane ride passed in silence until they approached

Fulton County Airport. Bob Cason checked in with the tower, received landing clearance, and within minutes the Cessna touched down gently. Cason had become infected with the grim determination of Cal and Striker. The last time that he had felt this way was during his last tour in Nam, where he had flown Huey gunships into Laos and Cambodia in support of SOG missions. As he met Cal's eyes, he was reminded of the look of cold fury that he'd seen in those days in the eyes of combat veterans who had lost buddies to the NVA.

He remembered with a trace of bitterness how he, and the other warriors of that era had been sold out by the yellow bellies in Washington, the long haired creeps who had made a habit of spitting on returning soldiers, and the harping newsies. None of them had watched their best friends bleed to death in their arms, or watched another gunship crash and burn. They had not known what war was all about. To men like Bob Cason, war was killing the enemy, making them pay for the screams of agony that still echoed in their minds when they tried to sleep.

He realized that the same burning anger that he'd experienced was what drove Cal to do what he was planning. Any trace of reluctance about his own participation vanished. Cason knew all too well the consequences of playing by chickenshit rules. Cal knew his enemy. He had found him, and now he was going to do what a warrior would do. He was going in and kill him, no rules were going to stop him. That's the way it should be.

Striker used his clout effectively to expedite the rental car, moving through the office almost non stop, pausing only to flash his badge, credit card, and to scribble his signature on the paper work. By the time Cason had secured his plane, a silver Ford Taurus was waiting for the threesome. Striker climbed behind the wheel, and as his two passengers settled in and closed their doors he accelerated out of the parking lot.

Taking Interstate 20 West bound Striker pushed the sedan hard, working his way through traffic with the deft agility of a former patrol division officer. The threesome raced past Six Flags Theme Park, then took the Austell exit, and drove another mile west before taking a turn into an office warehouse complex. He zeroed in on the office that housed Carlson's studio, and swerved into a parking place in front. He lurched across the curb, and used the bumper of the Taurus to splinter the glass window. The sign announcing that Creek Mark Builders had moved to another location slipped down, and draped itself over the hood of the car.

"He's all yours." Striker growled at Cal.

In an instant Cal was out of the car, and through the shattered glass. He crossed the vacant office and showroom in three giant strides. Without hesitation he drove his heel into the door leading to the warehouse area. In a shower of splinters it gave way, and he stepped into the empty space beyond. By now his fist had closed on the Glock resting behind his right kidney. As smooth as silk, he drew and trained the weapon on the interior. He didn't worry about seeking cover as his training normally dictated. He knew that Striker's aggression had given him the advantage of surprise. His eyes swept the murky interior as he sought a target.

To his vast disappointment, the building seemed completely empty. For an instant he worried that Strikers information was wrong, that they had crashed the wrong property. Fighting down a sense of frustration and disappointment that was so powerful that it almost brought tears, he studied the vacant building. Something wasn't quite right about it. At first he couldn't figure out what seemed odd, and then it struck him like a blow. The interior was far too small! Judging by the size of the outside of the structure, the warehouse area should be almost twice the size that it appeared from within.

The hairs along the back of his neck stood on end with the sense of danger that he suddenly felt. He was totally exposed in the vacant warehouse. If what he suspected was true, and there was a disguised interior room at the back of the structure, anyone inside would have an open field of fire from within if the designer had been clever enough to have provided a firing slit. Instinctively he closed the distance between himself and the back wall in a rush and huddled against the wall, pressing into it to provide as small a target as possible.

For long minutes he waited, listening for the sound of a weapon being cocked, or its action readied to fire. Hearing nothing, he breathed a sigh of relief and inched away from the structure and tried to get a perspective on it.

He was exploring the metal wall with his fingers when he became aware of a faint but persistent odor. He sniffed and evaluated. There was no doubt about it. There was a dead creature beyond the wall. It could be as small as a rat if the wall was really the exterior wall. If not, and it was only a facade to disguise an inner chamber, the origin of the odor could be much larger. As large as a human corpse. Cal thought about Beth Addison, missing now for several days. A dark sense of foreboding invaded his spirit, and seemed to settle into his very bones. Not only was he suddenly convinced that he wasn't going to find Heywood Carlson this day, but his imagination began showing him horrors that he didn't want to acknowledge.

Cal moved along the entire wall, searching for any sign that it was a false front. He found nothing obvious, but was still sure that his impression was correct. He would just have to have lights in order to find what he was looking for. He walked back to the front of the warehouse and flipped on the light switches. To his satisfaction, the lights flared on. At least Heywood had not had power disconnected. He stepped into the office, and waved Striker and Cason inside.

"Nothing here? Striker rasped as he stepped inside.

"Yeah, something's here. It's just not what we wanted to find." Cal said bitterly. Striker raised his eyebrows questioningly. Cal explained about his theory of a false wall and then about the odor.

"Hey, don't look so down. Carlson might still be behind that wall. I've a feeling that Ms. Addison had good reason to want out of their partnership, and I've also got a feeling that she'd be no push over. The only thing that I'd be willing to concede is that one of the two is back there, and the other is long gone. The only question is which one's still in play." Striker wheezed, lighting a Marlboro and exhaling a cloud of smoke. He broke off filters from two other cigarettes, stuffed them into his nostrils then extended the pack to Cal. "Let's get inside, and see what we got." Striker led the way back into the warehouse.

Cal stopped Bob Cason. "This is going to be nasty Bob. Why don't you wait for us out here?" Seeing Cason nod, Cal turned and followed Striker.

With the lights on it didn't take long to find the door. It was disguised behind a false air conditioning vent. Striker snapped the vent out, and went to work of the heavy padlock that secured the concealed door with a set of tools from his wallet. In less than three minutes the lock opened and Striker pushed the door inward.

The odor hit them like a physical wall as it rushed out of the room. The enclosure had been carefully sound proofed, and the effect that the insulation had was to trap the fetid air inside as well. Cal fought against nausea as he followed Striker inside. An unnerving scratching noise close by in the darkness stopped as Striker's searching fingers found the light switch. In the flare of studio lights that suddenly blazed on, the two men found themselves blinking owlishly at the grisly scene before them.

In the center of the room, lashed to a cross in a reverse crucifix position was what appeared to be the body of a black female. Some type of garment had been ripped away from the victim's shoulders and now gathered shapelessly about the waist. The victim was down on her knees, lashed to the crude whipping post in such a posture that the body at first appeared headless. A closer look revealed a cord around her neck that stretched the victim's throat across the top post of the cross cruelly, and forced the head down in an unnaturally strained posture.

When Cal forced himself closer, he saw for the first time the cascade of blonde hair hanging down. He quickly realized that what he was viewing was a Caucasian female, blonde, in her twenties, so badly beaten that dried and matted blood had provided the dark coloration that had caused his initial misconception. The sound that erupted from his throat wasn't human. He was incapable at that moment of rational thought. Instead, he was consumed by blind , unreasoning hatred, a dark force that enveloped him.

Striker knew by Cal's reaction that the body before them was that of Beth Addison. With that knowledge, he reached another inescapable conclusion. Heyward Carlson was gone. That identity, as well as that of Gordon Chase would vanish into thin air. If Carlson planned to continue living as either of the two identities, he would have made an effort to conceal the body of Addison. The fact that the killer made no effort to conceal his most recent crime, told the veteran cop that another identity was waiting for the murderer to step into. It meant that the search for Carlson would have to go nationwide, and involve the F.B. I. That meant that he would lose control of the investigation, and be relegated to a background role. There was no way in hell that he would let that happen.

Even as he put an arm around Dunforth's shoulder, and firmly pulled him away from the horror before them, his mind was working on this development. He realized that he wouldn't be able to find Carlson without interagency help, which he wasn't about to invite into his life, yet he couldn't let a homicide as high profile as this one would turn out to be, go unsolved.

As these thoughts raced through his razor sharp mind, the image of Claude Raynes flashed into focus. Raynes. He exploited death, made his living from it. He may not have actually killed anyone, but selling it, packaged neatly in video cassettes was just as bad. He deserved to go down hard. The possibilities filtered through Striker's consciousness. Yeah. He could put together enough pieces to make a case stick.

Instantaneously the decision was made. Claude Raynes would fall for the murder of Beth Addison. With that case solved, he could take his time looking for Heywood Carlson, or whatever alias that he would be using by now.

CHAPTER 20

Hannah had picked Cal up, and drove him back to her townhouse. The news of Beth's death had been a shock for her. She realized that everyone had underestimated Heywood Carlson. Hannah was particularly aware of this fact. She suspected that it had been Beth who had burglarized Heywood's safe, and it that was true, then Beth had cold bloodedly shot down the man that she had hired to crack Heywood's safe, yet somehow Heywood had gotten the advantage of her and slaughtered her.

She watched Cal pick at the plate of food that she had prepared for him. He looked drained. Maybe in a few days he would be ready to take up Heywood's trail again, but now he looked like he just wanted to curl up, and try to forget the nightmare that his life had become. She thought that she had discovered a way to keep him occupied, and safe for a few days. With luck, long enough for her to follow up the lead that she had developed on a possible place to start looking for Heywood Carlson. She decided to broach the subject.

"Cal, I've got to go out of town on business for a few days. You're welcome to stay here while I'm away. In fact, it would be very helpful if you would. I wouldn't feel comfortable taking Paula with me, but at the same time I wouldn't be satisfied to leave her with anyone except you while I'm away. She still needs to be with someone that she trusts. Could you manage for a couple of days?"

"I suppose so. I suppose I need to stay in the city for a few days anyway. I'll have to make the arrangements for Beth. She didn't have anyone that I'm aware of."

"That's so sad. I'm sorry. Do you need my help with that?"

"No. I can manage fine. I'll call Drew and talk to him about Paula. She needs a stable family environment. Maybe she can stay with his family until I can get settled down."

Hannah was surprised by his last statement. She studied his face. "It sounds like you're planning on her living with you. I had assumed that she would live with Drew or Matt. They are her uncles. Legally you wouldn't be considered a relative. You are her cousin, right?"

"That's right, but...."

His words trailed off. He looked at her with misery in his eyes. He seemed about to continue, then remained silent.

"There's nothing wrong with her living with you. It's just that I assumed... Well, anyway, that's something that you'll have to work out with Drew and Matt. That reminds me. Drew wants to see you, says he's found something important. I tried to pry it out of him, but he won't spill until he talks to you. Maybe you'd better give him a call."

"I guess so." He looked at her curiously. "Would I be prying if I asked where you're going?"

Hannah avoided his eyes. "I don't want to tell you Cal. For your own good."

"You're going after Heywood." It was a statement of fact.

"Yeah. I have a slim lead. I don't want to go into detail about it. It may not be anything." Hannah got up, and started clearing the table.

"At least tell me where you're going, and when to expect you back. I need to know that much in case..."

"Don't worry. I'm not going to try to take Heywood down, just find his trail. If I get that far, I'll call in the police. Believe me. I fully appreciate Heywood's capabilities."

"Still, you should tell someone where you're going. If you won't tell me, at least tell Striker," Cal said.

"I'll tell you, but you have to promise to sit tight until I get back."

"Promise."

"I'm going to Odesa Texas. I should be back in three to four days. As I said, the lead's thin, but it's all any of us have at the moment."

"When are you leaving?"

"I'd like to go tomorrow if I can get reservations. Are you sure that you can handle Paula?"

"Sure. She'll be fine. If I need help, I've got Drew, Matt, and Shanon." Cal said.

Finished clearing the table, Hannah poured a scotch and water for herself, and a Crown and Cola for Cal. She handed Cal his drink, and took his hand. Gently, she urged him toward the living room sofa. She turned on the stereo softly, and walked back to the couch. She nestled down with her back leaning against his chest, and rested her head on his shoulder. They sat quietly, enjoying the warmth of each other in the dim light, listening to the soothing sound of oldies playing on the radio.

Finally, reluctantly, Hannah broke the silence. "Paula's exhausted. She's been dragged around with me for the past several days. It will be good for her to spend some quiet time with you Cal."

"She certainly went to sleep early tonight. Of course, today has seemed like an eternity for me. I'm sure for a child it must have been even longer." Cal said.

"It has been a long day. A terrible day. We should turn in early too. Are you ready?" Hannah asked.

"Yeah. I'm not sure that I can sleep, but I'm ready to give it a try if you'll bring me a pillow and a blanket, I'll settle in." Cal said.

"I've got a better idea," Hannah stood and reached for his hand. She lead him upstairs to her own bedroom. They undressed by the reflection of light from the street lamps outside.

In bed they melted together as if the years of separation had never happened. Their lovemaking was slow, tender. Each took the time to reacquaint themselves with the other's body. Afterward they lay in each other's arms in silence, as if aware that words would spoil what they had shared.

****

By the next afternoon, Hannah was in Texas. She had uncovered the identity of one of Heywood's relatives. Mrs. Ada Parker, his great aunt, owned the Circle J ranch. She had been told by the lady that she had talked to at the county court house, that Ms Ada was quite a talker. The old lady was in her late seventies, widowed, and probably lonely in the sprawling ranch house that she shared with a live in maid.

Hannah fought down her rising excitement as she drove the rental car through the Circle J's gate. She reminded herself that finding one of

Carlson's relatives, and finding him was two different things. Still, her hunch that Heywood had relatives here had been born out. Maybe she would uncover his trail if she played her cards right, and was very lucky.

She parked in front of the house and got out. As she walked toward the front door it was easy to peel away the years, and imagine the rambling ranch house made of sturdy timbers and stone as it must have looked in the late 1800's when it had been built. To her right, a comfortable looking bunkhouse stood in front of a rail coral. Inside the fence, a beautiful roan stallion tossed his head, whinnied at her, and aggressively approached the coral fence. His demeanor of raw power was clearly evident.

Hannah rang the doorbell, stood listening for any signs of life from within the ranch house. In the distance, the low bawl of cattle could be heard. The door opened, catching her by surprise. Before here stood a tall erect woman whose skin was the color of mink oiled leather. The silver hair spilling out from beneath the wide brimmed Stetson was thick and luxurious, a mane of gray, proudly worn as a testament to the woman's years.

Hannah smiled, extended her hand, and introduced herself, noting that the fingers that closed around her own were hard and powerful. "You must be Ms. Parker."

"Friends call me Ada. Come in Hannah. I'll get us some coffee." The old lady's voice was pitched low, not masculine, but with a hint of strength in it.

Hannah followed Ada inside. Her eyes roamed the walls of the room. The mounted heads of two enormous deer looked down from above the stone fireplace. Over the mantle, which was made from a hand hewn log, hung a Greener twelve gauge shotgun, an old weapon with exposed hammers, and above it, nestled in a holder fashioned from horseshoes, was a Shiloh Sharps buffalo gun. On the wall to the right of the fireplace, a buffalo hide was stretched in testament to the efficiency of the old weapon.

Hannah followed Ada into the dining room, trailed her fingers across the broad smooth expanse of the heavy wooden dining table. She estimated that the expansive table would comfortably seat a dozen people.

"What brings a pretty young thing like you way out here? I don't often have guest these days." The old woman said as she filled an enormous coffee pot and set it on the stove.

"I talked to some of your friends in town. They told me that you knew more of the history of this part of Texas than anyone around. I was hoping that you would take some of your time, and share your memories with me." Hannah said, settling in at the bar.

"Friends." Ada snorted. "Acquaintances maybe. I don't have many friends left around these parts. Most of my generation's gone on. The young folks ain't got no time for us that's left. I figure you want something from me or you wouldn't be here either. No matter. I'm glad for the company. I hope they warned you that I can talk your ears off." The woman smiled.

Hannah wanted to get the conversation steered in the direction that would be most helpful. "Tell me about your family, how they came to settle here. I can almost feel the history oozing out of the walls of this place. It's beautiful, in it's own way. Pure, simple, yet elegant. I'm sure that a lot of work went into building it, and that you've put in a lot of your own effort to maintain it."

"You're very kind. Don't find many young folks who appreciate the past anymore." Ada paused, seemed to reach back into her memory for the threads of a story that she hadn't told for a very long time. "My Grandpa had the ranch house built, where he got the money, nobody seems to know. He was as colorful a character as you'd expect to find in any book about the old west. He was one of those men who built a reputation with his guns at an early age. His Pa was a General in the Union army during the Civil War. Legend has it that Ku Klux Klansmen hung the General right in front of his son, killed GrandPa's mother with him looking on, then drove the child out of his home. He drifted west. A six-gun in his hand, and hatred in his heart for everything about the South. Some said he once remarked that his Pa had lived through the war, only to be hanged by a bunch of Southern rabble, on the porch of his own home. They say that he was determined to own the biggest spread in Texas, and that he swore that he would kill any man that stood in his way. There must have been a lot of men in his way. I've still got his old six-gun, a cap and ball revolver, with eight notches carved in the handles." Ada paused.

"That's fascinating. Apparently he was successful. The circle J is most impressive." Hannah prompted. "What happened to him?"

"An old feud finally caught up to him.. He was gunned down by a man from Georgia in a saloon one night. Just a drifter they say. A man with ice in his veins, and lightning in his fist. He shot Grandpa and walked away. Not a hand raised against him. That's how it was in those days. The law was a gun, and a fast draw. My Papa was born two days after the funeral."

"How tragic. Your Grandmother must have been a strong woman, holding onto the ranch with her husband dead, I mean."

"Oh, she lost the ranch. Damn vultures at the bank foreclosed on her within a year. She'd borrowed to expand the cattle herd. Her ranch foreman was a thief. He threw in with rustlers, and stole her blind." Ada got up and poured coffee for the two of them.

Hannah sipped appreciatively. "This is the best coffee I've ever tasted. What's your secret?"

"Out here coffee ain't a luxury. It's a necessary part of life. I learned to brew a pot before I as this high." She held out her hand to indicate a child's statue.

"How did your family get the ranch back?" Hannah asked.

"Papa married the daughter of the man who bought it from the bank," a rueful smile traced itself across the woman's face.

"I see." Hannah studied the lines in the woman's face, and saw some barely concealed hurt in them.

"Papa was one of those men who was born into an era that he never quite fit into. The old west was tame. You couldn't shoot it out in the streets with another man anymore, and get away with it. He was always nostalgic for the times that his Papa and Grandpa lived in. He spent a lot of time brooding about the past. He used to show us kids pictures of this big white house, and tell us that it rightfully belonged to us. Mama would frown, and send me and my brother off to bed. Later we could hear them fighting about it. I've always wondered about that house, and where he got those pictures." The woman seemed lost in thought.

"I bet you've still got them." Hannah said quietly.

"As a matter of fact I do. I haven't looked at it for more than sixty five years though. I hid it away. Mama burned the rest of them after Papa died. I never knew what she meant by it, but she always said that house killed Papa."

"That's very intriguing. Did you ever try to find out what she meant?" Hannah asked.

"No. I never did. I found out later, after I was a grown up that Mama hired people to try and find out what happened to Papa." The lines in Ada's face deepened.

"You must have been young when he died." Hannah prompted.

"Eight years old. I remember it clearly. It was like a bad dream that wouldn't end. Papa went away one day, he used to do that a lot, I remember that, but this time was different. He had a terrible fight with Mama before he left. I heard her screaming at him to leave it alone, that we had all that we needed right here. He screamed back at her. I remember those were the last words that I ever heard him speak. He said, 'It's mine. I intend to have it, and nobody had better get in my way'. I never saw him again after that night."

"And you think that he was referring to the house in the pictures?"

"I'm sure of it. Mama burned them. All except the one that I kept hidden under my mattress. Somehow I always thought that if I could find that house, I'd find Papa."

"Did you ever try to find it?"

"Yeah. I tried. I never found it though. It's somewhere in Georgia. That's all I know."

Hannah almost decided not to pursue the conversation further, but some inner voice told her that it was important. "Would you mind showing me the picture?"

Ada looked startled, maybe a little afraid. "I... I don't know why not. Maybe I can stand to look at it again now. Maybe I should look at it. Come with me."

Hannah followed the old woman into the hallway, and waited while she pulled down the attic stairs. She felt tension building inside of her, but didn't know why.

Ada climbed the stairs slowly, but determinedly. "It's been years since I've been up in the attic. I've got so much junk up here that we probably can't even walk. I've never been one to throw anything away."

"Be careful. I wouldn't want you to fall and hurt yourself." Hannah admonished as Ada heaved herself up the last step.

She felt the old woman's withering gaze. "I'm not feeble. I'm probably in better shape than you are, young lady. You mind your own step." The last words were softened by the trace of a smile.

Despite her protests that she hadn't visited the attic for years, Ada proceeded unerringly to a leather bound trunk, opened it easily, and withdrew a tissue wrapped article. She handed it to Hannah and went to pull on the single bare bulb that hung from the ceiling.

When the light flared on, Hannah gasped. She found herself staring at a picture of White Columns. She felt her hand begin to tremble as she replaced the faded picture in the tissue. She sensed Ada standing beside her.

"You've seen the house." It was a statement of fact. The woman had noticed her reaction.

Hannah nodded.

"I don't want to know about it. I won't look at it either. It's why you're here, isn't it? You know about that house, and it scares you, just like it's scared me for all of these years. It took away my Papa. It's taken something from you too.

"Not yet. It hasn't taken him yet, but I'm afraid that it might." Hannah breathed.

"Dear God! Let's get back into the kitchen." Ada's shoulders shuddered as if she had experienced a sudden chill.

With fresh coffee before them, Ada resumed talking. "When I was a child I would dream about that house, a recurring nightmare. Papa was trapped inside of it, and I couldn't get him out. Sometimes I would be standing outside, knowing that he was there, but unable to walk up the driveway. Other times, I would dream that he was trapped inside, with strangers who wanted to kill him. I knew that I had to warn him, but I couldn't find the house. I would dream that I was searching for the house. I would spend hours searching, terrified that I'd be too late if I ever did find it. They were horrible. The dreams that I had as a child were so frightening that some nights I would try to stay awake, so that I wouldn't dream. That's how I learned to brew coffee. I would drink as much as Mama would allow before bed. It didn't work. Eventually I would go to sleep, and the dreams would come."

"I'm sorry. I hope I haven't upset you." Hannah said.

"You didn't upset me. I grew out of the dreams. I'm worried about you though. Your fears aren't over, are they?"

"No."

"I'd like to help you." Ada laid a weathered hand on Hannah's shoulder.

"You already have. I have to be going now. I appreciate your taking time to talk to me, and the coffee. It has been a pleasure talking to you." Hannah stood, and started to walk outside.

At the door Ada spoke again, "Will I see you again?"

"I'm not sure. I'm not from around here. Write your phone number down, and I promise to call you sometime." Hannah said.

She waited while the woman found pencil and paper, then accepted the folded note and tucked it into her purse.

"Goodbye Ada."

"Bye Hannah. Good luck."

When Hannah reached her car, she noticed that the woman was still standing in the doorway. She glanced down at the scrap of paper in her purse, and on impulse unfolded it. Instead of a phone number there was an address, and scrawled beneath it a note. Write me.

As she pulled onto the highway something about the note nagged at her. She worried it in her mind for a few minutes, and she realized what was bothering her. Write me. As much as Ada enjoyed talking, why would she give her address instead of a phone number? The answer came with a slight tremor of dread. A post mark! Ada Parker was still searching for something. A post mark would lead her to the house that had taken her father, or at least she was hoping that it would. What would she do if she found it? Hannah wasn't sure that she wanted to know the answer to that question.

As the empty miles slipped by, Hannah was troubled by the thought that had taken shape in her mind as she had listened to Ada Parker describe a family legacy of obsessive greed and ruthlessness. She wouldn't have to find Heywood Carlson. He would return to White Columns. Someday, in some guise, he would be back. He was as obsessed with White Columns as his Grandfather had been. He had married Marla Dunforth to gain possession of the house. When she had divorced him, he had murdered her. Why? Had her murder been an act of revenge, or was it a part of some macabre scheme to reclaim White Columns?

Putting the pieces of Heywood's scheme together, if indeed he had one, was like trying to put together a puzzle with the pieces lying face down. The only thing that Hannah was sure of was that he wouldn't give up, and that Cal Dunforth stood between Heywood and what he wanted most. She had to warn Cal. She had thought that Cal was the hunter in this deadly game, but now she realized that he could very well be the hunted.

****

In his dream, Marla glided through the dark waters just beyond his reach. Her laughter drifted across the river as she skillfully eluded Cal's outstretched hand. The long enticing legs that propelled her away from him were as dark as the river itself, and when he reached for them, seemed to disolve like water in his hand. She rolled gracefully onto her back and smiled invitingly, beckoning him forward. Striking out with powerful strokes, he tried to reach her, but could make no progress against a sudden powerful current that tugged him away from her.

The soft babble of the Alapaha's gentle current gradually grew until it reached a deafening cresendo. A powerful wall of water swept him away from Marla, and mocked his feeble efforts to swim against it. The water around him suddenly turned from the pleasant warmth of summer to the frigid cold of winter. The lush growth along the river banks disappeared, replaced by gaunt and bare skeletons of trees waving bony arms at him as he drifted helplessly downstream.

The overwhelming joy that he felt began to fade into a sense of impending tragedy as the black water began to swirl around Marla, forming a yawning vortex of eternal darkness around her. Before his eyes he saw her body begin to slowly disolve into the water and vanish into the whirlpool. He screamed her name, and tried to swim toward the spot where she had slipped beneath the water, but the inexorable pull of the current drifted him steadily downstream. His efforts grew more feeble as the water sucked the warmth from his body.

The cold water slowed the flow of blood through his veins and made his movements labored and sluggish. He felt himself slip beneath the surface, and begin an endless spiral downward. What little light that the hard gray winter sky had provided disappated as he slipped deeper into the frigid depths of the river. He opened his mouth to scream and the ice water rushed in, filling his lungs with an expanding coldness. By now there was no light filtering through the stained water, and he felt the last of his life draining away into the darkness.

Cal watched endless waves of gray cloud cover drift past as he floated gently in the water. All of his senses sharpened as an uncanny awareness gripped him. His acute eyesight was able to discern that it wasn't clouds that drifted over, but smoke, thick billowing layers of it. The acrid smell of black powder mingled with the sickening sweet odor of blood hung in the air. The roaring that he had thought to be the river was the steady firing of guns, and he could distinctly hear the labored grunts of horses, and the creaking of leather. Somewhere to his left, a bugle sounded. All around him vague shapes moved through the smoke. They smelled of sweat, and exuded a rank odor that he recognized as fear. A fleshy thud would be followed by a shape slumping to the ground, some to lie motionless, others to writhe and contort as aimlessly as the wind driven smoke.

There was a cold, heavy weight in his chest that was smothering the life out of him. When he coughed to rid himself of the obstruction, he tasted the salted copper of blood in his mouth. The heaviness in his chest was pressing him into the earth, and the scene around him disintegrated into fragmented pieces of a broken puzzle. Darkness engulfed him, but he could still hear. He listened to the rythmic thudding above him, followed by the sound of dirt trickling around him. Gradually the sounds diminished as the fresh earth covered the pine boards of his coffin lid. At first he thought that he was being buried alive, but then the awful coldness that penetrated to his very core convinced him that he was dead. The living, with warm blood flowing through their veins, couldn't possibly know such a cold emptiness as he had fallen into.

Somewhere deep within himself, Cal felt the slight flicker of life. He siezed it with all of his being and held on, praying that some slight breeze would fan it. Gradually the flicker grew into a light that burned down hotly at him. He opened his eyes and blinked into the hot summer sun.

The creature kneeling beside him, cradling his head in strong hands was the most beautiful that he had ever seen. Her smooth ebony skin seemed to glow with warmth. When she pulled him into her strong arms, the warmth from her body flowed into him and he felt his heart begin to beat stronger. The faint clean smell of fresh soap was what he would always remember. It told him that he was alive and safe. He felt his face stretch into a lazy smile. Hattie had found him. His sweet, beautiful Hattie.

Cal's dream jerked suddenly forward, and he was following Hattie across a field of cotton that stretched almost as far as he could see. The pail filled with black berries banged against his hip as he walked. He could almost taste the pie that Mamie had promised to bake if they brought her some berries. He lengthened his stride, determined to keep up with Hattie. After all, he was almost thirteen, and he should be able to keep up with a girl, even if she was two years older. As if reading his thoughts, Hattie reached back and took his hand in her own, pulling him forward. She liked Mamie's pies too, almost as much as she liked Mamie herself.

Mamie had given Hattie the scented soap that she so treasured. She only used a little each day, determined to make it last. Wearing it made her feel pretty, like on Sunday when she put on the dress that Mamie had told her was getting too small for her now that she was an old married woman. Hattie knew why the dress was too small for Mamie. She was as slender and graceful as a deer, and the most beautiful woman she had ever seen. Only in the past few weeks had the thickening at her waist become noticeable. Mamie was the Colonel's lady, and she was going to give him a son. Hattie didn't know how she knew that the baby would be a boy, but she did, as certainly as she knew that the Colonel would never see the child.

Cal sensed his companion slowing her pace and looked up at her. The sadness that he saw etched in her face stopped him in his tracks. Wet tears started streaming down her cheeks, and he felt his own eyes begin to sting. Looking far across the field to the house, he saw the lone horse, lathered and worn, hitched to the porch. He looked back at Hattie. She spoke for the only time in the dream. "De Colonel done met wid some misfortune. You hurry long fast as you can. I gotta get to Miss Mamie, We cain't let her lose dat baby."

Cal ran as fast as he could, but Hattie's long legs ate up the distance with amazing speed. She pulled away, and left him stumbling along with tears blinding him. His legs got heavier and heavier until he was barely struggling to walk. By the time he reached the edge of the field, he had collapsed onto the ground and was painfully clawing himself forward, crawling toward White Columns. Then he wasn't moving at all.

****

When Cal awakened, his face was wet with tears. For a moment the dream still claimed his mind, then gradually reality reasserted itself. He lay quietly in the darkness, wondering if the dream was more tragic than his real life. He decided that the real difference was that in the dream he had been a child, and could cry. Now he was a man, and although he felt like his very soul was bleeding from every pore, he couldn't do anything to ease the pain, except plot his revenge.

He thought about Heywood and felt the deep sadness being replaced by burning anger. It was the only way that he would be able to survive. He let his mind replay all of the ways that he would make Heywood suffer before he died. It occupied his mind for a few minutes, but then he felt the awful weight of sadness decending on him again. His mind went blank except for the dull ache that never went away.

He thought back to the dream, and now that he was awake, followed it through from his own memory. The rider had indeed brought bad news about his brother. Cal had arrived at the house and found Hattie trying to console Mamie. His sister in law had lost every shade of color, and looked as though there was no blood left in her body. He didn't remember her smiling again until after the baby had been born. After that, she seemed to have forced herself out of whatever darkness that had claimed her for the sake of her child. Cal shuddered when he remembered how bleak that year had been. He thought that now, after he dealt with Heywood, the rest of his life would be like that.

It was several minutes before an eerie awareness began to dawn. He felt the hairs on the back of his neck stir, and cold fingers counted his ribs. He turned on the bedside lamp and got out of bed. He quietly stole into the kitchen and started a pot of coffee. He waited for the familiarity of his own home to drive the thoughts that were suddenly hammering at his consciousness away, but there was no escaping from an enigma that wouldn't go away.

Only when the coffee was ready, and he was sitting quietly with a cup in front of him, did he allow himself to examine the insidious thought that had crept into his mind, and was threatening to push his sanity beyond his reach for good. The characters from his dream were as familiar as anyone that he knew. If he allowed his mind to flow, he could remember vivid details about each of them, but he was afraid that if he allowed it, his sanity would unravel and scatter like pieces of a puzzle that he would never put together again. The people from his dream that he knew so intimately had lived in another century.

CHAPTER 21

The atmosphere in the room was charged with tension. Cal could feel the under current of rivalry between Hannah and Shanon. His own guilt at having slept with both of the women added to the emotional charge. Beneath it all was his intuition that each of the women knew that he had recently bedded the other.

He and Shanon had driven to the airport earlier that evening and met Hannah's flight from Dallas. The ride had been strained, with Cal suffering from guilt pangs about resuming his affair with Hannah. Marla's words of long ago echoed in his mind. "You can't cheat on her, because if you do she'll know." He was certain that Shanon did know, and that it was responsible for her withdrawn behavior.

They had just arrived back at Hannah's apartment and were so far maintaining the uncomfortable silence that had marked the ride from the airport. Cal finally brushed aside his uneasiness, and broached the subject upper most in his mind. "What did you find out Hannah?"

"I know who Heywood Carlson is now. I know his motive for murdering Marla." She announced.

"My God! You know all of that and you've kept it under your hat this long? Why?" Cal exploded. "Heywood already has too much of a head start for comfort! Someone's got to get on his trail."

"That won't be necessary. He'll be back. I know what he wants, and how determined he is to have it." Hannah said.

"Enough with the damn riddles! What did you find out. What name is he using?" Cal demanded.

"Cal, you have to give Hannah a chance to explain." Shanon spoke soothingly.

"Fine. I'm listening."

Hannah patiently explained her visit to the Circle J, revealed her conversation with Ada Parker, then added, "I don't know what name he's using, or how he's disguised himself, but what I am sure of is that he won't give up. He'll be back, drawn by his obsession with White Columns. He's determined to own White Columns. His appetite for it has been whetted by the time that he spent there when he and Marla were married."

Shanon opened her brief case when Hannah finished speaking. She withdrew an enlarged portrait of General Jonathan Heywood that she had found in the book that she had checked out of the library in Emerald. She had made a photo copy of it on the machine in the library. She placed the copy on the coffee table and glanced from Cal to Hannah.

"General Jonathan Heywood, commanding officer of the Union forces stationed in southern Georgia during the early phase of military reconstruction, circa 1867." She reached into her brief case and withdrew another sheet of paper, laid it beside the first. "Heywood Carlson, a computer generated composite put together from his wedding picture, beard, calvary uniform, simulated aging, computer generated." She withdrew a third sheet of paper and laid it alongside the other two. "The intruder that my cameras photographed, computer enhanced, detail supplied by Paula Carlson while viewing the video screen of the new computerized police sketching system at Atlanta Police, homicide division. Boo Man, as described by Paula, Heywood Carlson, General Jonathan Heywood, one and the same." She sat back and waited for their reactions.

"Incredible!" Hannah was the first to speak.

"How?" Cal croaked.

"I convinced Striker that Paula had seen someone hanging around at White Columns prior to Marla's murder. He agreed to let Paula try to reconstruct the face that she remembered. This is the result."

"What does it mean?" Cal struggled to comprehend what lay before him.

"Unless I'm badly mistaken, what you are seeing is the first hard evidence ever compiled that supports the concept of reincarnation."

Shanon said.

"Reincarnation! That's crazy. It's no more than a strong family resemblance between Heywood and his ancestor." Hannah said derisively. "These pictures are no more alike than the resemblance between Cal and his Great, Great Grandfather whose portrait is hanging at White Columns."

"It's not merely a resemblance. In Heywood's case, and in Cal's they're replica's of a fifth generation ancestor. That doesn't happen as a result of random combinations of the gene pool. Something else is going on here. If you can't see that, you're blind." Shanon's cheeks colored with anger.

"You're saying that I'm the reincarnation of one of my ancestors. I'm not really me. I'm someone else. Someone from the past?" Cal's eyes bored into Shanon relentlessly.

"That's exactly what I'm saying. It explains how you got back to the past in your physical form, how you sustained the physical injuries that you observed when you awakened from what you thought was a dream. It wasn't a dream. It was real, and you were actually there in the flesh. I don't give a damn if you two believe me or not. I'm out of here," she gathered her purse and brief case, and started for the door.

"Shanon, wait. I'm sorry," Cal got up to follow her.

"I need to get away from you for a while. I have some things that I have to sort out for myself," she had stopped at the door.

Cal took a step toward her. "Please. Don't go now. I need you."

"I have to. Goodbye Cal." In the next instant she was gone.

Cal stood with her words churning in his mind. Goodbye sounded so final. He started to go after her, felt Hannah at his side and stopped. Outside he heard her car start.

"Let her go Cal. She'll be back." Hannah said.

"I don't know." He said.

"I do. She'll be back. She's in love with you."

Cal stared at Hannah for a few seconds. "Damn" He slumped down on the sofa, picked up the three sketches that Shanon had left behind. "Is it possible? Could she be right?" He looked at Hannah imploringly.

"Of course not. There's got to be a logical explanation. We'll find it, but not tonight." She changed the subject abruptly, but not before thinking, she'll be back all right, because she does love you, and I'm the unluckiest bitch on earth. "Have you heard when the lab is going to release Beth's body?"

"It'll be a few more days. The autopsy is complete. She died of shock, induced by torture and bleeding." He said it in the clinically detached way that cops use when referring to a victim. "The biggest holdup is that she has no next of kin that anyone is aware of, yet somebody could turn up. If they did, the lab would have a hard time explaining why they released the body to an unauthorized person."

"Damn. It's going to drag out isn't it?"

"Yeah."

"We have to come up with a strategy. Heywood will turn up again some day. I don't think that we can afford to let him choose the time and circumstances. He's too dangerous," Hannah said.

"We'll just have to keep looking for him. We might get lucky, catch a break. If not..." He shrugged.

"I'm scared Cal. Really scared. I know that you can handle yourself as well as the next guy, but we both know how tough it is to protect against a total stranger. That's what he'll be the next time he shows up. When he resurfaces he will have a new identity and a new face. You won't know who to suspect."

"There's nothing that we can do except keep looking." Cal said.

"No. We have to find a way to draw him out. It's the only way." Hannah said.

"I want to get back home for a few days. This sitting around for the past few days has really gotten to me. After Drew picked up Paula, I've had nothing to do but sit here and wait for the phone to ring. I'm going nuts."

"I understand. Tell you what, you can drive my car back to Emerald. I'll pick up a rental for a couple of days."

"No sense in that. I'll take a bus. I can use the time to try and sort things through. You can drive me to the station in the morning if you don't mind though."

"Sure. I'll be happy to. Are you hungry? I'm starving. Airline food has never been my bag." She said suddenly.

"I could go for a sandwich maybe."

They piled into Hannah's Taurus SHO and drove to Cumberland Mall. They had a sandwich at one of the shops, then spent some time wandering through the mall, just talking. They consulted the theater marquee and decided on a movie. Both of them needed the time to unwind.

As they waited for the movie to begin, Cal sat thinking about something that Shanon had said. Something about how history could have been changed if he'd taken a more active role in the raid on White Columns the night that the General had died. He was still thinking about it when the movie started..

****

Cindy's powerful winds churned across the Gulf of Mexico, howling like banshees. Her lust for blood unslaked by the victims that she had claimed as she had churned along the east coast of Jamaica, hammering Kingston with her Southern edge. Crossing the Western tip of Cuba, she had added more souls to the ones already groaning within the black whirling clouds spinning around her deceptively calm eye.

Within the quiet of the hurricane's eye, evil waited patiently, like a gambler idly playing with a deck of cards, head cocked to one side, listening for the unholy incantation that would signal acceptance of its master's offer. It knew that somewhere along its path, hatred would turn a heart to darkness, and render it vulnerable to temptation.

The storm hooked northward, toward Florida, feeding its voratious appetite for power with the warm moist air of the Gulf. As if realizing that its destructive life was nearing an end, it searched for a final target to batter, and beyond, a dark quiet place to deposit the restless spirits that had accompanied it across the expanse of water.

****

Striker turned the rented Taurus up the gravel drive of White Columns just as the sun hid its face behind the ridge. He parked, got out and stretched his aching back. He was stiff from the three hour ride, as well as having sat in his office for most of the day, working on the endless mound of paperwork that was an inevitable part of any homicide. At five, he had phoned Hannah Greene's home, and been pleasantly surprised to find Cal there. He had gotten permission for another trip to White Columns, and after an interminable fight with Atlanta traffic, had found the open spaces of rural I-75 a relief. He had set his speed control on eighty-five, and made surprisingly good time.

He wasn't looking for anything specific at the house. He just wanted a more thorough look at it, and an opportunity to search for any trace of Carlson. It was an opportunity to get away from the heat that was building now that bodies had started turning up. Bugosi wanted answers, and it was going to take him some time to supply them, even if he used his own creativity to do so. Besides, he couldn't tumble Raynes for the Addison murder too early. He wanted to give it a few days, to increase the credibility of his evidence, as well as to let the tension build, and give the media a few days to create an atmosphere that would enhance his statue for solving a major crime. No sense in not getting the most out of the situation.

As he started toward the house, he felt a hot breath of air close around him. Damn. It was a lot hotter down here than in Atlanta, he thought. The stillness, with only an occasional restless current of air, was almost tropical in intensity. Immediately he felt beads of sweat form on his lip. He paused, loosened his tie, and lit a Marlboro. He stood looking at the imposing home looming before him. He dismissed the sense that it was watching him as foolish, inhaled enough nicotine to satisfy his craving, and after grinding the butt out with his heel, resumed his pace.

He crossed the porch and unlocked the massive front door. Quickly stepping inside, he disarmed the security system. Flicking on the light switch, he looked around at the imposing room that he found himself in. The surroundings gave him the sense that he was visiting a museum, where the past century had been held at bay. For the first time since deciding to drive down, he lost some of his usual optimism. He had been right in assuming the house might hold a clue as to Carlson's plans, but it was so vast that it would take a team days to search it thoroughly. What could he hope to accomplish in the few hours that he had to spare?

As he stalked through the hall toward the library, he felt eyes boring into him. He stopped, turned, and looked behind him. Nothing. He stood listening. He could hear the old house breathing, currents of air stirring through the rooms, rustling a curtain here, setting up a faint tinkling in a chandelier there, but no sound of another presence in the house, nothing to justify his sense of being watched. He looked up at the portraits on the walls, and decided that all of the Dunforth eyes staring down was responsible for the eerie feeling. He moved on.

As he turned on the lights in the library, he was struck by the fact that although there seemed to be enough light fixtures to flood the area, they only managed to cast a soft glow over the cavernous room. White Columns liked darkness, and gave it up only grudgingly. If it had secrets hidden here, it wasn't going to give them up easily, he thought. He started a systematic search of the room, pulling books from shelves, and flipping rapidly through pages, searching for any loose papers, keys, or anything that might be worthwhile. As he worked, he became aware of the extensive wiring, all of it appeared new, and temporary.

White Columns...Dark Secrets

He followed a run, and found one of Shanon's cameras. What the hell, he wondered. A quick walk through revealed that the entire home was wired with surveillance cameras. He found the control center in an upstairs bedroom. He took a few minutes and learned how to activate it. When he walked in front of the camera, he heard it clicking and winding. Damn. Why would Dunforth go to these lengths to monitor what went on here, he wondered. Maybe Dunforth hadn't done the wiring. Carlson was into cameras, maybe he had set them up some time ago. But for what? It didn't make any sense to Striker. He shrugged. People were strange these days. He had long ago given up trying to understand people. He returned to the library and resumed his search.

As he was going through books again, he picked up one that claimed his attention: *Emerald, The Jewel Of The Alapuha*. He started skimming through it rapidly. Soon he was reading the history of the little south Georgia town, fascinated. He felt his way to a leather chair and sat down, engrossed in the saga. He was surprised, and pleased to find a chapter about White Columns, and the Dunforths. He read with keen interest the history of a family shrouded in tragedy. They had endured more than their share of loss. It seemed that almost every generation had been plagued by violent death. The deaths were more often than not murders, and chillingly, all had happened either inside White Columns, or on its extensive grounds. Striker thought of the Kennedys, and mentally compared their tragic circumstances to the Dunforths. What they had, the so called Kennedy curse, was only a mild case of what the Dunforths had been living with for generations. The damn house was an abattoir. He set the book aside and thought, why not get the hell out of a house that had brought so much sorrow. Why continue to live with the constant reminder that violent death was stalking you? Striker felt suddenly cold despite the warm air pumping through the old house. He lit a cigarette, then began a search for an ash tray.

He found one in the kitchen, along with instant coffee and a kettle. He helped himself to a cup from the cupboard, waiting with smoke from the cigarette curling around him, while the water boiled on the stove. With a fresh cup of coffee, he walked to the door of the largest downstairs bedroom. Standing in the doorway, he allowed his mind to travel back in time to the ghastly crime scene that he had just finished reading about. As he often did when viewing the scene of a crime that he was charged with solving, he let his mind replay the events as if seeing them through the eyes of the perpetrator.

He let himself see the sleeping couple in the bed before him. They would have been on top of any coverlet on a hot and sticky July night. The moonlight streaming in through the full length window, a thin gauzy curtain undulating in the hot muggy air. He focused on the woman, let his eyes roam up the expanse of leg exposed where her filmy gown fell open. He imagined the killers lust, felt his reluctance at having to deal with the man first. Striker imagined the intruder stealing quietly into the room to stand over the bed. In his mind, he raised the cane knife high overhead, and paused before the first bloody irrevocable strike, thinking that there was still time to sneak away, before starting the downward strike. The spray of blood appeared black in the moon's light. Instead of killing instantly as intended, it had brought the man fully awake, and although mortally wounded, prepared to defend himself and his family.

Striker imagined the weight of the man as he lunged off of the bed, wrapping desperate arms around his waist. He saw himself slashing downward with the long blade, hacking mindlessly at the back of the man's legs as he stumbled away from the bed. As he fought with the bloody mass of flesh entangled with him on the floor, long legs appeared above him, kicking desperately at his head. He lashed out with the evil blade, heard the solid chop as it buried itself behind the woman's knee, felt a fresh hot spurt of sweet smelling blood cover him as the artery erupted, gushing life all over him.

Striker felt steel hard fingers gouging into his throat, searching for his life force. He instinctively placed the sharp blade behind the man's neck, grasped it near the point with his left hand and began a desperate sawing motion. He heard the case hardened steel grinding against bone just an instant before the body on top of him started convulsing. He imagined himself crabbing away from the body as it twitched in death, clawing his way to his feet, and in a last act of destruction, slashing down at the exposed neck of the woman crawling toward her dying husband.

A chill swept through Striker as he stood there, as if the thin sheen of perspiration covering his body had suddenly frozen. The details might be wrong, but in essence he had seen what had happened so many years before. Striker had a keenly developed imagination that was able to supply surprisingly accurate details as he viewed crime scenes or photos. He wondered briefly how he was able to create such detail, and be so certain that the events had unfolded as he had imagined, from the sketchy description of the crime recorded in the book. It was a little spooky. He shrugged and turned away. No one had ever solved that murder. He wasn't going to do any good thinking about it either, he decided.

Striker walked to the window, pulled the curtain aside and looked out. The full moon was just climbing above the towering oaks of the river, bathing the yard with silver spears of light. A humid rush of air brushed past him, whipping the curtain in its wake. He looked out over the yard, and marveled at how the shadows cast by the trees, and the Spanish moss that clung to them, resembled the silhouettes of men slipping among the massive trunks. The thought crossed his mind that if Hollywood wanted to film a ghost story, this would make the perfect set. They wouldn't even need props. White Columns supplied its own, even to the sounds, like the faint jingle that he could hear moving through the old house. For a moment he would have sworn that he could hear the heavy clump of boots, punctuated by the faint metallic sound of spurs accompanying each footfall.

He had dismissed the sounds as imagination until he heard another, more modern noise join in. He had left the cameras activated, and now the unmistakable sound of the shutter clicking, and the automatic winding device on the camera in the hallway broke the silence. There was no mistaking what he heard, and it wasn't imagination. He was no longer alone in the house. His hand went to the Colt riding his hip, and he crouched instinctively. He let himself go dead calm inside, ready for combat. Whoever was inside, wasn't a burglar, or a prankster. His car was in full view outside, and the lights were on throughout the house. A sixth sense told him that whoever was in the hall had murder in mind. He felt the hairs rise on the back of his neck.

Just then the lights died, and a wall of darkness crashed down on Striker. He blinked, but still saw nothing in the gloom. He heard footsteps just outside the room, and then a harsh laugh, "Come on out Dunforth. I'm going to kill you." The voice was sepulchral, as cruel and heartless as Striker had ever heard. Despite a stoic disposition, and ample experience gunfighting, he felt a twinge of fear. You couldn't fight what you couldn't see, and Striker was almost blind in the sudden darkness. He groped behind him, felt the window ledge, and swiftly turned and climbed out.

Outside, the moonlight gave him enough light to operate. He moved behind the trunk of the nearest oak and waited. If his antagonist was stupid, he would come to the window and look out after failing to find him in the room. Striker would make sure that it would be the last mistake that he would make. He would put two rounds through any silhouette in the window in less than a second. Then he'd see who the hell thought he would just waltz in and kill another Dunforth.

It wasn't long before his patience was rewarded. A dark figure loomed in the window and the Colt roared twice, temporarily blinding Striker with muzzle flash, but he couldn't have missed he exulted. He was surprised at the roar of laughter from within the house. Damn. He hadn't missed. The bastard was wearing a ballistic vest, Striker felt sure of it. Knowing that he would have to even the odds, he sprinted to his car, clawing in his pocket for the keys as he went.

He opened the trunk and hauled out his own vest, weighted down with extra magazines for the Colt, a couple of stun grenades, and a pair of tear gas cannisters. He shrugged into the protective layer of armor, and then reached for the night vision goggles in his gear bag. With the goggles in place, he holstered the Colt, reached into the trunk for the Remington 870, and jacked a shell into the chamber of the battered shotgun. If some asshole wanted to play hardball, he'd picked the right guy. He opened the car's door, inserted the key and cranked the engine. He twisted the wheel hard right, pulled the headlights on, then jerked the shift into drive.

As he had hoped, the car started moving away. With the automatic choke on, the idle was high enough that the car began gaining momentum. As soon as it was away from him, he started back to the house. He hoped that his enemy's attention would be on the car long enough to allow him back inside. As he ran, he fumbled with the activator switch on the night vision optics, and got the device on in time to see the front porch looming up ahead of him in a greenish glow of artificial vision. He launched himself and landed on the porch with a heavy thud. Rolling and twisting he scrambled to the door, and without hesitation kicked it open, rolled inside, and trained the shotgun ahead.

A dark figure loomed before him, and remembering the vest, he aimed the shotgun at the menacing face and started firing. Mingled with the odor of burned gunpowder, he was aware of another odor so vile that he felt his stomach lurch. He ignored his sudden nausea, and worked the pump gun feverishly, the muzzle blasts slamming into his ears with physical force. Somewhere around the fourth or fifth round he began to sense that something was going horribly wrong.

****

Abe Lucas hit his siren, and turned on his lights as he sped toward White Columns. The report of gunshots had caught him by surprise. He'd thought Cal was still in Atlanta, but now he wasn't sure. Thoughts of his best friend, and fellow deputy in a gunfight spurred him toward the scene with more than a touch of anxiety. The highway flashed past in a blur as the powerful cruiser ate the distance to the plantation. Abe knew that he was in a bad situation. He was working alone, and there wasn't anyone else on duty within the department. If he had trouble and needed backup, he would have to depend on state troopers, and there was no way of knowing how far away the nearest would be. It was one of the hazards of a small department, deputies often found themselves on their own. But it wasn't the tactical situation that worried Lucas. Cal was already in trouble, and he could only hope that he wouldn't be too late.

There had been too much death at White Columns, he thought as he drove. He remembered finding Marla's body, and shuddered with revulsion. He didn't want to find Cal that way. He pressed harder on the accelerator, although he was already going more than one hundred miles per hour. He swept around a curve and had to ease off of the gas. He had just started to accelerate again when the old woman loomed before him in his headlights. "Oh Shit!" He growled through clenched teeth.

A twitch of the wheel avoided the pedestrian, but it also broke the tires grip on the pavement, and with a wail of protest the car went into a skid. Lucas fought for control, and was barely able to keep the cruiser on the road. He finally skidded to a stop facing back toward Emerald. He could see the old lady, still in the middle of the road, leaning on a cane—a bizarre apparition in the gloom of night.

He restarted the stalled engine, and drove back to where she was standing. He leaped out of the car and rushed to her side. "Are you hurt? For God's sake, what the hell are you doing in the middle of the road at night. Don't you know that you'll get hit!" His mind was racing. What to do with her. He couldn't just leave her here, but he had to get to White Columns. "Get in the car," He made the decision. He opened the door and helped her into the cruiser.

He wheeled the car in the road, and started back toward White Columns. She would just have to stay in the car when they arrived. There was no other choice. He had to help Cal.

"Doan go in dat house, chile," she said suddenly.

"What?"

"I say, doan you go in dat house," the voice rang with authority.

Lucas risked a look at her. He couldn't tell how old she was. Her face was partly hidden in the darkness of the police cruiser. The plain cotton dress and apron that she wore molded her into a shapeless form. There was something unusual about her that he couldn't put a finger on at first, and then it struck him. She would have been more at home fifty years earlier. The shapeless dress and apron, the red bandana knotted around her head, and the old fashion shoes made her look like she belonged in a picture on a flour sack. Where the hell did she materialize from? "What are you doing out this late at night?" He asked.

"Never you mind dat. You promise me you ain't going in dat ole house!" She reached across and clamped his arm in a wizened hand.

"Let go! How do you know where I'm going, anyway." He demanded angrily.

"I know chile! Dat's why I'm here, to stop you. Ain't nothing in there but death. It's waiting for you if you go in," she cried.

"I've got to go in. Cal, my friend's in there." Lucas said miserably.

"No chile, he ain't. He far away. Safe." Ain't no reason for you to go in."

"How do you know? Who are you anyway?" Lucas asked puzzled.

"I'm Tea Kettle Hattie. Ain't you heard bout me?" She lifted up a rusted old kettle that Lucas noticed for the first time.

A long buried memory stirred in Lucas' mind, something about an old witch that wandered around scaring all of the children. He had a faint memory of his grandmother telling stories about her. It had been long ago. He would never have remembered, but now he did. "No way. Old Hattie's been dead for over fifty years," he replied.

"Dat's right, but rest doan come easy to some," there was a weariness in her voice that suddenly made Lucas' spine tingle.

"We've arrived. Now you just stay in the car where you'll be safe," he said gently.

"Oh, I'm safe enough. It's you chile, dat's in danger."

Lucas tried to ignore her, but her words went through him like a cold knife, carving its way through his courage, and leaving gaping holes in its wake. The sudden irrational fear made him angry. "Just shut up, and stay in the car!" He ordered. He braked to a halt and was out of the car immediately. He the drew his Glock and cautiously started toward the house.

Inside White Columns, blood drooled down the walls, and puddled on the hardwood floor. Its smell mixed with gun powder, and an odor of rot. Malevolent eyes watched the deputy approaching, and a ripple of evil laughter drifted through the hallways. Air hissed past a bloody blade as it swept out in practice swings. At the entrance to the library, fingers still twitched reflexively at the end of a severed arm. In deadly silence, evil waited.

The spirit looked around with its one good eye at the carnage. What was left of Striker moaned and bubbled on the hall floor as blood and air leaked out of punctured lungs. A last wet feeble cough, and the corpse was still. With keen anticipation, the spirit waited for Lucas.

Lucas felt his guts sliding around inside of him. The pit of his stomach was cold and hollow, as if the blood that his racing heart pumped couldn't reach there and warm him. As he inched across the porch toward the splintered front door, he could smell fresh blood on the humid breeze that suddenly swirled around him. He knew he should be quiet, but he could stand the suspense no longer. "Cal! It's Lucas! Are you there?"

Silence. Even the night breeze died, as though waiting for his next move. He felt eyes boring into him. Every rational part of his mind screamed at him to wait, to get back up. But still he pressed forward. Cal might be inside, bleeding. He couldn't wait. As long as he could force his legs to move, he'd keep going. Moving had become a struggle against the fear that flowed out of his belly, spreading a gradual paralysis throughout his system. Already, he felt it squeezing his chest, making his breath come in short panting gasps. Still, he inched across the porch, his Glock trained on the doorway.

The first agonized moan almost stopped Lucas' heart. The sound of someone in the throes of death slammed into him like a fist. It came out of the silence, rising up until it filled the night around him. His skin crawled, and ice cold beads of sweat ran down over his ribs. He could smell his own rank fear. Not until the next sound had peaked, did he realize that the sound was originating from behind him. With that realization he turned, and looked over his shoulder at the mound of flesh writhing on the ground beside his car. The open door gave enough light for him to see that it was the woman, collapsed on the ground.

"Shit! Not now, God damn it!" He stood for a moment of indecision, then turned and ran to the woman. She was moaning loudly and rolling on the ground. When he placed an arm beneath her neck and raised her up, her eyes rolled until only the bloodshot white showed. A thin stream of spittle flowed from her mouth, and her breathing was a labored rasp. Lucas made certain that her airway was clear, then grabbed the radio mike. He called for backup, and an ambulance.

"It's going to be okay, lady. Help's on the way. You just hold on." He soothed, as he laid her gently back on the ground. He got a blanket from the cars trunk and spread it over her. Gradually, she stopped convulsing, and her eyes refocused. She seemed to snuggle into the blanket and a faint smile creased her face. In seconds she was lying peacefully, as if sleeping. Lucas felt for a pulse, but it was still. He felt a trace of deep sadness as he crouched beside her.

Inside White Columns, the ghost of Jonathan Heywood waited. He wanted to kill again. The first one had been a fool. Cursing and firing that shotgun like a madman. There was only one thing that could stop Heywood, and the cadaverous little man had not known. Cursing. It had made killing him so much easier. The other one was afraid. He could sense that, and he felt a twinge of worry. Frightened people prayed. And there was something else. He sensed the presence of the old witch, the one that he had raped so long ago, when she had been young and pretty. He hadn't known that she was a witch then. Damn his rotten luck! He cocked his head to the side and listened. He heard a distant rumble, and his lip curled into a snarl. Rebel Calvary. Damn that witch!

Lucas pulled the blanket over the dead woman's face and turned once again to White Columns. He felt a subtle sense of guilt at the sense of relief that he felt. Sure he wanted to help Cal, but that didn't mean he'd wanted the woman to die, he told himself as he walked back toward the house. As he approached, these thoughts were driven away. Fear consumed him as he faced the prospect of going inside the old house.

This time he moved to the doorway without hesitation, using the sturdy frame as cover. He shined his flashlight inside, and cautiously peered into the darkness. Blood reflected the light back at him as he swept it across the floor. He saw the body, lying in a heap in the hallway, and his heart crawled into his throat. "Cal! God damn it. Answer me!" He cried into the silence. He thought that he heard a jingle, and footsteps from deep within the house, but he couldn't be sure. The smell of blood mixed with another scent as Lucas cautiously made his way to the form lying in a pool of blood.

With his heart beating like a triphammer, Lucas cradled the shattered head, and turned the face so that he could see. "Striker. What the hell were you doing here?" In the distance he could hear a siren. He gently let the detective's head settle back to the floor, and carefully stepped away. With the Glock trained on the darkness, he backed out.

Horses! That's what he smelled. Lathered and sweat soaked horses. The house stank of them. He was glad to be outside again.

He started walking back to his car, and a new sense of alarm filled him. The woman. There was no sign of her. He broke into a run. Back at the car, he looked around in confusion. She was gone. Looking up, he caught a glimpse of a figure, bent over hobbling toward the river. "Hey! Wait! You can't go that way. There's nothing but swamp. Come back.," he cried.

The figure steadily plodded across the grounds and toward the river. At the edge of the swamp, she turned and looked back briefly before the mists swallowed her. Lucas stared after her for a long time. "That was a new blanket," he finally muttered.

Chapter 22

The phone shattered the stillness and jerked Hannah out of a dream in which she was wandering through a park, with an entourage of animals, rabbits, deer, and squirrels following along. She reached across Cal's form, trying not to wake him, but saw that he was not sleeping.

"Hello," she muttered sleepily.

"Hannah! Got any idea where Cal is?" The voice belonged to Abe Lucas.

"As a matter of fact, I've got a very good idea. Can't you guys down there get along without him for a few days. I'm just getting used to having him around."

"I gotta talk to him." Lucas ignored her banter. She checked the bedside clock and saw that it was after midnight. "Well, here he is." She frowned and handed the phone to Cal.

"What's up Abe?" Cal asked.

"Striker. He's dead." Lucas voice was flat.

"How." Cal sat bolt upright, then swung his feet to the floor. He had already started reaching for clothes. He listened as Lucas related the nights events.

"What was he doing back down there?" He asked when Lucas finished.

"I've no idea Cal. But I'm sure glad that I found you. Collins wants to put out an APB on you, thinks you've flipped out. What an idiot."

"He may not be that dumb after all. If I ever do flip out, he's the

234

one I'll be coming for." Cal laughed mirthlessly. "Any ideas on who could have killed Sriker? I would have bet that he could take care of himself."

"That's the strangest part. He was completely tactical, vest, night vision, and armed with an 870. He got off seven rounds, but someone sliced him up like Swiss cheese with a machete," Lucas explained. "How do you figure it?"

Cal felt a cold fist close around his heart. "Damn. Listen Abe, stay away from there. I'm on my way."

"What have you got in mind?" Lucas voice was laced with worry.

"I don't know. Just wait for me, okay."

"Know what I think, Cal," Lucas didn't wait for an answer. "I think we should burn the damn place to the ground."

Cal was silent for a long moment, then he said, "we just might do that Abe." He handed the phone to Hannah and started pulling on his pants.

"You gonna fill me in?" Hannah was also getting up. She dressed as Cal told her what had happened.

They gravitated to the kitchen, and Hannah started coffee. She broke their silence. "Damn it Cal. This is some weird shit. Could Shanon be right? It sounded like some off the wall crap when she was trying to explain it, but now, after what's happened it doesn't sound so far out. How could someone take out a guy like Striker with a blade, even a sword, while he was shooting back with a twelve gauge?"

"I don't know. Strange things happen when the balloon goes up. Maybe the first muzzle blast from the shotgun blinded him. Obviously he wasn't shooting in the right direction, or someone would have gone down with him."

"Unless Shanon's right," Hannah said stubbornly. "I think we should call her."

"Not yet. I'm going down and see for myself."

"I'm going with you," Hannah's chin jutted out defiantly.

"Good. You can keep the department off of my ass a little. They'll have no idea what to do. Collins will be shitting all over himself, but one thing that he will do is tie me up all day, unless there's someone that he would rather talk to. You can keep him occupied," Cal said evenly.

"What kind of bullshit is this. You think that I'm going to put up with Collins while you check things out?"

"If you really want to help, you will," Cal fixed her with cold eyes.

She heaved a sigh. "All right, another shit detail for Greene. What's your plan?" She brightened.

"My plan? Hell, I don't have a plan. I don't even have a place to start," Cal said bitterly.

"Hey. Why don't you hit the shower? I can tell you're going to be miserable company. I'm not riding all the way to Emerald with you smelling ripe as well," she said.

Cal agreed without protest. He had never felt so tired in his life. It was as though he were on a treadmill, and the harder he ran, the faster that it turned. He wasn't making any progress toward finding Heywood, and he was sick with grief. He had always known that Beth Addison was selfish and cold, but they had been together too long for him to be able to get over her death easily—and the inhuman way that she had died. No one should have to die like that. Now Striker. Cal's hatred of Heywood Carlson burned a hole in his stomach like acid. Sometimes he felt that it was the only thing keeping him going.

As the water pounded him awake, Cal started thinking about what Shanon had said. He tried to recall her exact words, but couldn't. He did remember her saying something about altering the course of history if he had taken a more active role. His head began to throb with the onset of a headache. It became harder to think, as pain built in his temples until it felt as though someone were hammering inside of his head. He felt a dark force sucking at his mind, as if there was someone inside his skull trying to take control. He fought it hard until the pain became unbearable. Then he slid down in the shower stall and let the cold rain fall over him.

****

He could hear the rumble of guns in the distance, probably Hood's. He prayed that it was so. If he was going to die here in the cold Tennessee rain, at least he could pray for victory. The rifle ball buried in his chest felt as though it weighed a ton. It grew inside of his lungs until there was no more room for air.

The cold rain in his face turned to warm sunshine. The guns faded, and he heard Hattie's laughter. He closed his eyes and stared up into the bluest summer sky that he had ever seen. He heard Hattie calling, telling him to come out, that it was time to go back up to the house. His last thought as he turned his head to look for one last time at the big white house, was that he wouldn't be going back with Hattie this time.

****

The pounding grew in intensity until it roused him. Slowly he opened his eyes, and found himself looking at the opposite side of the shower stall. The pounding was at the bathroom door. He dragged himself to his feet, and turned off the water. Who the hell was at the door, and just where was he? He blinked, and gradually he remembered. He heard Hannah calling his name. He toweled off and stepped out of the stall. Opening the door, he stood facing her.

"Damn Cal. Are you going to be all day?" She looked at him, and he saw her face twist with worry. "Cal, are you all right. You look a little green around the gills," she said.

"Yeah. I'm gonna be fine. Except for a killer headache. Got anything for it?" He rummaged in the medicine chest above the sink.

"Should be some Aspirin or something in there," she said. "Hurry and get dressed. We'll pick up some biscuits on the way out of town. If we drive like hell, we'll be in Emerald by daylight. We can work out a plan on the way."

"Yeah, I'll only be a minute," he answered. He didn't mention it, but suddenly he knew exactly what he had to do. He swallowed a palm full of pain killers and chased them down.

****

They drove straight to White Columns when they reached Emerald. The yard was filled with cars, and a van from the crime lab was also there. Daylight was just breaking, and a gray mist from the river cast a somber gloom over the scene.

Cal pushed his way past the outer ring of deputies and was about to step onto the porch when Collins reached out from behind him and grabbed his arm. "Where the hell have you been? You can't go in there. It's a crime scene," he snarled.

"Get away from me Collins," Cal jerked away from him, and walked to the splintered door. He stopped there, and stared at the grisly scene inside. He hadn't expected this much blood. Striker, as pale and fragile as he had been, couldn't have had this much blood in his body, he thought.

"Damn it Dunforth. I told you that you couldn't go in. Now I mean it. I'll have your ass in a cell so fast your head will spin," Collins growled in his ear and grabbed his arm.

Cal turned and shoved Collins violently. "Touch me again Collins, and I'll kick the shit out of you, and nobody will stop me. Look around, nobody here likes you any better than I do," Cal glared at him.

Collins started to respond, but instead stole a look around. He met icy stares wherever he looked. "Go ahead asshole, fuck this up. We got the G.B.I. here," he sputtered.

Just then a big man in a gray suit emerged from the house and intervened. "Frank Baxter. You must be Cal Dunforth. I heard that you were on the way. Let's find a place to talk." He reached out his right hand and clamped Cal in a firm handshake, while his left went around his shoulders, drawing him away from Collins.

The two men walked around to the back of the house where one of Baxter's agents was interviewing Abe Lucas. When Lucas saw Cal, he shot to his feet and strode up to him. Tears glistened in his eyes. He reached out, embraced Cal and said, "I thought that it was you when I first saw him lying there. Damn, it's good to see you."

"Take it easy Abe, everything's gonna be fine," Cal said confidently.

"You been thinking about what I suggested?" Lucas asked.

"I've got a better way," Cal assured him.

"I sure as hell hope so."

Baxter waited until the two men turned to him. "Well, Agent Douglas says that he's about finished with Lucas. Why don't you step over here and give me an informal statement while they finish up Cal, and then I think that we can cut you guys loose. It's been a long night for everyone."

Cal told Baxter in as few words as possible what had transpired in the past few days, not giving many details. The Special Agent in Charge, took notes, nodding occasionally, but not interrupting with questions. When Cal finished he said, "I think that will be all that I need for now. Of course, I'm sure we'll need to talk again when we begin to get some reports back from forensics. I'm really sorry about all of this Cal. I really am. I promise that we'll do everything that we can to get to the bottom of this."

Cal nodded.

"Are you gonna be okay?" Baxter asked softly.

"Yeah, but thanks for asking anyway," Cal answered.

Lucas and Cal walked back around the house, each now ready to get away from it. They met Hannah, and started walking back to her car. They agreed to meet in Emerald for breakfast and coffee. Cal climbed in the the car with Lucas and Hannah followed them back to town.

"So. You got a plan?" Lucas asked.

"Yeah," Cal answered.

"You gonna tell me about it?"

"No."

They rode in silence the rest of the way to Catherine's, a country style restaurant at the edge of Emerald. Inside they chose a booth in a far corner for privacy. The waitress who took their order was far too cheerful for the hour, and they were glad when she swooped up the menu's and darted into the kitchen.

Hannah was the first to speak. "Someone has to call Shanon. This shit will be on the news any minute now, and there's no telling how screwed up they'll get it. We can't let her hear it that way," she said.

"Give her a call," Cal nodded toward the phone on the wall near the restrooms.

"Maybe you should be the one to call her, Cal," Hannah said.

"She's pissed at me, remember?"

"I doubt that I'm at the top of her hit parade right now either. Don't be a chickenshit. Call her." Hannah retorted.

"How about giving her a call, Abe," Cal pleaded.

"Sure. I never mind calling a good looking blonde," he smiled. "Give me her number," he accepted the scrap of paper from Cal and started for the phone.

Cal and Hannah didn't speak while he was away. They busied themselves with the coffees that the young waitress set before them.

Lucas was back in minutes. "Man, she is a little frosty. What the hell did you guys do to her anyway?" He caught their guilty look, and the intensity with which they studied their coffee, and it hit him. "Oh shit. I'm out of here. This place will probably get hit by lightning, a bolt right from a clear sky. Dunforth, you always did live dangerously, but you ain't getting out of this one alive, and you ain't taking me with you," he pretended to slide out of the booth.

"Sit down Lucas. She likes you. She won't call down brimstone on me with you here," Cal said.

They laughed nervously, but the mood had subtly changed. They finished breakfast in silence.

After they plates had been cleared, Hannah finally broke the spell. "So, what's the plan guys?"

I think that you should go back over to White Columns, and

hang around with Baxter. He's a good guy, if you don't push, he'll keep you abreast of what they're finding, if anything,"Cal said.

"Sounds good. I'll play like a sponge and just soak up stuff," she grinned. "What are you boys going to be doing."

"Lucas needs some sleep. I can see all the way to Memphis on the road map in his eyes. I'm going to get away from everything for a few hours. I'll round you guys up when I get back,"Cal said.

Cal paid the tab, and they walked out. By now the sun was a hot ball of fire on the horizon. Hannah drove back to White Columns, and Cal caught a ride to his house with Lucas.

Lucas shook his head and grinned sheepishly. "I don't know what it is with you Cal. Most men would thank their lucky stars if they could get a woman like Hannah or Shanon to look at them. But you've got two of them. If you want my advice, not that you're ever smart enough to ask for it, although it could keep you out of a lot of trouble, you better decide on one and straighten up and fly right so that you can keep her," he looked at Cal across the car. "Otherwise old buddy, you're gonna lose em both, and end up crying the blues. Take it from someone who knows women better than you. Pick one and stick with her," Lucas declared solemnly.

"I've already decided," Cal's voice was laced with steel.

Lucas looked at the hardened face and kept silent. He dropped Cal off and started for his home.

Sleep was pulling at his eyelids as he drove, but he kept seeing Cal's stone hard face in his mind. Something was wrong. He couldn't shake the feeling, and by the time that he was home and undressing, he was almost too worried to sleep. He thought about all of the activity at White Columns, and decided that Cal couldn't come to harm until he could catch up on his sleep. After that, he would pin him down on his plan. He had an intuition that it was dangerous.

****

Cal fought his way through the dense undergrowth of the river bottom impatiently. He had parked his Jeep at the end of an old plantation road, and was brush busting his way to the river. As rough as the going was, it was the only way to avoid the circus at White Columns. He shifted the day pack that he had stuffed with lunch, and basic survival gear, and picked up the pace. He had a long walk. He only hoped that he could find the way. His plan depended on it. The river bottom had changed dramatically since he had last traveled up river. Old trails were completely overgrown, with no trace of their having ever existed. Still, he thought that he could find what he was looking for instinctively.

Low black clouds slid across the face of the sun, turning the swamp into a bleak and forbidding place. Overhead an unbroken expanse of charcoal cloud cover filtered out the sunlight, creating an artificial twilight. A sullen wind swept throught the hardwoods, stirring the drooping mantles of moss that hung from the ancient trees. Lightning flared suddenly, and the explosion of thunder sounded like a cannon firing.

Cal reached the river and used a game trail to make his way upstream for several miles. He ignored the steady pelting of warm rain that fell, and dared the blazing lightening strikes to take him. Across the river, he finally saw the mouth of the little creek that he was searching for, and without hesitation stepped off into the rising black water of the river. He swam across, the gentle current drifting him only a little way downstream. He followed the creek north, old memories guiding his footsteps. At the spring where the creek bubbled out of the earth, he found what he was looking for.

The old shanty was barely standing, and a towering pine had grown up through its roof. Muscadine vines draped themselves from the tree's uppermost limbs and supported what was left of the structure. The stone chimney still stood, but the door hung from only one rusted hinge. Feral hog tracks led up into what used to be the homes single room. A rusty old pot bellied stove fought to stave off encircling honeysuckle vines in the middle of what had been the kitchen. The tightly woven tangle of vines served as a roof, stubbornly resisting the incessant rain.

The swamp seemed to hold its breath here, where undergrowth was so tangled that breezes couldn't penetrate, and the humid air hung stagnant. The light dimmed more as the shadow of evil closed in. It had found the heart that it was searching for. Cal followed the animal tracks into the dark interior. He stood motionless for what seemed eternity. He closed his eyes and inhaled. At first there was only the musky scent of wild boar, rotting vegetation, and rain, odors that made up the swamp. Then, after what seemed forever, the smell of delicately scented soap drifted to him from across the ages. He smiled. She was here.

"Is that you Colonel?" The voice cracked with emotion.

He turned and she stood there, not as he remembered her, but an old woman, bent and leaning on a cane. She took a step closer, looking into his face, shielding her eyes from the midday sun with one wrinkled hand. Her face creased into a smile, and he saw just a hint of his Hattie in the twinkle of her eyes before they started to glisten with tears.

"Lord. It's my baby," her voice broke with emotion. She crossed the space and embraced him. "You done remembered Hattie after all these long years."

He could only nod. A flood of emotions kept him from speaking.

"I remember thinking when dey tole me you was going to fight de war, dat chile ain't ole enough to be in no war, why jest last summer we wuz swimming in de river, and picking berries together. You remember swimming in de river together, both of us jest chaps?"

He nodded, still holding her.

"Den I saw you in dat uniform, ridin up on dat ole gray stud hoss, hat pulled down over yo face, big ole pistol strapped on, and you wuz a man. Fourteen is all you wuz, but you wuz a man for sho. Then you wuz gone, and I never laid eyes on you again. I cried for a month when I heard how you got yoself kilt somewhere up in Tennessee. I knowed dat day, dat dey won't nobody coming home. Eveybody done kilt. Den de damn Yankees come. Dem wuz some hard days." She lead him to a chair, and they sat together at the table with cool breezes blowing through the house.

After a minute she continued. "Yo brother, de Colonel, come to me one night. I never forget dat night. It was de worse night I ever live through. De ole rogue took me dat night, and he done evil things, unnatural things, like something you expect ole Satan hissef would do. I was so hurt and so shamed, dat I tried to die. I cut deep, and de blood run out of my wrist like a river. Jest when I wuz dying, de Colonel reached out and took holt of me. He wouldn't let me go. He promised he'd see justice done if I jest hep him. He tole me what to do, and I went down to de river one night, and shook de bones, and called up de dead. After dat. Things wuz better til de ole rogue's ghost started comin round. Anyway, I got to thinking bout de gift. If I could call up de dead, I decided dat I call up somebody dat deserved to live, so one night I called you up, and gave you de body of dat chile de ole rogue kilt before it wuz even born."

They talked until it was time to go, and then they started through the swamp together. By now the rain was being driven by strong winds in advance of the storm. They huddled together as they picked their way through the swamp's rising waters. It was just after dark when they reached the spot across the river from White Columns. The full moon had already started to rise, but the heavy cloud cover obscured it, and covered the dripping swamp in pitch black darkness. They waited in silence for the moon to climb higher up the horizon.

CHAPTER 23

Shanon tried to bury herself in her work, but found her mind drifting from the paper that she was writing to Cal Dunforth. She was still trying to decide if she were angrier with him for sleeping with Hannah Greene, or for scorning her ideas. She told herself that it didn't matter anyway. She would not see him again. He had hurt her too much. It was better to allow the wound to heal, and resume her solitary lifestyle than to constantly expose herself to the aching pain that pervaded her very soul.

She found herself growing furious that she couldn't put him out of her mind, and concentrate on her work. Work was important. Men were not. At least she hadn't thought so before. Frustrated, she put her work aside and walked toward the kitchen. Perhaps a snack of cheese and a glass of wine would help her relax and concentrate. As she walked past the wall phone, it drew her like a magnet. She picked up the receiver and dialed Cal's number. She waited. After ten rings she replaced the receiver and fixed her snack.

She wandered into the den, clicked on the television and restlessly flipped through the channels. She settled on a program that dealt with the reintroduction of wolves into Yellowstone Park. She tried to listen to the arguments, and counter arguments advanced by a panel of experts as they expressed opinions about the reintroductions impact on game populations within and surrounding the park, and on ranching interests in the area as she munched on the snack. She wondered which side Cal would take in the debate, and realized that he was still very much a part of her life, and that no amount of denial was going to change that. She went back to the kitchen, poured another glass of wine and dialed his number again.

Since the call from Abe Lucas, and the news of Striker's murder she was more certain that the ghost of Jonathan Heywood was the killer than ever. Striker had been a formidable man, yet he had been butchered. It seemed that mortals were defenseless, except that she had escaped. She thought back to the terror that she had experienced at White Columns. Could something as simple as a prayer keep one safe from the ghost? She thought about Paula, and how she told of multiple visits by the evil spirit. Each time, she had forced it away by reciting the prayer.

Shanon replayed the terrible moment that the spirit had loomed over her, and remembered how it had reacted to her recital of Paula's prayer. It had recoiled as though from a physical assault. It was a slender thread of hope, but she desperately wanted to share it with Cal. He needed any veil of protection that was available. She knew that he was too stubborn to stay away from danger. "Come on Cal. Answer the phone," she pleaded.

She listened to ring back in frustration, decided that he was probably with Hannah, and experienced a tinge of hostility toward the red head. She hung up the phone, reminded herself that Hannah was actually a very nice person, and walked back to the den. The program that she had been watching was over, replaced by a sitcom whose dialogue didn't deserve the canned laughter in the background. She switched to the weather channel and watched as huricane Cindy stalked landfall at Apalachicola. She could see that the first bans of rain in advance of the storm were falling as far inland as Emerald. She curled up on the sofa, and wished that she could be there, safely snuggled into Cal's arms as the rain pelted down. Gradually sleep claimed her.

****

Hot wind whistled through the shanty, stirring up layers of dust, and gave life to cobwebs that clung from the ceiling. Torrential rain pummeled what was left of the roof, then as if in contempt of the feeble efforts to restrain it, poured through onto the red dirt floor. In seconds the powder turned to a quagmire of mud. Shanon struggled in the calf deep muck, looking around her fearfully. The decrepit walls groaned deep within their ancient timbers, the sound as soul wrenching as the cries of living beings. It was as though the structure realized that it was doomed, that this was the storm that would finally sweep it into oblivion, and it mourned its own death.

Suddenly a strong hand clutched Shanon's wrist in a grip like iron. She felt herself torn from the clinging muck, and led outside. There she watched in wonder as the rotted wood died in a last shriek of agony. She saw the roof cave in with with a final groan, and a crash that was barely audible above the howling of the wind. She turned at last to the person still gripping her hand.

The woman was so dark that she almost blended into the storm blackened night. And she was old—wrinkled and withered, with leathery skin that looked as though it might tear, or simply disintegrate beneath even the gentlest touch. She smiled, revealing a toothless cavern that was as bottomless as her soul. She was hunched over, the hand not occupied with Shanon clutching a cane, and the handle of a tea kettle. For a moment she seemed to totter, as though unable to stand against the wind. Then she steadied herself with an effort, turned and lead Shanon away from the house, down to an overgrown trail that lead along the river.

The pair seemed to walk for miles before the old woman finally stopped in the trail ahead of Shanon. Breathing heavily, she simply pointed.

Shanon peered through the darkness at something looming up ahead, across the river. There, glowing with a pale light stood an enormous white house. Shanon recognized White Columns, and reacted with a sharp intake of breath.

"Dat's right. White Columns. You know bout dat house, doan you Honey. You got de gift, des lak I had it, only stronger. You been able to see wid out de bones. You got it powerful. Tonight goan be a full moon, and storming. Spirits goan fight all night long." The old woman hunkered down on the river bank. "My name's Hattie. I know yo name. I goan show you how to bring up de dead tonight. Goan let you shake de bones."

Shanon was shaking her head. "No, she croaked. I don't want to know."

"Ain't got no choice. You goan see. Ole Hattie goan show you. I's gettin too ole. Now you pick up dat kettle, and rattle dem bones des a little. After dat, dey rattle and shake like you never see. Go ahead gal, you do what Hattie tell you!"

Shanon shook her head and tried to back away. "No! Please", she cried out, but felt the kettle drawing her hands to it with an irresistible force. The old woman held it out to her.

"Come on gal. You take de bones. Des shake em a little, de words come," she coaxed.

Shanon touched the kettle and her fingers tingled with electricity. Tentatively, she shook the old vessel until the contents began to rattle With the first sound, a jolt of pure agony shot throughout her body. Her throat filled, and when she opened her mouth, she spoke in a language

246

that she had never heard, yet the words were completely comprehensible. What she was pleading for in the hissing clicking dialect, filled her with a visceral fear such as she had never known. She heard herself moaning in agony as pain consumed her. Her vision dimmed as though life itself was slipping away. The only way that she could be sure that she was still alive was the unrelenting sensation of being torn apart.

Shanon awakened abruptly. She was suddenly violently sick, vomiting onto herself before she could react. Every fiber of her being ached and throbbed. She slid off of the couch and onto the floor. She lay moaning and gagging for several minutes before she was finally able to move. Her head whirled, and her stomach contracted until she was dry heaving. She felt near death.

At last she was able to pull herself up, drag into the bathroom, and get cleaned up. She changed, cleaned up the mess that she had left on the couch, and heated a cup of soup. The warm liquid restored some of her strength, and better still, stayed on her stomach. Gradually she began to recover. It was miraculous. For a time she had been certain that she was coming down with flu.

Only when she was feeling better did she remember the dream. She wondered if the terror of it had been enough to bring on the physical symptoms. Certainly she had never been so frightened by a nightmare. It was more terrible even than her dream of Marla's death. It's most salient characteristic had been the fear that she'd experienced at the end. She shuddered, wondering if this dream had a hidden meaning that she simply couldn't comprehend. Was something as horrible as the dream about to happen? No. She pushed away from the table and started pacing. Let the dead stay dead. She felt an incredible yearning for the living, and to feel comforting arms around her. She found herself picking up the phone again.

Again there was no answer.

She walked out onto her deck, slumped down in a lounge chair and stared out into the night. The glowing lights of Mountain Brook slowly dissolved into the flashes of lightning bugs. The artificial glow of night lights in the upscale neighborhood gave way to silver gleams of moonlight reflecting off of dark oozing water. Gradually the silhouettes of houses was replaced by towering water oaks. Looking down, she saw a reflection in the river—an old woman bent painfully over a cane. Looking back across the river, she saw the big house on the bluff, arrogantly looking out of its glass eyes. Mossy gray beards hung from thick trunked trees that rose up out of rich black earth. Fear squeezed icy droplets of adrenaline into her stomach as she recognized the view of White Columns from across the river.

Overhead dark ominous clouds whipped past, almost low enough to scrape the tops of the towering trees along the river. Rain was falling, and intermittently the sky was torn asunder by jagged streaks of lightning. Thunder shook the earth with resounding claps that came so frequently that the rumble of one had barely faded before the explosive blast of another shattered the night. At that moment, the moon brushed the clouds aside and bathed the scene in silver light.

Shanon's spine froze as she realized that she was seeing through the eyes of the old witch from her dream. What new horrors was she about to witness? She had no control over the scene that the aged eyes focused on. She tried to urge the old woman to get closer because, as frightened as she was, she had a desperate need to see what was going to happen. As if in response to her urging, Hattie crossed the river, moving with supernatural speed. In seconds she was standing on the porch of the house. Her old eyes swept downward, studied the moonlight slowly creeping across the smooth boards of the porch, then out over the driveway, and focused on a dark sedan parked there.

The light was too dim, and the old woman's eyes too weak to make out the lettering on the side of the car, but its profile, and the antennas protruding from the trunk told Shanon that it was a patrol car. Cal's car!

She had to warn him away. There was more danger at White Columns on this night than even she had imagined. Words from her dream reverberated in her mind. *Spirits goan fight all night.* She had to find a way to get him away safely.

Like a sleep walker, she stumbled back inside— unable to use her own eyes, she had to feel her way into her bedroom, grope desperately for the phone. There! She had it in her hand. She had difficulty orienting the phone in her hand, and realized that dialing a number would be hopeless without her sight. She was able to punch zero for an operator. She waited until a bored voice answered, then gave the number for the Alapaha County Sheriff's department.

"Ma'am, you can dial that number direct." The operator said.

"No. I'm blind. I can't see the digits on the phone. Please hurry It's an emergency." Shanon begged.

She waited, watching a thin gray mist slipping toward the old house from the river. The dispatcher came on the line. "Please, this is an emergency, I need you to patch me through to Cal Dunforth's radio. He'.

in grave danger. I have to warn him."

"Lady, if this is some kind of a prank..."

"Please help me. My name is Shanon Lee. I have to talk to him!"

"Yeah. I remember you now. Hold on, I'll try his car, but I doubt if we get through. He's off duty tonight, and most of the phones in Emerald are dead from the storm. Did you try his home number?"

"He's not home."

The line went silent for half a minute before the dispatcher came back on, " Sorry Honey. I can't raise him on the radio."

"Shit!" Shanon slammed the phone down, desperately punched at the keypad until the operator came back on the line. She asked for assistance dialing the phone at White Columns. Maybe Cal was inside. She waited. The frustrating sound of busy circuits told her that the lines were down.

Shanon dropped the phone as a wave of helplessness swept over her. Whatever was going to happen, she was helpless to stop it. She sprawled across the bed, and buried her face in her pillow, concentrating on the image before her. "Damn you Hattie, look around. Find Cal!" She implored.

The old eyes seemed mesmerized by the shaft of moonlight gradually creeping across the porch. Finally, the gaze shifted, and Shanon saw polished black boots. Her heart lurched. Cavalry boots! No. Wait. More like the ones that Cal wore with his uniform. Gunmetal gray Dockers! The ones that Cal had been wearing the first time that she had met him. She saw his hands then, big and powerful, wrapped around the butt of some kind of antique pistol. She knew those hands. Now, it seemed like a very long time since they had explored her body.

"Cal. Thank God! Why are you at White Columns?"

The sinister shaft of moonlight crept into view, and revealed the jagged edge of a dark spot just beyond the toe of Cal's boot. A slashing blue saber of fire reached down without warning, fiery fingers searching the night. Shanon screamed then, an agonized sound from the core of her soul. The reason for Cal's presence at White Columns struck her as suddenly as the lightning strike. "No. Oh God Cal, no!", she wailed.

As she watched the sinister beam of moonlight creep inexorably closer, she tried desperately to connect with Cal. She knew that he was going to risk more than his life to try and change the course of history. She racked her brain for a way to try and stop him. She concentrated as hard as she ever had in her life, sent all conscious thought down into the deepest recesses of her brain. She brought her entire being into focus behind a single utterance. "Cal! For God's sake! No!" She cried out desperately.

She prayed for the storm clouds to blot out the silver glow of the moon, but it stubbornly persisted, its light edging steadily closer. Suddenly she knew that the old witch was responsible for the patch of cloudless sky. It was as if Hattie were holding the sky open, letting the light through. Shanon realized that it wasn't the moonlight, but rather the power of the witch that opened a door to the past. She focused her mind and felt the first tremor of pain. She ignored it, and feeling her throat fill, opened her mouth and uttered the unspeakable, in a language that she had never spoken before. She felt herself being torn apart, the flesh flayed from her bones, but she endured the pain, and allowed the words to flow. If she couldn't stop Cal, then she would go back with him.

Her vision went black, then gradually she saw white hot particles of dust rushing past, and finally an exploding burst of white light that lasted for only a slit second, enough to temporarily blind her. Gradually, she was able to see shapes moving around her, big lunging shapes that sharpened into men on horseback. Faces gaunt and haunted, covered with dusty beards, and the dark stubble of whiskers came into focus. Eyes buried deep in cavernous sockets blazed with fury beneath the shadow of wide brimmed calvary hats.

The river exploded in glistening silver geysers as the lead horses plunged in without slackening pace. A sinister metallic whisper swept through the troop, and then moonlight glinted off of polished blades. Ahead, gleaming white on top of the bluff, White Columns beckoned to the avengers, silently urged them on.

The horsemen reined up in front of the house. The Colonel leading them turned briefly toward his men. The familiar face was hardened into a lean and hungry mask that bore a striking resemblance to Cal Dunforth when he was angry. With a savage jerk on the reins he whirled his horse, dug in his spurs and vanished inside the house. In seconds he rode through the door way with a sniveling prisoner clamped in his powerful hands.

A rider dismounted, slipped a noose around the prisoner's neck, tossed it over the sturdy main beam overhead and remounted. He dug his spurs into his horse, and dragged the frantic man off of his feet, securing the rope to the porch railing.

The Union General did a macabre dance step in the air, as the rope choked the life out of him. Suddenly, smoke and flame spurted from the huge revolver clutched in the Confederate Colonel's fist. The body of his enemy jerked and spasmed as the heavy caliber balls impacted yielding flesh. Again and again the flame and concussion split the night air, the final shots eliciting no more than a lifeless jerk from the hanged man.

Shanon witnessed the event, holding her breath with anxiety. As the scene unfolded uninterrupted by Cal, she began to regain hope. Something had spoiled his plan, whatever it had been. Perhaps in his former life, he couldn't remember why he wanted to change anything. In any event, the chances of his returning unharmed were far greater. At least that's what Shanon hoped.

A face peering out of the window, young and hard, with cruel compassionless eyes, watched his father's killers reform into columns and canter off toward the river. The youth didn't notice the lone rider watching from the shadow of the oak at the edge of the yard. He disappeared from view, his attention diverted to something inside the walls of the mansion.

Shanon watched the marble steps pass beneath Cal's boots, and saw the shattered face of the lynched officer as Cal brushed past. Inside, bathed in the glow of a single kerosene lamp, she saw the body of the woman on the floor. Shanon watched in morbid fascination as she extended an imploring hand toward the young man standing over her.

In a flash Cal's plan suddenly crystallized in Shanon's mind. He had never intended interfering with the hanging. That wasn't what he was there for. He had another, more ruthless plan to carry out. His real purpose manifested itself in the intense glare that he directed at the youth before him. All of the hatred that he bore for Heyward Carlson was focused on the thread of life that would lead to murder so many years later. A murder that would shatter his very soul, and render him incapable of living with it unavenged. His plan was to sever the thread, and unravel the series of events that had destroyed Marla.

In vivid slow motion she saw the youth whirl toward Cal, saw the yawning maw of the Colt clutched in his fist coming to bear. In the next instant, she saw Cal's outstretched right hand, saw the front bead of the Lemat steady on the thin chest. She saw the jet of flame from the Colt's barrel, the cloud of smoke obscure the menacing figure just as Cal's own weapon fired. Gray smoke swirled around her. She saw the floor rushing toward her, then darkness closed on her.

****

Shanon Lee groaned as the sound of her alarm clock jarred her out of sleep. She rolled over toward the nightstand, and fought at the clock until the piercing sound died. She rubbed her eyes with delicate fists, threw back the covers, and padded to the bathroom. The dream that she was having when the alarm sounded was terrifying, something about dying, of being shot. She couldn't remember the details. She didn't want to. She studied her image in the mirror. Not bad, she thought, not bad, even after a night of bad dreams.

What she needed was a man in her life, she thought as she turned on the shower. It was time. She wasn't getting any younger. As she stepped into the warm flow, she couldn't help thinking that out there somewhere was a man that she could love. It was odd, the feeling that she had met one once, that something terrible had happened, and she had lost him. She wondered if that was what she had been dreaming. Must have been, she told herself. There certainly wasn't any Prince Charming in her life now, nor for that matter could she remember ever meeting one. Still, there was this feeling that out there somewhere someone was waiting.

She emerged from the shower drying her hair with a towel and made her way to the kitchen. Coffee. She needed it desperately. She was going to be late for work unless she hurried. She reached for the kettle on the stove and stopped, her hand hovering over it uncertainly. Instead of the cute little white kettle with red flowers that she expected, the kettle on her stove was old and rusty. When she picked it up, it gave a faint rattle, as though something brittle was inside. She set it down quickly, feeling queasy. Now where the hell did that come from, she thought.

EPILOGUE

In the soft glow of the bedside lamp, sweat glistened off of Cal Dunforth's muscular body. He heaved a satisfied sigh, and rolled off of the lithe body of the woman who had shared his pleasure. He lay staring up at the towering ceiling of White Columns, his mind overwhelmed with a sense of wholeness. He had never been happier in his life. He felt soft delicate fingers exploring the tangle of hair on his chest. When the hand reached the puckered, nickel sized scar over his heart it stopped. The larger scar on his left shoulder blade tingled as the soft fingers traced a circle around the entry wound on his chest.

"I'm so happy that you've given up your job as a Deputy. It was so dangerous. I don't think that I could live if anything happened to you." The voice was husky with the aftermath of sex.

"It'll take all of my energies to turn this place into a first class hunting lodge. There's dogs to train, forage to plant, advertising campaigns to organize. It's a lot of work, but I'm looking forward to it." Cal said.

"I'm so happy for you. I know how much you love the outdoors, and working the dogs. We'll have the classiest operation in the Southeast. Wild quail, no pen raised birds like the other plantations, and trophy deer."

"Don't forget the boar hunting along the river bottom."

"How could I forget that. Listen to those crazy bulldogs barking their lungs out. What do you think they're after?"

"Who knows. I better go see. They usually don't bark unless there's something prowling around outside." Cal rolled out of bed, and pulled his pants on. As he was reaching for his shoes, the English pointer bird dogs began whimpering in terror.

"Cal! Listen!"

He pulled open the night stand drawer, and stuffed the Glock semi-automatic into his waist band. The wail of the pointers had a desperate pitch by now, and he could hear the two bulldogs ripping at the kennel doors. Something was definitely out there in the darkness. He hurried toward the door.

"Cal, be careful!"

He looked at the woman in his bed. Her long dark hair fell down over her shoulders, stopping just short of covering the rose colored nipples that adorned her firm breasts as she sat up in bed. She was the most beautiful creature that he had ever seen. She owned his heart and soul. He would walk through the fires of hell for her, he thought as he drank in the visual stimulus. He felt himself stirring again at the thought of her in his arms. "I'll be back soon. I promise. It's probably just an old boar wandered up from the swamp, nothing to worry about."

"It could be something else, Cal. Be careful." She repeated herself.

"I will."

He disappeared into the hallway, leaving the woman alone in the room. She climbed out of bed, knelt on the floor beside it, and her lips started forming the words of the simple prayer that her Grandmother had taught her so many years earlier.

After the words had tumbled out, she got up and walked into the hall. She saw the door to the bedroom across the hall swing open, watched as the figure of a three year old emerged. She gathered the child into her arms, padded down the hall, and stared out the window overlooking the backyard. It could have been her imagination, but Marla was certain that she caught a glimpse of a dark figure slinking down the footpath toward the cemetery.